THE FALSE PROPHET

CHRONICLES OF THE SUPERNATURAL: BOOK FIVE

JM HART

First published by JMH World Publishing in 2022
Copyright © JM Hart 2022
www.jmhartwriter.com

The False Prophet:
Chronicles of the Supernatural, Book Five

EPUB: 978-0-6450396-5-8
Print ISBN: 978-0-6450396-6-5

ACKNOWLEDGMENTS

I would like to thank my supportive family and friends for their encouragements. Thank you to invaluable editor Susan Bischoff and, proofreaders, at BookBaby and cover designers at Creativindi as well as JMH World Publishing's ARC team who have been a tremendous support throughout the process. No book is complete without the vital service of editors, proofreaders, and great book cover designers.

But we are all as an unclean thing, and all our righteousnesses are as filthy rags; and we all do fade as a leaf; and our iniquities, like the wind, have taken us away.

Isaiah 64:6

PROLOGUE

The death of Sophia has hit everyone at the estate hard. But the clock is ticking and none of them have time to grieve or debrief each other on the happenings during the past seven days, because the atmosphere around the earth rumbles and moves in strange ways and no longer can they deny the existence of demons and monsters from the ghostly realms.

After the return of the Emerald Tablet to the Tomb of Thoth, they expected good fortune to rain down on earth and mankind, but nothing but the opposite has happened.

1

JADE: THE GROUND SHOOK

Out front of Casey's estate, by the plane wreckage, Jade opened her soul and let go of the earthly realm, losing herself within the rhythm of her shamanic drum. With each beat of the drum, a beautiful resonance reverberated through her entire body. It silenced all other sounds. The wind, Tim and Seth's chatter from inside the camper van, the scream of the foxes, and the howling of the wolves. The warmth of the light from her crystal wand settled upon her face. It was good to have her parents back, but her heart was heavy, as were everyone's at the estate. But none more than Casey's heart. It was as if life had drained from his pores. Each time Jade went back to her room, Casey would be on Sophia's bed with his back towards the door, clutching her pillow. It was easier to sit outside in the dark with her wand.

Focusing inward, and on the rhythm of the drum, was the best thing she could do as she searched the astral planes for Sophia. Even if it was only a fragment of light, a simple sign Sophia was okay. But there were no signs, just an empty void that reminded her Sophia was gone.

With the fluffy tip of the drumstick, Jade struck the deer skin drum faster and faster. If anyone watched her, they would think her arm was rubber—it moved so effortlessly. She gave one mighty bang, and the ground shook underneath her. Slowly, she opened her eyes and sat her drum beside her and placed her hands on the dew-covered grass. The ground moved beneath her.

Jade stood up and looked into the darkness, pivoting until she was facing the house. Around the corner of the house, a blue light swarmed like an alga bloom floating in to shore. She watched the luminescent light in wonder as it approached; it was Shaun. Shaun and Rachel arrived back from Israel two days ago, and Shaun had glowed ever since. It fascinated her. The light from her crystal wand was no match for his sapphire icosahedron, now embedded in the palm of his hand. The light it produced was not of this world.

Shaun had changed so much since they first met nine months ago, she hardly recognized him. He had been sitting on the rooftop of his house hurling insults, taunting Kevin and Tim. Shaun's and Rachel's battle against the Leviathan in Israel sounded epic, and they were lucky to be alive.

Jade already updated her diary with a drawing of the icosahedron embedded in Shaun's palm, which illuminated when the sapphire activated. Coming around the corner in the dark, he looked like a blue angel.

"Why have you activated the sapphire?" Jade asked. She still felt a little uncomfortable in his presence, afraid he'd turn back to his old ways, lashing out and belittling her.

"I went to Alex's grave to get the obsidian I left for him to keep safe. I'm curious if it increases the power of the icosahedron and if it, too, might activate."

"All the stones might activate eventually," Jade said.

"I don't know if I'm excited or afraid," Shaun said, picking at the skin at the edge of the sapphire.

Did he just say he was afraid?

"What are you doing up this early?" Shaun asked.

"Oh, nothing," Jade said.

"Bullshit. You're always up to something. I don't think your brain ever stops. I can see your brain ticking over with ideas as you gaze into space. Kevin does the same thing."

"Well, I'm trying to quiet my mind and align with the universe, so I can find Sophia in the astral plane," Jade said.

"Any luck?" Shaun asked.

"No, nothing. I'm surprised, because I thought she, of all people, would be in the spirit realm, ready to help us. Don't mention it to Casey. I don't want him to get his hopes up. I know he has tried astral traveling, in his own way, to find her, but he's not having any luck."

"Did you feel the tremors? Do you think it's an earthquake?" Shaun asked.

"Yeah, no, I felt it, but I don't think it was an earthquake. It was more like a stomp," Jade said.

"Back home, we lived near an army base where they conducted war games with heavy artillery. The bombs felt like this. The ground shook, and windows rattled for a couple of seconds. This sounded muffled, like the explosion came from under the ground." Shaun said, moving closer and surrounding her in his light.

"I don't think that's the army," Jade said, reaching out her hand, touching the rim of the blue light that had expanded into a sphere.

"Congrats on finding your dad, by the way. What do you think of the newcomers from London?" Shaun asked.

"Seth's okay. Tim seems to trust him. Poor Tim. His heart is aching. He's been hiding his grief, just like Casey, but I can see his face light up when he's with Seth."

"What are you guys talking about?" Kevin's voice came out of the night.

"Where did you come from?" Jade asked, stepping out of Shaun's blue light and moving towards Kevin.

Kevin put his arm around her shoulders. "You must be freezing."

"I'm okay. Drumming keeps me warm." Jade bent down and picked up her drum, placed it inside her crocheted bag, before slinging it over her shoulder and tucking her crystal wand into her back pocket.

"It seems like a lifetime since I heard the army practice bombs," Kevin said.

Shaun looked at Kevin. "I know, right? It hasn't even been a year since we found and returned the Emerald Tablet. I've defeated a monster, lost a kidney, and Rachel's been to the stars and back."

"But the demons and monsters continue to emerge from God knows where," Jade said.

"The past nine months were mental," Shaun said.

Jade reached out for Kevin as the ground shook for a third time. She was the only one who swayed and took a backward step to find her balance.

"I think we're going to have to get Casey to push past his pain; we need to work as a team to find out what's causing the tremors before things get worse." Jade shivered.

"I don't know, Jade, he's so distraught. We need to give him some space," Kevin said.

Shaun must've noticed her shivering because he stepped forward until she felt the warmth of the energy that was coursing through his being, emanating from the icosahedron.

"After what I saw in Israel, we can't assume anything," Shaun said.

Kevin pulled his arm off her shoulder and brushed his hand across his head, stopping to feel the scars where the bats had clawed it opened. After thinking for a few seconds, he nodded. "I'm picking up some terrible vibes. I don't think we can clean away the emerging evil. It's saturating the earth. Where's it all coming from?" Kevin asked.

Shaun dug his hands in his pocket, reaching for his leather pouch of sacred stones. "Rachel doesn't want to talk about the message she received from the stars without Casey. But she believes heaven is amongst the stars in the Pleiades," Shaun said.

"Why are you all up?"

Jade jumped, startled by the sudden sound of Tim's voice.

Tim was rubbing his eyes, walking down the steps of the camper van parked outside the barn. Tim and Seth had been talking most of the night but had fallen quiet in the last half hour. There was plenty of room for them in the converted barn, but they didn't want to disturb

Hugh, Gwen, and her daughter Bo, along with Seth's dad, brother, and sister. Jade's mom and dad were staying in the rooms in the barn with the newcomers. Kevin's and Casey's families would be surprised when they returned. Sophia had said people would come, and they had.

Jade missed Sophia, and she believes in her heart what Sophia was fighting for, so she will follow in Sophia's footsteps and listen to her heart. Hopefully lead by her heart and not too much with her head. To align the two, to become one with the universe, would be perfect. Something Jade's great-grandmother, Great Turtle, had tried to get her to understand throughout her life. To open her heart and let the universe show her the way. She thought about her memory stones, upstairs in her bedroom with her medicine pouch. No longer did she feel fear and trepidation towards them, she felt love and curiosity.

"Tim, Casey hasn't said how Sophia died, just that it was his fault for taking her necklace. What does he mean? He would never take her necklace from her," Jade said.

"I don't know what he's talking about. The last I saw, her necklace was in the Emporium when she was making holy water," Tim said.

Tim glanced at Kevin and continued, "I wasn't there. I didn't see how she died. Casey told us to leave the city to get as far away as possible. So, we left. I should've stayed with them."

"If you hadn't left, all those people in the barn, including yourself, might have ended up dead, too. You did the right thing, Tim. We have to trust Sophia knew what she was doing," Jade said.

Kevin placed his hand on Tim's shoulder and quickly pulled it away. Jade knew, Kevin had just received an emotional surge from Tim. Kevin's clairsentience ability was getting stronger. She had noticed, most of the time he avoided touching anyone other than her. She had also noticed the same thing about Casey a few weeks back; everyone's powers were getting stronger. But instead of bringing them together, it was pushing them apart.

Kevin raised his eyebrows, silently questioning Tim.

"It's okay," Tim said.

Kevin wiped his hand on his jeans. "Whatever happened in London was pure evil. What occurred in London, and too Shaun and

Rachel in Israel, is just the beginning of something of biblical proportion."

"How. Can. Things. Get worse?" Shaun asked, drawing out every word with his frustration and worry.

Jade watched Shaun as he spoke and she saw a change in his facial expression, as he realized things could get a lot worse.

"You know what? Don't answer that." Shaun said, drawing in the blue light until it clung to him like a glove.

"The sun is going to be up in a little over an hour. Why don't you get Rachel and meet us in the basement?" Jade asked Shaun.

"It would be better if you woke her up, and I'll see if I can get Casey to join us. Rachel has to tell everyone what the message is, whether Casey is part of it or not."

"Tim, do you want to get Seth and Hugh in on this? I think it's something everyone should hear," Shaun said.

"Sure, will do," Tim said, stretching out his arms and yawning.

"Oh, and Jade, be careful. She's still sleeping with the bowie knife." Shaun said.

"What do you mean by that?" Jade said.

"Nothing, I'm just fooling around," Shaun said, smiling.

Jade pulled her eyebrows tight and drew her lips together as if scolding him with her gaze. "You're even making jokes now? Bad ones, I might add. Someone should've ripped your kidney out a long time ago," she said, nodding her head.

"What about Joe?" Kevin asked.

"Let him sleep. He hasn't slept for the last two nights," Tim said.

Behind Shaun, Jade walked up the front steps into the manor. Everything had a strong sense of clarity. The feeling of the still air on her face, the darkness of the night, and the warmth of Kevin's hand in hers. It was a moment she would never forget, because, as she paused on the top step, it felt like it was going to be the last time. Kevin stopped her just before she walked inside. He turned her towards him.

"I have the same feeling," Kevin said.

The darkness was impenetrable as she stared out into the distance, but in her mind's eye, the canopy moved under the strain of an unseen force.

Boom.

Boom.

"What the hell is that?"

2

CASEY: FALL INTO THE DARKNESS

Casey breathed in the smell of Sophia from her pillow. He lay still, listening to the darkness, hoping to hear her voice, or a whisper of her breath against his ear. His heart chakra, like a wilted flower, tightened in his chest, making it almost impossible to breathe. Everyone he loved died. The universe and God didn't have his back. He was only a puppet, just like Sophia. Metatron let her die—for what? To kill, banish an evil spirit, a demon that he could've destroyed with his blade. Instead, Sophia had sacrificed herself to send the demon to its end. She probably believed it was the will of God.

To hell with this world.

Knock, knock, knock. The sound startled him. At first, he thought it was because he had said the world could go to hell. But it was just Kevin again, trying to get him to leave the room. Soon they would send up Shaun. Eventually, Casey knew, he was going to have to leave the room. But he felt like, if he did, he may never see it again.

Casey ignored the persistent banging.

"Come on, mate, open up," Kevin said.

"Go away!"

Casey heard Kevin walk away.

Why can't I see or feel you, Sophia? Casey thought, breathing in deeply. The scent of her filled his heart and soul with memories of her smile, her soft skin, her joy, doubts, and certainty. Her certainty in God. The thought of God angered him. He clenched his fists, twisting the ends of her pillow. She was selfless, willing to step into the unknown, with only faith as her companion. Something had ignited within him the first time he had met Sophia. His heart had opened. And when she unveiled the realms beyond this world, showing him the light and the glory of God, he was in awe. But the glory of the light had abandoned him, and darkness coursed through his veins. How could he believe in something that destroyed and stole away the things he loved? How was he expected to keep an open heart, mind, and spirit while his heart shriveled like a rotten apple fallen far from the tree?

Powers beyond his wildest dreams were now his to employ at will, and he also had two books full of mystical knowledge he knew he wasn't worthy of owning. People that had certainty and strength in their beliefs wrote those books, with the kind of faith that he will never have again. How could he continue to believe in a power that continuously destroys the earth, humankind, love, hope, faith—everything precious upon the earth?

Darkness traveled, slithered deeper into his mind, as his own doubts snuffed out his inner light. He clenched his jaw tight. Curled up like a frightened dog, Casey pressed the pillow against his face and screamed until he had no breath. Then he drew in the scent of Sophia, as deep as it would go, trying to capture her essence.

A blood-curdling, horrific cry escaped his paralyzed body. Suddenly, he lashed out his arms and threw the pillow across the room. All the furniture in the room lifted off the floor, into a whirlpool of chaos banging against the walls and ceiling. A hurricane of emotion tore through his room. The anger churned in his stomach like a pit of snakes. From deep inside, a dark energy force exploded from his being. He stood up and entered the center of the whirlpool, hoping to get hit. The chest of drawers just missed his scalp. He screamed out. "How can I continue to serve God? How can I believe?"

The walls expanded outward under the pressure of his force. He trembled with fear. The force of his anger frightened him so much he held up his hands and the table, chair, shoes, books, cups, all collapsed to the floor with a heavy thud.

Frustrated and ashamed, Casey glanced down at the scattered objects. One book he found at the Emporium in London, the notebook that had belonged to Isabella Sumer, lay staring up at him as if scolding him for his rage. Underneath the leather notebook was the book of Enoch. Sophia's pillow lay at his feet. He picked it up and dropped to his knees. Clutching it to his chest, he bowed his head and sobbed until he was numb.

His skin crawled. Silence amplified. Something was behind him. He turned. A dark shadow disappeared into the corner of the room. "Sophia?" Casey leaned backwards against the wooden frame of Sophia's bed. He scanned the room, watching as golden light washed away his dispelled emotions. He focused inward to calm his thoughts. Sophia would want him to go on believing in the grace of God and that it would cleanse the earth of evil.

His ears hypersensitive, and, for a moment, he imagined her breath as if she tried to whisper in his ear. Calmness and hope washed over him. All he needed was to connect with her. Into the stillness of the room, Casey spoke, "Sophia, is that you? Are you there? Speak to me, please."

Heavy footsteps moved up the staircase and along the hallway, breaking his connection. Casey squeezed his eyes tight and tried to hold the sensations. A breeze passed through his hair. He imagined her soft hands that wielded great power, raking her fingers through his curls. Light from the memory entered his being but came to an abrupt stop as his mind doubled back to the image of the shadow.

It had worn a hat! The dark shadow wore a hat, the same type of hat worn by the ghost from his nightmares. He pinched himself to make sure he was awake and not trapped again in a nightmare illustrated by the *Homoharenae*, the sandman. Casey was sure he had destroyed the creature. But the shadow was a great likeness to the evil warden from the old Newgate prison, which was, at one time in history, very much alive. It can't be the same ghost. It was just a shadow. Nothing but a shadow, and shadows can't hurt him. He tried to convince himself. He sat on the edge of Sophia's bed, opened the book of Enoch, and read out loud from where the book fell open.

. . . 8 And now, the giants, who are produced from the spirits and flesh, shall be called evil spirits upon the earth. 9 And shall live on the earth. Evil spirits have proceeded from their bodies; because they are born from men and from the holy Watchers is their beginning and primal origin; 10 they shall be evil spirits on earth, and evil spirits shall they be called. As for the spirits of heaven, in heaven shall be their dwelling, but as for the spirits of the earth which were born upon the earth, on the earth shall be their dwelling. And the spirits of the giants afflict, oppress, destroy, attack, do battle, and work destruction on the earth, and cause trouble: 11 they take no food, but do not hunger and thirst. They cause offenses but are not observed. 12 And these spirits shall rise against the children of men and against the women, because they have proceeded from them in the days of the slaughter and destruction.

Knock. Knock. Knock.

"Go away!" Casey yelled.

Giants; there's no such thing, Casey thought. How long is this evil madness going to last? We came together with the others; we returned the Emerald Tablet. It should've brought world peace, but billions of people are dead or missing. It's worse than ever. Hell is earth.

Sophia's bedroom door burst open, and the book of Enoch slammed closed.

Shaun surveyed the clutter in the room, picked up the desk chair and sat down. "You can't stay locked up here for the rest of your life."

Casey pretended Shaun wasn't there, but it was harder to ignore the majestic colors in his aura and the soft vibration of the blue light around his physical being. Casey wanted to know what happened in Israel to create such a dramatic change in his aura. "What are you glowing about?" Casey stood up and tossed Sophia's pillow back onto her bed. "Second thoughts, I don't want to know."

"I think you do. It's the sapphire, the icosahedron." Shaun held up his hand, and the sapphire glowed from within his palm. "It's fused with my body. We were trapped in an underground bunker the size of the city. It was being ruled by a giant evil monster that shape-shifted into anything it wanted, and it controlled the minds and the emotions of the people. It called itself the supreme master. I had to destroy it, and when I did, I woke up minus a kidney and this fused to my hand."

"I'm glad you and Rachel are safe. But just leave me alone." Casey said, still hearing the word 'giant' in his head.

"I can't imagine what you're feeling right now. I would perish if I lost Rachel. But you have to come downstairs and hear what Rachel has to say."

The house rattled, and Casey raced to the window. He searched the darkness with his mind. Something was coming. The lights flickered in the room. He turned for a split second and in between the light and dark, black entities entered the room. They turned into entrails of gray smoke as the light returned.

Shaun stood up as if someone or something touched him from behind and turned to take a swing.

"Okay. I'll listen to what Rachel has to say. Then I'm leaving," Casey said, walking from the room, not wanting to be left alone with the entities.

He checked over his shoulder to make sure they weren't being followed. "The timeless dagger!"

"Your what?" Shaun said.

"Dagger. Wait here." Casey raced back to Sophia's room and picked up the book of Enoch and Isabella's notebook. He shoved them into his backpack and put on the holster with the silver medallion of St Benedict's cross and the timeless dagger. He had the feeling he was going to need it. As he stepped from the room, Jade, coming down the hall, looking at her feet, deep in thought, bumped into Shaun. "Where are you going?" Shaun asked.

"I'm just putting my things back in my room," she said, turning her body sideways to show her drum on her back.

"Okay, meet us in the basement," Shaun said.

"Will do" Jade said.

"It might be better if you keep your stuff with you," Casey said.

Jade reached out for the doorknob. "I'm glad you're coming to join us," Jade said, searching his eyes. "I'm sorry Sophie's not here."

She cast her eyes down as he teared up. He wiped his hand hard against his face as if it would press the tears into nonexistence.

"I prefer to keep my wand, drum, memory stones, and pouch together in my room. They're precious to me. I'll be quick and just place them on the bed and meet you downstairs. I won't be far behind you. Promise," Jade said.

"Everything you hold precious, keep close to you," Casey said, but not really understanding why.

"What do you mean? Why? What aren't you saying?" Jade said.

"I'm not sure if we're safe here anymore," Casey said.

"Because Sophia's not here to shield us with the psychic dome? Did you feel the earth tremble? We all felt it outside. That's why we're meeting in the basement," Jade said.

"No. It's something else. It's hard to say. I could just have the jitters, after what happened in London, the exorcisms." Casey shuffled his feet and pushed his hair back. He pursed his lips, preventing his words from being said out loud.

"What happened, Casey?" Jade asked.

"Let's just go downstairs and get this over with," Casey said.

"There's a wooden box of memory stones and a medicine pouch under my pillow," Jade said.

He wanted to ask her about the memory stones and the medicine pouch. He hadn't talked to her since they got back. "Okay, I'm coming with you," Casey said.

As soon as Jade opened the door and entered her room, she turned on the light and stopped in her tracks. "What in tarnation happened in here?" Jade glared at Casey. "What did you do?"

"Whatever, just hurry and get your stuff," Casey said.

Jade searched his face. He could see her concern. She drew her brows together as she peered deeper into his eyes.

"Never mind!" Jade tiptoed through the mess to her turned-up bed. "Help me, Casey. I need my memory box and pouch."

"What do they look like?" Casey felt his cheeks flush with shame as he surveyed the mess he'd created. He had discarded Jade's and

Sophia's belongings like insignificant objects during his outburst. His head was aching. He felt the tightness in his throat.

"What's happening to you?" Jade asked.

"What's happened is I've lost my best friend. My soul mate. We're all puppets!" Casey said.

Casey lifted the bed up over Jade's head with his mind as she searched the floor for her things. Slowly, he lowered it back to where it belonged. The springs squeaked as he dropped the mattress onto the frame. He chucked the bed linen onto the bed.

Jade sat back on her heels and sighed. "If you want to help me find my things, you'll have to get on the floor and sift through all this mess."

Casey picked up the desk, chest of drawers, bedside tables and chairs and flew them across the room, placing them where they belonged. Then he pushed the smaller items into the center of the room for Jade to sort through.

"Shit!" Jade rocked back, holding her knee. Sticking out of her knee was a fragment of glass. Last night, she had brought him a glass of water and a plate of food, which he'd dismissed.

"Wait, let me . . . ," Casey said.

Jade reached around for the crystal wand sticking out of her back pocket. He had wanted to ask her about it but didn't feel like talking. It was such an effort. Carefully, she touched it to her knee around the shard of glass. Slowly, the glass moved as if being pushed up and out of her body from the inside. Her knee glowed with green light. The glass dropped to the floor.

"I'll get a bandage to stop the bleeding," Casey said, heading for the opened door.

"Don't bother. It will be okay. The bleeding will stop. Just a few seconds more. There," Jade said.

Casey squatted beside her and looked at her inflamed knee, it was red, but there was no cut; it had healed.

Jade handed the wand to Casey. "Searching for my dad, I met Chief Thundercloud. He gave it to me. It's a healing wand. My great-grand-mother, Great Turtle, left it for me, along with the box of memory stones, shamanic drum, and the medicine pouch. I'm just learning how to use them. My great-grandmother trusted that one day the spirits of our ancestors would bring Chief Thundercloud and me together. I crawled through a narrow tunnel and found a cave, trying to find my father. That's when a vampire bat took a chunk out of Kevin. If it wasn't for Chief Thundercloud, I could've lost my father and Kevin."

Jade shook her head. "It sounds crazy saying it out loud. To find my father, I had to open my heart and travel through the spiral of the drum to the realm of lost souls. It was amazing and terrible. The things I saw terrified me. I will never forget the wretchedness of the realm. Heartbreaking pleas from lost souls still ring in my ears. They weren't all evil, just lost in the depths of their own despair. There were thousands, buried up to their necks along the shore of the sea of tears. And bones that I thought were coral covered the ocean floor. It must be the darkest realm within this multiverse. And I fear that dark and evil realms are merging with ours."

She looked up at him for a moment, then waved a hand. "Forget it. Don't listen to me. I'm not sure of anything anymore," she said as she scanned the items on the floor. She picked up her hairbrush.

"There was a shipwreck of flying heads—cursed souls," she quickly added.

"You're right. I've been seeing it since the beginning," Casey confided. "Evil from the surrounding realms is merging, and that scares me. I feel the darkness all around us. There are things I'm not seeing. The evil tricked us. It kept Sophia and me apart. I wasn't there for her, Jade," Casey said, pulling Sophia's necklace over his head and putting it over Jade's.

"I can't take this," Jade said, reaching for the necklace.

"I don't deserve the protection of Solomon or Penelope's cross. If you don't take it, I'll give it to Rachel." Casey watched Jade turn the pendant between her fingers, looking at the Seal of Solomon and the protective web of Penelope.

"I'll keep it for you. If Sophia gave it to you, it was for good reason," Jade said, tucking it under her shirt.

"Look at these." Casey removed the book of Enoch from his bag.

Jade stroked the cover. "A lost book of the bible. Have you read it?" Jade asked, taking the book from him. Her enthusiasm changed the colors in her aura to shades of yellow and purple.

Casey crouched beside her. "I just read something about spirits of the children of the watchers' fallen angels, and evil spirits rising and destroying humankind. That's why I think you're right. The evil spirits and the demons must be everywhere or come from another realm. And look at these." Casey showed her his drawings, and remembered the feeling of the charcoal poised between his fingers. He had closed his eyes, refusing to watch the images unfold. He didn't know if they were from the past or the future. His hand had moved methodically over the page, turning the charcoal on different angles. In his mind, he had floated upon waves of celestial energy, searching for a sign of Sophia. Energy had poured down through his head, neck, and arms until it flowed out of his feet, connecting him with heaven and earth. Waves of energy had rocked gently around him. He had drawn dozens of pictures of demonic creatures since Sophia's death.

"You drew these?" Jade said, flicking through the images quickly. "Since when do you channel images?"

"A week ago when you first saw Hugh, just before you left to find your father, leaving Sophia and me here," Casey said, shuffling, rubbing his hands on his legs, trying to generate some heat. He was feeling cold.

"What do they all mean? They're all so scary. The angels look angry."

"I think it's because they're fallen angels, the watchers who had children with the females of earth. God has cursed those children and the watchers, forbidding them from ever returning to heaven, their place of creation," Casey said, trying to take back the images.

"These are hideous." Jade said, refusing to hand them over. She pushed her bracelet up her arm while looking at the picture of a man's face with a snake filtered through his eye and mouth. "Surely that's not an angel, but a demon." She moved to the next one. "At least this isn't so bad. What's with the silhouettes and the one wearing a derby hat?"

"I don't know what, or who, they are," Casey said. Casey rolled up the images and tossed them aside. A sudden chill filled the air and his breath turned to fog.

"We have to tell the others. Warn them. Maybe without Sophia's protection, we are open for psychic attacks or worse," Jade said, looking around the room as if suddenly afraid they were being watched. "Is it getting cold in here, or is it just me?"

"I feel it, too. You tell the others. I don't want any part of it. Now that Sophia's gone, there's no point. I would only be a burden. She was the light in my life. I could always sense her spirit, even when she was on the other side of the earth. I felt her as if she was as close to me as you are now. Her presence has gone—I can't feel her anymore. I don't know what to do without her."

Jade put her hand on his shoulder and pulled him towards her. She held him tight. His hand settled on the deerskin drum.

"Casey, you will see her again. This isn't over. There is so much more I want to tell you. We can journey to a place amongst the stars that is constructed out of crystals and gemstones. We can travel through the windows in the head of my crystal wand. I have seen it. We're not alone in this universe, Casey. We are being guided, and we can only do what we can."

A small leather bag was lying on the floor, under the edge of Sophia's bed. "Is this your medicine pouch?" he asked, retrieving the bag and holding it up. From Jade's back pocket, her wand sparked and shot a solid beam of light towards the ceiling.

"Yes. And there's my memory stones!"

"What are memory stones?" Casey asked as Jade pulled a wooden box from the pile in the center of the room.

"Come on, let's get out of here. I'll tell you later. I feel like we're being watched, like something else in the room with us," Jade said, standing up and putting her medicine pouch in her pocket and her memory box of stones into the bag next to the drum, and flung the bag over her shoulder onto her back.

Casey took one last look at the room and saw Sophia's pillow. He breathed in deeply and closed the door gently behind him.

3

JADE: MESSAGE FROM THE STARS

W alking down the basement stairs in front of Casey, Jade could hear the murmur in the room fade out. Everyone was there, except Tim and Seth, who were still to come. Joe was missing, too. Someone must've woken up her parents, because they were sitting on an old travel trunk by the hole in the wall that led into the passage ways. It was nice to see them together again. Her dad still looked frail. It was going to take a few weeks for him to build up his strength after being in the realm of lost souls. He was doing alright, though.

Rachel looked nervous.

Jade sat down on the couch next to Kevin. He had saved Jade a seat opposite Rachel and Shaun. Carefully, she put her drum bag between her feet so she could feel it next to her in easy reach, it gave her comfort, and she was glad she had listened to Casey. She tried to relax and sat back. She could feel the warmth from Kevin's thigh against hers as their auras merged. Their life forces amplified whenever they were together. Just like Casey's and Sophia's had—poor Casey. She watched Casey fold his arms across his chest as he leaned against the stone wall, away from everyone else. Rachel pushed herself up out of the comfy sofa, and paced the floor, nervously rubbing her hands together. Shaun smiled at Jade before standing up and speaking quietly to Rachel, who sat down and tried to look relaxed, which only made Jade feel more anxious. Rachel was ex-Israeli military and didn't scare easily, if she was worried then Jade was too.

Kevin leaned into Jade, brushing a hair off her face. She readied herself for his kiss. "How's Casey?" Kevin whispered in her ear.

She blushed and turned her head slightly, wanting to kiss him. "He's here. That's a good start. But he's not doing too well."

"Why is he wearing his backpack? He looks like he's about to leave," Kevin said.

"Something upstairs has him spooked," Jade said.

Kevin sat forward and spoke quietly to her. "I woke up spooked . . . and for the past few hours, I've had the urge to run. Something has got me worried, looking over my shoulder; it's an awful feeling of dread."

"Me too," Jade said.

"Why do you still have your shamanic tools? I thought you were taking your drum and wand back to your room?" Kevin said.

"Casey suggested I keep them with me," Jade said.

Kevin pushed his long fringe of hair off his brow to the side and studied Casey. "That doesn't sound good," he said.

"What do you mean?" Jade said, tracing the lines of the raven tattoo on her wrist.

"I've got the feeling I'm not going to like what Rachel is about to say. She's been holding it close to her chest. Shaun knows, but he's not talking. He said it's Rachel's to tell. I've had a bad feeling ever since we got back to the estate. I can't believe Sophia is gone – we all need time to grieve." Kevin reached out for Jade's hand.

The warm, excitable energy between them amped up a few more notches. Her stomach fluttered. He smiled, and she knew he could feel what she felt. It relieved her to know only Casey could see and read their auras. But shrouded in grief, Casey wasn't seeing or reading anything.

Tim and Seth hurried down the stairs, then pulled up an empty chest, parking themselves next to Hugh and Gwen. Jade smiled at her parents then looked through the hole in the wall, into the first chamber of the labyrinth of tunnels that snaked their way underground. Her body involuntarily shuddered as an icy chill filled her veins. She had been down in the labyrinth a hundred times over the past couple of months, and the tunnels had never felt foreboding until now.

"What's got your wheels spinning?" Kevin said, moving to the edge of the couch.

"I'm not sure," Jade said.

"Now that everyone is here," Rachel began, standing up.

The murmuring stopped. Rachel inhaled a deep breath and let it out. "Okay, everyone, I realize Casey's and Kevin's families aren't due back until tomorrow, but I think it's important to tell you all what I know. And Ellen, if you could bring the others up to speed when they arrive back, that would be great.

"As most of you know, four days ago, Kevin opened a portal for Shaun and me to go to Israel to find my mother and brother. In a bunker the size of an underground city, we found thousands of people who were under the control of a tyrant, a shape shifter; a demon the resistance called the Leviathan. My mom and brother weren't in the bunker. They had been part of a group on a pilgrimage that walked from Jerusalem to the Sphinx in Egypt. They had a 'calling' in a dream and blindly followed it."

"Just like the dream we had about the pilgrimage to Stonehenge," Hugh said to Gwen, loud enough for everyone to hear.

"Eventually, on the last day, before Kevin open a portal for our return, we went to Egypt in a Blackhawk to see if my family and the pilgrims were there. It's a long story, so I will not go into details. The place was deserted. Not one pilgrim was there. Not one. But I found steps between the Sphinx's paws, and while Shaun, heavily sedated, slept in the chopper, Eitan, the pilot, and I entered an ancient chamber that I can only describe as a portal." Rachel paused for a couple of seconds for everyone to understand what she had said.

Jade sat on the edge of her seat, wondering what she was going to say next. There were so many things that intrigued her that, even if she had a hundred lifetimes and remembered each one, there would be still so much more to learn and explore.

Rachel cleared her throat. "Together, Etain and I, on a beam of light, teleported up to the heavens. The room we arrived in was circular, the floor was smooth as ice, and the walls were a beehive of clear crystals. It looked cold, but I felt warm. I could have been deep inside a sparkling diamond. I had no physical clothes; I was cloaked in light. I felt solid, but I was pure energy," Rachel said.

Jade, fascinated, sat forward, and let go of Kevin's hand.

"What is it?" Kevin whispered to her.

"I don't know. It reminds me of the place I travelled to through the windows in my crystal wand," Jade said, leaning forward, focusing on Rachel's every word.

Rachel zipped up her leather jacket, as if she felt a chill. "We weren't alone, light beings were in the room and they separated Eitan and I. They ushered him into another room, and I remained in the crystal room alone until they returned. They never spoke, but we had an understanding as if they had.

I became aware of a change in the atmosphere in the room, as a wave of energy joined me. The energy was sparkling matter, like converging fireflies, until it divided into two groups and two light beings shaped like humans were standing before me. A tall woman and an even taller man. I imagined, by the constant movement of their energy, that if I reached out to touch them, their energy would compress into a dense solid form able to withstand a blow."

Correct, I heard inside my head.

"They're gods, I thought. Telepathically, they corrected me. 'We are elders, messengers of the creator.'

"It was as if they shared the response. It was strange to hear the words internally and not to see their mouths open. They spoke again.

"'You and your friends were not forgotten. You did not ascend because a patriarch of earth, begged the creator to show mercy, and allow time for the remaining survivors to be gathered and guided to ancient portals around the earth, for one last ascension before the cleansing of the planet. That is your task, and this is why, you are still on earth. Our creator will hold off the order to whitewash the earth of the abominations of the fallen angels for as long as possible. If you do not ascend before the house of Leo is in the sky over egypt, you will be trapped and destroyed along with the evil.'"

"How is God going to whitewash the earth?" Tim asked.

"Rain, floods, earthquakes, and fire. Probably," Seth said, glancing towards Casey. "Casey, do you have Isabella's notebook with you? Can you see if there's anything written in there that can tell us what the abominations of the fallen angels are?"

Head bowed, his eyes glued to the floor, Casey had pulled up his hoodie. He could have been sleeping, for all Jade knew, but she doubted it. He was still as a statue, and the silence in the room was impatient.

"I can go get it for you," Tim said, getting up.

Casey pushed away from the wall, pulled his backpack round to the front, and took out the notebook. He secured his bag on his back, then flicked through Isabella's notebook as if he was angry. Jade thought about the image he had drawn in the sketch book and shivered. Casey began to read, then as if it was too much bare, he pushed off the stone wall and placed the thick stuffed notebook on the table in front of Jade. The leather looked old and worn, but tough. It reminded Jade of a beloved journal. At the top of the page, it said 'The Watchers - Fallen Angels.'

Casey stood at the edge of the table, between her and Shaun. "This is the notebook we found at the Emporium in London, where we also found the flyer about the dream, or the 'calling' to go to Stonehenge. The notebook helped us to kill the *Homoharenae*. Sophia . . . ," Casey paused.

It was painful to watch him swallow his sorrow and anguish. Sadly, there was no time for him, or anyone, to grieve. He grappled with his emotions.

Seth moved to the edge of his seat, closer to the notebook.

"Sophia said Isabella's family most likely passed the notebook down through generations, and that it's about two thousand years old . . ."

Casey turned the pages carefully. The oldest text was in Latin.

Jade, excited, wanted to touch the old leather and study the overstuffed notebook. It fascinated her; it was oozing with information and ideas.

Casey read the heading below an image of a hooded angel:

The fallen angels. Semjaza the leader of ten angels God appointed to watch over humanoids. Ten watchers ruled over two hundred angels appointed as watchers. They became known as the fallen angels, and the gates of heaven were closed to them forever because they stole the daughters of men, and their offspring would not have immortality like the angels, their physical bodies will perish, and when they die their spirits will not be welcomed into heaven, they will be banished, trapped for a thousand years within the realms around the earth. If you're living in this time, the thousands of years are up and the spirits are no longer bound, and they will seek you out. You are only a vessel to them. May God help you.

Casey met Shaun's eyes.

Jade wondered who Isabella and her family were to have created a book with such knowledge. She held back her questions.

"So, humans are the children of the fallen angels?" Shaun asked.

"How am I supposed to know?" Casey snapped.

Jade had never seen Casey's face contorted in such anger before. "Is that all it says?" she spoke softly, trying to promote calmness.

He glared at her. "See for yourself." He turned the book upside down and pushed it towards her, without the care or respect he gave it a moment ago.

Jade scanned the pages, taking in the images of half-human and half-animal beings, giants eating men, angels seducing women. "Are these creatures the abominations?" she asked, more to herself, as she studied the sketches that were made with a pot of ink and fountain pen. It reminded her of Isaac Newton's sketches, and how he needed to be discreet in case the crazy mobs lynched him as a heretic, along with other alchemists; could Isabella's family hidden, afraid of the authorities.

"It's possible. In Egypt, an Ammit that had the head of a crocodile, the body, part hippopotamus and part lion, hunted us. It quenched its hunger on human souls," Rachel said.

At the bottom of the page, it read: "Enoch, chapters 1 to 36."

"What's or who is Enoch?" Jade asked, looking up at Casey.

"You've got to be kidding me. I don't think we ever had a will of our own," Casey said, removing his backpack again.

That was out of left field, Jade thought, trying to understand where Casey was going with his comment.

"Why do you say that?" Ellen asked.

"Because, along with the notebook, I took another book." Casey opened his backpack and removed a white leather-bound book with gold writing—*The Book of Enoch*.

"Maybe it seems like we don't have free will to you, but what about looking at it as divine intervention?" Kevin said.

"I'm sick of divine intervention," Casey said, dropping the book onto the coffee table. "It can leave me the hell alone and give me back Sophia!"

Casey opened the book and read, "Chapter 1: The words of the blessing of Enoch, with which he blessed the elect and righteous, who will be alive in the day of tribulation, when all the wicked and godless people are to be removed from the earth." He closed the book again. "Great, more riddles."

"It seems clear to me," Ellen said.

Casey made no sense and wanted to pick a fight with someone. He put the book back in the bag and stopped to stare at the corner of the basement. His eyes squinted, then widened in horror.

"What's wrong?" Rachel asked.

"Nothing," Casey said, turning his back on whatever he saw.

Rachel turned and looked behind her. "What did you see? I know you well enough to know that look, Casey. What is it?"

"If you're finished, I'm out of here," Casey said, heading for the stairs.

Jade searched the room. There was nothing she could see that would justify his behavior. But that meant nothing. Casey saw spirits, demons, and the dead, things they didn't see. "Do you feel anything?" Jade whispered to Kevin.

"Yeah. I'm picking up a menacing dark hunger," Kevin said.

"No, I'm not finished, Casey!" Rachel said.

"Then hurry up, and spit it out," Casey spat.

"After the light beings relayed the message, I saw my mom and my brother. They, too, appeared as light beings. But when my mom went to wrap her arms around me, I expected to feel nothing and for my arms to float in the fog of light. But she was solid, firm, and warm. She smelled of flowers. It was surreal. Like a dream. All communication was telepathic. Casey, you will see Sophia again. I was in a place beyond this planet, far away amongst the stars, in a world of crystal that was pure. I was in heaven, or some part of heaven. Together, we can find the survivors and get them to the ancient portals around earth before the last ascension," Rachel said.

"But what about the demons and evil spirits? They will stop us. They will kill all of us, just like they killed Sophia," Casey said.

Rachel walked up to Casey, where he held onto the basement wooden banister with one foot on the first step. "We will see more and more of these evil demons and spirits as they enter our world, Casey. Some will need vessels. They might take our bodies and eat our souls, but we have to try. There are survivors out there that might not know what is going to happen, and they will become vessels for the evil entities if we don't help them. If we help them, they will ascend if we help them. We need to find the survivors and give them a chance to ascend, even if we need to sacrifice ourselves, just like Sophia did," Rachel said.

Jade could feel her heart beating faster, as if it were keeping rhythm with a speeding, drum. She touched her drum between her legs for comfort.

Rachel's smile at Casey was sympathetic. "Shooting stars, like dazzling bright lights, whooshed upwards from the earth into the heavens. They twinkled when they flew past me, shooting into the night sky. Casey, I was traveling within a beam of light, and still the power, the energy of the shooting stars filled my heart with love, and I knew one of those stars was Sophia. I didn't want to believe it, but it was her. Her spirit is safe. You will see Sophia again, I promise," Rachel said.

The sound of Sophia's name echoed in the room's silence.

Casey stepped away from the stairs and shoved Rachel to the ground. It was as if Rachel expected Casey to lash out, and she let it happen. Jade knew Rachel could easily take on Casey, as long as he didn't use his powers, that is. Shaun was up on his feet and grabbed Casey by the backpack as he turned to go up the stairs. Kevin got to his feet and tried to pull Shaun off of Casey.

"I'm okay, let him go!" Rachel said.

"How can you be so certain?" Casey said, shaking off Shaun's grip.

"I don't know. But it was her—I'm sure of it. She's not here, but she has already ascended," Rachel said.

Dust fell from the ceiling, and the ground trembled beneath their feet. Casey lost his balance and Shaun caught him.

"I need to get out of here. I have to get Bo," Gwen shouted.

"Everyone, wait a minute. Don't go running scared. When is the next ascension?" Jade asked.

"I've got to get to Bo," Gwen said to Hugh.

"Just a few more minutes, and we can get Bo and head off for the portal at Stonehenge," Hugh said.

"I'm not waiting," Gwen said, leaving.

"Let's reconvene after breakfast, guys?" Hugh said.

Seth stood up, and Tim followed. "That's a good idea. Joe should be here," Tim said.

The trembling stopped. And Rachel spoke in a loud voice.

"The eighth day of Leo is a full year from the first moon after the last ascension. If we miss that day, we all die, and the judgement of the demons and the fallen angels will fall upon us. We will never return to heaven. We will never see our loved ones ever again," Rachel said with the authority of a soldier heading into battle.

"So, before we can ascend, we have to gather the survivors and not get killed by fallen angels, demons, or evil spirits, and God knows what else, or we will die anyway when God cleanses the earth," Hugh said, heading for the stairs after Gwen.

Rachel nodded repeatedly. "That's right."

"I'll head to Stonehenge. Anyone who wants to come is welcome," Hugh said.

"Gary and I will wait for the others and meet you there," Ellen said.

"Are you sure, Mom?" Jade said.

"Yes. Your dad and I will make sure Casey's and Kevin's families know what's happening and get them to Stonehenge," Ellen said.

"Okay, those that want to come with us to Stonehenge, we'll leave after breakfast," Hugh said, climbing the stairs.

Jade took Kevin's hand. "I think I should go back to Black Mountain and warn the community there. Maybe they should all head to Devils Tower, where Chief Thundercloud headed. It could be an ancient portal."

"I'll come with you," Kevin said.

"Kevin, there must be survivors all over the world, and you can connect us all together, you're the only portal master we've got, we need to keep you safe, so you can open portals all around the world for others to find the survivors," Jade said.

"I'm going with you. I will open portals for everyone that needs one, and then I'll open one for us to go to Black Mountain; we are going to stay together. I'll need to find people with emotional memories of traveling to other countries," Kevin said.

"Shaun and I can head back to Olivet in Israel and inform everyone in the city to be at the portal at the Sphinx by the eighth of Leo. Let's all agree to meet back here in two weeks. We have a little over three months to circumnavigate the earth."

Jade felt her awareness expanding, allowing her to see things from a greater, objective perspective. With the drum between her feet and her healing wand in her backpack, next to her medicine pouch, she felt like a warrior, ready to defeat whatever demon dared to challenge her. *I'm ready, Great Turtle. Chief Thundercloud, I'll do you proud*, she thought. She felt as though she was about to enter a great battle. A battle against unseen forces that she felt weren't coming but were already here.

The ground shook.

"That one was closer," Kevin said. "After breakfast, we should all prepare ourselves and leave."

"Don't you worry about us," Ellen said. "I'll stay here with Joe until the others come back from Scotland. Hopefully, they've found survivors. On that note, Joe will probably be awake soon to start break-fast for everyone. I will go get it started for him."

Jade's dad put his boney arm around her mother's shoulders.

"Stay safe," Jade said and watched them leave worried she might not see them again.

Casey was still standing by the stairs, watching everyone else leave. Jade looked over at Kevin, and his face was turning white. "What's wrong?" she asked.

Kevin kept his lips sealed tight, holding back the words. He screwed his face up, struggling for the right word. "Something's coming. We have to leave the estate, now," Kevin said, turning to Casey.

Casey held up his arms for everyone to stop talking and to keep still.

Deep beneath the ground, the earth quaked and shuddered, as a shockwave passed violently through Jade's body and everything in the house. It happened again and again.

"Take cover!" Rachel shouted and clamped her hands over her ears. "I hate that sound. It's like bombs exploding!" Rachel suddenly looked up, and Jade followed her gaze. Jade had no time to move as the ceiling collapsed.

The sound of her own screams filled her ears. The lights went out. And the sensation of her body ceased to exist. An infinite space of darkness surrounded her. She breathed, though she felt as if, she had no lungs to fill. She stretched out her arms, though there were no arms to stretch. The darkness did not swirl or move as she tried to get a sense of physicality. The darkness resembled a vortex, like one she had opened through the rhythm of the drum. *Drum, my drum, drumming. Am I drumming now?* No answers penetrated the darkness and entered her mind. Suddenly, a high-pitched ringing filled the infinite space. If she could use her hands, she would press them hard against her ears to stop the painful noise.

Pain. Pain is good. Sound. Creaking. The ringing stopped. A low hum. A baseline of vibration. Then the intense ringing returned, disbursing out her thoughts.

It was less than a week ago the Shaman had drugged her to steal her power. Power that she didn't even know she had. Jade's mind crystalized and her senses heightened. Cautiously, she scanned the darkness for anything that could cause her harm. The place she was in resembled the space between wakefulness and sleep, a relaxed, safe place when her body was aloof, but her emotional spirit was awake. In the past she had laid in bed, not wanting to leave the wonderful, blissful state, and she would hold on to it, hover between sleep and awake for as long as possible, or until her mom or dad opened the drapes, letting the sun stir her into full consciousness.

There was no cause for alarm, she told herself while she allowed one thought to lead to another, as she floated in the stream of consciousness. Kevin. His portals: she always wanted to stay in the portal's warm membrane that embraced her with love. But she couldn't stay swaddled within the membrane. Eventually she would have to step through, or Kevin would reach in and pull her through. *Kevin, where is Kevin?* Jade struggled to remember what was before the darkness. *Had I been meditating? Did I forget to tether myself to my physical body? Or was I stepping through a portal, traveling to another realm?* Jade struggled with her memories and tried to move and feel her fingers and toes, like Sophia had taught her to do when coming out of a meditation, but it was no use. She couldn't feel them, but gratefully, the ringing in her head had stopped. As annoying and painful as it was, it gave her a sense of having a head, and that was good.

Jade imagined her blood, red and blue, whooshing through her veins. If she could see herself, she would see a warm smile that lit up her face as she rode upon the life force flowing in her veins. Like an artist sketching a faint outline of a portrait, Jade traced herself slowly back into existence. The words of Rachel, describing the light beings compressing into solidity, entered her mind and Jade imagined her own being taking form. Pain shot through her body as her nervous system fired up. Quickly, she pulled back from her body and returned to the darkness, away from the physical pain. *You chicken shit, there's no going back now!* Jade merged into her body again pushing through the pain. Every fiber in her body hurt, bolts of pain shot up her legs and back. She pulled away from her body and the shooting pain. Separated from her body, the darkness was bliss, liberating, peaceful and pain free. Now she knew at the crucial moment when death was inevitable, a separation took place, freeing the soul from the suffering physical body, turning it into pure energy. Is that what is happening? Jade looked into the darkness, the emptiness, the loneliness, it was like being at the outer limits of space, but not the space that's above the earth, above the clouds with twinkling stars, amazing nebulas, and wonderful colored planets, she was in between realms, held up in the astral plane. Her body waited for her on earth—something bad must have happened to her body to leave her stuck in limbo.

People murmured in the distant darkness. She turned to scan the emptiness once again. Sparks of light formed it was like twirling in an ocean of thoughts. In between the light, an ominous shadow moved towards her, taking the form of a silhouette of a group of men, and one wore a derby hat from decades ago. They floated between the sparks of light. There was something odd. As the shadows got closer, she backed away with an urgency to be in her body before the shadows caught up to her. Casey's drawing flashed in and out of her mind. Then Rachel's words, came through loud and clear. 'Evil demons and entities need a vessel.' *Heck no!* Jade wasn't ready for a meet-and-greet with a demon. She had to get back to her abandoned body before evil took up residence. Jade focused and searched for the rhythm of her heart. *There you are; you're beating way too fast.* She pushed into her heart, and flashes of pain pushed her back from her body. Her heart raced like a vagrant running for the last carriage on a freight train that quickly built momentum. She jumped into the pain. Every part of her body was on fire as she lay on the basement floor, broken.

4

CASEY: THE INVISIBLE BECOMES VISIBLE

Instantaneously, Shaun generated power from his icosahedron sapphire to create a hermetic shield around Rachel and Casey as the ceiling of the basement collapsed. Casey was powerless inside the shield, and he could do nothing to stop the furniture from the kitchen above falling on top of Kevin and Jade.

It felt like forever before Casey saw movement from under the drywall. Shaun reduced the hermetic shield and Casey, with his mind, lifted the slab of drywall covering Kevin and Jade. The kitchen table and the refrigerator hid Jade from their view. Kevin lay motionless with white dust caked over his clothes and hair. Casey kneeled and checked his breathing.

"Be careful. Is he alive?" Shaun said, trying to get the kitchen table and chairs out of the way.

"Hurry up get them out of there before the rest of the ceiling could come down," Rachel said stepping over the debris with care.

Casey looked up as Lucy barked down at him from the kitchen. "Move back, girl," Casey yelled at the sandy retriever. He put his hand over Kevin's nose and mouth and felt the warmth of Kevin's breath on his hand. "He's breathing," Casey announced.

Kevin stirred, then moaned. His hand was wedged under the refrigerator where Jade had sat.

"Can you move, Kevin?" Casey asked.

"Yes. yes, I'm fine. Help me, I can feel Jade's wrist, but there's no pulse. I'm squeezing, but she's not squeezing back." Kevin winced with pain, forcefully removing his hand from under the refrigerator, as he moved into a sitting position. removing his hand from under the table.

"Don't move so fast, you could be seriously hurt. You don't want to be a dead man walking," Rachel said.

"I don't care. Help! Casey, help me get this off her," Kevin said, struggling to his feet.

Shaun and Rachel positioned themselves to lift the refrigerator, when Casey raised his hands and moved the refrigerator and debris off Jade and over to the far side of the basement, the very spot he had seen the shadows enter the basement right before the tremor. He let the refrigerator drop heavily, hoping the black shadows were still hiding in the corner.

Jade lay at an odd angle, her hips probably broken. Jade had received the mass of the debris. It was strange how most of the kitchen furniture had fallen on top of her, as if targeted, but Casey knew that was ridiculous. Casey looked back to the corner just as the black shadows stepped through the refrigerator.

"Shaun, put up the shield. Put it up now!" Casey said.

A zap of blue light is all it took for them to be safe. Sophia would have loved to have seen Shaun create the hermetic shield.

Within the shield, Kevin touched Jade's neck searching for a pulse. "I can't find her pulse," Kevin said, starting compressions. "I need to create a portal; I can't create one from inside your shield. It's the only way to save her," Kevin pressed down on Jades chest. "Shaun Reduce the hermetic shield."

Casey stepped forward watching jade's aura. "We must be quick; she is only linked to her body by the thinnest cord of light. Hurry before her spirit disconnect from her body forever. She's close."

"I'll open the portal just in the first chamber of the tunnels. Casey, get ready to lift her and carry her into the portal membrane," Kevin stopped the compressions and rubbed his hands together, anxiously.

Casey picked up Jade, her body was on fire with unbearable pain, he pushed back the crippling pain of the multiple broken bone and internal bleeding from her crushed organs, he was worried she wasn't going to make it. "I can feel her spirit. Hurry up and get us outside into the open," Casey said, looking at the three shadows floating towards them. "You better be quick! We're not alone down here."

"Okay, now, Shaun," Kevin said.

"Drop the shield," Rachel said.

"I've got this. Just calm down," Shaun said.

"You've got about five seconds, three dark silhouettes are coming for Jade's body," Casey said to Kevin.

Sparks and light crackled in the small space. Beautiful colored waves flowed within a space wide enough for them to step through. Pure energy moved around Kevin's hands as he quickly opened the portal. Casey held Jade's broken, limp body close to his chest as Shaun dropped the shield. The intense pain throughout her body as her nervous system was firing one more time passed into his body causing him temporary paralysis. Casey forced his legs to step into the energy of the portal, and the pain and lifelessness of Jade's body instantly dissipated once immersed in the portal's healing membrane. He could feel her body repairing – coming alive in his arms.

If only Kevin had been back in time to have saved Sophia, Casey thought. He'd saved Tim's life the same way, and Rachel's and Shaun's. It's not fair! Why did Sophia have to die? The energy of the portal wrapped around their bodies, restoring every cell.

Inside the membrane of the portal, Kevin, Casey with Jade in his arms, Shaun and Rachel stepped from the basement to the field at the back of the house, he felt Jade's hip and leg being reconstructed and put back into place. Casey watched and felt the light of the membrane renew Jade's cells and her crushed organs. She lay in his arms as good as new. Glittering silver light from Jade's aura forged her totem animal. A white deer filled his vision as healing golden light touched his heart. He resisted; he didn't want to let go of his pain. He stepped from the portal and placed Jade on the ground. Kevin collapsed the portal. Outside the air was fresh; he drew in a deep breath glad to be out of the basement. The sun was yet to peek over the horizon and shine upon the dew on the fields that would sparkle like diamonds.

"She's going to be fine," Casey said, watching her chest rise.

"It's a miracle. Thank God she's alive!" Rachel said, holding Jade's bag with her drum and memory box inside.

Kevin checked Jade's pulse. "She's coming around." Her eyes fluttered open as a tiny spark of starlight disappeared inside her chest. A flicker caught Casey's eye, in the fields by Alex's grave. A white deer watched on. Then it turned away, disappearing into the woods.

"What happened? Where's my drum?" Jade said.

"I've got it," Rachel said, holding it up.

Kevin and Shaun helped Jade up. Jade wrapped his arms around Kevin's neck. "I thought I lost you," Kevin said.

Casey felt alone.

"How do you feel?" Casey said.

"A little dazed. For a minute, I was dead and stuck between realms, and preyed upon by dark entities. Including one that wore a derby hat." Jade laughed. "That's stupid, right?" she said, laughing, but quickly stopped, seeing the look on his face. "You've seen them too?" Jade said to Casey.

"You were dead. They were after your body. We need to warn the others," Casey said, looking back at the house.

In the distance, he could see the damage to the main house. Lucy ran out of the back of the house and towards a cluster of trees that hid part of the road out front. She skidded to a halt and barked ferociously as the canopies thrashed violently. The ground trembled. A section of the trees disappeared as if torn out of the ground like a weed. A huge ripple of energy created a haze against the woods in the shape of a giant man that stood forty feet high. As if bending forward, it folded downward. The grazing cows at the back of the house, one after the other, were lifted into the air as the giant haze unfolded to its full height. Shaun and Daniel had spent weeks collecting the cows. They were part of their family now. Lucy, fearless, continued to bark at the giant. The cows' moos stopped as they disappeared into the haze. A leg and a head dropped to the ground and landed at their feet as if spat from the giant's mouth. Casey shot up into the sky and Shaun ignited the hermetic shield. He could see the ripples as the giant moved across the trees and stepped onto the plane wreckage on the front lawn.

Seth's father ran with his son Ernest in his arms. He fell, dropping Ernest before he disappeared under the giant's foot. Billie, Ernest's sister, ran fast and grabbed Ernest's hand. Casey pushed out a concussive energy blast towards the giant humanoid haze that was slowly becoming a solid form. He may not be able to protect everyone like Sophia had, but he could easily push anything a mile away with his telekinesis.

The blast sent the giant stumbling backwards, toppling on to the house, which it crushed like a pile of matchsticks. As the giant crashed to the ground, what was left of the house vanished under the giant's invisible form. Shockwaves moved like rolling waves of water, tripping Billie and Ernest as they tried to get into the idling camper van. Tim, standing on the camper-van step, with one hand holding on to the side of the van door he reached out for and grabbed Ernest. The giant snatched up Billie by the hair. She dangled in midair, slapping at the hazy giant's hand as it lifted her closer to what Casey imagined was its face and mouth. Casey zoomed towards her and snatched her out of the giant's clutches.

A foul-smelling gust of air consumed Casey and Billie as the giant gave out a thunderous roar as it suddenly revealed it the giant hideous form. It had three eyes, one in the middle of the forehead that blinked as Casey and Billie passed it by. It wore a necklace of bones, and it dressed like a Viking in the middle of a winter storm. Three giants surrounded the estate.

"Put me down, I have to get Ernest," Billie yelled, struggling against him.

"Tim has him." Casey searched for the camper van. It was heading out the main gate and onto the road. Casey flew over, holding onto Billie. Tim opened the door of the moving camper van and Casey let go of Billie and levitated her into Tim's arms.

"Come with us," Tim said, putting a protected arm across Billie's chest so she didn't fall out of the van.

"Who's with you?" Casey asked.

"Everyone but my dad," Seth said.

Ellen stuck her head out. "Jade and Rachel, Shaun and Kevin, are they okay?"

"Yes," Casey said, hovering in the doorway.

Boom! Boom! Boom! Casey turned. The giant he stole Billie off pursed Casey and swatted him out of the air and sent him flying across the adjoining fields. Casey, tumbling backwards, hitting tress and limestone boulders, breathless, he finally regained control of his body, and sped back towards the estate. With a mighty push of energy, he upended the giant sending it crashing to the round. Casey's nose was bleeding, from the force of the psychic push, the blood was warm, he could taste it on his top lip. The giant, dazed, struggled to stand.

Tim closed the camper-van door and Seth speed off swerving, getting traction and clearing the fallen giant. Casey made sure the camper van had some distance between the giants before he headed back for Shaun and the others who were secure within the hermetic shield but one of the other giants poked at the blue sphere that protected Shaun, Jade, Rachel, and Kevin, pushing them like they were in a hamster's plastic ball. The screech of tires coming from the road caused him to stop and look back at the road. The giant was up on its feet trying to catch the swerving camper van. Casey pushed out with his mind and the giant moved like a drunk, on the fourth of July. The van gained speed. Casey uprooted a tree and used it as a club. He was at least a mile from the estate when the giant fell. He thought of catching up to Hugh and Tim in the van but felt compelled to go back and help the others.

The giant continued to push the hermetic sphere over the back fields.

Shaun had expanded the hermetic shield to the size of a house, but the giant shoveled the land under it and picked up the hermetic sphere with his friends inside. Casey pushed the giant over and then levitated it off the ground and propelled the giant up through the clouds. Casey soared into the morning sky. The blue air thinned out as he reached the edge of the ozone. Fatigue and a lack of oxygen made him sleepy. He heaved and thrusted the giant as far out into space as possible. He hoped it would sail forever and never return to earth. Rapidly he blinked, trying to keep his eyes open. He fell into a micro sleep and tumbled down through the ozone layer. Quickly snapping awake, his heart racing, from the lack of oxygen and extreme exertion, he let himself free fall for a mile or two before taking control of his descent entering a whisper of cloud. Meters away from the ground, he slowly lowered himself down next to the hermetic shield. "We have to get going. Kevin, open a portal for Shaun and Rachel to go back to Israel."

Shaun looked at him and said, "Come with us, Casey?"

Shaun was like the big brother he never had. "I'll be fine," Casey said.

"You're not fine," Shaun said.

"Come with us, Casey," Rachel said putting her hands on her hips.

"There's no time. The giants will be back," he looked up into the early morning sky worried the giant he tossed into outer space was going to drop down on his head any moment. Kevin, open a portal now," Casey said.

"Stay safe," Shaun took his hand and then pulled him into a brief hug, the releasing him for Rachel to give Casey a hug too.

Kevin moved his arms like a magician weaving a magical spell and opened a portal back to Israel. Quick hugs with Jade and Kevin, then Shaun and Rachel were gone. Quickly, Kevin closed the portal and started to generate another.

"Wait! We should search the rubble for the others," Jade turned back towards the pile of rubble that was once the house.

"We also, need to find a way to let Terry, Amy, and your parents know to be weary of the giants and to head to Stonehenge. There's left-over paint in the barn. I could write a quick message on the road for them. Help Jade. It won't take long," Casey said, running off towards the barn.

Quickly, he found the tin of paint and wrote, *Keeping going, beware of giants. Head to Stonehenge.* Casey soared across the sky towards the rubble. Jade and Kevin together, removed wooden beams, cracked blocks of sandstone as they search for their friends. Casey, from the air searched for Lucy, but the dog was nowhere to be seen, praying she was with Tim he set down next to Jade.

"I can't find Joe." Jade went deeper into the rubble, pieces of wood collapsed under her feet, she sank down, reached out and held herself up from falling any further by holding onto a water pipe. Kevin went after her.

Casey stopped him. "Wait!" He stretched his arms our toward Jade and she slowly raised out from the rubble and floated over to Kevin, where Casey set her down on the ground.

The ground shook. They all looked over their shoulders, the remaining tress toppled, as the giants headed for them.

"Let's pray he's with Hugh and Tim," Casey said, looking back at Jade and Kevin, as a mass of dark figures of all sizes began popping into existence across the paddock, floating towards them and one wore a hat. "Turn around, guys."

"Oh no," Jade said.

"Let me guess, they're what you saw in the astral plane?" Kevin said.

"Whatever you have to do, Kevin, do it now," Casey said.

"You don't need to tell me twice," Kevin said as he created a portal back to Black Mountain in North Carolina. Together they jumped into the portal as a giant stomped down.

5

JADE: BLACK MOUNTAIN USA

With her drum slung over her shoulder and her wand tucked into her back pocket, Jade stepped from the early morning light into the darkness of the night at Black Mountain, on the other side of the North Atlantic Sea. She expected the residents of the campground to have a couple of lookouts standing guard. Across the dark field, not one cabin light was on. She removed her wand from her back pocket and her bracelet slipped down her wrist and clicked against the gemstones on her wand. She pushed her bracelet up from her wrist and held her wand lighting their way forward. All the familiar sounds of the forest hushed.

"What is it?" Kevin asked.

Listening, she looked up into the sky, straining to hear anything out of the ordinary. Kevin looked down at the ground, trying to pick up a scent of emotions. A wolf yelped and its pack howled in pain. Jade calmed her breathing as one of her animal guides stepped silently out of the forest. The white deer's ears pricked up, and Jade heard dripping, panting, and running; it drew near. She raised her healing wand up high but could not reveal what hid deep in the forest. The deer bolted, so Jade ran after it across the field.

"Wait! Where are you going?" Casey said.

"Come on," Jade yelled. "Stay within the light." As she approached the steps of the community hall, a light came on and the deer disappeared.

Kevin and Casey stopped on either side of her. Clouds floated across the clear sky, dimming the natural light of the moon.

"Should we hide?" Casey asked.

Butterflies filled her stomach. Jade changed her grip on her wand. The community hall door burst open. The light coming from inside hid the details of the man stepping onto the verandah. But she knew who it was. Her body instantly reacted to his pheromones. She felt betrayed by her own body's chemical response. She hadn't given him too much thought and hadn't prepared for his magnetism. It bothered her because she liked everything about him—his strength, his crystal blue eyes, even his shoulder-length black hair was perfect, and not to mention Great Turtle had chosen him to teach the shamanic healing ways instead of her.

"Raven Wings," Mingan said.

Raven Wings was the name her great-grandmother, Great Turtle, had given her. No one called her Raven Wings except Great Turtle and Chief Thundercloud. A gentle tug on her forearm caused her to lower her wand, and she rubbed her forearm as if to stop her Raven tattoo from taking flight. Mingan had no right to call her that.

"Back so soon," Mingan said.

Mingan put his arm on Jade's shoulder. She pulled away. Embarrassed, she dared not look at Kevin in case he could feel her tension.

"Honestly, stay here." Mingan was a man of few words, but when he spoke everyone listened.

"Why? Because I'm a female?" Jade snapped. It frustrated her that she acted out of character—around him she was reactive instead of proactive. There was something about him that made her want to get to know him better, but she feared they were all the wrong reasons.

"Jade?" Crazy Bear pushed past Mingan. "You and your friends better get inside."

"Why? What's happening?"

"We can talk when we get back." Mingan headed down the verandah steps.

"Mingan, wait! Crazy Bear, what's going on?"

"There's a terrible infection that might be spreading through the camp and Russell's son, Bob, seems to be infected. He has gone mad with fever and escaped from the infirmary. We're worried he will hurt himself or someone else. He is the third person in two days to fall ill and flee to the forest. Something is terribly wrong. You should stay here, Jade." Crazy Bear moved aside for Russell and his eldest son, Mitch, as they burst through the doors of the main lodge.

Russell and Mitch jogged across the field to the woods.

A loud cry came from deep within the forest.

"Maybe we can help?" Casey said, watching the men enter the woods.

"Maybe? Come on then. It's your funeral," Crazy Bear said, putting his hand out to Casey.

Casey looked at the simple gesture.

"He doesn't shake," Kevin said.

Jade didn't wait for permission and took off after the others who knew their way around the forest. They were moving fast, and she found it hard to catch up. She took out her wand for light as Casey kept pace with Crazy Bear, and Kevin wasn't far behind. Frightened night animals fled through the brush. *What's going on?* she wondered. Kevin moved fast and passed her by, quickly catching up with Russell and Mitch. *What was he doing?* she thought. The forest thickened, and they fell into a single file. A stitch in her side was becoming unbearable. She had to stop. She wasn't a runner, she was and academic who ran her eyes across sentences until ocular vertigo forced her to stop reading

Mingan was behind her. "You should have stayed behind."

How did he get behind me? I thought he was out in front? "You don't have to babysit me. I'll be fine." Jade stepped off the trail to let him pass, but he stood his ground, waiting for her to move on.

"I will not leave you here. You need protection." Mingan said.

"Oh, please," Jade said. She only needed a few seconds to pull out her wand and draw a line across her side where it hurt the most. The stitch gone, she took off after the others.

She stopped running after a few minutes. The bobbing flashlight beams disappeared. She couldn't see any lights up front, and there was no sign of Mingan behind her, and where was Casey. Suddenly the hairs on the back of her neck tingled and her skin puckered. She looked up at the sky. The trees swayed slightly. The clouds had thickened, blocking out the moon and the stars. She could feel the change in the air. A storm was coming. "Really!" she said as it sprinkled. "Now? It has to rain now?"

Jade calmed her breathing, raised her arms above her head, closed her eyes, vulnerable in the darkness, she imagined a clear night, stars twinkling bright enough for her to see. She opened her eyes and the clouds parted. From her heart, light glowed, everything went still, and the rain stopped. It frightened her to have such power. Only Great Spirit should be able to control nature.

She waited for guidance. The feeling of the pounding hooves of the animals fleeing the area had stopped, along with everything else. A foul stench and a sudden chill tainted the spring air. It was deathly quiet. A large branch crashed down at her feet. She jumped back when a boney, human-like creature leaped down from the tall trees above. Jade screamed. Bits of flesh stuck to its ribs. It roared releasing a foul stench, hot air and a forked tongue like a snakes soaked up the air. Jade covered her nose and mouth as its forked tongue reached out for her. She stepped backwards as it advanced, the spirit of a gray wolf intercepted, and the gory creature dematerialized.

Then the wolf was vanished, and the sounds of the forest's nightlife returned. As the forest breathed an owl hooted, which she imagined was telling her to go.

Kevin came running. "Jade! I heard you scream?" He twisted around, searching frantically for what had frightened her. Mingan stepped out of the shadows. "Where did you go? I thought you were watching Jade?"

Mingan walked past Kevin without a word.

"I'm not sure what I saw," Jade said.

"Over here!" Crazy Bear called out. "I've found him."

Jade and Kevin followed the sound of Crazy Bear's voice. Russell and Mitch were already there. Bob was on the ground naked, with blood over his mouth and chest. Crazy Bear moved, making room for Mingan. Mitch covered his brother with a blanket as if this wasn't the first time he found his brother naked in the forest. Jade searched the surrounding forest. The blood on Bob's face made Jade think Bob was the hunter, not the hunted. He looked like a wild man. He certainly was not the same guy she had met a few days ago.

"What are you doing?" Kevin said in a soft voice.

"Searching; the same as you."

"Over here," Casey whispered.

In the brush, using her crystal wand for light, Jade stepped over fallen branches to see what Casey and Kevin had found. A dead wolf, with its stomach torn open and its intestines spilling out, lay at their feet. "That's probably the wolf we heard yelping when we first arrived," Jade said.

Casey reached down and touched the wolf's paw. His face contorted in pain, and he withdrew his hand. "Bob did this. Bob hunted the wolf down and tore it open with his bare hands."

"Back away," Kevin said.

Casey wiped his hand on his jeans as if it would wipe away the wolf's memory from his mind. "What is it?" Casey said.

Kevin started generating a portal. "We're being watched. We have to go."

"We can't leave the others," Jade said.

"Close the portal. I've got this," Casey said, stretching out his arms, generating energy, ready to blast anything that jumped out at them. "Start walking back to the others."

Jade and Kevin did as he asked, trusting Casey had their backs. Crazy Bear looked up from where he was crouched over Bob.

"Where did you go?"

"There's a gutted wolf over there," Jade said.

"We have to get out of here," Kevin told him. "We're not alone out here."

* * *

CHANTING, Mingan moved his hands in a circular pattern over Bob's body. "I'm afraid it's what we feared. He is only going to get worse," he said to Russell.

"I don't care. I'm taking him back. Pick him up, Mitch," Russell said to his son.

Mitch did what he was told, but not before he locked eyes with Mingan, as if daring him to stop him. Mitch wrapped his brother in the blanket like a burrito and slung him over his shoulder. Bob could have easily been mistaken for an old floor rug.

"Walk in front," Mingan said to Mitch. "So, I can keep an eye on Bob. Crazy Bear, watch our backs. There could be more like him."

When they were back on the path where it widened, Casey moved up beside Jade. "What's going on here?" His voice was soft but rushed.

"I don't know. It wasn't like this when we left two days ago," Jade said.

"Take him to the infirmary," Mingan said when Mitch made a beeline for his family cabin.

"I'm not letting anyone chain up my son like a wild animal," Russell said.

"I can't let you take him to your cabin," Mingan said.

"He wouldn't hurt us. He didn't attack a person; he killed a wolf, dammit!"

Mitch stopped walking and turned to Russell. "He's got the fever, Dad. We can't risk it. He has to go to the infirmary. If the doc says he hasn't got the fever, then I'll take him back to our cabin," Mitch said.

Russell seemed defeated. "Okay. I know you wouldn't let anyone hurt your brother. Just don't leave his side."

"The cabin assigned to your family is still empty. You can stay there for now," Russell said to Jade as he hurried to follow Mitch.

So much has changed in such a short time. There were no infections when she had left a few days ago, whatever it is, it develops quickly.

"I have something important to tell you all," Jade said as Mingan walked off. *Why the hell is Mingan so dismissive? Is it because Kevin is with her?* she wondered.

"Jade, we can tell them in the morning," Kevin said, trying to get her to move away from Bob.

Mingan turned around and Jade nearly had her face in his chest. "Maybe it's time to listen to the stones," he said and walked on.

* * *

WHO THE HELL *does he think he is?* Jade thoughts were reeling as she entered the cabin.

The cabin was an open area, on the left the kitchen with a window, and a circular table with four chairs, on the right was a small couch and a one-seater; it looked exactly how they had left it. Kevin showed Casey around before they both came outside to join her on the tiny porch.

"What happened to Bob?" Kevin said.

Casey leaned against the wooden porch rail, gazed at the sparkling stars, and Jade wondered if Sophia was watching him from heaven. Casey, smiling he pushed away from the railing then squatted down on to the step beside her.

"How well do you know these people, Jade?" Casey asked.

Before she could take her eyes off the sky, Kevin answered Casey's question.

"Not very well, but they are all acutely aware of Great Turtle, Jade's great-grandmother which puts Jade on a pedestal." Kevin scratched the back of his head.

"We'll have to wait. Maybe Bob's gone mad," Jade said.

"He was sweet on Jade when we first arrived, he offered her his seat in the dining hall, and offered to teach her how to protect herself using a knife," Kevin said.

Casey chuckled. "Really. Well that was nice, but I don't think anyone can use a knife as well as you," Casey said.

"Except Rachel," Jade said.

"Yeah," they both said and nodded.

Jade was stuck on a thought she had when Casey implied, she was good at using a knife. The first thing that flashed into her mind was a memory of Great Turtle slicing open a snake.

"Jade, I know we haven't talked much about what happened to you during your search for your dad, but I would like to know more about what happened to you, when you're ready to talk. Joe did tell me that Kevin had had ant mandibles used as sutures in his head," Casey said without taking his eyes off the stars. "I'm glad you found your dad, Jade, and I hope you're okay now, Kevin."

"Yeah, I'm alright. There is so much we still need to tell you, Casey," Kevin said. "But we didn't want to say anything, because of Sophia. Man, I cannot tell you how sorry I am that she's gone."

Kevin placed his hands over his solar plexus and turned side on protecting himself from Casey's emotions. "This is a friendly community. If we want, we could bring everyone in the UK here; they will welcome everyone. And I've been thinking, why get all the people to go to different portals around the world? Why not just channel them all to this one space, to the one portal, whether it be the one that Rachel found in Egypt, or Stonehenge, or the temple in Peru? We can congregate in any place in the world. Why can't we just get everybody in one place?"

Jade got up off the step and dusted off her pants.

"I don't know, as much as I hate to say it, there seems to be a reason for everything," Jade said as she walked up onto the porch and opened the cabin door. "Kevin can fill you in as to what happened searching for my dad. I'm going to lie down for a while." Jade went to close the door.

"Where are you going?" Kevin asked.

"I'll be back. There's something I need to do in my room."

* * *

JADE TOOK out the black onyx stone from her medicine pouch. It seemed like such a long time ago that she was studying over books of quantum physics, studying courses way beyond her years. That stuff was easy. Nervously, she took the box of memory stones out of the cream crochet drum bag and placed it on the bed. The seashells glued to the lid felt familiar, just like they had when Chief Thundercloud had given them to her on behalf of her great-grandmother less than a week ago.

Her stones, her memories. Jade pushed down, and the lid slid easily in its groove. She closed it, afraid of what the stones might reveal. She needed to look and move beyond her fear. Taking in a deep breath, she slid the lid to reveal six onyx stones. She placed them next to the first onyx that had a tribal drawing of a drum with wings. Drawn to the black stone with the spiral of a snake eating its own tail, she picked it up. "A good place as any to start."

The height of the bunk bed was a little too low, and when she tried to get into a comfortable position to meditate on the memory stone of the snake, her hair got caught on the springs above. Outside would have been good, but for now, the floor was going to have to do. She untangled her hair, then shut the bedroom door, crossed her legs and sat down. She cupped her hand around the onyx with the snake.

Jade sat lotus style, like Sophia had taught her, and imagined her feet sinking into plush green grass and deep into the ground to connect with the roots of the earth. Relaxing, she held the image of the stone in her mind as she searched for the door to the dream lodge. Her body was covered in bear skin. It felt heavy, keeping her grounded as she moved deeper into her subconscious mind and into the dream realm, where she found the door to the dream lodge. She hoped Great Turtle would be there, and for a fleeting moment, she hoped to see Sophia. She calmed her thoughts because all she was doing was planting potential scenarios into her mind that would only confuse her when she made genuine connections.

Suddenly she was inside a tree, in its belly, like a child waiting to be born. The door opened, and she stepped out of the tree into a cabin. She could hear men talking and arguing outside. She went to the window and peeked outside. Snakes obeying someone just out of sight surrounded four men. A shadow. Jade had to slow her breathing. The snakes slithered up over the men. A coral snake went into the man's ear. From above, a wolf dropped into the center of the circle of men and landed on top of the snakes. The men ravished and tore at the flesh of the wolf and ate feverishly.

Jade couldn't understand the message of the stone. She could see the connection with the snakes, but that was all. What did these men have to do with her stone? They didn't have the feeling of the past. Then Great Turtle appeared. She was young and beautiful. She was shaking, a rattle advancing in on the shadow. The image disappeared. Jade sat on the porch of Great Turtle's home, watching her crush the vertebras of a snake that had bitten Jade as a child. Her two-year-old self got down on her haunches, mesmerized by Great Turtle's actions, and sang along with Great Turtle's rhyme.

Hisss. Hisss. Hisss. Hunger and pain,

the infernal shall slither,

into your minds again.

Poisoning your thoughts,

Feeding on your fear,

Luring you into the darkness,

Boiling your blood as he nears.

Hiss. Hiss. Hiss. Hunger and pain,

Feast from the vessel,

starvation is the game.

Snakes circled around her two-year-old self. Great Turtle turned to her and said, "Remember! This snake is not one of good fortune; it is the sign that evil is near. Take up your wand and cast the light . . . at the end, the fight begins."

Jade couldn't quite understand Great Turtle's muffled words, but she could see herself in the memory standing near Great Turtle's cabin, when she saw in the far corner of the property by the forest, snakes slithering up the leg of a shadow of a man, until they were one dark mass. She put her baby hands over her eyes no longer wanting to see. Frightened, her tiny body hiccuped with tears as she wailed.

Great Turtle comforted her, "Shh, child. You are the warrior. The poison in your blood will protect you. Hush now and watch how easy it is for you to destroy the beast." Great Turtle raised her arms and gathered the light down from the sky, and as she prayed to Great Spirit, a pool of light expanded from her being, forcing the snakes back into the darkness, back to the shadow of the infernal standing at the edge of the forest.

Jade cried and watched the shadow, filled with snakes. A cobra sat on top of its derby hat.

"Jade, wake up!" Kevin said.

He was crouched down beside her. "Are you okay? I heard you cry out."

It took a few seconds to register she had crawled under the bed and her hair had entangled with the bed springs again. "Help me, will you?" Jade said.

Kevin got down on his belly. It reminded Jade of the snakes, and she was afraid he would turn into one. She searched the floor, making sure there were none in the room.

Free of the springs, Jade wormed her way out from under the bed. Rubbing her sore head, she said, "I was meditating against that wall when I saw a vision from my memory stone. Suddenly something happened, and I was yanked out of the dream lodge. I saw a shadow filled with snakes and it was wearing . . ."

"A hat," Casey said, tossing her the onyx as if it were a hot potato.

"Yes, and a . . . ," Jade said.

"A cobra was sitting on top," Casey said.

"But how did . . . ?" Jade looked down at the stone. She looked up at Casey. "You held the stone for a second, and you saw all that?" She got up and sat on the edge of the bed.

"You were singing a nursery rhythm or song," Kevin said.

"I can't remember. Why can't I remember? Tell me what you heard," Jade said.

"Something about a vessel, starvation, and hissing," Kevin said.

"Casey, why don't you hold the stone and tell me what you see? If you saw the snakes and the hat, maybe you could see the whole thing?" Jade said, holding out the onyx to him.

"I don't know, Jade. Maybe he shouldn't?" Kevin said.

Casey met her eyes. He allowed her to drop the onyx into his hand. Then he crumbled to the floor, dropping the stone.

"Casey!" Jade slapped his face gently. "Casey." She touched Casey between the eyes with her wand. The terminator crystal radiated a light so blinding that she had to close her own eyes. In her mind, she saw an angel wrapping its wings around Casey's body, protecting him from the onyx. The light disappeared as if someone had flicked off a switch. "What happened?" Jade said.

"I saw the dark form filled with snakes, wearing that stupid derby hat with a live cobra on top. It struck out at me. Its fangs were so long, I had no time to protect myself. But the bite never came. I blacked out," Casey said.

"An angel protected you," Jade said.

"I felt the power of the darkness and the light," Kevin said.

There was a knock at the cabin door. Jade looked out the bedroom window. "It's daylight. How long was I . . . never mind," Jade said and stuffed her wand back into her pocket. "I'll see who it is. You help Casey up."

It was him. Mr. Blue Eyes. Somehow, he looked taller, broader, and more handsome in the early morning light. She felt like a silly schoolgirl all over again. Even though it was the end of the world, the development of a teenager continued. She could feel her cheeks warming, and fury at herself of being so easily distracted, and her hormones raged. She wanted to lash out at Mingan for being so gorgeous and making her feel so uncomfortable.

"Are you ready to learn?" Mingan asked.

There was a lot that he could teach her, and she wanted to learn.

6

KEVIN: JEALOUSY BITES

On the front porch Kevin watched Mingan's eyes darting from left to right, up and down, as he studied Jade. Tension built up between them. Mingan turned his face away, but he continued to watch her out of the corner of his eye. Clearly pleased at what he saw, he nodded.

Kevin raised his eyebrows at Casey.

"He's reading her aura," Casey said leaning into Kevin from behind.

"Well, Mingan? What do you see?" Jade asked, annoyed.

Mingan was twenty-six, ten years older than Kevin, and an inch or two taller, and a hell of a lot more confident. Around Mingan's strong tense neck, a chunk of clear quartz crystal dangled on a piece of black leather and sat comfortably on his defined chest. Suddenly the porch like veranda seemed small. Kevin felt the intensity in which Mingan scrutinized Jade, as if he was seeing beyond her clothes and skin. The magnetism between Mingan and Jade was so obvious that Kevin could see the moment when Casey must've sensed it because he took a few steps back, as if Mingan's and Jade's auras had expanded forcing everyone back.

Kevin, annoyed. "What the hell? Are you right!" Kevin feeling hostile towards Mingan stepped into his space breaking the invisible connection with Jade.

Mingan ignored Kevin and kept his eyes fixed on Jade's. She was the first to pull away.

"All good. Very interesting. A deep thinker. Loves to learn. Feisty," Mingan said.

Jade took the first step down from the cabin verandah and stumbled. Kevin reached out and caught her, felt her butterflies, her confusion, and uncertainty. He pulled his hand away, not wanting to feel and know about the emotions she was trying to hide. His body perceived her doubts so clearly, it made him feel uncomfortable. But there were deeper feelings, desires, questions she felt only Mingan could answer.

She pushed Kevin away, angry at him for reasons Kevin didn't understand. He only knew he could feel her heart racing, the swirl of her confused thoughts. She wasn't doing a good job keeping her feelings and thoughts close, despite knowing that he could sense them.

This had often happened to Kevin as a child. When his mother was afraid, she would be unable to rein in those feelings, and he would find out things she didn't want him to know.

And that's where he was now, looking from Jade to Mingan. A fire had ignited in Jade's belly, and he knew!

"What was that all about?" Casey asked Kevin as they passed the other cabins where people were stirring inside. Clanging breakfast bowls and spoons; the sounds of a family breakfast seemed so odd, in the scheme of things, that Kevin shook his head in disbelief.

"I don't know, Casey, but I don't like it." She seemed to be mesmerized by him and yet repelled at the same time. Her emotions were confusing. And Jade was normally clear-headed.

They walked across the open field to the main building used as a community hall, where the singles boarded above the infirmary. Couples and families were assigned to the cabins. Jade fell into step and smiled at him. She touched his hand. Warmth and certainty filled his being. Her emotions were conflicted, and it confused him so much, he let go of her hand as soon as she interlocked her fingers with his. From the first moment he'd met her, he had been there for her, allowing her to see inside him, to feel his energy, to know him from the inside. It was sheer stupidity to have allowed himself to be so vulnerable. There had never been a person in his life to whom he had opened himself that way. But now it didn't seem like such a smart idea to wear his heart on his sleeve. He'd thought they were falling in love —maybe not.

Jade, hurt by his rejection, quickened her pace to walk beside Mingan.

"I have memory stones. I'm having trouble extracting the memories. Can you help me?" Jade asked Mingan, avoiding eye contact.

Kevin slowed his pace. It was like being kicked in the stomach. *She could have asked me,* he thought. He'd at least be able to tell her every emotion she had felt contained inside the stone, during the creation of the original memories. Why didn't she ask him to help her?

Mingan put his hand on the small of Jade's back, encouraging her to walk up the steps to the community lodge first. *Mingan's just being caring, after she had stumbled on the steps of the cabin,* Kevin told himself. But it felt like so much more. In his mind's eye, he saw the image of a bird stretching out its wing to protect its partner. Kevin felt his own anger stirring inside him.

"What's wrong?" Casey asked.

"Nothing, why?" Kevin said.

"Your aura is all over the shop. You need to stop reading other people's emotions. It's going to mess with your energy and your head. Later, you need to open the portals. You know when you overuse your clairsentience ability, you can get overloaded and unable to open portals. When Alex died, you were in burnout for three months. Take it easy and control your ability, or it will control you," Casey warned, stopping on the community verandah.

"It's not an ability; it's a curse. I'm not a clairsentient; I'm just a pussy," Kevin said.

"You're an empath at least. We need you, Kevin," Casey said as he went to put his hand on Kevin's shoulder to comfort him but stopped and pulled away.

The door closed behind Mingan, as if Kevin and Casey weren't even there.

* * *

UP THE STAIRS, Mitch stood guard at the infirmary door.

"What gives?" Mingan said to Mitch.

"I didn't want anyone going in until you checked on Bob. He's been making crazy sounds throughout the night. I don't know if it's even safe to go in," Mitch said.

The door creaked as they all entered the infirmary. Two rows of ten beds, evenly spaced, filled the room.

"Somebody needs to open a window," Jade said.

The room smelled funky, of stale sweet and urine. It left a metallic taste in Kevin's mouth.

There was one unkept bed at the far end of the right-hand side of the room, the farthest away from the windows, but close to what Kevin imagined would be a consultation room or a nurses' station, which was now unoccupied. As they drew close, they could see an empty bed the bedsheet covered in stains. On the end of the bed was a long, papery strip, like a strip of tissue paper or the shed skin of a huge snake. Mitch lifted the bedsheet hanging over the edge and looked under – Bob was curled in the fetal position under the bed, and away from the light coming through the window. Hidden in a shadow, he had pulled his legs up so the light couldn't touch him.

"Oh shit! What is that? What's wrong with him?" Jade said.

Mingan crouched down and Mitch joined him. Casey pushed his hands deep into his pockets, careful not to touch anything. Kevin wished he could do the same. Bob was naked, his skin pale, scaly, glistening with moisture, and his hair thinned. Clumps of hair like tumble lay on the floor.

"Bob, can you hear me?" Mitch said.

"Help me get him out," Mingan said.

Mitch touched Bob's leg. "He's wet." Mitch rubbed the substance between his thumb and forefinger. "It's slippery."

"I'll draw the blinds. Give us a hand, Casey," Kevin said.

Mingan and Mitch reached under the bed for Bob and tried to uncoil his body. Bob hissed at them. Kevin opened the window then pulled the blind closed. He looked over his shoulder, back at the bed, where Bob continued to hiss at his brother.

"He hissed," Jade said. Her eyes narrowed in concentration, her head tilted up diagonally as if the hissing triggered a memory. Something important for her to understand. He loved watching her mull things over in her mind.

"What?" Kevin said.

"The onyx stones. My memory stones. The one with the coiled snake. There was a song, a nursery rhyme, or maybe it was a poem. It couldn't be a nursery rhyme. It's too morbid. One line was 'Hiss, hiss, hunger and pain — that's right — hiss, hiss, hunger and pain, the internals will rise again . . .'"

"Do you think it has anything to do with Bob's illness?" Casey asked.

"I don't know how," Jade said.

Mitch and Mingan put Bob on a clean bed and covered him up.

Mitch picked up a skin flake and rubbed it between his fingers until it crumbled into a fine powder. "He's shedding skin."

Casey moved his head from side to side. "This doesn't look good."

"Mitch, clean this up before the doc comes to check on him," Mingan said.

"Too late," Kevin informed them as the infirmary door squeaked open.

A man in his early forties walked through the door. "How is he this morning?" The man moved over to a metal canister, withdrawing an old-style thermometer, and came towards them, shaking his wrist and the thermometer. "It has mercury in it. I suppose you younglings have only seen digital thermometers. He doesn't look so hot. You should have sent someone to fetch me. I don't need a thermometer to know he still has a fever. We need to cool him down." He looked over at the bed and frowned. "What's that?" He, too, picked up the skin and rubbed it between his thumb and index finger. "Skin."

Mingan looked at Kevin. "Come with me."

Mingan opened a storeroom door. Kevin followed him inside.

"You can help. Like you helped Sue, the pregnant woman you helped last time you were here. You do whatever it is you do and heal Bob," Mingan said.

Mingan's right, the portal's vortex membrane was healing, and it would cure Bob as long as he wasn't evil, or possessed by evil, or carrying a firearm. "I'll need privacy," Kevin said.

"Easy." Mingan opened the door. "Mitch, come here."

It was getting a little claustrophobic in the storeroom. Kevin banged against a mop and bucket, stepping back to avoid feeling and knowing Mitch's emotions. His own emotions were enough. Kevin's adrenal glands were on hyperdrive.

"What gives?" Mitch asked.

"We need to get the doc out of the room so Kevin can get his mojo on," Mingan said.

Mitch stepped into Kevin's space. Mitch was agitated. "Your what?"

"Mojo. His thing. His magic. The doctor can't help him," Mingan insisted.

"But he can. He said he's got psychosis brought on by eating too much meat," Mitch said.

"It's okay. Trust me," Mingan said.

Kevin didn't like it when people said, 'trust me.' He always thought it meant that there was a time when the person wasn't forthcoming with information or was not initially truthful.

"Okay, okay," Mitch said, rubbing his temples.

Glad to be out of the closet, Kevin watched the doctor struggle to uncoil Bob's body. He was like a fetus; or coiled up snake. The doctor struggled with his arm, and, with Jade's help, stretched out Bob's arm out flat to insert an intravenous drip. "He needs fluids. There's not much I can do for him. I'm surprised he's as stiff as if..." The doctor stepped away from the bed.

"As if what?" Jade asked.

"Never mind." The doctor quickly turned his face away.

"Do you think you can go see my parents and let them know how Bob is doing while I watch over him? I don't think we should let them see him like this," Mitch said.

"No problem. It's not like I have an influx of patients," the doctor said, taking off his gloves and balling them up.

"You can't come in," Kevin said to Mingan.

"What's happening?" Jade said, looking from Kevin to Mingan.

"He's going to get his mojo on and do his thing," Mitch said, looking at Mingan. "Isn't that right?"

"Stand guard. Make sure no one comes in," Mingan said.

"You can't come in," Kevin repeated.

Mingan nodded with reluctance. "Whatever gets your mojo going is fine with me. I'll wait outside. Jade, let's talk in the hallway," he said with his arm out as if to guide her out of the room.

"She has to stay. I need her help," Kevin said.

"If you're going to . . . you know what, you don't really need me," Jade said.

"I've got your back, K. What do you need me to do?" Casey said.

"Unlock the bed wheels. Help me push him over to the storage room," Kevin instructed, trying not to let his anger show.

The wheels swiveled around. Kevin touched the doorknob, giving himself a static shock. His energy was already building. He walked backwards, pulling the bed in with him. Kevin slipped past the bed and grabbed the handle, ready to pull the door closed. "As soon as I have the portal wide enough, I'll push him through. Be ready to pull him out."

"Will do."

Kevin felt the sorrow that filled Casey and paused to meet his eyes. "I'm sorry. I'm so sorry I didn't make it back in time to save Sophia."

"Me too," Casey said.

With a quick nod, Kevin closed the door, not wanting to make eye contact with his friend any longer than necessary. The pain was visible in Casey's eyes and sadness would only block Kevin from opening a portal.

The energy built up in Kevin's hands. It tingled. The sensation traveled through his body. A vortex appeared at the foot of the bed in front of the door. Currents of electrical energy sparked and sparkled inside the membrane when they made contact. It cracked like a stockman's whip. The energy grew stronger. The portal filled the supply room with color. A low hum pulsed through the room like a sound from a subwoofer.

The portal was ready. Kevin could trust Casey to be ready, waiting for Bob's bed to come through the door out of the supply room and into the infirmary's main room. He pushed the bed forward. The bottom of the bed disappeared. Bob's feet touched the edge of the vortex and he howled in pain. Bob reached up over his head, grabbed Kevin's wrist, and bit his arm. The portal collapsed. Kevin stood back from the bed.

"Open the door!" Kevin yelled.

"What's up?"

"Move! It didn't work," Kevin said, pushing the bed out, cradling his arm. "He bit me!"

Mitch, Mingan, and then Jade, flicking her hair off her shoulder, returned to the infirmary.

"What happened?" she asked.

Jade went to touch his arm. Kevin pulled away from her. "I'm fine. He's the worry."

"You'll need stitches?" she said.

Bob coiled up on the bed, his snake eyes fixated on Kevin. He hissed, and his tongue darted from his mouth.

"I can't do it. It won't work. He can't go through the membrane of the portal. Evil is with him. Nothing can go through the portal that is evil."

"What do you mean *evil*?" Mitch grabbed Kevin's shirt. "What do you mean? There is not an evil bone in my brother's body."

"I feared this would happen," Mingan said. "Take him to my cabin so we can ask the ancestors to enlighten us with the knowledge of what evil has cursed Bob."

"The doc won't allow it," Mitch said.

"If we don't work out what's going on, Bob is going to die," Mingan said.

"We'll have to carry him." Mitch picked up Bob and Mingan moved to help him.

"I've got him. He's my brother," Mitch growled.

"Jade, go ahead and make sure the coast is clear. Do you remember which cabin is mine?" Mingan said.

The energy oozed off Jade. Kevin stiffened, feeling as though he was violating her most private thoughts.

"It's not what you're thinking," Jade said to Kevin. "This way, everyone."

Mitch struggled to carry Bob down the stairs. They went through the kitchen and exited the community lodge out through the back door. Not speaking, they snuck around the cabin and, just as they were about to step out around the back of Mingan's cabin, to head up the few stairs to the front door, the doctor came out of Mitch's cabin with Russell. They were deep in conversation, rushing to the infirmary. Russell, highly agitated by the news, was insisting on seeing his son, Bob.

As soon as they were inside Mingan's cabin, he saw Crazy Bear and Charlie at a tall wooden bench, mixing herbs with granite pestles and mortars. Charlie wanted Mingan for herself and didn't like the way Mingan had gravitated towards Jade when they first met a few days ago.

"When did they get here?" Charlie said, giving Jade the eye, then she hit Crazy Bear in the arm. "Did you know Jade was here and didn't tell me?" Charlie said.

Kevin could tell Charlie felt the energy between Mingan and Jade. Jade loved to learn, she was a sponge, soaking up knowledge, diving into anything she didn't understand. She always had to learn all about it until she was finished. *That's all it is*, Kevin told himself. *Mingan has knowledge that's a mystery to her. Knowledge and answers that maybe only he can give her. Maybe I should just leave them to it. Go back to the estate and find Tim and the others, or maybe even head off to Israel and help Shaun and Rachel. Not that those two would need my help.*

Casey leaned into Kevin. "You need to go heal yourself, man. Your aura is suffering," Casey said in a low voice.

It was a good idea. "Where's the bathroom?" Kevin said to Charlie.

"Third door on the right."

When he heard the door lock click behind him, Kevin took in a deep breath and let it out and tried to generate enough energy to create a portal big enough to stick his arm through. That's all he needed to help himself, but he couldn't get his mind off Jade to do so. "Dammit!" He slammed the toilet seat down and sat on top. His arm was sore. The tissue around the wound was bubbling as if Bob's bite had injected venom.

"What the hell!" Kevin closed his eyes to clear his head and create emotional distance from Jade before trying to open a portal again. Standing up, he readied himself and this time, the portal membrane formed, and energy swirled around his arm, repairing the tissue. Though he felt a little ill, he was lucky. As the energy traveled up his arm and into his body, he stepped all the way into the membrane, healing his emotional state too.

Casey was right, Kevin thought, closing the portal. He must get out of here before he was no good to anyone. He had to shut out his feelings for Jade, somehow.

There was a knock at the door. "You okay in there?" Crazy Bear asked.

"Just a minute," Kevin said and splashed water on his face. "I'm good, thanks," Kevin said, pushing past him.

"Your arm, man? It's healed!"

"Once I washed the blood off, I realized it wasn't so bad," Kevin said, pulling down his sleeve.

Kevin followed Crazy Bear into a back room where Mingan had set up a healing work room. Branches with herbs, crystals, powders, drums, and rattles were just a few of the items that cluttered the bench space, as well as books. Ancient books that Jade practically salivated over as she read, her focus so complete that she didn't notice he had joined them.

Mingan concentrated on laying crystals around Bob body; starting at his feet. "Don't touch those," Mingan said to Jade, without taking his eyes off Bob.

Jade pulled her hand away from the books. She was so deep in awe of Mingan and his books that when Mingan had spoken it frightened her. Kevin looked away and pretended not to have noticed her shame.

"We should call a meeting," Jade said, watching Charlie assist Mingan, who waved his arms across Bob's chest.

"That's a good idea," Charlie said, not even knowing why they were there. "Why don't you run along, like a sweet girl?"

Charlie wanted Jade gone. She felt threatened by Jade's presence. Kevin was thinking she ought to be. Jade and Mingan had a thing going on between them.

"Let's go, Jade. We came here to deliver a message. We need to stay focused," Kevin said, stepping back towards the door and away from Bob's body on the floor surrounded by crystals and now smoke as Mingan waved a shell smoking with herbs over Bob's body.

Instead, Jade moved close to Mingan, so close their shoulders touched Kevin was sure she could smell his natural perfume. "Jade?" Kevin agitated clenched his teeth stopping himself from saying something he might regret. Disappointed and frustrated at his rising jealousy he pushed his fringe back off his face and bit down on his bottom lip.

"Watch and learn, Raven Wings," Mingan said.

Jade slipped quietly into the fold of energy Mingan channeled and knelt beside him.

Mingan spoke as if entranced. "The healing energy from Great Spirit will talk to you if you listen with your heart and stop thinking, Raven Wings."

"Jade!" Kevin said. He touched her and broke the spell. "We have to call a meeting and tell everyone why we're here."

"You do it. You and Casey. You don't need me," Jade said.

"It has to be you; you're the descendant of Great Turtle, not me.

They will listen to you. Then you can do what the hell you want, but I'm going back to help the others. Our families are back at the estate. We need to be there for them," Kevin said.

"No, they're not. Mine are on their way to Stonehenge, and yours . . . yours are . . ." Jade hesitated. "All the more reason why you should go without me, so you can get back to the estate. I'll meet you up there," she said, pointing to the stars.

This wasn't like her. Kevin was confused. "What?"

Casey gave Kevin a half smile and raised eyebrows.

Jade tried to lock eyes with Kevin, but he let his fringe drop back over his eyes to avoid contact. "I'll be outside."

The air cleared the fog of emotions inside the cabin. "I'll come with you," Casey said.

Kevin didn't want company, she had been so dismissive, how could she be like that? She was had distanced herself emotionally from him, and it felt awful! "Stay here. Watch out for Jade. I don't trust him." He snapped at Casey.

"I don't think he has bad intentions towards Jade," Casey said opening the door for him.

"But he has intentions, right?" Kevin said.

"I'm not sure," Casey lent against the rail.

IT DIDN'T TAKE LONG for the small community to come together, and Kevin did his best to relay the message. At first, they were skeptical about the ascension to the stars, but then Mingan and Jade appeared, and an elderly man, on the top of the community hall stairs, rang a bell that Kevin hadn't noticed before. It could have been a dinner bell or a fire bell, either way it was effective. People came out of their cabins, earlier risers by the lake changed their direction and headed towards the hall and the ringing bell. The elder cried out. "Great Spirit is calling us home and has sent Raven Wings, the great-granddaughter of Great Turtle to give us this message. It is a sign. It's time to return to Great Spirit."

The elder re-told the community the message about the journey to the stars, the final accession before the world as they know it ends forever, and most of the people were suddenly excited about the departure from this world, but the doctor looked furious. Kevin was confused and he sensed trepidation.

"A feast! A feast to farewell Mother Earth, this wonderful land that has fed and sheltered our ancestors and our bodies while our spirits experienced the wonders of Great Spirit's creations."

"All those in favor of traveling on foot to Bear Lodge, raise your hands."

The majority raised their hands.

"Bear Lodge was the traditional name for Devils Tower. I just read it in one of Mingan's books," Jade smiled at Kevin, looking a little embarrassed, but her energy was full of excitement. She was trying to hide her emotions from him.

"In one week from now, we will begin our journey to the portal of our ancestors, who knew that one day we would return to the stars. They have passed the story of the seven sisters down through the generations and we will be ready for the great ascension that will take place two and a half-moons from now."

It sounded strange. Crazy. It reminded Kevin of so many cults that believed they needed to vacate their bodies to return to a place amongst the stars, and they all had to commit suicide to do so. *How was this any different?* He wondered listening to the elder convincing the community to pack up and leave everything and walk hundreds of miles with the promise of accession to heaven. A year ago, he would have thought it was crazy to believe he could open portals to any place he could emotionally connect with. The world had become a very different place, and he still had trouble adapting. Walking in the school halls between classes, knowing what people were feeling or wanting . . . that was a game and not important. But now, feeling the willingness of these people to believe and follow blindly the word of one person because of who their family was seemed problematic.

Once the elder was finished addressing the crowd, Kevin watched Jade and Mingan rubbing shoulders with the community, answering questions like superstars. They worked well together, like a power couple. Mingan brought out a level of confidence in Jade that Kevin never had. He had waited patiently for the gathering to break up, to tell her he was leaving, but he couldn't wait any longer; he didn't belong.

7

CASEY: SNAKES IN HIS BELLY

Casey moved to the outskirts of the crowd when he spotted Kevin walking off into the forest alone.

"The hunting party is due to return this afternoon," Russell said from behind him.

Concerned for Kevin, Casey stopped listening and watched him walk with his hands shoved deep into his pockets, his head focused on the ground at his feet, and his aura was shaded deep blues and washed-out mustard yellows—Kevin was sad and confused as he disappeared into the woods. He was leaving. He would be back, but would he be back before the community headed for Devils Tower?

"Sorry Russell, I don't mean to be rude, but I need to find out where my friend is going." Suddenly, Casey feared his friends would die one by one, and he would be the last man standing if they separated now. This wasn't the time for Kevin to go off on his own. It would be his worst nightmare if they all joined Sophia in the afterlife but him. Casey ran, propelling himself up into the air and went after Kevin. Casey could see him through the dappled trees and he let himself drop quickly to the ground landing in front of Kevin blocking his way.

"Where are you headed, man?" Casey asked. He heard an edge of desperation in his own voice.

"That's impressive," Kevin pushed passed him.

"Wait. You can't leave," Casey stepped in front of Kevin again.

"You're the one who suggested that I leave," Kevin said, shouldering past him.

"But not like this. Weren't you even going to tell us? At least you should tell Jade," Casey said.

"She doesn't look like she'll even notice I'm gone," Kevin said. "I'll be back in a few days," Kevin said as he checked behind him. "This should do."

Kevin had spoken more to himself than to Casey and began to gather energy to open a portal.

Casey felt in Kevin's mind he had already left, there was no turning him back. There was nothing he could think of to make Kevin stay. Not one positive idea came to mind. He felt hopeless as he watched Kevin and the portal disappear, before he walked back to the community, where he didn't belong either.

Jade was jogging towards him. "Where's Kevin?"

Casey read the slogan on her purple shirt about never trusting an atom as she came to a stop and pushed away a strand of her dark hair at the side of her mouth and tucked it behind her ear. He'd read it a hundred times, and it always reminded him how quirky Jade was, and his mouth turned into the slightest smile. "Sorry. He's gone," Casey said.

"What do you mean *gone*?" Jade demanded, the hands on her hips digging in with her frustration. She pulled the hairband from around her wrist and pulled her long black hair back to tie it up, before pulling it around the front and setting it neatly on her shoulder. She never wore her glasses or contact lenses anymore. She didn't need them after traveling through the portal dozens of times, but every now and then, she would push up a pair of phantom glasses when she was trying to get clarity. She had trouble gauging emotions in the past, but lately, she seems to be more aware of other's emotions. But since last week, she had made changes and seemed somehow more aware. One minute she was deliberating over an idea, the next she opened up her heart and her aura changed to magenta and soft sky blues as she became mindful of someone's feelings, mostly Kevin's. She understood the theory of an empath or a clairsentient, but she couldn't feel it like he could. But she was trying. Her obvious interest in Mingan was insensitive, but she was unaware. Casey could understand why Kevin was so confused by her emotions.

"He left. He said he'll be back in a few days," Casey said.

Jade looked over at the trees. "A few days . . . he's left us? Where's he going?" Jade said. She didn't wait for an answer. Instead, she jogged off into the woods after Kevin.

"Wait! He opened a portal and vanished. He's gone." Casey watched Jade freeze. She stared at the trees for a full minute before turning around. Her aura had changed from peachy oranges to deep blue and red. She was angry at Kevin and disappointed he was gone.

"Did you guys get Bob back to the infirmary?" Casey asked seeing the pain in her eyes, he tried to distract her, get her out of her emotions and back into her head, where she wouldn't feel the pain of Kevin's sudden departure so much.

"Yeah. His behavior is so strange," Jade said, looking past him and into the forest where Kevin disappeared.

"Who, Kevin? What do you mean?" Casey said.

"No Bob's. His tongue is forked. I asked Mitch if Bob had a piercing or a tongue bifurcation in the past. Mitch said it wasn't like that before he went out hunting. And the skin shedding. And now . . . ," Jade said.

"What's a tongue bifurcation?"

"It's a body modification; a splitting of the tongue, anyway Bob is now sitting up and eating. He's gulping his food down as if he hasn't eaten in a very long time. And the scaling on his body has gone; very peculiar," Jade said.

"So Mingan's healing worked," Casey said.

"Well, sort of," Jade said.

"You're not making sense. Did it help him or not?" Casey said.

"Why don't you go see for yourself and tell me if the healing helped or not?" Jade said.

"I will. Did Mingan get an answer during his meditation from the ancestors? Does he know what's wrong with Bob?" Casey asked.

"If he did, he didn't think to tell me," Jade said.

Casey and Jade walked back to the disbursed community, Jade stopped, and joined Mingan and Charlie sitting under a tree, talking to the hunters who had just returned. Casey smiled at them as he continued to the community lodge – they looked odd, distanced, and their eyes had glazed over.

He took the steps to the infirmary two at a time. This time, Mitch wasn't standing guard. An excited group of women chatting about preparations for the coming feast passed him by as he pushed through the squeaky infirmary door.

At the far end, Bob was sitting up in bed with a bowl and spoon in his hand, eating, while his mom sat talking about the coming ascension to him. His mother was fussing over him, and his little sister, who looked about eight or nine years old was standing back from the bed. She was afraid—her aura colored with fear. Casey hadn't met Bob's family, but the woman and the girl had similar features. They looked like a family. Bob's mother's aura was a ray of violets, pinks, bright yellow, and cherry red as she tried to keep up with her son's appetite. Pleased her son was healing, she encouraged her daughter to sit on the side of the bed while she went to fetch more food.

"You stay here with Bob. I'll be right back, sweetie," Bob's mom said to her daughter.

Casey smiled as she passed. The girl pulled back from Bob as he reached out for her to come closer. She took an extra step back as he leaned over the edge of the bed trying to touch her. She turned to leave, and he pushed off the bed to grab the back of her hair. "Bob, isn't it?" Casey said as the girl took off after her mother.

The girl stopped at the door. "That's not Bob!"

Bob hissed at her like a cat, and the girl screaming, ran from the room.

"Who wants to know?" Bob said, with a lisp, and sat back up on the bed.

"It's a little dark in here. Why don't I open the shades and let some light in?" Casey said, moving towards the window.

"I met you while you had a fever. I'm a friend of Jade's," Casey said.

"Don't open the shades!" Bob yelled.

"Okay," Casey said, lowering his hand away from the cord.

"Jade, Great Turtle's descendant?" Bob said.

Casey got closer and would have sworn he saw Bob's eyes blinking like a reptile.

Jade was right, Bob didn't look normal. His pupils were yellow with black slits in the center. His skin looked wet and was a slight resemblance to fish scales. He looked yellow, jaundiced. His forked tongue flicked around his mouth, collecting pieces of food before it darted towards Casey, tasting the air in front of him. He was even acting like a reptile.

"Yeah, she's outside with Mingan. She helped Charlie and Mingan heal you. You had a fever, Bob," Casey said.

"Well, besides an incredible hunger, I'm fine. Where's Jade now?" Bob said, getting out of bed and pulling on his pants.

"She's outside with Mingan," Casey repeated.

The door to the infirmary opened, and Bob's mother walked in with another tray of food. "You shouldn't be out of bed. Bob, Where's Ruby? where is your sister?" she demanded.

"Hi, the girl, Ruby, she went after you. I'm Casey; Jade's friend," Casey said, trying to give her his best reassuring smile that felt so fake.

"I'm Sue-Anne, but everyone calls me Sue. You're one of the messengers. I was just told the good news. The men and women in the kitchen are already preparing for the feast to celebrate the ascension. We knew Jade would be back. We knew she was the one," Sue said, brimming with enthusiasm.

"The one for what?"

"To lead us to Great Spirit, to guide us like her great-grandmother," Sue replied.

"I better go after Bob and bring him back," Casey said.

"I think that's best," Sue said, avoiding his eyes.

He heard a yelp and a hoot from outside. Bob was moving fast, not quite running. It was more of a lumbering as he entered the woods at the very spot where Casey had seen Kevin go. Mitch and Mingan gave chase.

Casey flew straight up off the community lodge steps, nearly hitting the awning of the porch. He propelled himself straight at Bob, passing Mitch and Mingan. He was getting faster all the time and should slow down because, if he hit a tree at this speed, his head would crack open like a cantaloupe. Casey pulled himself up and blocked Bob's path. Bob's face was covered in blood, just like the night before. Mitch and Mingan came up behind him and tackled Bob to the ground. Bob screamed like a banshee, trying to get free.

The forest on his right drew his attention away from the struggle. *When the group of men that had gone hunting arrived back, their eyes had been glazed over, something was going on inside the forest,* Casey thought and it was about time that he checked it out on his own. He had nothing to lose. Mingan and Mitch took care of Bob, freeing Casey to head off the track.

"Wait! Where are you going?" Jade called, alarmed. He could almost hear her begging him not to go.

He hadn't noticed Jade in pursuit of Bob. "Something is out there, and I'm going to find out what it is," Casey said over his shoulder.

"Wait!" Mingan said, struggling to keep hold of Bob.

"What for?" Casey said.

"We can all go. But first, we need to get back and talk to the hunters. They know something." Mingan gave him a look, and Casey saw Mingan's aura transform around him, into the spirit of a wise old wolf. Casey had never seen that happen before. It intrigued him. Jade looked back at Mingan, knowing Casey had seen something that she couldn't.

"Okay." Casey said, turning around and following. "But we came to give the ascension message and, when Kevin returns, Jade and I will be leaving. It's not safe here."

Mitch had his hand over Bob's shoulders, acting as if they were having a friendly, brotherly chat. But he, too, was having trouble keeping Bob from fleeing.

Jade frowned and scolded Casey. Her aura blazed with anger. But she held her ground until he had walked by.

* * *

CASEY LISTENED as Mingan questioned the hunters that were lazing under the tree, as if they had just finished a feast of their own.

"What happened out there?" Mingan asked the men. Casey could tell Mingan was picking up something from them.

Casey watched as the wolf spirit sniffed around the men's dark auras. They had deep gashes taken out of their auras, leaving empty black spaces that differed from the black spots he had seen in the past, which had signified cancer. This was different. It was like black holes, a nothingness.

"Nothing. We saw nothing. We found the traveling pastor and his churchgoers. They gave us a hot meal and read the scripts from Mark. Something about those that take up serpents, or something or other. They seemed like harmless church folk. A little mad, drinking strychnine, but hey, the world is a different place, right? Each to their own." The man twirled the end of his handlebar mustache.

The youngest man of the four stood and hiked up his trousers before he wiped his nose on the back of his sleeve. "Early this morning, when we were hiking back, we found a dead pack of wolves. It was a bloodbath. We could smell it before we even saw it!" he said, biting his bottom lip as if to stop a smile.

"Shut your mouth. Can it!" the first man snapped and stopped twirling his moustache.

Casey watched intently as the four men lied.

"We should hunt close to camp for the next few days and let whatever is out there find a new place to feed," Mingan said.

The tall man studied Jade and Casey. He condescendingly patted Mingan on the shoulder. "Now, if you don't mind, we're going to get cleaned up and get us a little something to eat. We're famished, right, boys?" he said to his men with a smirk, as if they all shared a private joke.

The four hunters stood, picked up their guns, and carried them on their shoulders. They tipped their hats at Jade as they passed.

The sound of the birds in the trees returned. Casey hadn't noticed they had stopped. He heard the door of the community lodge close behind him as they headed up the stairs to the first floor where Bob was resting in the infirmary.

"How is he?" Mingan asked Mitch.

"Well, the doctor has administered something to help Bob rest, for now," Mitch said, concerned.

"Maybe we should all just concentrate on leaving this area," Crazy Bear said, walking up behind Casey with Charlie.

"The sooner the better," Casey said.

"I think he's right," Mingan agreed.

"It's a shame Kevin has left. He could've opened a portal for us all," Jade said.

"It's a good time to learn about your memory stones, and I can teach you a thing or two while you wait for him to come back. You can join us on our journey to Bear Lodge. You can catch up with him after the ascension from up there," Mingan said.

"Might as well," Jade said. "Do you mind, Casey?"

"No. Why would I mind? I'm not Kevin. I've lost the only person who meant anything to me anyway, but I still think we should leave with Kevin when he gets back," Casey said.

"Why don't you come and have a healing session?" Mingan said.

"I'll do it," Charlie said.

"That's a good idea. His aura could do with a cleansing," Mingan said, staring at Casey.

Casey wasn't sure who Charlie was, but she obviously wanted to keep an eye on Jade and Mingan.

They headed back to Mingan's cabin, and Charlie led the way. "I'll use the mediation room for Casey's healing while you teach . . . ," Charlie said.

Casey didn't need her to finish her sentence to know she was jealous of Jade.

Mingan smiled at Charlie, and she blushed. "Who better to help him transform the festering caused by his grieving self into a new clean form of energy, than you?"

So Mingan, too, could see that he grieved. Casey felt betrayed by his own body and emotions. He supposed that's what it felt like for others when he read their auras.

Fresh bird droppings added to the old white dots that covered the small porch of Mingan's cabin. Mingan, being a gentleman, stretched his arm out for Jade to go up the stairs first.

Just as irritated as Kevin had been, Charlie pushed past Jade and entered the cabin first. The best thing Casey could do for Charlie was to distract her. "How are you going to do the healing? Do you use crystals like Jade?" *Bad choice of words,* he thought as he followed her into a room with drawn blinds and the smell of sage.

"I like your butterfly. It looks like it's going to fly off your arm, like Jade's raven. Did you get them done together?" Casey said.

"What? No. I earned mine over years of practice and dedication. Jade's just a novice. If she wasn't Great Turtle's great-granddaughter, nobody would give her a second glance," Charlie said, looking at Mingan.

"Well, it's a nice butterfly. Very girly," Casey said.

Charlie frowned and screwed up her face as if she had just eaten something sour.

"No. I'm more advanced than a 'girl,'" Charlie sneered as she walked them through a doorway.

"This is the healing and meditation room. This is a sanctuary," she said, dropping her jacket on the edge of a couch covered with a giant rainbow-colored crocheted blanket.

"That's nice. Did you make it?" Casey asked, trying to establish some sort of connection with her. He could see her aura settling down. The wavelengths became longer, and the colors changed and softened. The thought of the blanket had an instant healing effect on her, as did the room.

"I did. I made it with Great Turtle before she returned to the Great Spirit," Charlie said.

"So, did you know Jade before she came here to find her father?" Casey asked.

"No. Great Turtle mentioned her a few times. How she wished Jade would embrace who she was and follow the ancient ways. She had constantly said that Jade would begin to walk the path when all else fails. But she never did—until now. I don't understand why she would abandon such a gift, and her own great-grandmother, Great Turtle," Charlie said.

Her aura changed again. Red flowed out from the lower part of her body into her aura. She was angry at Jade long before now. "So that's why you're mad at Jade?"

"Maybe. Enough about me. I need to focus on you. Your body is harboring massive grief and resentment. So don't talk to me about anger. I'm going to need a few minutes to get into the right headspace. Wrap yourself up in the healing blanket and sit cross-legged on the floor over there."

Casey grabbed the blanket off the couch. It was one rainbow of zig-zags after another rainbow of zig-zags. It was huge and soft and smelled of freshly baked chocolate cake, which reminded him of his mother baking when she was alive and life was normal. *How can a blanket smell of warm chocolate cake?* Tears welled in his eyes. He felt a lump in his throat. It was suddenly hard to swallow.

He did what Charlie had asked and moved to the far side of the room and found spruced, comfy cushions around a woven mat. He crossed his legs and looked at the contents of the room as Charlie sat opposite him, studying him as he tried to forget the smell of the freshly baked chocolate cake that covered him in the disguise of a woven blanket. The lump in his throat was getting bigger. His eyes pooled with unshed tears. Just sitting down in lotus style reminded him of Sophia.

I can't do this, he thought. The fresh baked cake, reminding him of his mother, and the meditation, reminding him of Sophia—terrible combinations. It would be impossible for him to relax. He felt his stomach churn.

"I can't do this," he said, standing up and dropping the blanket.

Charlie sprang to her feet as if anticipating his reluctance and his need to flee. "It will be alright. You need to release your bottled-up emotions to transform and reach a state of harmony with Great Spirit," Charlie said. Her aura had turned to a beautiful, gentle violet, casting a softness she hadn't shown before. Her body was covered in flowers. It was like she was part of a bouquet. The flowers reached out to the edge of her body and that's when the butterfly wings opened. A butterfly in the garden. She was beautiful. Full of love.

"No, I can't. Sorry." Casey stepped out of the blanket surrounding his feet. Suddenly, his stomach moaned, and gurgled, a surge of fire and pain exploded inside. He grabbed his sides, held his stomach, and dropped to his knees. "What are you doing to me?" Casey gritted his teeth.

"It's not me. It's you. You are hurting yourself. Let it go," Charlie said, helping him up and moving him back towards the cushions and the mat.

Casey coughed. His throat, already tight, felt as though it was going to close completely. He wanted to scream, to release the trapped anger and grief, but his throat forbid the cries to surface. Balls of squirming pain engorged his abdomen. He had to get them out. What's happening! He grabbed his throat.

Charlie lowered him down to his knees and draped the blanket and her aura around him. The tightness in his throat extended down to his chest. His whole body was seizing up. *What has she done to me?* Casey thought. Flashes of the past week unfolded in front of him. One horrid moment running into the next. He tried to squeeze his eyes shut, but his muscles were no longer obeying his thoughts as he sank into himself, drowning. No longer caring, as his head fell below the surface of the dark ocean of grief and anger within him.

"Good. That's it. Stop resisting and let go." Charlie's voice became muffled by the pressing darkness.

A shark was in the waters with him. Casey sensed it, but he couldn't move. It swam past, in and out of sight. Then his lungs opened. His eyes widened in the darkness. Fear filled his being as a hat floated down in the murky water around him. It paralyzed him with terror. A hand reached out of the darkness towards him and grabbed the hat. The same freaking derby hat. Another black shadow figure dropped into the water, and another, and they all swam towards him.

Get me out of here! he imagined yelling at the top of his lungs. He struggled with his body. *Move, damn it! Sophia! Sophia!* he called out in his mind.

Laughter filled his head. His veins filled with ice. It was a combined sound from the black shadow men—a voice of menace. Casey could sense their loathing towards him. It was as if they held him responsible for their plight. They were out for revenge. There was something else amongst the hat man and the black shadows, something he couldn't see until they parted. A hideous monster that he couldn't find words to describe.

They had Casey trapped in his own ocean of grief. The stingray turned on its side and had the legs and head of a man, a man with the shadow of wings. It moved closer, laughing, enjoying Casey's fear. It reached out its arms, ready to squeeze the life out of Casey.

Then behind, Casey felt a gentle touch, and a flash of light entered him. Life, golden with joy, returned to his body. He raised his head up as goodness entered him through the back door of his solar plexus. It was warm as a summer sun rising as it traveled through his body.

Sophia, he thought. She was the only one who ever filled him with golden energy. Relief gave him new hope. His chest rose. He let out a scream that forced all the shadows out of his murky ocean, and he saw streaks of light in the turquoise ocean of his subconsciousness.

"Sophia. Sophia. Is that you?" His arms moved. He felt himself swimming out of the depths and rising into the light of consciousness, back into the healing room on his knees, doubled over under Charlie's healing blanket.

Still, he felt disassociated from himself as he heard and felt a long scream erupt from deep within, forcing the blockage in his throat to clear as the scream, wrenched out from deep inside him, sending chills down his spine. His mouth stretched wide as a stone fell from his mouth. It was more like a cocoon—larvae covered in spit. It rolled on the mat in front of him. Something was inside of it.

Charlie, holding a smudge stick of sage, blew smoke into his face. As she moved her arm, Casey saw it as a butterfly wing fanning the smoke. She was in a trance. Casey could see her face transforming. He looked back at the wobbling larvae, disgusted it had come out of his mouth. The sack-like ball cracked open from the inside, releasing a rush of fluid and a baby snake out onto the mat. Casey wiped his mouth.

"Kill it; you must destroy it," Charlie said. Butterflies danced around her. The words seemed so out of place. She handed him a mallet and pestle.

The snake had yellow rings around its body. It was growing at the speed of lightning. "I can't just kill it." But something inside him knew that if he didn't, it would kill him.

"This is the grief and anger that grew inside you. If you don't kill it now, it will kill you." Casey moved back as the snaked moved closer. Its head turned and faced him as it reared up. He couldn't.

"Grab it; kill it now!" Charlie yelled. She clicked two pieces of flint together and a flame burst out of the bowl at his feet. "You must cast it into the flame!"

It was way too big to just scoop up. Reared up, alert, waving backwards and forwards, as if looking for the best place to strike. Casey thought about reaching out and grabbing its tail when the door to the healing room burst open and Jade, in a flash, snatched up the snake by its head. She held it out to him.

"Kill the snake or it will kill you," Jade said, handing it to him.

Carefully, he took hold of the back of the snake's head where Jade had been holding it. It almost appeared placid and harmless in her grip. The snake instantly coiled around Casey's arm and squeezed as it grew bigger and bigger. He tried to pull it off with his other hand.

"Now, Casey. You must put the snake into the flame!" Charlie yelled.

Building up the energy inside, he ignited his telekinesis and repelled the snake off his arm. It slid across the floor. He concentrated on the snake lifting off the ground. It floated in the air, across to the bowl and into the blue flame. The flames hissed as the snake's flesh burned. The flame stretched up and out as the snake turned to ash.

"You have much more to purge; your emotions are curled up inside you. If you don't purge them, they will kill you from the inside," Mingan said.

"More?" Casey spat into the bowl. "I'm not afraid to die. Bring it on."

"It's not what you want. You're not thinking straight. You don't mean that, and you would miss everyone. This isn't the way you want to meet Sophia again," Jade said.

"Everyone I loved is dead. It's best not to care," Casey said.

His throat was tightening again as he chocked backed his emotions. He felt the tension in his neck and back. Casey burst through the front door of the cabin and the cool air hit his face. He bent his knees and propelled himself up into the sky. He rocketed beyond the safety of the ozone and drifted into unconsciousness as the air thinned.

8

JADE: FINDING GRAY WOLF

J ade raced outside to find Casey. She looked into the sky until her neck hurt. There wasn't even a whisper of him in the sky for her to focus on.

"He's intense. Incredible. Broken," Charlie said, walking down the steps into the open.

Jade stood on the porch looking up, searching the sky for Casey. Clouds drifted in and blocked her sight. Quickly, she silenced her mind, breathed in and out, relaxing after two long breaths, she connected with nature. Moving the clouds, feeling the warmth of the sun upon her face, she smiled. Behind her eyes, her lids turned red with sparkles—she opened them and tilted her head upwards again to search the skies. The clouds floated to the west, but still, there was no sign of Casey. She knew that there was only so far, he could go before he blacked out.

"Did Great Turtle teach you that?" Charlie said.

"I suppose so," Jade said in a dreamy voice; still feeling the connectedness to nature.

Mingan tapped her on the elbow.

"What the hell! Why did you do that?" Jade snapped, frustrated at having her trance broken. Suddenly, she had the feeling that Mingan knew more about her than she had thought. Her mother and Great Turtle had done the same thing—tapped her on the elbow to draw her attention and to focus. Like a reset button planted on her elbow. She hadn't even noticed Mingan had left the cabin and joined them. *How long had he been standing behind her?* She wondered.

"Why did you run out of your session? It's bad for your aura to disengage from the other realms so quickly it can cause a psychic tear. You need to relax, Raven Wings, and let the stones speak to you, they will ignite your memories through action. You are faster than the snake. You can see the goodness and the bad and you can slither into someone's thoughts and transform them," Mingan said.

"But the song is a warning. I'm sure," Jade said folding her arms across her chest.

"Then, when you need to be warned, the stone will speak to you through song. Be patient, and always give yourself time to draw in your aura and reconnect to the 3D realm, before ending an astral learning session, " Mingan said.

"Can you make it rain?" Charlie asked.

"You too Charlie, pull in your aura."

Jade looked up again, worried about Casey. When she turned to answer Charlie, she had gone. Jade watched Charlie and Mingan return to the cabin. It was time to get back to their session. "I'll be right here when you get back, Casey," Jade said into the sky.

THE ROOM SEEMED DARKER and colder than it had before she'd ended her session with Mingan to help Casey. The room smelled like the forest—musty. Cold, she sat back down on the meditation mat in the circle of her stones, with Mingan on the edge of the mat and Charlie as well.

Jade closed her eyes. It was as if she was sitting outside, surrounded by trees and not her onyx memory stones. The trees spoke to her in feelings. Like ancient elders, they towered over her, comforting her, inspiring her. Swirls of energy moved between the trees as if they were playing catch, pushing the energy back and forth between them. It reminded her of the spiral dance of the plains grouse bird that assisted her on her travels to the realm of lost souls.

She understood which memory stone represented the spiral dance, and she knew what the stone with the curling winds represented—her ability to control nature. Now the snake swallowing its own tail turned like a wheel in front of her, anticlockwise. The true nature of this memory stone hadn't been fully revealed, and she was going to have to be patient.

Jade picked up the shiny black onyx with the rotating snake, then but put it down again and pick up her wand instead. The head of the terminating crystal glowed. She turned it around. The facets were doorways and windows to different realms. Jade found what she was looking for; the window Chief Thundercloud had revealed while teaching her how to travel to different worlds, through the crystal. She wondered if she should go into the crystal and through the window now.

Mingan watched over her. She wished Gray Wolf, the teacher Chief Thundercloud had talked about, would appear and help her understand the old ways of her ancestors. With a desire to know, Jade twirled the wand clockwise and gazed into each window.

Suddenly, she stopped. Deep inside a window facet, it looked like a snowfield, another world, a gray wolf partly blended into the horizon, watching her, then disappeared beyond the horizon. It resembled the wolf that chased away the threatening emaciated beast that she had seen on arrival at the campsite. Jade, without hesitation, focused into the crystal's depth until she waded in knee-high snow. She spotted the wolf and followed it over the horizon to green pastures. The snow was behind her, in front was greenery, and Jade felt a childish urge to roll down the hill. Below to her right was a cluster of trees, and to her left was a campsite by a tranquil river. Smoke trailed from a fire, and next to the fire the wolf waited. Without the blinding whiteness of the snow, she could see it was a gray wolf.

Gray Wolf, her teacher. As fast as she could without falling, she ran down the hill towards the wolf and the river, as the wolf disappeared inside a tent. At the door of the tent she hesitated, listening, then slowly, pulled back the flap and peered inside. There was no wolf. She stepped inside and turned from left to right, but there was nowhere for it to hide.

But as she turned to leave, she felt a presence behind her. Glancing over her shoulder a man appeared a man sitting by a fire, wearing the head and fur of a wolf. Once Chief Thundercloud had spiritually appear to her. She believed the same thing was happening now. The man had old skin; it was so tight against his bony chiseled face that, as he drew on his pipe, his cheeks sunk inward, and his cheekbones protruded even more. He puffed on his pipe, then handed it up to her.

"Are you Gray Wolf?" Jade reached out for the pipe and sat next to him. He scooped up water into a cup and poured it over the stones at the bottom of the fire. Steam rose, and the tent heated quickly becoming a sauna. He nodded at Jade and raised his hand to his mouth as if he was still holding the pipe. Jade brought the pipe to her mouth, fearing an asthma attack preventing her from opening her lungs and breathing deeply, she inhaled. Gray Wolf was patient and made the motions of taking in a deep breath. She looked into his blue eyes, opened her lungs and drew in the smoke. Instantly, she was floating in a warm blue lagoon.

Jade moved her arms, treading water while she got her bearings. The water against her body reminded her of swimming under the boardwalk in her hometown at Myrtle Beach. She missed her home, wished she had spent more time enjoying her life and celebrating who she was rather than hiding it. It was the first time that she saw herself in a new light.

Jade paddled further out, but the water became shallow, so she waded through the shallows, feeling the warm sun and warm water, as she looked around to find why Gray Wolf had brought her here. What was she to find?

Suddenly, cliffs wrapped around the lagoon. Jade looked up at the rising ridges. A single star in the sky grew bright. She assumed it was the morning or evening star; it didn't matter they were one and the same –Venus. Jade waded towards the star until the lagoon bed dropped, her head for a moment went under, breaking the surface, no longer able to wade, she slowly swam towards the star, and the closer she got to the star, the closer she was to the sharp rocks surrounding the base of the cliff. She breast-stroked towards the cliff and could now see the rocks at the bottom were still some distance away.

The star shone brighter. It expanded in size. Jade turned onto her back and floated, looking up at the star, before she turned upright and bobbed in the water. The star was so crazy bright that it was getting hard to see the rocks at the bottom of the cliff, and she knew the water rocked her towards them.

The star grew brighter still. She dove under the water to get away from the blinding brightness, but to no avail. It followed her. When she lifted her head out of the water, it was directly above her. She swam to the water's edge and wished she could swim as fast as Kevin.

The thought of him took her back to the river where she had seen a beacon of light that had guided her in the middle of the night, deep under the water and into a cave where evil Shaman waited to steal her power.

The thought frightened her, so she swam faster, but the light was enveloping her. She hit the shore, but the glare off the sand was too bright to see. The idea of people trapped in the realm of the lost souls, reaching out from under the sand and pulling her under, entered her mind. She shivered, dived back into the warm water, and washed the negative thought away. Then she walked out of the water, onto the sand warm feeling it between her toes.

She stretched out on the sand with her eyes open, watching the star turn and swirled into itself, getting smaller and smaller, but it wasn't moving away, it was just getting smaller. It hovered above her before it slammed into her. She grabbed her chest. And that's when she recalled the memory of the morning star. Its light filled her chest as two wolves fought nearby. She bathed in the glorious light, feeling the sensation of a breeze on her body, drying up the droplets that clung to her skin.

Slowly, she opened her eyes. She was back in the cabin, inside Mingan's healing room, and he was waving a fan of feathers over her body, which was covered in sweat.

"Take it slow," Mingan said.

The room was steamy, the air thick. Slowly, she sat up. She didn't recall lying down on the rug. A cough rattled its way up her chest until she expelled it. "I met my spiritual teacher," Jade said.

Mingan handed her a glass of water. "When you're ready. Come outside and help prepare for the feast."

Dazed, Jade tried to stand, but the room spun around. She sat back down. "What about my memory stones?"

"Pick up the one with the turtle. Use it to ground yourself. But don't go into a trance," Mingan said.

"It's not like we have a lifetime for me to learn," Jade said.

"You need to be patient," Mingan said.

Jade took another sip of water and picked up the onyx with the carving of the turtle. She spotted her crochet bag, the one with her drum and other belongings, resting against the wall. She pulled it over and fished out her notebook.

She had forgotten she had it. She wrote everything that she could remember about Gray Wolf, the sweat lodge, the meadow, and river. Jade pictured his old leathery face and his eyes, full of wisdom. She smiled. *Maybe he had been her great-grandfather,* she thought wistfully. But she had seen pictures of her great-grandfather and it wasn't the same person. Gently, she placed the stone of the turtle on her knee. The onyx with the star on it must relate to the star that entered her being. She looked over the stones.

No way! The onyx with the stick figure and a maze had changed. The stick figure had moved. It was inside the maze.

Jade smiled, excited. Joy filled her heart, but she didn't know why. She felt like fist pumping the air. She finished up writing in her journal and packed up her things. Reaching her hand out, she touched her drum. A vibration passed between them. Like a joyful child, she slammed the door and rushed out of the cabin into the daylight and Charlie.

Charlie looked over Jade's shoulder, as if expecting to see Mingan behind her. "What's got you glowing?"

While Charlie was in her personal healing power, she was sweet, gentle, oozing with love and compassion, but when she wasn't, she was a green-eyed monster. It was an extreme transformation of character.

"He's not here. I thought he went to find you. Mingan left our meditation before I came out. He might be helping with the preparations for the feast or the journey to Devils Tower," Jade said.

"It's Bear Lodge, and you better wipe that grin off your face or people are going to think something's going on between you and Mingan," Charlie said and marched off. Jade blushed. Embarrassed, she turned away and gazed into the late afternoon sky, wondering where Casey and Kevin were.

* * *

JOYFUL MEN, women, and children busied themselves setting up long tables outside for the feast. The four hunters had gathered around the back stairs of the community lodge, looking like they were conspiring. The man with the brown hair and beard seemed a little hunched over. It reminded her of a group of football players in a huddle. Quietly, she moved between two trees to catch what they were saying. They weren't talking at all; they were sharing a jar, drinking the clear liquid inside.

Mingan came out of the back door and saw them. "Maybe you want to save that moonshine for later. Didn't know you fellows had a still and were cooking up your own brew. There's plenty of free alcohol down in the town nobody wants."

The man with the jar placed a golden lid on top and gave it a tight seal before slipping it into his coat pocket. The way they were dressed in utility vests reminded Jade of strong masculine game hunters. They walked off into the forest. Jade wondered if she should follow.

"Jade, come help me pick the herbs for the venison," Sue said.

Ruby ran over to her. "Where's your friend, Kevin?"

Jade's stomach turned at the thought of venison. There was no way she was going to eat any deer. "I don't know," Jade said.

"I hope he comes back soon," Ruby said.

Ruby was in love with Kevin the first time she had laid eyes on him five days ago. "So do I, Ruby," Jade said.

"Who are those men?" Jade asked Sue.

"They're harmless enough; mostly they're out hunting. They brought some of the meat from that nice preacher man they were talking about. It'll be at the end of the table if you want a piece of blessed meat. The men keep to themselves, mostly. Been no real trouble. They were nice, ordinary men when they worked at the mill," Sue said.

Jade allowed herself to draw in the smell of the fresh herbs and tried to identify each one by smell. Ruby quizzed her.

"When's Kevin coming back?" Ruby said, blushing.

"I told you, I don't know. Definitely not today. He was here earlier, but he had to go help the others back at our community," Jade said, hoping it was the truth.

"Are your people from across the ocean going to join ours, too? Mama said we're all going on a trip out into space, that we came from the stars and it's time to go home. I don't enjoy flying," Ruby said.

"Ruby, take a breath. Stop asking so many questions," Sue said.

"That's okay," Jade said, smiling at Ruby.

Jade was more worried about Casey than Kevin at the moment. "You all seem to have this under control. I think I might find Casey, my other friend," Jade said.

"See you at the feast," Sue said.

Jade made her way around the whole campground and even checked the lake. He was nowhere to be found. Maybe he headed back to the infirmary to check on Bob again. But then she saw Bob with the hunters, drinking the moonshine. She was going to have to be patient and wait until he returned.

9

CASEY: BEWARE OF THE FALSE PROPHET

C asey fell from the air without a care for life; as the wind pushed his eyelids back, he closed them tight, as he plummeted to the ground, jostling between trees and branches – longing to meet the earth, he barely flinched, but suddenly, he stopped. Excruciating pain radiated up from his groin, his crown jewels crushed. He screamed out, furious he was alive to feel the radiating pain. He opened his eyes and cursed.

The sun had passed over the canopies like the hands on a clock and it was now on his other side. An hour or more passed as he sat on the branch replaying Sophia's death over and over in his mind, listening to the carousel of loathsome thoughts, wondering what he could've and should've done differently to save Sophia, it was exhausting. There were no suitable answers to his questions; thinking tied him up in knots of regret, blame, frustration, bitterness, and anger at God for the death of Sophia. He was no good to anyone. Casey wished he had died with her. He screamed at God until his rage subsided and sorrow and emptiness took its place. He swung his legs over the edge dangerously and screamed one more time, causing a sonic wave of energy to topple the surrounding trees.

Casey cried. He cried for the pain he caused the trees, the pain he caused his family, and most of all, Sophia. Glad life on earth was coming to an end, if it was going to stay like this forever, he would rather die. Days and weeks would roll by, and his friends and family would stop missing him.

As he sat amongst the trees, in the distance, beyond the toppled trees from his sonic blast, trees fell one by one as if something was pushing them aside. He couldn't see anything approaching, but he could see the devastation in its wake as it advanced towards him. He slowed his breathing and searched the air for a change in the atmosphere. These days, anything could step out of the forest. The giants at the estate weren't like Godzilla or King Kong or something out of Gulliver's Travels. They were energy. Vapors, shimmering mirages with a hunger for humans. They were camouflaged predators.

As the birds and the forest hushed, Casey stood on the tree branch, and kept perfectly still, worried an invisible beast was coming. The slight sensation of being held around the waist morphed into a definable growing pressure as it tightened. Then a pungent gust of air covered his face and assaulted his nasal passages. Something had a hold on him. He repelled his telekinetic energy down to the ground to propel himself upwards and off the branch, away from what was standing unseen in front of him. He could go no more than a few feet. Something in the haze of energy in front of him was holding him back as if he had a rope around his waist that bound him to the tree. Casey pushed out his energy in all directions and burst free from the invisible bind.

Flying high over the Black Mountains, Casey headed back to the campsite to warn the others, while searching the terrain for signs of the unseen creatures when he saw a river parting the trees below. It was a little over an hour away from the campsite and still no signs of the unseen, no toppled trees or unusual movement among the canopies, which was good. He glided over the waterfall and down to the river, landing at a small sandy cove. Kneeling at the water's edge, he scooped up a handful of cold water and splashed it over his face, washing away the trails of salty tears. The sudden coldness was like a slap in the face, which he welcomed, and he threw more and more cold water into his face. Thirsty, he scooped up one more handful and drank, soothing his sore throat from screaming. Casey took off his shoes, rolled up his jeans and soaked his feet in the cold mountain water until they were numb. His stomach rumbled, which made him think of Tim. Tim eating Joe's boiled fruit cake. It made him smile. Tim was good-hearted and Casey was glad that he had found Seth. Everyone seemed to have someone. He sighed.

The water lapped against his shins and to his rolled-up jeans. Casey lifted his leg out of the water, ready to roll down his pants, just as a snake swam around his other leg. Quickly, he pulled his leg out of the water and rolled his jeans down. The water rippled into life as dozens of snakes surfaced and zigzagged their way towards him.

"What the hell! Where did they come from?" Casey looked up and saw snakes tumbling over the edge of the waterfall into the pool of water. Searching over his shoulder for his shoes, the small sandy bank turning into a collage of colored snakes, wriggling out from under the warm sand. Dozens of species he didn't believe were native in these parts—an Indian cobra, a tree viper, a green python, a rattler. They were coming from every direction. Perplexed, Casey skipped over a couple of rocks to reach his shoes, and as he picked them up a rattlesnake struck out at them.

The snakes climbed over one another, to get to him. It was as if they were being controlled by one mind. The python slithered towards him over rocks. Anybody else would be trapped. "This is nuts!" Casey pushed off into the sky and snakes reared up to strike.

He landed on the other side of the river to put on his shoes. The snakes in the water turned around to face him. *Shit!* He chuckled, realizing the irony. If he dived into the river, he would end up dead for sure. It made him mad to know that really, he didn't want to die. He just wanted the pain to stop. He shook his shoes, making sure nothing was inside.

As he walked in the direction of the campsite, a cloudy mist rolled in around him. The smell of smoking meat filled his senses, and a melody echoed through the trees and fog. Casey followed the choir of voices, trying to make out the undulating words; something about angels from other realms, a natal star, and the birth of the messiah. Christ is reborn. Just before Casey came upon the choir's campsite, he slowed down as the words rang clear: 'Come and join us, welcome Christ the newborn king.'

He peered between the trees and watched as a man in a hat preached. Casey's blood ran cold. He had never seen the man before, but he looked so much like the silhouette in the corner of his basement back at the estate. Women, men, and children danced and sang between the preacher's sermons. Casey squatted and listened for a while, then silently backed away and headed for the Black Mountain campground. If he couldn't end his own life, he might as well help Jade out and get everyone to the portal at Bear Lodge.

Casey turned and looked back. He could still hear the people singing. He should tell them about the ascension. They don't know. He swallowed his fear and ignored his instincts and jogged back. He stopped behind the people in the last row, so the preacher, when finished, would see him. He swallowed his sudden unrealistic phobia of hats and smiled at the preacher, who beamed at him.

Casey clapped along. He sort of knew the hymn, so he sang along to be sociable. Happiness and positivity radiated off these people. Their auras were one as they danced and sang. *It must be nice inside that bubble of joy and certainty.*

"People! We have ourselves a vis-i-tor!"

The small ground turned and looked Casey over.

"Come on up here, boy, and tell us how the good Lord guided you to our little ol' circle."

The congregation parted for him to walk down the middle. "Come on up, boy. I know ya want to speak."

Suddenly, Casey didn't think it was a good idea. Everyone was so quiet, he heard a twig snap behind him, and he wondered what made them feel so joyful. Just because they radiated conviction didn't mean they found their joy in the light of goodness.

Like a rag doll, a young girl held a viper snake by her side. "Take it if you believe God will save you," she said with her head tilted and a cheeky smile, as if to say I dare you.

"Just like the book of Mark 16:18, 'He that believeth and is baptized shall be saved; but he that believeth not shall be damned. And these signs shall follow them that believe; In my name shall they cast out devils; they shall speak with new tongues. They shall take up serpents: and if they drink any deadly thing, it shall not hurt them; they shall lay hands on the sick, and they shall recover,'" the preacher said.

Casey smiled. The little girl hurried through the congregation to the front, next to a row of logs used as seats. From the back, Casey hadn't seen the logs or snakes that surrounded the preacher. The old women closest to the logs seemed not to notice the snakes, or weren't concerned by their presence.

Casey tried not to stare at the preacher as he recalled the snakes nestling inside the shadow man with the derby hat back at the estate. His body trembled. He searched all their faces. Off to the side was one person, away from everyone else, cooking meat over a fire. It must have been what he had smelled. The man carved into the meat, slicing pieces off what looked like a human torso.

Ashamed he had found the smell inviting, Casey covered his mouth. His stomach churned with pain as if something were eating him from the inside. Shaking and numbness held him on the spot.

"It's all right, son. If you believe in the good Lord, no harm shall come to you," the preacher said.

"Sorry to intrude," Casey said.

"No intrusion, boy. We are all God's children here. He has graced us with a warm sun that penetrates the depths of the mountains. Come into the light, son," the preacher said.

Everyone was waiting for him to move to the front of the congregation, but he knew he had to be ready to leave quickly, so he stood his ground. "There is going to be an ascension. You all need to head to Devils Tower to return to our creator. The days are few until God will welcome us into heaven. Ten weeks from now, on the eighth day of Leo," Casey said.

"I told you all he had something to say. Hallelujah!" the preacher said, and the congregation answered.

"If you're feeling blessed and you are a messenger of our divine

Lord, come pick up a snake. Drink the poison and ye shall be saved," the preacher said, and the parishioners close to Casey reached out to touch him.

"Now, now, folks. We don't know if he's good or evil, yet. Come pick up a snake and show us who you might really be. Who is this God you speak of?" the preacher said, looking at him with hooded eyes.

Dark shadows covered the preacher's face. The happiness and joy in the people quickly changed. There was tension between them, waiting for Casey to respond to the preacher's challenge. Their auras turned black. The aura around the preacher expanded like a vortex towards him. Transfixed, Casey watched the man basting the torso, unable to tear his gaze away. He closed his eyes, waiting two seconds then met the preacher's, which turned yellow with thin slits for pupils, like Bob's.

Casey weighed up his options. He could propel himself into the sky and forget about the preacher and his congregation. He had delivered the message. It was up to them to believe him or not. Or he could pick up a snake. Neither of those options pleased him. Casey had nowhere to go but forward. With each step, Casey projected his aura outward, pushing everything within three-feet radius out of the way.

The crowd murmured.

"What is this trickery?" the preacher said as the snakes slid away from Casey. A forked tongue darted out of the preacher's mouth. The woman next to Casey, and the men and women nearby, were under the preacher's spell. They all were. Casey stretched out his arm and motioned his hand upward, raising a cobra into the air. The congregation gasped.

"Devil! How dare you mask yourself as one of God's chosen? Pretending to be his messenger," the preacher boomed. "I am his original messenger and history has ended!"

A tight circled of snakes and people got as close as they could to Casey, but they could not step over his energy boundary.

"Beware of the false prophet! Hissss," said the preacher.

"Hisss, hisss, hisss," said the congregation.

"You will make a fine vessel," said the preacher.

Casey would not stay any longer. He propelled himself up into the air.

"See, I am the newborn king, and the devil sent his servants to trick you. Drink the poison with me and you shall be blessed. Pray and give thanks to the Lord . . . ," the preacher said.

Casey moved higher and higher until he no longer heard the preacher and they could not see him.

He changed his trajectory towards the campsite. Passing through a dense fog again gave him the creeps, so he rose higher into the sky, towards the light of the sun until it cleared and he could breathe easy.

* * *

"HELP ME WITH THE PINEAPPLE," Charlie said, lifting one of the four pineapples onto the cutting bench.

Casey watched as she sliced the pineapple with swift movements. She handled a knife well, and he bet she could throw it, just as good too. He had just arrived back at the campsite, and he was slow to move to help, still somewhat stunned by what he had witnessed today.

"Hey, Casey! Jade's been looking for you everywhere," Crazy Bear said, entering the kitchen from the back entrance, letting the screen door slam shut.

"Where is she?" Casey asked.

"By the lake," said Crazy Bear.

"Hey, can I ask you something?" Casey said.

He noticed Charlie move a little closer to listen discreetly.

"Who is the preacher in the woods with the congregation?" Casey said.

"We don't know about any preacher in the woods," Crazy Bear said.

"The hunters mentioned something about blessed meat from the preacher, didn't they?" Charlie said, tasting a piece of pineapple.

"Yeah, that's right. But that was the first time I heard of the preacher and his congregation," Crazy Bear said.

The kitchen was a beehive. People walked in and out with trays of food for tonight's feast. He didn't want to say too much in case someone overheard him, and it sent an anxious ripple through the camp.

"Come, come outside," Casey said to Crazy Bear and Charlie.

She handed him a piece of pineapple, and he took it. It was cool and sweet. He threw the peel into the bushes near the stairs.

"What's up, man?" Crazy Bear said.

"Let's talk while you show me where Jade is," Casey said. He could see the questioning look on Crazy Bear's face.

"What's got you spooked, man?" Crazy Bear said.

"In the woods. I saw the preacher and his congregation. It felt like a group of people you would find in any church on a Sunday, but these guys had snakes. They controlled the snakes. Maybe you should stay clear of the preacher for now. And there is something else out there; it's gigantic and is camouflaged, unseen, it blends into its environment like a chameleon, it might be best if you mentioned it to Mingan, to keep the campsite safe," Casey said.

Jade and Mingan were walking towards them. As soon as she recognized him, she started running. She wrapped her arms around him and hugged him tight. "Where the hell did you go? I was so worried about you. Don't take off like that. First Kevin splits, then you rocket yourself to God knows where," Jade said.

"He was just telling us about the preacher in the woods. The one the hunters spoke of," Charlie said.

"What about him?" Mingan said.

"They're about an hour's flight west from here," Casey said.

"Flight? Sorry, go on," Charlie interrupted.

Casey described his walk and discovery of the congregation. "I turned to leave when I remembered why we're here, to tell people about the final ascension. I went back and told them to go to Devils Tower," Casey said.

"Bear Lodge," Charlie corrected him.

"Bear Lodge. But then the preacher wanted me to prove I was a messenger from God, and he wanted me to pick up a snake. So, I did, but telekinetically. There was no way I was going to touch anyone of those snakes. I'd swear they were all venomous. Then, the preacher turned the congregation against me. I could see them tense with fear, and their auras turned black. He told them I was from the devil. I think if they see me again, they will tear out my heart. And that's not all. They were cooking a torso," Casey said.

Jade frowned. "What do you mean a torso?"

"A human body with no head legs or arms." Casey rubbed his eyes as if trying to rub the image out of his head.

"Cannibalism? That's disgusting." Jade closed her mouth tight.

"What else can you tell us about the preacher?" Mingan said.

"It was like the congregation were hypnotized. And he was tall—seven or eight feet. I thought he was standing on top of a box, using it for a pulpit, because he was at least three feet taller than the congregation. But when the crowd parted, I could see the snakes. They slithered around his feet that were firmly on the ground."

"Walk with me," Mingan said to them all.

Mingan walked with a sense of urgency. He studied the ground, then the sky. Then his eyes fixed on Casey. "Could you lead us to them?"

"Yes. I think so. There was a river and a waterfall that spilled into a pool of water with hundreds of snakes," Casey said.

"I know that place. There are caves behind the waterfall. That's where I found my father and Chief Thundercloud," Jade said.

Casey could feel nothing but love coming from Jade. So much had changed within her in such a short time. "I can take you right now," Casey said.

"No, the sun will set soon," Mingan said.

"Everyone should stay close to camp at night," Charlie said, as if directing it at Jade.

"I remember. I wasn't suggesting that we head out now," Jade said.

"We need to prepare," Mingan said, stopping out the front of his cabin.

"Prepare for what?" Charlie said.

But before Mingan could answer, Crazy Bear spoke. "What about the celebration, the feast? Everyone is expecting Raven Wings, the descendent of Great Turtle, to be present."

"They'll have to wait. We have more pressing matters to attend to," Mingan said, walking into the dim cabin.

Mingan, Charlie, and Crazy Bear's kitchen was small, and it didn't look like they ever cooked.

"Do you have anything I could eat?" Casey asked.

"You should have gotten yourself some of the good food up at the big house while you were there. But go ahead, help yourself, man. Whatever you can find in the refrigerator is yours," Crazy Bear said.

Jade and Crazy Bear went with Mingan into the back room. Charlie hung back in the tiny kitchen with him.

Casey found it difficult to look directly into Charlie's eyes. He still felt embarrassed about storming out of her healing session. He grabbed a piece of cheese, put it between two slices of thick bread, and set it on the table. Then he fished inside his backpack for the notebook, but as Charlie pulled out a chair and sat down, the sketchbook fell out of his bag first as he pulled on the notebook. He knew Charlie was watching and trying to see into the book, just like Jade had in the basement. Maybe they were more alike than they realized.

Abruptly, she stood up and pushed her chair back. "What the hell are those?" she demanded.

Casey snatched the charcoal sketch of boney, human-like creatures that had hair or fur on their bodies and bits of flesh hanging from the chest, face, arms, and legs as if the creatures were in the final stages of metamorphosis. They surrounded the preacher and the congregation like sentinel guards. He had forgotten he had drawn them the night before they left the estate, but now he understood his gut reaction upon seeing the preacher and his congregation. "Maybe it's the preacher I met today. But I didn't see the creatures. Everything was strange. The preacher and the congregation auras were unusual. Dark masses of energy floated around them, like cancer. And the fog I passed through before I heard them singing was strange, thick, and I could've sworn I saw an invisible giant something, while I was amongst the trees beforehand," Casey said.

Charlie, who had been leaning over his shoulder, straightened up. "The gigantic chameleon-like creature you mentioned? What did you see if it was invisible?"

"Yes. A shimmering distortion in front of the trees," Casey said.

"Like a mirage on a hot day?" Charlie said.

"Yeah. Exactly," Casey said.

"There's been a lot of weird sounds in the woods since the white-out. We only go into the woods if we must. Mainly the men go off hunting when it's necessary. It's usually the same four guys you met earlier, and occasionally Bob and Mitch would go with their dad," Charlie said, taking a bite of his sandwich.

"It's a long shot, but I was thinking maybe I would see something in this notebook that would trigger me. Like this here. These are infernals—fallen angels—and these giants and creatures are their offspring. It's mentioned in the book of Enoch that they will be unobserved. Could that mean invisible? I was really hoping for an idea on how to destroy them," Casey said.

"How many are there?" Charlie asked, looking at the list of names of the fallen angels.

"Two hundred, and these ten are the leaders," Casey said.

"This is terrible. But the ascension isn't for another ten weeks. If the fallen angels and those creatures are roaming freely around the earth, then we're all fucked," Charlie said.

"In this book, there are many mythological creatures and how to destroy them, but nothing about destroying the infernal," Casey said, closing the book. "We better join the others." He stuffed the last piece of crust in his mouth before Charlie could swipe it.

Mingan was standing at a high bench, working on molding a piece of silver. "I think I know what we're up against," he said.

"What are we preparing for?" Charlie asked, sitting down on a stool next to Mingan at the workbench. Checking out the bench, with all its herbs and bowls of potions, reminded Casey of Sophia so sharply, it left him breathless. *God help me,* Casey thought, and under his breath he muttered, "Please, God, grant me the sincerity to accept the things I cannot change, courage to change the things I can, and the wisdom to know the difference. Amen."

Jade sat upon a mat with a zigzag weave that resembled mountains. It told a story. She ran her fingers around the edges of her drum. Her aura washed with pastels as she pulled the feather out from behind the drum and caressed the white deerskin.

"Since the whiteout, we have been experiencing strange events. Evil spirits and creatures that hide in the shadows. Beasts from long ago," Mingan said.

"I can relate. Who hasn't?" Casey said.

"The ancestors told me we are in a time when Great Spirit will allow the evil banished from this realm to roam freely upon the earth. Each day, more and more seen and unseen creatures emerge into our realm. One of these unseen creatures has taken Bob, and he is now only a vessel for evil. I will need to see the preacher for myself to know what we are up against," Mingan said.

"These creatures and evil entities we have seen and heard; I believe are the sins of the Fallen Angels—their children. The preacher could be a vessel for evil, like Bob," Casey said.

"I'm like you, Casey. I can see beyond the physical form into their spirit and see their auras, I can see into the abyss, I can see what others can't, as you can. But you don't look deeply in case you see evil; you only want to see the good." Mingan picked up another piece of silver and started carving the same symbol on it. "Casey, pick up a piece like this and watch me. Jade, drum, create a vortex of protection. Let the spirit guide you."

"Casey has a book which shows us the fallen angels. I too believe it's their children who haunt us in the woods. What do you want me to do?" Charlie asked, bouncing off the stool.

"Do what you do best, go watch over Bob, and the hunters, something strange is going on within them. Don't let them out of your sight. Warn us if there is any change in their behavior," Mingan said.

Charlie's whole body seemed to sigh. Her enthusiasm to help was gone. It was clear to Casey that she wanted to do so much more than be a watcher. She stormed out of the room, her aura showing she was hungry for Mingan's affections and approval.

"Was that necessary?" Casey said.

The buzz of the engraver drowned out anything Mingan might have said, though Casey doubted he said anything in reply.

Mingan concentrating on the fine lines of his carving, briefly looked up at Casey. "Bob is cursed with wendigo fever, a low form of spirit that has been on the earth for centuries. Like the sin of the fallen angels, they seek our bodies to use as vessels."

Jade stopped her arm in mind motion as she was about to beat on the drum. "If we kill Bob, and if they're evil entities inside him, what's stopping the evil spirit of the wendigo from leaving Bob's body and finding a new vessel?"

Casey didn't care to know, and picked out a piece of silver. "I'm tired of battling God's demons and evil entities. If they want my body as a vessel, they can have it if it's going to get me closer to my spirit ascending to be with Sophia again. There really isn't anything more I need."

"I don't have all the answers, Jade. But, Casey, if those entities get inside you, you will never see Sophia again. You will be a puppet to the devil, like those poor lost souls during the plague; but this time it will be forever," Mingan said without taking his eyes off his carving.

Casey flattened out the silver and watched the carving take form. It resembled the seals of Solomon on Sophia's necklace.

10

JADE: THE PURGE

The oscillation of the drum evoked peace as it touched Jade's soul. Calmly, she watched Casey as he attempted to engrave the special symbol that she couldn't see. He was tense and hunched over, trying to focus on the detailed task. She wondered where Kevin had gone and when he would be back. She missed having him close. The light and color in the ether seemed different when he wasn't around, and as much as it irritated her, she also liked how he knew her feelings and needs. After watching Charlie storm out of the room, and Mingan clueless in her wake, Jade realized how special Kevin's gift of empathy was. Mingan, with all his charms and . . .

"Concentrate on the drumming," Mingan said.

His sudden words made her body jump in fright and sent a shot of adrenaline through her system. Her cheeks flushed, wondering if he knew what she was actually thinking, or if he was reading the changes in her aura.

"Quiet your mind. Did Chief Thundercloud and Great Turtle teach you nothing?"

"She's really amazingly intelligent," Casey said.

Mingan stopped working on the engraving. "You're not ready for your teacher," Mingan said.

"Yes, I am. I've already met my teacher. His name is Gray Wolf." Jade had lost her rhythm and tried to get back on track. Now her senses were off and her anxiety returned. *Thanks a bunch, Mingan,* she thought.

Fear and darkness overlay peace and calmness. She closed her eyes and tried to connect to her teacher, or Great Turtle, to find balance and grounding. She took deep breaths, opening her lungs, and imagined sitting by a brook under a full moon, paddling her feet in water.

The brook moved with the pull of the moon as it journeyed into streams. Her thoughts flowed upon the streams until she felt peace again and her body relaxed, giving in to the distant sound of the drum. A vision appeared in her mind's eye, she was alone, walking deep into the forest, when she found a reflective triangular door, as if it had magically appeared from another world.

Jade cautiously walked around it. There was nothing of it from behind. She moved back to gaze into the front, imagining the face of the triangle was perhaps a doorway.

A figure within the triangle, as if on the other side of a mirror, moved towards her. It looked female, with long white hair. The woman glowed, radiated joy, hope, and freedom, which were only a few of her emotions, and Jade felt them as if they were her own. The woman reminded Jade of her studies of the European Neolithic period and a discovery near Stonehenge of a burrow that was over five thousand years old that contained the remains of a high priestess. Jade touched the end of her hair in disbelief and wondered if this woman was a high priestess.

Sophia replaced the woman, stepped to the threshold, and smiled. She was beautiful, ageless, and wise as an old woman. All that she ever was glowed from her light being. In Jade's mind, she heard Sophia's voice, as if she were standing next to her.

"It's up to you, Casey, Kevin, and Shaun. No matter how much the others want to help, the four of you must stand together. Tell Casey not to forget the dagger or Isabella's notebook. Tell him I'm watching, and soon his pain will ease," Sophia said.

Beside her, Great Turtle appeared, and a rush of love brought tears to Jade's eyes.

The further into the triangular doorway Jade peered, more light beings revealed themselves. "But how, Sophia? What do we need to do? I don't understand. We are already getting as many people together as we can."

Sophia faded, and the doorway vanished. The forest filled will dense misty clouds, and she knew it was an infernal shroud to befog her senses. Suddenly the warm loving vision shifted. She had lost her way once before and didn't want to make the same mistake. She looked behind her for the deer. It stood waiting for her to follow. The grounded clouds thickened, and she drew out her wand from her back pocket. The light only glared back at her, unable to penetrate the infernal shroud. Whispers of black smoke, patches of gray whipped past her like smoke streams. *This isn't good,* she told herself.

The deer guided her deeper and deeper into the forest, the deer one step in front of her at all times. Never did it turn to meet her eyes. "Wait," Jade called out to it. She reached out to touch it, to place her hand on its back in case the fog grew even thicker. But the deer moved faster.

Something was wrong. The gentle energy that radiated from the deer vanished. The energy turned evil and strong. It turned and looked at her. Its eyes were gorged out, the sockets hollow, blood tears trailed down its muscular cheek.

"You're not White Deer." Jade, horrified, turned her head from left to right, trying to decide which direction to run. There was no way out of the fog. She was trapped. Her breathing increased; hyperventilating, she tried to hide her emotions from the creature and get herself under control. She turned to run in the opposite direction as the image of the deer turned to black trails of smoke. She swallowed her fear and waited to find out what form it was going to take next. She was certain it was not of this world.

This is not the time to analysis the energy, she scolded herself. Searching for a way out of the fog and back to her body in Mingan's cabin at the campsite, Jade ran blindly until her throat hurt. The fog didn't subside. It was more like thunderous rolling clouds. She stopped and listened for the sound of her drum. Not once in her dash did she run into a tree, or trip on a rock. *Where am I?* she wondered and recalled it was vision. She had to return to her body. It was time to get out of the vision.

Jade sat down in the forest and closed her eyes, holding her wand to her chest. She imagined her memory stones around her, especially the stone with the image of the wind, and she concentrated on the warm summer wind in her hair, the smell of the sea, and sand between her toes. She breathed in and out. In the space of one breath, the fog backed away from her until it was all clear. A whisper of black smoke drifted down from the clouds. An evil trickster was in their midst. The wind picked up the evil, pushed it across the mountains and into the sky like tumble weed.

Her drumming increased as she opened her eyes and she was once again in Mingan's healing room, drumming a steady rhythm. Casey rubbed and blew away shavings from the carved arrowhead he had created.

"You did good, Raven Wings," Mingan said.

"Casey, I—"

"Not now, Raven Wings," Mingan said.

Jade wanted to argue, but she knew he was right. Something about the intense energy in the room encouraged her to keep drumming. She increased the speed of the drumming determined to keep the evil that had tried to spy on them away. Her memory stones floated around in her mind's eye, faster and faster. She opened her eyes again and quickly closed them to see if they were still there, but as soon as she opened them, she saw the stones had actually lifted off the ground around her and her bracelet carvings glowed. As soon as she thought about what was happening, her stones clanged to the floor and her drumming stopped.

Casey's concentration had been broken by the sudden clang of the stones and the end of the drumming. He looked at her wide eyed, as if he had drifted far away or had gone deep within himself and had to return suddenly.

Mingan was unaffected. "That's enough for today's lesson. You are quick to learn."

Jade was confused and unsure of what lesson he was talking about. "What?"

"All the knowledge stored in your stones circled around you. Soon it will penetrate the layers of your aura, then into your ethereal body, and then into the physical. You will know when this happens."

"How did you do that?" Casey asked in a dreamy voice.

Jade wanted to ask Mingan more questions but couldn't think of the questions. He poured two glasses of water and handed one to Casey, and then he squatted down and placed one beside her. She reached for it, accidentally touching his fingers. Her heart skipped a beat. She drank without meeting his beautiful eyes. It made her a little angry, as if her hormones betrayed her.

"Casey . . . ," Jade said, trying to speak, but her throat was tight and dry. She couldn't finish her sentence. She cleared her throat and tried again. "Casey . . ." But her voice came out a dry rasp. She tried to swallow.

"Not now," Mingan said to her.

"How did you do it?" Casey asked again, sitting beside her. He looked pale.

"Are you okay?" she asked him.

"Fine now. How did you do it?"

"Do what?"

"The storm. It nearly tore the roof off. Then the fog came in under the door. Mingan said we had to keep working on the carvings and you would take care of everything else," Casey said.

"I . . . I don't know what you're talking about." But then Jade remembered her vision of the fog. It was an infernal fog. And the hollow eyes of the deer, an evil entity, had tried to lead her astray. She recalled the stone of the wind and clearing away the fog.

"Yes. Clearing the evil that had entered our sacred space," Mingan said. She wished he'd say more.

"Casey, you have bitterness growing inside you like a poisonous snake," Mingan said, brushing the shavings off the workbench. He picked up the carving on top of the pile. The two of them had made six carved arrowheads.

"What? Did Charlie say something?" Casey said.

"Casey . . . ," Jade said.

"No, she didn't," Mingan said. "I can see the tiny snake curled up inside your spleen."

"But I already vomited up the snake," Casey said.

"Hang on, I'm confused," Jade interrupted. "That snake I snatched out of the air earlier on? You puked it up? That's crazy." As soon as she said it, she realized it was redundant, because everything that was happening was crazy.

"Yeah," Casey said, wiping his mouth.

"If you're ready, I can help you expel it now. Get rid of it forever. Be done with it," Mingan said.

"Jade, you can do it. You know how," Mingan said.

"Casey when I—"

Mingan cut her off again. "No, not like that. Use your shamanic gifts and heal him."

"Now? I thought lessons were over for today," Jade said sarcastically.

"I'm ready, Jade," Casey said.

"I've done this only once before."

"I trust you."

"Okay, lie down on the rug. While I prepare." Jade reached for her drum bag. She took out her medicine pouch tools and positioned them on the ground beside Casey, along with her wand. She placed her singing bowl at the top of his head. Her drum was at his side, ready for her to use. "Close your eyes, Casey," Jade said.

Mingan picked up a box of matches and scratched the flint. He held the flame against a stick of sage; he blew against the flame until smoke drifted into the air. Jade held out her oyster shell for Mingan to place the burning sage. Gently, she picked up her raven wing by the edge bound with turquoise suede, fanned the smoke over her body, and silenced her thoughts.

Next, she needed to cleanse Casey's aura. She started from his head and smudged across every part of his body, down to his feet, using the shell. He breathed in deeply, welcoming the scent. A tear bubbled at the edge of his eye and slipped down his face. "The smell. It reminds me of Sophia," Casey said. His chest heaved.

"It's only been a couple of days. It will get easier." Jade finished smudging Casey and put the shell down at his feet, letting the sage continue to burn and keep him grounded. She held his feet, squeezed his toes.

Her movements were fluid as she picked up her singing bowl. Standing at the top of his head, she gently tapped the side of the bowl and watched the vibrations travel over Casey's body. The vibrations were like ripples on the surface of a lake, undisturbed until they came across a blockage in the flow. The waves fractured as they passed his spleen. Jade tapped the bowl again, moving closer to the left side of his body, the waves distorted over his heart. Then she concentrated on the right side, where the waves moved down his body without breaking. His troubles were on the left side of his body. Jade pushed her own questions aside and focused on the areas.

Jade held her hands over Casey's spleen to feel the fractured vibrations. She listened with her hands. Her left hand stayed over his spleen while her right hand moved over his emanating physical energy, which had peaks and dips. Her hand stopped just above his belly button, and she knew the two points were connected—his spleen and his sacral chakra. In her mind's eye, she saw a murky orange, slow swirling energy, as if weighed down. The flow was stifled by the heaviness of something growing in Casey's spleen.

She heard laughter, as if it was coming from the next room, Casey's and Sophia's combined laughter. The room filled with joy. Then the sound of a slamming door and the handle rattled across the floor. The joy now trapped inside the room with the memory of Sophia and Casey on the outside. The door handle floated into space. Jade need to retrieve that door handle. It represented a part of Casey that had been lost in the void.

Jade tapped crystal dust from her brown medicine bottle onto Casey to mark the spot over his stomach and spleen. She tapped the singing bowl again and watched the vibrations travel over his body revealing the next spot that needed healing, which was the heart. But first she thought she saw a slight ripple over his brow. She concentrated on the heart area, placed the bowl down gently and raised herself up on her knees. She focused on the energy around the heart until she felt a difference in the energy. Her hand dipped down, as if the wave had lost momentum and become stagnant.

Her right hand settled over the area. The energy was a dark, murky olive green with a dark core at the center. Casey's life force was heavy with grief. He could never ascend to heaven with such a heavy heart. This was a paradox. Because Casey wanted to connect with Sophia, he had tried to astral travel to see her and failed, and it was because of his pain trapped in his heart. If Jade could not clear this area and help him heal, she feared he would descend into the depths of despair with the evil forces close by.

Suddenly, she realized the importance of emotional pain. Anyone blocked emotionally with a wounded heart may not be able to ascend. A black onyx stone with the symbol of the heart came into view. It was the last stone she needed to understand.

The energy in his aura kept her right hand buoyant over Casey's heart. Jade felt compelled to turn her left palm up and raised it away from the body and towards the sky, as if she were waiting to receive healing light to channel into Casey.

In her mind's eye, she saw a golden light. It traveled down from the universe and into her heart. She felt it pulsate like a second heartbeat. Her mind sparkled with the transcendent light which was for Casey. It crossed her body and through her right arm, into her hand, and into Casey.

His body arched towards her hand, welcoming the flow of energy. Jade hummed, holding a single note that sounded like the word air, which she held constant—eheheheheh. With each long breath, she repeated the sound. The energy continued pouring into Casey. Jade opened and closed her eyes, checking on Casey's physical state. As she did this, she saw the color of his energy reflecting off his body. His nose was red and his eyes watered.

She felt compelled to speak, but when she did—it was so gentle she almost didn't recognize it—she knew the energy of the deer as it influenced her speech. "You will journey without distance. You will soar like the eagle through all realms. Balance the heart, leap into flight. See your spiritual self in all things. Revive the passion, the warmth, no judgement, but compassion for all things."

As she spoke and the energy filled his heart's energy center, the murky green turned into vibrant emerald green, and the center turned from black heaviness into a light, soft pink. His heart filled with unconditional love from the universe and Great Spirit. "God watches over you, Casey, as does Sophia."

The tears poured down Casey's checks unencumbered. His mouth turned in to a smile. He swallowed. Things were happening inside Casey. Private things which were not for her to know unless he chose to tell her when they were finished.

It was time for Jade to find the missing part, the door handle. She picked up her wand like a surgeon's knife and cut the air around the spleen. Gently, she placed the wand in the center of his body and the terminator crystal head glowed. Jade sat by his side. Breaking off a piece of the sage from the bottom of the stick, she popped it into her mouth and chewed, remembering not to swallow.

The touch of her drum, drumming stick in hand, she began drumming to journey into the void for Casey's lost part. Her focus was on the sprinkled crystal shavings that marked the areas for healing as she let herself fall into the vortex that was like a deep, narrow funnel. She dropped through the bottom of the funnel and saw a trail of sparkling crystals. She didn't have to journey too far before she saw the door handle floating out in space alone.

Jade reached out and connected with the handle until it merged with her. She felt it bang into her spleen, where she would carry it back to Casey. Back up through the spiraling funnel and into the room, she quickly put down the drum and leaned over Casey's body. Placing her hands on either side of his spleen, she pulled at it as if to open it wide, and she breathed into it until she had no breath left.

Mingan offered her a bowl, and she spat the sage into it. Something squirmed inside the bowl of spit. She breathed into Casey and saw the room inside him where he had hidden his joy open wide, saw the positive energy flow into every part of his being. She breathed into his spleen seven times and spat seven times, removing all residual energy of the darkness that had settled inside his spleen. With both her hands, she pushed the skin together and used her wand like a laser to heal the ethereal scar.

Casey started coughing. Jade sat him up just as he violently vomited squirming tiny black snakes. Mingan handed her matches. Casey watched the flame fall as the snakes frantically wriggled, releasing high-pitched sounds, then he lay back down. "I'm just going to check your heart and sacral chakras have cleared, just to make sure we haven't missed anything in the spleen," Jade told him.

She picked up the singing bowl and gently tapped the edge as she walked around his body. The vibrations rippled over him with no disturbances. Jade picked up her drum and held it up so her raven's feather, attached to the underside of her drum, trailed over his body as she strummed and covered him with a web of golden energy to protect and continue his healing.

"How do you feel?" Jade asked as she softly placed her hand on his shoulder. Casey's eyes widened, and he blinked rapidly as he tried to focus. "Take it slow. You've been in a deep meditative state."

She gathered her tools, put her medicine pouch back inside her medicine bag, and smudged her wand before putting it away with her singing bowl. She smudged her drum before going to the bathroom to rinse her mouth out and wash her hands.

"You okay? How do you feel?" Jade asked and smiled at Casey as she wiped her hands on the back of her jeans.

He smiled back. "I feel like someone drugged me."

"That's because you were in a deep state. It will wear off shortly. But you're grounded. No flying for the next couple of hours. You should go eat orange and leafy green foods. Drink plenty of water," Jade instructed, her voice stern.

Casey sat up. "I saw her; I saw Sophia."

"Do you feel connected to her again?" Jade asked. She noticed

Mingan had strapped the arrowheads to the top of four staffs, turning them into spears.

"I feel connected to everything again. I'm lighter. My stomach isn't churning, and I don't feel fear and anger festering inside me anymore. I'm not alone. I never was," Casey said, wiping his eyes and mouth.

"Casey, I saw her before, when you were engraving the arrowheads," Jade said, taking another sip of her water. "She told me to tell you, she is with you, and we all have to work as a team."

She waited to see if he was going to share what he saw or what Sophia had said to him. But he got to his feet and stretched. He looked out the window into the twilight of the evening. "Where did the day go? I'm famished. When does this feast begin?"

"For you, it starts now. Go. Enjoy yourself. I will catch up with you. Find Charlie and Crazy Bear," Mingan said.

Healing Casey, gave Jade an elated feeling that remained from the energy that had travelled through her being into his. There were so many questions pushing to the forefront of her mind that she wanted to ask Mingan.

"Now's not the time. Now is the time to celebrate," Mingan said to Jade, as if he read her mind.

How does he do that? she wondered.

11

CASEY: SPIRIT WALKER

S tepping out of the cabin and into the coolness of the evening, Casey gazed into the sky, searching for Orion's belt and the star cluster alongside it. He took in a deep breath and released it. Walking back to the community lodge, he took out the arrowhead from his jeans pocket and studied it. In its center, two lines interlaced to create a wheel of circles and the stars, all joined as one. The hardest part of the carving was keeping everything connected, starting at the center and using only two lines. It was just like Sophia's necklace; it was a ten-spoke wheel with stars at the end of each spoke. Each star had twenty outward points—the sign of protection, the amplified protection of the Seal of Solomon. There was no stopping and starting. Mingan had him drawing it repeatedly until he was ready to engrave his first head of silver.

"My backpack. I forgot it. I need to go back. It's beside the kitchen table at Mingan's cabin," Casey said, breaking the silence.

"Don't you want to get something to eat first?" Jade said.

He was standing near the community lodge, surrounded by tables with fresh food and fire pits. The feast had begun. His stomach groaned, but he struggled with the idea of eating. The smoky smell reminded him of the torso the preacher had on the spit. The mood of the people was joyful and energized with hope, their auras colored like a bed of spring flowers.

Sitting on a log, Crazy Bear was playing the guitar and Charlie sat next to him, nervously fiddling with a string of pearls around her neck. He didn't recall seeing them before. They looked out of place amongst the handmade turquoise jewelry she wore around her neck and wrist. He wondered if they were a family heirloom, like Sophia's necklace. "It's inviting, but I better get my things. Sophia had made a point of mentioning Isabella's notebook. There must be something that she wants me to see."

When Jade turned back to him, Casey added, "You don't have to come. You can go get something to eat. It's been a while since I saw you eating."

"I can say the same for you; get something when you're ready. Maybe vomiting up those baby snakes spoiled your appetite," Jade said, pulling her long black hair to the side and over her shoulder. Gently, she brushed her face with the ends of her hair. Casey knew it soothed her. When stressed, Jade would twirl her bracelet around and around her wrist, or lightly brush her face with the ends of her silky black hair.

"I wonder where the shells are?" Casey said.

"What shells?" Jade asked.

"Snakes lay eggs. They had to come out of a shell, no?" Casey said, digging his hands deep into his pocket.

Jade screwed her nose up at the thought and smiled, her face radiating strength and confidence. "I've been trying not to think so much and accept there are some things I can't understand or explain," Jade said.

Casey ducked under a tree branch as they walked around the back of Mingan's cabin. "Healing suits you. When did you learn . . . what did Mingan call it, shamanic healing?"

"Great Turtle taught me a long time ago. Only now the teachings are coming to the surface, because of the memory stones. Let's go down to the lake for a minute first? We'll collect our things on our way back," Jade said.

He had hold of the wooden banister that led up the three steps to the cabin door. "Sure, why not?" They strolled towards the lake as if it was an ordinary evening. It was good to a have a moment of normality. Normal seemed like a long time ago. The reflection of the lights and moon sparkled on the placid lake. "You're a good healer. Thank you," Casey said.

"It emerged when I was looking for my dad. I met Chief Thundercloud, and he triggered the resurgence of the teachings Great Turtle taught me when I was too young to even remember. Chief Thundercloud had my memory stones. Great Turtle gave them to him until I was ready. Oh, and there's a trigger point."

"What do you mean by a trigger point?" Casey asked, rubbing his stubbly cheek. He was going to have to shave or let it grow out. In-between made his face itchy.

"Before all this, I used to sit on the verandah to watch the wind roll over and through the trees and admired everything around me, in awe of Mother Nature. I would lose myself and drift for hours, deep in thought, until my mother gently tapped my elbow. I always thought it was because she didn't want to startle me, but now I know it's an anchor point. When searching for my dad, my mom tapped me on the elbow. When I was with Chief Thundercloud, he tapped me on the same elbow. They had programed my brain to respond in a particular way when someone tapped my elbow—it aligns me to the universe and my teachings. Early today, Mingan touched my elbow in the same way. How did he even know about it? Did my great-grandmother tell everybody but me about it?"

"I don't know. You should ask him. But thanks again for the healing," Casey said.

"Come on, let's get our belongings from the cabin."

The lights were on, generators hummed, and the air smelled of the fumes. They knocked and waited, but no one answered, so they let themselves in. Casey's backpack leaned against the wall in the kitchen where he had left it. He checked everything was fine and put it on his back. Jade came down the hall from the healing room with her bag and drum. "I'm famished," Casey told her, surprised to realize it was true.

They passed the fire pits where people talked and ate. "Let's get something to eat, sit by the fire, and go through Isabella's book together. See what jumps out." He adjusted his dagger that he had buckled around his waist. The dagger rested against his thigh, and he pushed it towards the back.

Jade wrapped her arms around him tight and gave him a big squeeze. "I love you, Casey—we all do. Don't go off on your own. Let's stay together until this is done and we've ascended."

Casey kissed her on the top of her head. Her hair smelled like sage and shampoo.

"I would love to have a look through the notebook," Jade said as she pulled away. "But how can you touch it? It's so old and full of memories. Aren't you affected? Can't you feel its past?"

"I'm not affected when I touch it. I'm somehow protected and I would like it to stay that way. You can look through it, but no one else."

"I wonder if it has anything about the wendigo in it?"

* * *

SITTING on logs around a fire with their new friends, Casey was surprised how hungry he was, and tried not to eat fast. The twins spoke to each other, and Charlie ate her last mouthful. Crazy Bear was sitting close to the female of the twins and his aura was touching the edge of hers. Jade has yet to introduce the twins to Casey.

The food was delicious. "Where did you guys get the mango from?" Jade asked.

"You'll have to ask them over there," Charlie said, pointing to a group of women with small children that ran around playing tag.

Mingan walked past the table of food. Jade watched him make his selection. "When do you think Kevin is coming back?" Jade asked Casey.

Casey had just taken a bite of his roast turkey sandwich, and pretended not to have noticed she was watching Mingan, He chewed as fast as he could and tried to swallow quickly to answer her. "Maybe tomorrow? You miss him, don't you?"

"How can she miss him when she's always got her eyes on my man?" Charlie said, dropping her empty plate at her feet. The flame in the pit seemed to stretch out, as if something flammable had just been tossed in.

"He's not your man," Crazy Bear told her. "Gray Wolf is no one's man."

"Gray Wolf?" Jade said.

"Yeah, that's what Mingan means, Gray Wolf."

"What?" Her face turned red. "I'm so stupid," Jade said.

"You said it!" Charlie looked at Jade.

"So, where's your significant other?" Charlie said to Casey.

"She left this world," Casey said.

Jade put her hand on his leg. He squeezed her fingers and smiled.

"I'm sorry to hear that." Charlie shifted her position on the log.

"Her name was Sophia." Casey studied the food on his plate, losing his appetite.

"Like the Greek goddess of spiritual wisdom?"

"She was." Casey smiled at Charlie because she was right, Sophia was a goddess.

"How did you learn to fly?" Charlie asked.

His paper plate was buckling under the weight of the untouched food. The twins, hearing Charlie's question, asking him how he learned to fly, looked up from their conversation. Casey could see the soft peach and blues in their combined auras, reflecting the deep balanced level of communication they shared.

Breaking the twin bubble, he and his sister were in, the guy stood and offered his hand. "I'm Jackson. You can fly?"

Casey ignored the offer and Jackson sat back down and picked up his cup next to his plate on the grass and took a sip.

"Sorry, sometimes I prefer not to shake hands. I can fly, but not 'flap your wings' kind of fly. I sort of propel myself off the ground, like the opposing side of a magnet," Casey said.

"Like a rocket?" Jackson said.

"Pretty much," Casey said, trying to keep his ego in check.

"That's so cool," Jackson said.

"Hi, I'm Emma."

"Hi. How long have you all known each other?" Casey asked, referring to the whole group.

"We went to school together. Great Turtle picked us to learn the old ways." Jackson's sister explained.

Emma wore a choker around her long neck, and her short black hair curled inwards and touched the sides of the choker. Jackson's black hair was a little longer and touched his shoulders.

Crazy Bear started playing the guitar, and Emma sang. She had a beautiful voice. It was a song about the moon. "The moon she is waiting, waxing and waning, the moon she is waiting for us to be free."

Casey looked into the sky. *Sophia is waiting, and soon we will be free of the evil taking over the earth.*

"Have you been amongst the stars? I mean, physically, not spiritually," Jackson asked, moving next to Casey. Casey shuffled over on the log, closer to Jade.

"I tried, but I passed out when the oxygen in the air got too thin. Don't quite make it to the stars. Free falling is a rush, though," he said with a self-deprecating smile.

"What, you flew as high as you could until you passed out? And then free-fell until you regained consciousness?" Jackson said.

Casey raised his eyebrows and nodded.

"You're crazy!" Jackson said.

"But you're not going to do that anymore," Jade said, banging her knee against Casey's.

Crazy Bear paused his playing to grab Casey's hand in a shake, then punched his fist against Casey's. "That's my man. Hell yeah!"

Violence, blood, pain, and suffering entered Casey's mind. Images of Crazy Bear crying over a child, his sister, a victim of his parents' violent rage. They had had the virus, the shape-shifting demons that started all this eleven years ago. His parents, controlled, were merely puppets of the evil that had plagued the earth. It took ten years for everything that was called civilization to be destroyed. Crazy Bear had watched his parents go insane until they killed his little sister. The military came to take them away. Crazy Bear ran out the back door and into the woods. He met up with Charlie and Mingan at Great Turtles cabin where they had practiced their art with Great Turtle before she passed away.

"Let go of my hand. You're hurting me," Crazy Bear said, trying to pull his hand from Casey's grip.

Casey was shaking. He blinked wildly, trying to get rid of the images, and loosened his grip enough for Crazy Bear to pull his hand away. "Sorry. All good. Sorry. Are you okay?" Casey said, wiping his hand on his jeans.

"Yeah. All good. What was that, man? What happened to you?" Crazy Bear said, rubbing his strumming hand.

"It's not what happened to him; it's what happened to you. He sometimes feels and sees people's past," Jade said.

Crazy Bear locked eyes with Casey, as if trying to know what Casey had seen. It was a few seconds of awkward silence around the fire, then Crazy Bear nodded in acceptance.

"If you're cold, move closer to the fire, or get a blanket from one of the cabins," Jackson said to Casey.

"You can move a little this way, and I'll keep you warm," Charlie said.

He wasn't sure how to respond to that. He just smiled. "I'm warm enough, thanks. Don't mind me," Casey said.

Rugged up in a blanket, Bob came over. He was very pale. He shivered. Oils from his pores made his face look wet. Casey wondered if Bob had gone through another shedding. In his right hand was a big turkey drumstick. He chewed down on it as if he hadn't eaten in weeks. Just when Casey thought he was going to plonk down between him and Charlie, Bob mumbled, then threw the savaged drumstick into the fire and headed back for more. This time, he stayed and ate as much as he could until Russell pulled him away.

The clapping and dancing were infectious. "Sophia loved to dance. She had been a ballet dancer, you know," Casey said to Jade.

"Yes, when she leaped over the river of fire in the Tomb of Thoth, she was incredible." Jade stood up and offered her hand.

"No, I'm not dancing."

"Come on, I have two left feet. You can't be any worse than me." Jade pulled him to his feet. "One dance."

Mingan sat beside the elders, smoking a pipe. It looked odd, because it wasn't so long ago they were all forbidden to share food or drinks. They passed the pipe between one another.

For a moment, Casey felt like he was being watched. He looked into the dark woods that surrounded the campsite. The trees seemed taller than in the daylight. He pivoted around and checked the cabins. Like Japanese lanterns, the yellow glow of the cabin porch lights streamed down towards the lake. It looked haunted. The shadows of the forest seemed sinister.

"What is it, Casey?" Jade asked as the silhouettes of five men wearing hats moved out from under the shadows.

"Over there, on the overside of the field, coming out from behind the trees," Casey whispered.

"I see them. Do you think it's the same as . . . ?"

He wasn't listening. The blood pounded in his ears. He breathed out, letting his shoulders relax as the first shadow stepped into the light, twirling the ends of his moustache. It was the four hunters. The young guy, constantly hiking up his pants, wiped the back of his mouth as if he had just finished eating something extremely enjoyable. The closer they got, the less frightened Casey was, but something was still very odd.

"Did you see something in the forest?" Casey asked the moustache man, whose shadow was way too long. All their shadows were elongated.

"Na. Why?" the young guy said.

"What you looking at?" the mustache guy snapped.

"You have blood on your lip," Casey said.

"Well, what do you know?" the man said and wiped his mouth with the back of his hand, then licked the blood off.

They all laughed. One man, who seemed to always walk behind the mustachioed man, grabbed Jade by the wrist. "Let's have a dance."

"Let me go!"

Behind Jade, Mingan stood, and the wolf in his aura stood at attention.

"Let her go," Casey warned.

"Or what? You're going to make me?" the man sneered.

The man smirked with plump red lips. They seemed way too red, and grossly over-moistened. Casey tucked his chin down and mentally pushed the man over. The mustachioed man struggled to breathe, and the other men tried to help him up. He was only winded for a few seconds. Casey hadn't pushed him too hard, just a little nudge to knock him off his feet.

"What did you do?" the mustachioed man snarled, spitting in Casey's face. Casey could smell the blood.

"That's enough," Mingan said, blowing out smoke.

"You lot and your voodoo. You shouldn't be allowed to stay here," the mustachioed man spat, spraying the words through his moist red lips.

For a second, Casey thought he saw a forked tongue dart out and lick the air. The young guy was laughing like a hyena. Casey fixed his gaze on the man's lips, waiting to see if it happened again.

The men moved on. Casey watched them prop their guns against a tree and get themselves some more plates. They stood next to Bob, who no longer had a blanket wrapped around him. Bob was a skinny, lanky fellow, but his stomach bulged, engorged with food. The guy with the mustache pointed to the spot where they had just emerged from the forest. He whispered in Bob's ear. Bob turned away from the tables of food and hypnotically walked past Casey towards the woods.

"Join us," Mingan said, nodding his head at Casey. The gray wolf in Mingan's aura turned to smoke.

"You too, Raven Wings," Mingan said without looking back at her.

Casey did and Jade hesitated, then followed along.

The elders shuffled around, making room for them.

"Welcome to the elders' circle. This is Rising Eagle and Spirit Walker," Mingan said, gesturing to the two elders across from him. The others just nodded as a welcoming gesture, but Mingan didn't mention their names and they didn't offer them either.

Rising Eagle relit the pipe with a burning stick from their fire pit. Casey rubbed his hands nervously on his knees, watching the men pass the pipe around. He would receive the pipe before Jade. Casey took it. Not sure what to do, he stuck the tip of the pipe between his lips and drew back, and instantly he coughed and choked. Mingan patted him on the back. Casey braced himself for the overwhelming images and feelings he would see and feel from that touch, but he saw only an image, an image of an old, wise Native American man with a braid and one feather sticking out of a red sash that was tied around his head. His skin tanned and taunt over his bones, his eyes all-knowing, reminding Casey of a wise old wolf. He was soft, kind, and patient, and strong like a buffalo. Casey wondered who the man was. Mingan's father, or grandfather perhaps?

"More," Spirit Walker, the only female elder in the group, said.

"You heard her," Jade said with a smirk on her face.

The tip butted against his teeth. He drew on the pipe.

"Hold it," Mingan said. "Hold it. Now, blow it out until you have no breath."

Casey's chest convulsed. He stifled a cough. But as he blew out, the smoke took on the form of an owl and hovered in the air, staring at him with enormous eyes in a heart-shaped face.

Rising Eagle said, "Hmm, the Night Eagle. Deep insight you have, clairvoyance and strong intuition. The owl brings medicine of illumination and wisdom. You must go inward. Ancient knowledge is being given to you. Many fear owl medicine. Owl medicine represents the power of the woman. Imagine you are the owl, soaring in the night sky, moving through the darkness, and seeing clearly. You too shall perceive the truth in the darkest situations." Rising Eagle intoned. Though his voice was gentle, he spoke with conviction.

Casey could see in his mind the owl flying around unseen in the night sky. It also reminded him of his astral travels at night and how he moved around in the realm unseen. The owl evaporated into the air and Casey passed the pipe to Jade. She coughed and spluttered, to the amusement of the elder woman next to her. Jade puffed again on the pipe and held it back like Mingan had instructed. Jade blew it out and the smoke, like his, took the form of an animal. A white buffalo.

"White Buffalo calf woman, a powerful medicine. An honor. She promised long ago to return at the end of an age. Raven Wings, white buffalo medicine is calling you. Significant forces in the universe have chosen you to bring about a time of miracles and a balance for all things. You are a channel for the greater forces in the universe. With their help, all things are possible, Raven Wings, but if you deny their help, things can be troublesome. Surrender to the support of Great Spirit and lead with your heart. You do not have to do everything alone. Call on white buffalo medicine to multiply your energy. Imagine the weight and warmth of its coat and call the energy of white buffalo into your life," Rising Eagle said as the other elders generated energy that held a tight ring of protection around the group of elders.

Around the circle the pipe went, and each time a spirit animal appeared with a message. The visitation of the trickster bothered Casey more than he let on. He focused on the owl for the sight beyond the darkness, which he was feeling all around him. Even though people were laughing and dancing, he felt it like the calm before the storm, a feeling he knew all too well.

Clearly visible behind the Rising Eagle were the hunters. Bob had disappeared into the forest and hadn't returned. The hunters were getting rowdy, throwing their moonshine jars into the steel fire drum they stood around for warmth.

"Keep it down, boys," Russell yelled. "Is Bobby with you?"

"Yeah, for sure. He's one of us now. He'll be back soon, old man." The way he twirled the left side of his moustache irritated Casey. It was slow, deliberate, hypnotizing.

"Casey, show them the book and dagger," Jade said, pulling his attention back into the circle.

He'd told her he didn't want to show anyone or have them touching it, but they were all looking at him expectedly. Casey went back to the fire pit, where Crazy Bear and Emma were making out, and grabbed his and Jade's belongings. He stepped back over the log and retook his spot in between Mingan and Jade. He pulled out the book and put the bag behind him.

First, he drew the dagger from its sheath. The elders, sitting cross-legged, relaxed from the pipe and connection with spirit, perked up with fresh interest. Their old backs straightened.

"Old magic," Rising Eagle said.

Casey handed it out towards him to hold. Rising Eagle looked uncertain, contemplative. "Maybe not, Casey, the magic called to you."

"It's okay. You won't feel the pain of the past; you may see the creatures it has slain. For centuries, it has destroyed beasts and evil. When I lay my hands upon things, more often than not, I'll see visions I wish I hadn't. This is the only thing I have touched and not felt pain and suffering, though it's been part of many harrowing battles against the evil. If you give me your knife, I will feel the suffering or peace from the animals you've slain. But when I touched the dagger, the sense of its timelessness fills me. The flashes of history were painless. It was like traveling through a wormhole of time, back to before the construction of the pyramids, and beyond, into the light of the universe," Casey said.

Spirit Walker reached out for the dagger. He handed it to her. Her eyes rolled back into her head and her body shook. "She's having a seizure." Casey got to his feet.

"Sit. Spirit Walker needs no help. The spirit of the Dagger speaks to her," Rising Eagle said.

Spirit Walker spoke in a deep-timbered voice, "Cum postestate omnipotentis, aut spiritum daemonii immundi, et terebrare in te judicia, et non erit ultra ferrum: et hoc non factum est, in nomine spiritus sancti." Her eyes rolled back from within her head and held his gaze.

Casey was surprised to hear the words from Spirit Walkers mouth. "That's Latin; it means, with the power of the Almighty, unclean demon or spirit, I pierce you with the blade of judgement and you shall be no more, and it is done, in the name of the Holy Spirit: Amen. Sophia translated the Latin text that accompanied the dagger. The text, along with a drawing of the dagger, was inside Isabella's notebook. I had found the dagger hidden on a shelf in the Emporium, and Sophia believed I was meant to find," Casey said.

Spirit Walker bore through his eyes and spoke to his soul. "You are a warrior. The dagger comes from our ancestors in the sky. They showed me the beginning and end of the age. They, too, have honored you with the power of Great Spirit. You cannot leave; you must fight. Your tears are self-pity. Embrace the goodness for your friend that has returned to Great Spirit. Fall from the sky if you will. Jump off the cliff or tie a noose around your neck, but you cannot leave; you will not die. No more free falling for you. It's time for you to fight like a warrior," Spirit Walker said.

Casey could feel Jade's glare at the side of his head. He nervously glanced around at the leathered faces. How did Spirit Walker know?

"The blade will not harm you. Press it to your neck and it will feel blunt. Press it to another's and it will slice through as if the skin and bones were dust. But it's the black heart which you must pierce," Spirit Walker said.

He could feel Jade's questions pouring out from her aura one after another, compelling him to turn and answer her.

"What is she talking about? You're not going to...?" Jade asked.

"No. I don't want to die. I'm fine now, thanks to you, Jade," Casey said, not sure if she believed him. She was probably going to watch him like a hawk until they ascended.

"Spirit Walker? You said you saw the past and the future?" Casey said.

"Yes," Spirit Walker said but did not elaborate.

"What did you see?" Jade asked before he could get the words out.

Spirit Walker didn't answer. She kept her mouth closed. She reached out and touched Rising Eagle's hand, and he closed his eyes. Casey could see a connection in their aura as she passed the visions on to him. He opened his eyes and spoke. "It is not for us to tell you about your journey. It is your journey to live."

"Okay. What about your future, the dagger's future? What does it look like?" Jade said.

"You both have travelled far and wide and have seen where all things come and go, and you have all you need to find the answers to all your questions," Rising Eagle said.

Casey took back the dagger. He placed it in the sheath before opening Isabella's notebook.

A woman screamed, and the music stopped.

"My children are missing. Their beds are empty."

Rising Eagle closed his eyes and tilted his head up to the night sky in prayer. "It is time."

12

JADE: WENDIGO FEVER

A faint pathway of light streaked across the lake as Jade checked the banks for the missing children. The surface of the water looked serene and undisturbed. There was no obvious sign anyone had gone into the lake. People called the boys' names, Peter and Steven, but there wasn't any return cry for help. Alone, she kept an expanded awareness of her surroundings, afraid something might creep up on her. The trees had an ominous presence, as if they knew something. Jade turned her attention inward, listening with her heart and a powerful sense of caution, woken by an even higher state of awareness came over her.

Casey and Crazy Bear walked out of a cabin they had just searched for the missing boys. They waved her over, and she headed in their direction, cautiously looking up into the trees as she walked. "Nothing. What about you?" she said, wishing to hear something other than the foreboding whisper of the wind in the trees.

"Something is here. I can feel it," Casey said, turning his head from left to right, trying to find what he was sensing.

Jade understood what he meant. Her skin crawled, and everything around her seemed to vibrate, as though things could change at any minute. "Same."

"Me too. It's like we're walking into a lion's den," said Crazy Bear.

Jade stared into the darkness of the dense canopies. They all swept their flashlights up into the trees when someone ran out of the forest near the edge of the lake on the other side, where the hunters had sent Bob.

"Bob!" Mitch yelled and ran around the top end of the lake towards him.

The figure ran hunched over and didn't stop. He ran past Mitch, who gave chase. They headed for their cabin.

Crazy Bear went to join the chase but halted and stayed with Jade and Casey. "He's messed up with some bad mojo. Mingan and Rising Eagle are going to put Bob in a sweat lodge for sure. They have to release the evil spirit inside him, regardless of what the doctor thinks. Russell and Sue loved Great Turtle, but the doctor has them convinced *modern medicine* is the way. The doctor thinks the old ways are not medicine. He forgets where his medicine came from," Crazy Bear said and resumed scanning with his powerful flashlight, searching for the missing boys.

"I know. In the old days doctors used to have to study botany as part of their training. The plants and the trees around us have all the medicines we need, but it has to be extracted and prepared for bulk administration. But things are different now. There are no pharmaceutical companies. The plants and trees are all we have," Jade said.

"What's that awful smell?"

A loud thud came from behind, as if something heavy dropped from the trees. They all pivoted. A beast, upright as a man, lanky, and over ten feet tall, had sunken yellow eyes and a forked tongued. It growled like a canine, showing its sharpened teeth. It was smaller than the one she had seen in the forest, but its skin was just the same, decaying and wrapped tight over its protruding bones as if it had risen from the grave. Her hair moved gently as an arrow whizzed past, hitting the beast in the shoulder. Gray smoke trailed up from the beast where the arrow burned its flesh. It howled in pain and deconstructed, disappearing into thin air.

"Damn it! I missed the heart," Charlie said, picking up her arrow.

"What was that?" Casey asked.

"A wendigo. Mingan thinks Bob is turning into a wendigo. Wendigo's were nothing more than a myth, a representative of winter, hunger amongst the tribes, a warning against greed, selfishness, and cannibalism. But since the disappearance of billions of people and the whiteout, they have become something more. The elders say if you eat human flesh, hungry evil spirits will devour your soul and possess your human body until the body eats itself from the inside out. Then it searches for another host. The only way to kill it is a silver arrowhead or blade into the heart," Charlie said, putting the arrow in the pouch hanging off the side of a belt she had around her waist.

Casey flinched and touched the dagger around his thigh. "It moves to a new host unless you pierce its heart?" he asked. Jade knew what he was thinking. The elders had voiced the verse he needed to say when he used the dagger. He took out the arrowhead he had made with Mingan.

"That's why you guys were carving the arrowheads," Jade said watching Casey rub it between his fingers.

"Yes, it not only kills the beast but it also destroys the evil spirit inside from taking on a new host," Mingan said.

"Just like my dagger," Casey said.

Charlie looked at Casey as if she didn't know what he was talking about.

"Charlie, when did the elders tell you this?" Crazy Bear said.

"They didn't. I overheard them telling Mingan. That's why Bob has an insatiable appetite, because his body is eating itself from the inside. His hunger can never be satisfied. What we didn't know was who was serving human flesh. Until Casey found the preacher," Charlie said.

Jade thought about Bob, how he ate and ate and didn't seem to get enough. "That's the evil spirit you think is with Bob?"

"Not with but *in* Bob. If we don't do something soon, to get it out of Bob, it will consume him until there is nothing left but skin and bones, and then it will take someone else as a host," Mingan said.

"Old wives' tales," the doctor said, rushing up from behind. "Shouldn't you be helping with the search?"

He didn't stop for an answer. It was more of a statement. The doctor kept moving, disappointed. She watched him head for Bob's cabin.

"We need to destroy that thing before anyone else becomes a victim of its evil," Mingan shouted to the doctor.

"I don't think your herbs are going to do him much good. This is nothing more than psychosis. He needs modern medicine, or he'll lose his mind forever and do unspeakable things," the doctor said.

"What is the unspeakable? And what do you mean by 'his mind will be lost forever'?" Jade asked, rushing to keep pace with the doctor.

"Come, Jade, he's right. We should help try to find the missing children," Casey said, touching her elbow.

"Don't do that!" Jade yelled in his face.

"What?"

"You touched my elbow!" Jade said.

"I meant nothing by it," Casey said.

Jade knew she had overreacted, but she thought Mingan had touched her. The raised brow and pleading look on Casey's face told her he had forgotten about the trigger point anchored at her elbow.

Mitch was on the small porch of the cabin, as if keeping guard.

"Let me in, son," the doctor said.

Mitch looked from the doctor to Mingan, unsure of what he should do.

"So, you know what's wrong with Bob?" Jade said to the doctor, who was holding onto the porch rail with one foot on the stair and one on the porch.

"Yes, it's psychosis, and known amongst the superstitious as wendigo fever. And the unspeakable, young lady, is an intense craving for human flesh, which causes a neurological degeneration," the doctor said.

"Let him in," Jade said to Mitch. Boldly, she walked past Mitch and opened the door for the doctor.

The front room of the cabin was modest, with a lounge chair covered with a crochet blanket next to the kitchen and breakfast bar.

Sue braced herself against the kitchen sink, crying and barely holding herself up. Jade went to Sue and helped her into a chair before she fell to the floor. "Bob . . . Russell." Sue couldn't get the words out. Neither the doctor nor Mingan waited for an invitation to head further into the cabin. They rushed down the hallway to the back room.

Russell lay on his back on the floor, his throat torn open. Blood pooled around his head and neck. Bob was cowering in a corner, shielding himself from the bright flashlight Russell had dropped on the floor. Mitch stood outside, guarding the cabin, protecting his family, when the danger had been on the inside. Not realizing his brother, Bob, was capable of killing his father.

"Jesus!" the doctor said. He placed his bag on the bed and drew out a needle. "Hold him. We need to sedate him."

Crazy Bear looked at Mingan.

"Come, let's do it together," Mingan said.

Bob's strength didn't mirror his withering frame. Mingan and Crazy Bear had equal trouble restraining Bob. The strongest weapon in the room was the light. Jade flicked the light switch, driving away the shadows from the room. Dark blood pooled around Russell's neck and shoulders. Bob stopped struggling and covered his face from the light. The doctor administered the sedative, and Bob moaned before going limp and passing out on the floor. Crazy Bear and Mingan lifted Bob up onto the bed.

"What the hell happened!" Mitch cried, checking his father for a pulse. Blood and flesh covered Bob's mouth and chin.

"Mitch! Leave us. You can't help here. Find your sister and take care of your mother," Mingan said.

Jade wanted to step forward and see more of what the doctor saw. Mingan was itching to get to Bob. He whispered to Crazy Bear. Jade stepped forward, leaving Casey at the back of the room. The last thing Casey should do was touch the body.

Because of her curiosity, the doctor looked at her, hoping to find an ally. "Look here. See his response to the light, the uncontrollable shaking? Touch his body, he's burning up. All signs of psychosis, a neurological disease brought on by prion. A disease brought on by eating human flesh. It causes delirium which would account for Bob's unusual behavior in the hospital," the doctor said.

"Unusual behavior! Shit, are you blind?" Mingan said, moving closer to the bed. "You call shedding skin like a snake unusual behavior? And only a type of mental disorder?" Mingan cried.

Mingan stepped back as Crazy Bear returned with Rising Eagle. In the commotion, Jade hadn't noticed that he had left the room.

"Bob is your patient. We honor the wishes of the family. You are to respect that, Mingan," Rising Eagle said.

The look on Mingan's face was one of shock. He must have expected Rising Eagle to side with him. He stepped away from Bob and around Russell's body. Rising Eagle knelt down and shook a rattle, one that looked like a dried-up pumpkin, over Russell's body. Jade watched Casey take a step even further away as a mist rose from Russell's body and exited the room. Unbelievable. Never had she seen a person's soul rise after death. She couldn't help being curious. "Did you see that?" she asked the doctor.

"See what?" he muttered, looking up from the syringe he was preparing for Bob.

"Never mind," Jade said.

"But you saw it, Raven Wings," Mingan said, with the tiniest hint of pride lingering on the edge of his lips. If it hadn't been under such horrific circumstances, Jade believed he would have openly smiled at her.

"We must leave the room, Doctor. Come with us," Rising Eagle said.

"We can't just leave him!" the doctor exclaimed and turned back to Bob. "Help me. Hold him and make sure he keeps still, so I can give him another shot." Once it was administered, he peeled back one of Bob's eyelids.

Mingan and Crazy Bear held Bob still even though he appeared to be out cold.

Bob twitched. Jaded watched, waited, and willed the twitching to stop.

"Mingan, check and lock all the windows before leaving," Rising Eagle said.

In the kitchen, the doctor put his arm around Sue's waist and helped her to the infirmary. "Where's Ruby? Ruby!" Sue said.

"Mom. Mom!" Ruby ran out of their cabin.

Sue held her daughter and pushed the doctor out of the way, as if he disgusted her. "You did this! We shouldn't have listened to you. We should've listened to Mingan! Now I have lost a son and husband!"

Jade looked back over her shoulder at Crazy Bear nailing the kitchen window shut. The window that overlooked the lake.

It hadn't taken long until every cabin had been searched, and still no one had found the missing boys. An armed party of men had assembled to go into the forest to search for them. The mother wept on her husband's shoulder, begging him to find her boys before he headed off with the search party. The woman saw Jade. "Help me. Where are my boys?"

Jade didn't know what to say. What did the woman expect her to do?

"Casey, can you see auras in the dark? Would you be able to check from above? Maybe look for heat signatures or something?" Jade said.

"I haven't tried it before," Casey said. Without hesitation, he shot into the sky and threw Jade and Sue off balance as he propelled upwards.

Jade watched how quickly the goodwill of the feast had turned into fear. Some people scattered and hid in their cabins, afraid their children would be next to go missing, while others continued to search the campsite again. The search party had just penetrated the forest when a man screamed in pain. The mother of the boys must have recognized the sound of her husband screaming out in grief.

Jade, Mingan, Charlie and Crazy Bear ran after the woman. She entered the forest and screamed with equal pain. The woman could barely stand. Jade watched as Charlie helped the boy's mother as she crumbled to the ground in front of the empty carcass. The woman rocked back and forth in pain while Jade followed the blood and entrails. Something moved in the trees. She aimed her flashlight as if a gun and Casey lowered himself down from the sky.

"What did you see?"

"Very little," he told her.

Charlie had her hand on the woman's shoulder. "There is not much we can do until daylight. Maybe we should get everyone to stay in their cabins until the sun is up," Charlie said, looking at the father.

The boy's father sprang to his feet, looking for someone to blame. "I will not listen to a teenager, no matter whose great-granddaughter she is. I will not sit around and let whatever attacked my boys get away," he said, leaning on his gun to stand. He pulled his wife away just as the doctor showed up.

The doctor examined the remains of the boys. "A wolf, maybe. Your wife's in shock. Let me take her to the infirmary," the doctor said.

Bob had come from here, Jade thought. She couldn't look at the face-less boys. The hunters were laughing a few feet away, snickering like mad men. They were the only ones who hadn't searched for the boys. Casey made for the men. Jade grabbed his arm. "Don't. They're not worth it."

A loud explosion drew everyone's attention to Russell's cabin as it burst into flames. Everyone rushed over to help. Mingan, and Mitch were already standing outside the cabin, watching it burn.

"What are you doing?" Jade hissed. People started collecting buckets of water from the lake to douse the flames.

"Where's Bob?" Getting no answer from Mingan, she turned to Mitch. "Where's your brother?" Not one of them answered or looked at her. They kept their eyes on the flames.

"You're crazy. You can't do this," Jade said. The people formed a line from the lake and passed buckets of water, but the flames were too hot to get close.

"Bob has gone, Raven Wings. He killed his father. He probably killed the missing children too. To the wendigo, children would be a delicacy," Mingan said.

"That's disgusting," Casey said, helping with the buckets of water.

Two men dragged a fire hose to the cabin. One aimed at the cabin and sprayed it with water.

"What about the arrow? It turned the beast to smoke," Jade pointed out.

"The arrow doesn't destroy the wendigo unless you get it in the heart, otherwise it dematerializes and reappears elsewhere," Mingan explained.

"We sedated Bob. It would have been an easy shot!" Jade ran around the back of the cabin, looking for a way in. The window suddenly exploded outwards, and through the flames, the thing that was once Bob tried to get out of the cabin but slumped dead over the windowsill. Jade and Casey walked away, steeling themselves against the hideous sight and smell of burning flesh.

The hunters stopped laughing at the sight of the flames and returned to the woods. "The hunters, they're returning to the forest. We have to follow them," Casey said, tightening the straps on his backpack.

They had only gone a few feet into the forest when Casey turned off his flashlight.

Jade turned off hers as well and then wrapped her hand around the clear quartz crystal at the apex of her wand to shield the light as she encouraged it to dim. Twigs snapped behind them and a light bounced as a group of people headed their way.

"Jade, Casey, it's us," Crazy Bear said.

"You can't go in there alone," Jackson said.

Mingan and Charlie were with them, too. They had staffs in hand and Charlie sported a bow and arrow. Her pouch of arrows hung off her hip.

"What do you expect to do?" Charlie asked Jade.

"The hunters, they were acting strange," Jade said.

"Where's Mitch?" Casey asked, looking across the open field for him.

"He's not coming. He has to protect his mother and sister now."

"Jackson, take the lead," Mingan commanded.

Jackson walked a few feet in front of Casey and looked around. He pointed his flashlight to the ground, searching for a trail. "That way. Four of them," he said.

"Stay behind us," Mingan told Jade. She didn't feel he was also referring to Casey, but Casey fell into step with her.

"Crazy Bear, watch our backs."

"Charlie, keep your eyes on the top of the trees," Mingan said, and his voice seemed authoritative and old, wise beyond his years.

Jade slowed to check the canopies for herself. The view of the night sky was scarce the farther into the forest they went. They hadn't been walking long when their pace slowed. Jackson seemed to have lost his sense of direction. They should've waited for daylight. Her grip on her wand was tight as she held fast to it in order to refrain herself from speeding up time towards dawn. She hadn't attempted to manipulate time since that one day at the Catawba Falls, when she agreed with Kevin that messing with time and nature wasn't a smart thing to do. There were bound to be consequences. But it was so dark, a sliver of light between the trees was all she wanted. Or maybe a strong wind to blow back the incoming fog. What's the point of having the power if she didn't use it?

"What is it?" Charlie asked. She had her bow and arrow drawn, pointing it up into the trees, sweeping from left to right.

The silence made the night sounds of the forest come alive, as the fog continued to blow in from the west drifting through the trees.

"I've lost the trail of the wendigo," Jackson admitted. He swiveled around like a lost child. Fog messes up my senses. We need to slow down and be ready for anything.

"Stay close, everyone. I've seen this fog before," Casey said.

"Me too, searching for my dad, but it was much thicker," Jade said.

"Lead the way, Raven Wings," Mingan said.

"Casey, it's a good time to focus on the energy of the night eagle. Let it guide you. Let it be your eyes. Join with Raven Wings and guide us through," Mingan said.

The fog thickened. Jade pocketed her flashlight and tried to see beyond with her wand, but the more she did, the harder it was to see anything. Mingan, Charlie, Jackson, and Crazy Bear vanished. Casey held fast to her hand.

"You have the power of the night eagle, Casey. Tell us which way to go," Mingan shouted from within the fog.

Jade squeezed Casey's hand for him to let her go, but he refused and squeezed back. "I'm not going without you. Kevin will never forgive me if anything happened to you. I know you can look after yourself, but please, don't make let go," Casey said.

Jade understood. After losing Sophia, there was no way he was going to lose her, too. She wanted to stay and watch him like a hawk, anyway. Even though she couldn't physically see him, she could feel his energy and the warmth of his hand.

Casey led Jade forward. She felt Casey concentrating on the dense mist, and she hoped summoning the power of the night eagle too. She listened, waiting for a hint of sound, trying to catch whatever hid in the ominous ground clouds. A strong smell of decomposing garbage mingled with the misty fog.

Jade closed her eyes and focused inward, slowing her breathing. She imagined the wind, the sound of it blowing through the trees, and the movement of nature. Casey drew her closer as the wind picked up around them. She thought of the white buffalo and the weight of its coat grounding her as she called out to the universe to strengthen her energy, to help magnify Casey's sight as they moved through the fog.

After what seemed like forever, she opened her eyes. She was back-to-back with Casey. Mingan, Crazy Bear, Charlie, and Jackson had formed a tight circle around them. They were chanting. Only a few feet beyond, a circle of four figures blended into the fog. Possibly, the hunters were watching. The air reeked, making her eyes water.

That's when she saw the glow of yellow eyes in the dark and fog, as the resonance of the chanting flowed around them like a barrier. The beings kept their distance. The harmonious sounds Jade hummed in her head stopped and were replaced with the haunting verse Great Turtle had taught her.

Hisss. Hisss. Hisss. Hunger and pain,

The infernal shall slither,

Into your minds again.
Poisoning your thoughts,
Feeding on your fear,
Luring you into the darkness,
Boiling your blood as he nears.
Hiss. Hiss. Hiss. Hunger and pain,
Feast from the vessel,
Starvation is the game.

The eyes of beings retreated as if they feared the harmonized chants from Mingan, Charlie, Crazy Bear, and Jackson, who didn't seem to take a breath till the beings disappeared back into the treacherous fog. Jade wondered if the creatures had brought the fog to conceal their presence, or if the fog was part of a greater darkness.

"What happened?" Jade whispered as the yellow eyes blended into the night shadows. It was hard to tell if they had truly left or not. Jade turned around and shone her wand forward.

"It was too hard to tell. But whoever they were did not bring good tidings. It might have been the hunters," Mingan said.

13

CASEY: THE SERPENT IN THE FOG

I t was hard to see in the fog, but it had thinned enough for Casey to look over his shoulder and see the others. In his gut, he knew they were heading towards the preacher and his snakes. The stench subsided, but it was still there in the fog's background. The yellow glowing eyes had kept their distance, but Casey stuck close to Jade, determined not to let anything happen to her. Casey had felt Jade's light grow brighter since they entered the fog, which was adding to the blinding reflection. It was like they were a vessel lost at sea. There was a haunting energy that followed alongside.

Casey looked back again. Charlie had her bow and arrow aimed up high, as if she expected something to swoop down and attack. She glared at him as she followed behind Mingan. She leaned in to speak to Mingan but was loud enough for them all to hear.

"If Jackson's lost the wendigo's trail, we should head back and wait till morning. We shouldn't be out here. It's suicide. And why is Casey leading? Jackson's the tracker. Sorry, Casey, but you're only a city slicker. Where is he leading us to? He should get us out of here, not lead us deeper into the fog."

"A city slicker that can fly by repelling his energy," Crazy Bear said. "Let me see you do it without invoking your spirit animal."

"Calm down. Balance your energy. Trust," Mingan told Charlie.

Casey let Jade walk up front and take the lead as the track narrowed. He whispered in her ear, "Stay close."

"You feel it too?" Jade said.

"Yes," Casey said.

Charlie went quiet. Casey waited for her to speak; sure she hadn't finished. He turned back. Charlie, Mingan, Crazy Bear, and Jackson were gone. "Jade, stop! We've lost the others," Casey whispered.

"What?" Jade said, turning around and holding her wand out. "Where did they go?"

"Shh, do you hear that?" Casey said, swatting at a moth.

"No, nothing. What do you hear?"

"An inconsistent vibration, a fractured resonance in the air."

Jade put her hand out and touched the air. A scream ripped through the silence. "This way, quickly," Jade said, going off track.

He pointed his flashlight down to see where he walked. Something heavy had pressed into the foliage when it recently passed through.

"I can feel Mingan. He's close by, but I can't see him," Jade said, stopping and turning, trying to find where she felt Mingan.

"Mingan!" Casey called out. A faint reply, as if Mingan had whispered in his ear. "Did you hear that?"

"No. What?"

"Mingan. I could hear him as if he was standing right next to me," Casey said. Twisting around at the hips, he looked around, afraid to move. He reached out his hand, and Jade copied him. "Feel anything?"

"Charlie, Crazy Bear!" Jade called out.

Casey wished they would answer. The energy caused his skin to prickle. "We have to keep moving. We have to get out of this fog."

"I think I heard Charlie. It sounded like it came from over there."

"Okay. Go slow, we don't want to get separated, too," Casey said and followed closely behind.

"There, did you hear it?"

"Nothing, I can't hear it."

"What's happening?" The fear in Jade's voice sent ripples of dread through Casey's body.

"I don't know, but we're close to the preacher and his congregation. I'm starting to think it's not a coincidence that a fog has separated and blinded us from the others," Casey said.

"Should we go back to the trail and find them?"

The stench became almost unbearable. "We're being stalked. We better keep going and pray this fog ends. Crazy Bear!" Casey called and shifted the weight of his backpack. The charcoal and pad loomed into his mind. A strong urge to sketch came over him.

"Why did you stop?" Jade said.

"I need to draw."

"Not now. This is the wrong time, and the energy is all wrong."

"I have to!" Casey insisted, fumbling to remove one arm from his backpack. He tugged the bag around to the front of his body and wrestled to free the sketch pad and find a piece of charcoal. He rested the pad on his forearm, closed his eyes to calm himself, and drew.

Hurried, his hand darted across the page as if on fast forward. He sensed he was drawing a lot of small parts, detailed images. Casey listened for Jade's breathing, making sure she was still close. The charcoal quickly heated his thumb and forefinger and, as soon as he finished the image, he dropped the charcoal and opened his eyes. A carnage of limbs splayed across the page, and the preacher stood at the center—his followers dead and torn apart. Snakes slithered over the body parts, and in and out of skulls. Casey shook his head in disgust and frowned. "It's awful." He locked eyes with Jade's. "We have to find the preacher before it's too late," Casey said, tucking the pad into his backpack.

"Do you know what it means?"

"Not sure. It's definitely the preacher and his congregation. I think the wendigo is going to attack the preacher and his flock. Honestly, I don't want to go to their campsite. I had a terrible feeling when I was last there, but we need to save them. The fractured haunting energy we feel right now is the same energy that emanates from the preacher, but worse. He dreaded going deeper into the fog because the darkness felt as real as the adrenaline surging through his veins; it was too much.

Maybe we should just head back and hope we run into the others," Casey said rushed.

Jade squinted. Confusion covered her face. She looked sad. He felt ashamed. His checks flushed. Embarrassed, he turned away.

"But you just said we need to help the congregation? Running away – this isn't you, Casey. It's the energy in this terrible fog. It's heavy and foreboding. It makes me want to run; I'm afraid of what we can't see, but we have to keep going," Jade said, scratching her shoulder.

His heart told him she was right, but he didn't want to go any further into the forest. He'd seen enough gruesome dead bodies to last a dozen lifetimes. Casey didn't want to meet up with the preacher again, but how could he not? He knew, no matter how much he wanted to flee, he had to go on. "You should go back, Jade," Casey said.

"Don't be stupid. We need to get out of this fog! I don't have any sense of direction. I'm relying on you, Casey," Jade said, pivoting around.

Each direction looked the same. Casey checked the foliage to see if he could determine which way they had come from.

"When I had searched for my dad, I got lost in a fog like this. I didn't know which way to go. The white deer found me and guided me to an opening. This fog isn't normal. I think it might have something to do with infernals. I've been calling on the deer to guide us, but I can only see her in the astral plane, as if we're worlds apart."

Jade called out for the others, and the echo of her voice was absorbed by the wall of the fog. Casey focused ahead, not knowing where he was going.

"This way," Casey said, taking her hand.

"Are you sure?"

He raised his eyebrows and gave her a half smile. "Who knows? Shine your wand forward and stay close."

Jade continued to shine her wand forward, guiding the way through the fog. Casey stepped into the spaces the light penetrated until it lifted.

"It's getting thinner," Jade said.

It was still night, and the fog had made the night look strangely brighter than it was. The illumination of the quartz crystal at the pinnacle of Jade's wand kept the dense, overwhelming darkness at bay. The purity of the energy reminded Casey of starlight and Sophia's ascension to heaven with the archangels.

Casey stopped.

"Are you okay?" Jade asked, looking tired, and alert at the same time.

"The sound of our footsteps has changed. Does this dirt feel different somehow?" Casey bent down to pick up a handful of soil.

Pain rushed through his arm and struck deep into his heart. He dropped the dirt and grabbed his chest.

"Casey, what's wrong?"

He couldn't answer. It was like a fist had grabbed at his heart, squeezing the life from him. He felt the veins in his head and neck swell with blood. Unable to catch a breath, Casey fell and curled up onto the forest floor.

He waited for Metatron to come for him. Sophia might even be the one to take his spirit to heaven. He embraced the idea. Never had he imagined feeling joy while experiencing pain.

Then agony tore through his leg and groin. He screamed, as if he were being torn apart, limb by limb. None of the pain was his; it was from the soil. The soil held the memory of deaths. Jade was wrestling with his hand. She wedged the crystal up into his tightly clenched first full of dirt, until all the small particles fell back to the forest floor and the pain subsided. He had to stand.

"Help me up. Don't touch the soil. Oh man, the dirt smells like burning flesh, and the air, is that sulfur?" he asked, brushing the dirt off his forearms and clothes.

"Yeah. Mingan! Charlie!" Jade cried out for the others, and they waited. "Did you hear that? It's faint. But it's there." Jade pocketed her wand. The light lit up her face.

"You look creepy like that," Casey said.

Jade removed the wand and held it by her side. "What happened to you?"

"I felt what happened to someone else. Their hearts were crushed, and their limbs torn from their bodies until they died."

"Something is wrong with this part of the forest. I can't hear the trees or feel them anymore. Mother Nature is quiet, as if she's not even here."

Casey smiled. *She has no idea how special she is.*

"Come on, I think the faint sounds of the others were from over there somewhere. That's where your eyes darted to," he said, leading the way, but cautious not to touch anything unnecessarily.

They walked for a few hundred feet. The crunch of the fallen leaves under their feet was dull, suppressed. He couldn't recall if this was what he'd experienced when he had stumbled onto the preacher before. The night was getting colder. Jade started shivering. They should have brought their coats.

That reminded him of the whisky flask Sophia had kept inside her coat pocket, filled with holy water. If they had the holy water now, he imagined it would sizzle if he splashed it on the soil. He took in a deep breath and tried to relax. Jade must have been in tune with him because she, too, took in a deep breath.

"Wait." He strained to hear. Nearby were the sounds of singing, as if behind a double-glazed glass panel.

"I can just hear them. Why would they be out at night?" Jade whispered.

"I don't know. It's the same song I heard this afternoon."

"It's strange. It's the same song. What are the odds of that?".

"Downright creepy, but it's got to be a coincidence," Casey said.

"If we heard it, maybe the others did, too."

"I've got to admit the suspense is freaking me out. The whole place smells of death. Over and over again, I smell death. It makes me want to puke and scream. I don't feel one bit of optimism about the outcome of leading you to the preacher and his congregation. They'll see you as a witch, and . . ." Casey stopped himself from saying anymore.

Jade moved half a step. Her nose was nearly touching his. She gently reached out and touched his chest, pressing her wand against him. She breathed light into him. Her eyes sparkled like diamonds. His heaving chested slowed, and the intense uncertainty and fear calmed.

"You're stronger than you know, and I am stronger than I would like to believe. We've got this. That's what Tim and Kevin would say. We've got this, Casey."

Colors mapped up and down the crystal wand, balancing out his energy centers calming his insides. He felt as if he was taller, stronger, and more capable somehow. The darkness from the gray fog had pressed upon him and clouded his judgement, using his sadness as a catalyst to put him off balance. Harmony returned to his being.

Jade was right. She was much stronger and capable than she realized. "Let's warn the parishioners about the wendigo. The preacher, well, the wendigos can have him," Casey said, giving Jade a quick hug. "Thank you."

Staying vigilant, they moved closer to the campsite and the closer they got, the louder and less muffled the singing was. Casey readied himself to do anything to protect Jade. Hoping the others would find the campsite too, because Mingan would double Jade's chances of survival, he would lay his life on the line for her. There was a connection between them that seemed ancient.

After five long silent minutes, the glow of the campsite pierced the trees, guiding them towards it.

Jade crouched down behind a tree, but first looking up, as if checking nothing was perched on a branch, waiting to pounce down on them. "Is that them? You've got to be kidding me. He's wearing a derby hat."

"I know, right?"

The singing stopped mid-verse. The congregation as one turned and looked in Casey's direction. Jade's eyes widened, as if asking him if he thought they had heard them talking. Jade stuffed her wand down the front of her pants like a gun and pulled her shirt over the top of it. She kept her back to the congregation until the light of the wand faded to nothing.

"Come!" the preacher said. "Welcome to our guests!"

"I don't think they can see us yet. We must appear confident. Leave your things," Casey said, taking off his backpack, feeling anything but confident. Jade put hers next to his, and they covered them with branches.

"Is that you, boy? Have you come for redemption? Are you ready to cast off your Satanic ways?" the preacher said and chuckled.

"Stay here. Maybe they don't know you're here." Casey stepped forward and out into the clearing, revealing himself. The slither of snakes was unmistakable. It was night and too cold for snakes. *Where did they get the energy?* he wondered. As he walked forward, the snakes moved to greet him. It was like he was a magnet as they turned and headed his way.

"My loyal pets won't hurt you unless I tell them to." The preacher smiled.

How can the people not see the evil inside the preacher? Casey took his eyes off the snakes and searched the people, and the parishioners hissed, as he moved.

"I'm only here to warn you about a creature, we call the wendigo, they eat human flesh," Casey said slowly as realizing the preacher, vile and evil ate, and feed human flesh to his parishioners. Casey had made a mistake coming here. "I've seen it. At our campsite an hour away from here. It took two young boys right out of their beds and devoured them in the woods." No one moved. No one responded. They were all transfixed. "Can you hear me?"

"I hear you, boy. I'm just waiting for your girlfriend to come out of the woods and to stand by her man," the preacher said.

So, he knew Jade was there. Casey would not tell her what to do. It was up to her. "This has nothing to do with her. Forget about her."

But before he spoke another word, Jade walked out from the fog to his side, and all the snakes turned back towards the preacher, as if Jade repelled them. Were they frightened of her? Casey sensed a fear. What did they fear, the wand, or Jade?

"Well. If it's not another imposter of the creator. Behold! See how the devil hides behind the face of beauty," the preacher said, holding his hand out towards Jade for his congregation to gaze upon.

"We mean no harm," Jade told him. "Times have changed. We need to trust each other. We have not come to cause you harm but to prevent you from being harmed. In the woods, a creature stalks the living. It is out for meat and blood, and it has the taste of human flesh on its tongue. You must protect yourselves. Arm yourselves. Be vigilant."

Her words were falling on deaf ears. They watched her, amused and curious. A few parishioners stepped towards Jade. Casey didn't like this.

He turned, startled by a sudden sound from behind. With a pustulated face, its skin hanging off its cheekbone, a wendigo stood behind Jade. Casey reached out and pulled Jade behind him, protecting her from the creature. The face still looked human; it was one of the hunters. It had not yet completely transformed. Another wendigo crawled out from the brush, then another, and another.

The four hunters had recently mutated into wendigo! The preacher didn't move, nor did the parishioners, who seemed more afraid of Jade than the wendigo.

"Raven Wings!" Mingan called.

Casey tried not to react to the sound, and Jade kept steady as well. Casey could hear Mingan, but he couldn't see him.

"Don't come any closer, Mingan. Stay back!" Casey yelled.

Casey stepped back, and the congregation parted. The preacher sent his snakes forward.

Something unseen stood in the middle of the congregation, then moved off to the side and around them, as if blind to what was happening, and inspecting an abandoned the area. The congregation moved and parted again, as if allowing something to pass through. Even though he sensed Mingan and the others, Casey couldn't see anyone. He tuned into the energy between the people and saw a spirit wolf moving amongst them.

Mingan.

"We have to go," Casey whispered, reaching out his hand to Jade. He glanced up at the dark sky, pulled Jade hard, quickly unto him, slamming her up against his chest and throwing his arms around, embracing her. Behind Jade the wendigo its claws through the air, as

Casey propelled himself, and Jade, up into the night sky, praying he wouldn't slam their heads into a branch as they rapidly ascended. The wendigo simultaneously leaped towards them and consequently slammed into each other. its claws through the air.

14

JADE: THE DISTORTION OF REALITY

From the sky looking down, the moon reflected off the surface of the dense gray fog below that stretched out for half a mile in either way. At first, she thought it looked like a tightly woven cocoon over the forest. But then it looked dense, like a brewing storm cloud. Jade could smell Casey's strawberry breath and found it interesting how the smell of something he had eaten hours ago lingered.

The higher they went, the colder it got. Jade recalled the snakes that slithered over the ground, the huge python around the preacher's neck, and the smell of the barbecued human flesh. She thought it should have smelled bad, but it didn't. It had smelled like pork. She was glad she didn't eat pork. The preacher and his parishioners had resorted to eating human flesh. *But whose?* she wondered.

It was so beautiful in the sky. A magical romantic moment, to be clutched to a strong, handsome young man's chest, feeling his heart racing against hers, and the exhilarating power he expelled propelling them into the sky. She placed her head on his shoulder, sad for him. Never again will he be able to share moments like this with Sophia. She thought of Kevin and wondered where he was, she missed him and wished he would hurry back. *When Kevin gets back, he can open a portal to where we left our bags, so we can pop in and out before we draw the congregation's attention,* she thought.

A carousel of questions rotated in her mind that she wanted to ask Casey, but she didn't want to interrupt his channel of energy keeping them in the air. She wished for Kevin to come back. Her wand glowed, lighting them both up in the dark night. If anyone looked up from the ground and spotted them, they would think they were a shooting star.

In the distance, the cabin lights twinkled. Casey started their descent. In Jade's mind, she mapped the angle of velocity from their rise to descent and estimated their distance and time of travel. Flying was a great way to travel.

Suddenly, she was out of Casey's embrace and falling. Just as quickly, her fall stopped, and she rose. Casey caught her again.

Jade's heart raced. She caught her breath. "What happened?"

"Something hit me from behind," Casey said.

"A bird?" *That's a dumb idea.* But she didn't want to think about what might fly around in the middle of the night. Nocturnal birds were few, but even if there were birds, Casey, with the sight of the owl, the night eagle, would have known. It had to be something else. "We've got to get down."

"I'm with you. I see nothing that could've hit us with such force," Casey said.

Her stomach rose with the sudden acceleration of descent, creating an awareness of the lack of gravity. It was like being on the Tower of Terror at Disneyland. Jade stifled her natural desire to scream. When they hit the ground, they were partly crouched, as if waiting for their organs to settle back into their bodies.

"The others won't be back for a while. We should head back to the cabin and try to get some rest," Jade said.

"I don't think I can sleep."

It was well over an hour before the others emerged from the forest tree line beyond the lake. Jade jumped off the porch step.

"They're back," Jade said, resting her hand on Casey's shoulder. He was sitting cross-legged meditating. She had tried to meditate, but she constantly thought of Kevin. Then, when she found her focus, she kept seeing rich green meandering mounds that resembled snakes. People lined up along on top of the mounds. Her imagination was on double time. Once again, many questions rolled around in her head, searching for answers.

Jade and Casey stood up under the porch light to let Mingan and the others see they were there waiting for them. They waited in silence, mindful of the few people that had been able to sleep after the trauma of finding the remains of the missing boys. Since Jade had returned from the forest, she had heard people talking in whispers from inside the safety of their porches. Some people had gathered, but they finally separated and went back to their own cabins.

"What happened to you two?" Charlie asked as they got closer.

Crazy Bear didn't give them a chance to answer. "At first, we thought you were dead. We saw body parts scattered in a clearing. That looked like the preacher could have used it for a campsite. There was so much fresh blood. The smell of the corpse on the barbecue was horrendous. I'll never forget the sound of the crackling fat as the body cooked . . ." Crazy Bear doubled over and vomited in the bushes surrounding the porch.

"Where did you go? We called out for you; we found your bags," Mingan said.

Jade hadn't noticed Crazy Bear had her gear slung over his shoulder, and Charlie had Casey's backpack. "Thanks," Jade said, reaching for her belongings.

"Where did you go?" Mingan said

"We got lost in the fog and stumbled upon the preacher and his congregation. We warned them about the wendigo, but they turned on us and accused us of being evil. Four wendigos surrounded us, as if under the preacher's command. It was the hunters transformed into wendigo—I'm sure of it. They weren't interested in the congregation, only us. Casey sensed the danger and got us out of there," Jade said.

"What bodies?" Casey asked.

"Don't act surprised," Jackson said.

Jade, perplexed, shook her head. "Why wouldn't we be surprised?

Let's go inside." Jade shivered. The sudden cold pierced her skin and touched her bones.

Charlie with her bow and arrows, Crazy Bear with his sheer presence, and Mingan looked like warriors taking refuge. They put their stuff on the floor beside the couch and sat down heavily.

"Show him!" Jackson said, pulling out a kitchen chair and aiming his next words at Casey. "You knew what we would find at the preacher's outdoor church. You'd been there before, right? Drop the act."

"I told you I had. I ran into them earlier on that day," Casey said, confused.

Jade was confused. She didn't understand what Jackson meant. Charlie took Casey's bag off her shoulder and opened it. She pulled out Casey's drawing pad. Casey tried to grab his backpack, but Crazy Bear stood in his way.

"What's going on?" Jade demanded.

"We have to ask," Crazy Bear told her.

"Ask what?"

Charlie opened the book to the last drawing and held it up like she was about to give a presentation. "This is what we saw," Charlie said, tapping the picture of carnage. "Why did you kill those people at the preacher's campsite?"

Mingan sat watching Casey closely.

"This is ridiculous," Jade said, trying to snatch the book from Charlie's hands.

"Is it?" Charlie said, challenging Jade and pulling the book away from her.

"Yes, it is. Casey drew that image because it was a vision. He quickly draws what he can see before it disappears from his mind," Jade said, looking at Casey for confirmation.

"Pretty much," Casey said.

"We just came from there and the preacher looked alive to me. No one appeared dead. Everyone animated," Jade said.

"We called out to you," she continued. "We heard you close by in the woods. Didn't you hear the singing? There was no way the wendigos massacred the preacher and his parishioners. They are under his command. We didn't know that until we got there. And no one was dead, not when we were there."

"They were all dead. The last time we heard you was from inside the fog. Once out of the fog, we heard nothing. We saw your bags. We saw the body parts. The so-called preacher was nothing more than a hat on a post," Mingan said.

"And there was the barbecue. We both saw that," Crazy Bear said.

"But how could you see one thing and we see another?" Casey said.

They went silent. Jade took a seat at the kitchen table, tired. She pondered the question. No one could really think Casey killed all those people. There had to be another explanation. But why did he draw the image? "Maybe we were in parallel universes? We were in one realm and you in another," Jade suggested.

"Which realm was the real realm?" Jackson said.

"Where do your visions come from?" Charlie asked.

Crazy Bear looked confused. "What?"

"Where do visions come from?" Charlie repeated.

Jade understood what she was getting at. If they can have visions from Great Spirit, God, the positive life force of the universe, then there must be an opposite.

"The devil made me do it?" Jackson said.

Crazy Bear's head snapped to stare at Jackson. "What? *You* killed them?"

"No, I'm referring to the saying 'the devil made me do it.' The devil put the thought into the person's mind," Jackson explained.

"That's what I'm thinking," Charlie said.

Mingan rubbed his jaw thoughtfully. "You could be right."

Charlie straightened up in her seat. Mingan's simple words gave her a huge energy burst. Casey noticed it too. Jade would love to ask him what he saw in Charlie's aura at that moment.

"Were we both being played with by the dark force in the woods? Which one was the true reality?" Jade asked.

"I hope ours was the true one. Otherwise, that would mean all those people are dead," Casey said.

"How long have you been communicating with spirit through drawing?" Mingan asked.

"Not long. A little over a week," Casey said.

"What are you thinking, Mingan?" Jade asked. Her heart fluttered in a bad way.

"I think what we saw was reality, because of your drawing," Mingan said.

No one spoke. Jade settled into a state of deep contemplation. Casey took his bag from Charlie.

Hisss. Hisss. Hisss. Hunger and pain,

the infernal shall slither into your minds again.

Poisoning your thoughts,

Feeding on your fear,

Luring you into the darkness,

Boiling your blood as he nears.

Hiss. Hiss. Hiss. Hunger and pain,

Feast from the vessel—starvation is the game.

"Hiss. Hiss. Hunger and the pain . . ." Jade's verse transfixed the group as if she had opened a deep memory inside them all.

"What does it mean?" Jackson asked.

The others kept staring, making Jade feel self-conscious. "Great Turtle taught it to me. It's a memory embedded in one of my onyx stones." Jade fished the box out of her bag, pulled out the stone, and showed them. At first, she wasn't sure if she wanted them to hold it but then thought it might be interesting to see what their reaction was or even if they had one.

Thinking like a scientist often comforted her. It stopped her from making rash decisions based on fear, but she also didn't want to dismiss the signs coming from her intuition and the universe. Now definitely wasn't the time to be analytical. Jade placed the stone in Mingan's hand. He flinched as if he got an electric shock and paused before passing it along. Charlie also flinched. They all did. Crazy Bear held it out to Casey. Jade watched him refuse the stone. Jade reached out and took it.

"Did you hear it?" Mingan asked the others.

They all concurred. "Hear what; what did you hear?" Jade asked.

Mingan smiled at her and his beautiful blue eyes pooled with tears. "Great Turtle. A vision of Great Turtle singing with a toddler as she cleaned the skin of a rattlesnake. The toddler, I assume, was you, Jade? You were playing with its tail. Shaking it up to your ear, listening to its rattle," Mingan said.

When Jade had meditated on the memory stones, she had heard the nursery rhyme, if you could call it that, and she was the toddler, and parts of that snake were now in her medicine pouch.

"What do you think it means?" Casey said.

"It's a warning," Charlie said.

"She is right. We need to take greater precautions. We're . . . ," Mingan said.

". . . living in the days of tribulation, when all the wicked and godless people are to be removed from the earth," Casey said.

"Yes," Mingan said.

"But does that make us the godless and wicked?" Charlie asked.

Jade could sense the horror the thought of being godless and wicked brought Charlie. "You're not wicked or godless," Jade reassured her.

"Come, I need to consult the elders. And we need to visit the dream lodge, Crazy Bear," Mingan said.

"What about us?" Jade asked.

"We should stay together."

"Safety in numbers," Charlie said, giving Jade a solemn smile as a sign of a truce.

Apparently, Charlie no longer felt the need to compete for Mingan's approval. He had just told her she was correct, twice, and there was no competition, anyway. Jade's pursuit was for the light of the creator.

"Share your memory stone with our ancestors, the ancient ones. They will help you understand its meaning," Mingan said.

They all entered the healing room, where they had made arrow heads not so long ago. Jade sat in between Mingan and Casey on the woven mat.

"Mingan, if you are my teacher, Gray Wolf, why do I see an old man in my visions?" Jade asked.

"Because I have lived many lifetimes. You are a pupil of the spirit of Gray Wolf. I, as you, am having a human experience. One of many over the centuries. We are all spiritual beings, and we all have a soul that is older than this world. We, Raven Wings, have shared many lifetimes. Sometimes you have been my daughter, son, brother, or sister. You are always part of my family tree. We all are part of one family, and I think that is why we're all quested with the gathering of the people for the ascension."

"Because we're from the same family? You're not making sense. Jade and I are from different families," Casey said.

"We are all from the stars. That makes us one family. Those creatures out there, the wendigo and that demon, the preacher—I believe he is what your books call an infernal. One day, they may have had a connection to heaven and the stars, but not anymore. They do not shine with celestial light. They are not part of our family," Mingan said.

Jade watched Mingan light-footed walk behind everyone, turning off the light and lighting the candles, creating a more peaceful atmosphere. The smell of burning sage trailed over her head as Mingan positioned the candles around them—there was strength and mystery in his profile. As she followed him with her eyes, her heart raced. He picked up the bowl of sage and a wing with leather along the edge. He stepped behind Jade, and she felt him whisk and snap a feathered fan over her head to cleanse her aura before moving on to Casey. The smell of sage lingered in the air.

Jade closed her eyes and, with her mind's eye, watched Mingan put the sage in the middle of the circle and take his place alongside them. He drew in a few deep breaths, and everyone followed suit until everyone's breathing synchronized.

Jade drifted deeper into herself as the others started chanting. She wasn't sure if she should also join in. She leaned slightly towards Casey and clearly heard him chanting along with the others. Eeeeeeee. Ahhhhhh. It surprised her how the vibrations of each cycle of vowel expanded the energy centers in her body and aura. Her body tingled like effervescence. Probably from all the oxygen in her bloodstream.

"Focus!" she told herself. It's not the time to be trying to work the science behind everything. Airrrrrrr. Her breath was endless, and her crown filled with violet. Her entire body no longer existed. She was pure energy.

The sound of the chanting hummed in the room. She would have liked to open her eyes to see if she could see physically all the energy in the room, but she dared not peek. She feared if she did, she would slip out of the induced state that Mingan created for them to unite. So, when he spoke her name, it startled her, but the energy flowing through her body increased.

"Raven Wings, slowly, move your arms and pick up your drum. Do not open your eyes or lose the connection to the universal energy," Mingan said.

Jade did as he said. Her arms were so hard to move. She was grateful that her fingers on her right hand were already clutching the woven waxed string on the back of the drum. She couldn't recall taking it out of its bag. Slowly, she slid her left arm off her leg and let it rest on the wood of the drumstick before wrapping her fingers around it. She placed the head of the drumstick in the middle of the drum and lightly tapped. The sound and vibration were like an earthquake. She beat her drum softly, then a little harder, getting faster and faster.

"We will all enter the dream lodge with the spiral of the drum. Raven Wings, take us on our journey to the dream lodge," Mingan said.

Jade drifted in and out of consciousness. The energy was so strong she found it difficult to remain focused. It was like trying to fall asleep while not falling asleep. As if tricking your unconscious mind into thinking that the conscious mind was in la-la land and it could step forward, opening up the dream world. It reminded her of a cat. How they pretend they're not interested in the tiny mouse hiding behind a dumpster, so the mouse thinks it's safe, and as soon as it pokes its little head out, the cat pounces. But in this case, as soon as the unconscious senses the conscious mind is still active, it hides.

She waited for further instructions on how to take everyone into the center of the spiral to the dream lodge, but none came. She wondered if Mingan was alright. Maybe she should stop drumming and check.

"Let your fears and doubt go," Mingan said.

Thank God, he is okay. Was he talking to her or everyone? Shit. She felt herself slip out of the trance state with all the thinking. She had to stop thinking. Jade tilted her head up and surrendered to the energy, allowing it to flow freely. She focused on the vibrations of the drum and the spiral in her mind. She imagined it expanding out from her and touching Casey on her left and reaching out to Crazy Bear on her right and expanding until it touched each person in the circle, connecting them together. A slight push outward, expanding the vortex until they were inside its center. The room disappeared, and they floated in space. She smiled. It was like being underwater. They all floated within the energy.

"Crazy Bear, you're up. Lead the way," Mingan said.

Like a formation of geese, they glided downward. Jade stretched the vortex until Crazy Bear stopped. An image appeared, and she knew it was the entrance to the dream lodge. One by one, they entered and were welcomed by an ancient one. The atmosphere inside the lodge ignited her inner senses to a level that she could only describe as ecstasy. She needed to sit down. Her limbs felt like they were heavy lead pipes, and if she tried to flex her arms, she would be powerless to do so. She just hoped that her body was still drumming in the healing room and able to provide a way home for their spiritual bodies. Never had she felt the intensity of the energy, not even when she had been drugged by the shamans that had tried to steal her power. She wondered where all the energy came from. Just when she thought it couldn't get any stronger, it did.

An ancient one sat on her knees in the middle of the room, stoking a fire. Steam rose above her head as she sprayed water over the rocks within the flames. The ancient one wore traditional clothing, as if she had passed away centuries ago in her ceremonial clothes. She looked beautiful, with long, shiny black hair.

She gestured for them all to sit by waving her arm around in a circle. Jade noticed they all sat in the same position as they had in healing room. Jade focused on the flames to stop her mind from taking her back to her physical body and the cabin. She needed to stay here in the dream lodge with the rest of them. This time, she was responsible for them all. With Crazy Bear's guidance, she had brought them here quickly, and she had a strong feeling she would need to the do the same to get them out.

There was a strong sense of something coming, lurking near their bodies. Always, the future seemed to be about to roll in on her, not giving her enough time to prepare. The flames rose higher. Jade followed them up and into the sky. Her mind wanted to count how many levels she had gone down into her subconscious, instead of believing she was a guest in the spirit realm. It felt different from astral traveling. Astral traveling was more like being on a highway that anyone could jump on and off. Like Route 66, it just kept going.

She could feel, but not see, an abundance of energies and activities happening around her in the dream lodge. They weren't scary or malevolent. It resembled being in the middle of a city rush, everyone minding their own business, going their own way.

Jade looked down at the lodge from above and the ancient one rose with her. That's when Jade noticed the woman wore a white buffalo skin. She touched Jade on the forehead, opening up her third eye even more. It expanded outward and a fountain of blue and red poured into the universe and floated away into a stream of stardust. They moved into a pale blue sky and rolling green hills formed, like paint dripping down a canvas, revealing the hidden masterpiece of a perfect landscape.

They all became the center of the landscape and below them were trails of people walking. The sky tore open; the opening got bigger and bigger. Murky brown and black smoke poured through the opening and took form, heading down from the sky towards the hundreds of travelers nearing a giant granite rock that had burst up from the ground.

People, scattered over chiseled granite face of the mountain, climbed to the top. Above the towering rock were the seven Palladian stars alongside Orion's belt. Jade knew it was just a vision, but when the dark entities trailing the sky suddenly knocked the climbers off the face of the rock, she gasped as the entities slaughtered the people.

She saw herself on the top of the towering rock and holding her wand; she raised her arms up. It was like she was watching herself from the inside. She hadn't even noticed she had her wand with her. She watched herself point it up to the heavens, drawing unbelievable amounts of energy and channeling it downward. Dry lightning burst from her wand, incinerating the evil entities in mid-flight.

Suddenly, it all stopped and disappeared. It was dark. Jade looked at Casey and the others. They were all still together, floating in nothingness. The ancient one called out for Casey. Jade couldn't quite tell if he floated towards her willingly or if she pulled him reluctantly towards her.

The ancient one embraced him. It looked like he was being crushed. Jade wanted to call out, "Let him go!" but she knew there would be no sound. She could do nothing but watch. Failure filled her being; she needed to help her friend. She was letting Sophia down, allowing Casey to be hurt. But why would the ancient one hurt him? Jade had to trust the universe, that what was happening was for the greater good. Like thought bubbles, pictures burst from Casey as if the ancient one squeezed them from him.

15

CASEY: THE FLOOD OF EVIL

C asey watched the scenes birthed from Jade's spirit. When the old woman summoned him, he resisted her pull, but out in the universal energy, he didn't seem to have the will to pull himself back into the folds of the circle. He surrendered to the old woman and, as Metatron had done time and time again, the old woman squeezed him until he had no breath left in his body and he was on the verge of passing out.

But this time, something different happened. The old woman let go and the images flew out from him as if he were the world's historian. Like thought bubbles, images formed in the surrounding nothingness, and he watched time roll back through the ages. It was a collage of history. Time spun all the way back to earth's beginning. Angels descended, and humans were small, passive, and in awe of the wonders, grateful for the bounty of life. Children were born into a blissful state of being.

But the angels envied the humans' gifts that God had given them. They saw the humans as another mistake, like the previous race from the flame of the fire. To the angels, humans were docile, so the angels together decided to take some of the earthly pleasures for themselves and copulated with the females of the earthly species. Females of all creeds gave birth to abominations of the fallen angels.

The waters rose and fell, destroying the abominations and giving birth to a new era for humans. But still to this day, the dark entities, condemned by Great Spirit, played with the human soul like toys of war. The history of mankind presented itself exhaustingly to them through Casey. War, greed, lust, and envy, woven through the years to the very day when the lights of heaven would fill the sky and the earth would shake and rupture—the end of time—the end of history. The winds would howl as the seas rose and once again, the earth would be cleansed of all living creatures of all creeds. The slate would soon be cleaned. Their memories would not be erased, but they would have the choice to start again somewhere new, because Great Spirit loved all.

Casey understood why the world needed the coming change. Life as he had known it couldn't keep going the way it was. Everyone had wanted change. Everyone wanted wars, famine, the destruction and pollution of earth to end. But people feared change. People had stopped having children before the apocalypse because they saw no positive future in which to raise a child. The earth had made its plea to the heavens, and it was heard. The fallen angels, the banished races that came before humans, other dark entities, the abominations of the fallen angels, all wanted revenge. God had promised them the time would come when they would get their time on earth. But he hadn't promised them the human race.

Once the images faded and nothing else emerged from his being, Casey floated back into his spot in the circle next to Jade. Two down and four go. Jackson sailed willingly to the old woman and dreamed the hidden dreams within him. Milky Way star clusters and colorful nebulas were all inside of him. He was a traveler moving from galaxy to galaxy. Casey wished what he was seeing were possible, then remembered he could fly. Maybe one day Jackson could guide him around the galaxy. The endlessness of space. Colored waves floated through all of them as Jackson's galaxies expanded and contracted.

Crazy Bear was the keeper of the stars, protecting the night sky. The door keeper for this world. At first, the images of despair, as the flood of evil toiled with this world, made it look like Crazy Bear had failed at his purpose in the universe. Until the images of a great battle. A bear, the size of a great tower, had held back a surge of darkness from entering the world for millennia and only trickles of evil had entered.

If all the darkness in the world through the ages was just a trickle, then . . . Casey didn't need to think about what the next two months were going to be like. But he remembered one night, when he and Sophia had been lying in the fields looking up at the night sky back at the estate, feeling blessed to see a falling star. She had said, "You know the apocalypse hasn't marked the end. It had marked a new beginning."

He thought she was just being positive, trying to stay optimistic about the future. They were the survivors. They should be grateful. But now, watching Charlie's cosmic unfoldment, he understood. It was just a cycle, and the earth was just one spoke on the wheel of life. Today Casey realized God was in the middle of the wheel of life, and each spoke was a pathway to a different universe. There were endless possibilities. Now they need to fulfill their purpose on earth and get as many survivors as possible ready for ascension. Casey could feel a tingle in the middle of his forehead. It felt like what it must have been like for Jade when the fountain of blue and red poured from her brow.

Charlie floated back to her position in the circle with expanded wings behind her. The wings had eyes. She was a seer, and he was a scribe. He saw himself writing in many positions, at a desk with a quill, carving on cave walls, writing with a laser pen. So many lifetimes and so many more to be had.

As soon as Mingan entered the center, the darkness turned to a thick ink, and it was hard to breathe. Casey's senses heightened, and it felt like Sophia, with the hand of God, ran a finger up his spin. He didn't feel the physical sensation, but the energy inside him burst into overdrive, as the darkness turned to brown. Thick brown clouds boiled around them and out flew countless creatures of darkness, evil entities flying, and armies of shadows marching towards them like ancient Roman soldiers ready for battle. Whoever and wherever they had come from, they had come prepared. They had glimpsed these entities during Jade's visions.

Boiling clouds compressed into a single entity, a shadow of a man wearing a hat. Casey recognized it, and the snakes that slithered out of the clouds and into the body of the shadow until the face of the preacher appeared.

But his features changed and changed again. The images multiplied until there were millions of the entities filling every inch of space. The preacher was just one of hundreds. It would be impossible to defeat each and every one of them. How were they going to make it to the ascension date? The clouds broke and an image of a man with a bow and arrow pointed at the preacher's head materialized. It was Mingan. Maybe Mingan was going to destroy the preacher with his arrowheads.

The images stopped. Casey heard distant screaming. He didn't believe it was part of the shared visions in the dream lodge. He felt they were coming from below him, far below on earth. Slowly, he turned his head towards Jade and reached out his hand towards her. For a moment he thought he saw Kevin, his signature of golden sparkling light. But it was gone in a flash.

The ancient one disappeared from the circle, then Mingan, Crazy Bear, Charlie, Jackson, and Casey left the dream lodge, leaving Jade behind.

The beat of the drum echoed in the healing room, but still, from outside, screams penetrated the walls of the cabin. Casey labored to open his eyes, to move, to get up, anything, but it was useless. His body was so deep in a trance he couldn't bat an eyelid. The drumming stopped. Did that mean Jade was back, or she was dead?

"You're okay. Take this cup and sip it," Charlie said. She pushed a cup into his hand and lifted it up to his mouth. He tried to sip. Some water trailed down his chin. He took in a deep breath and started coughing. Slowly, he forced his eyes open, desperate to know if Jade was safe and if she had returned with the rest of them.

He knew they were back at Mingan's cabin, but it had happened so fast he was having trouble reconnecting with his body. It was like being twisted inside a sweater you had put on the wrong way and trying to spin it around the right way while your arms were still inside it. It reminded him of when he had drowned and struggled out of his school blazer that had soaked up the river water, dragging him down as he sank to the bottom.

"It's okay, I've got you," Charlie said.

She put one hand on his head and another on his back, behind his stomach. His energy settled, no longer part of the cosmic. He could feel its flow. He breathed in and opened his eyes. Jade was next to him, rocking back and forth as if wriggling back into her own body.

"She'll be okay. She had to shut down the vortex to prevent the dark matter entering our space. Not sure if it's going to do much good. There seems to be plenty outside the cabin already."

The face of the preacher appeared before Casey. He pushed himself back in fright, away from Charlie, until he had backed up against the wall.

"He's here," Casey rasped. The night never seemed to end. He wished the sun would rise.

"We know. We have to get out of here and find out what is going on outside. I want everyone to arm themselves," Mingan said.

"What about Jade?" Casey asked.

"She'll be all the way back in a minute. Get her gear ready to move."

Crazy Bear handed Casey a staff with the carved arrowhead on the tip.

"I'll be alright," Casey said.

"Come on, man, you need to protect yourself," Crazy Bear said, pushing the staff into his hand. They made the staff from willow.

"Seriously, man, I'm good," Casey said, showing him his holster with the dagger. "I'll take the staff for Jade."

Jade opened her eyes and raised her brows as she blinked, as if she had something in her eyes. "That was heavy. Help me up, will you? I feel like a hundred-year-old right now."

Screams penetrated the safety of the room. "What the hell is going on out there?" she said.

"It's the preacher. He's here, but I don't know why the people are screaming and running for their lives." Casey handed her the staff. "This is for you."

"Wait. Drink this." Charlie handed her a cup with the same mixture of herbs and water she had given him. "It will help you ground yourself a little faster. Once you go outside, your spiritual and physical body can be a little more vulnerable after being in the dream lodge. It's always best to isolate yourself for a couple of hours afterwards, or go for a walk in nature, under normal circumstances."

"Do you know what is happening outside?" Jade asked.

"No. But I think Mingan has an idea, because he is arming us all with the arrowheads. Aim for the heart. If you miss, they will dematerialize and take form again. It gives you enough time to get yourself away," Charlie instructed.

"Let's do this," Mingan said.

The backpack seemed to weigh a little more than usual. Casey tightened the straps before helping Jade with her drum bag. They were as ready as they were ever going to be to face the horror beyond the cabin.

He didn't have to wait long to find out. He emerged from the cabin to see, through clouds of fog, people being run down and attacked by the wendigo. Gunfire cracked through the night, but the wendigo didn't fall. Casey heard breaking glass, then screams, as a wendigo broke into a cabin and attacked.

Casey stood in the middle of the open field. "Back-to-back," he shouted to Jade. He could feel her drum push against his backpack as she jabbed out with her staff. He glanced over his shoulder in time to see the wendigo vaporize and another one run at her.

Casey maneuvered his body, rolling around to her side, keeping contact with Jade's body until he had placed himself between Jade and the wendigo. He held his dagger out and waited for the right moment when he saw the chest of the wendigo. He lunged forward and drove the knife through the ribs into the heart and said, "With the power of the Almighty, unclean spirit, I pierce you with the blade of judgement and you shall be no more, and it is done, in the name of the Holy Spirit. Amen."

The wendigo turned to smoke and was gone, but the body fell to the ground and looked almost human again. Jade tapped him on the shoulder and pointed to Mingan. Mingan, Charlie, Crazy Bear, and Jackson protected a group of people they had saved from the wendigo. "Stay close," Casey said to Jade.

The preacher stood on the top step of the community lodge. Casey feared the wendigo was inside, attacking the people. "We have to get inside," Casey said to Mingan.

"How can you get us in there?" Crazy Bear asked.

Casey pointed to the roof. "See the windows on the second floor? I'm going to put you on the roof of the verandah, and you can get access through the windows."

Those that didn't know him looked at him as if he lost his mind, one of them offered to get the ladder from the maintenance shed, which would have been an okay idea, but Casey was sure that the preacher would stop them before they had time to climb halfway up.

"Okay, four at time. Ready?" Casey said.

"Ready," they said in unison.

Casey channeled all his energy outward and lifted the men up off the ground. He had only intended to raise four, but he had the six of them up in the air. A few wobbled. "Relax, I've got you," Casey said. Jackson stretched out his hands as if enjoying the sense of being up in the air. Jackson looked down at him while the others were focused on looking up to where they were going. As soon as they landed on the roof, they headed for the windows, crashing through the glass.

Casey could see the silhouettes of them battling against the wendigo. There must be at least half a dozen in there. How many wendigos did the preacher manage to acquire vessels for? Probably most of the congregation had been fed human flesh, turning them into vessels for the incursion of the evil spirit of the wendigo.

The preacher's attention turned to the wendigo climbing up onto the roof. "We have to move," Casey said to Jade. She looked in the direction of the preacher and agreed with Casey. The preacher stepped down the first two steps and raised out a hand.

Jade doubled over in pain. "My stomach, it's like he's twisting my intestines."

Casey went to help her when he, too, was afflicted with the same pain. The preacher kept walking towards them, and the closer he got, the more severe the pain became.

Casey aimed his dagger at Jade. He couldn't control his hand. He was aiming for her heart. The blade was inches away from her body.

Jade was frozen. Her face contorted in pain and horror as the tip of his blade touched her chest. Crazy Bear jumped off the roof and landed on the preacher, breaking the connection he had over Casey and Jade. Casey pulled the dagger back away from Jade as her body collapsed, nearly falling onto his blade.

Crazy Bear went flying towards a tall oak tree. Before he hit the tree and broke his back, Casey reached out and grabbed him with his mind, levitating Crazy Bear back up onto the roof. The bang of his body against the iron roof made the preacher look up. Before the preacher could do anything, Jackson was thrown through the second-story window. Casey grabbed him with his energy and set him down on the ground. The preacher fixed his stare on Casey, and Casey pushed back.

"Get out of here, Jade. Get the others and get out of here!" Casey shouted.

"I'm not leaving you!".

"I'll catch up with you. Get as many people as you can and hide in the woods. I'll get Mingan and the others and find you. Go!"

Casey felt for Sophia's necklace, which he forgot wasn't under his shirt, but it didn't matter. He knew he was not alone. She was with him every step of the way. The idea of her being with him gave him an enormous amount of strength.

A wendigo dove through the window, as if thrown from the second story. Mingan was on its tail—he leaped, bow and arrow drawn, aiming at the wendigo. He fired in midair, hitting the wendigo in the back. It dematerialized. Casey wondered what happened to the victim's body, which had become its vessel.

He couldn't think about that now as he pushed back harder against the preacher's energies. Casey had never come against a force like this before. Not even the battle with the She-Devil for Kevin's brother and sisters' lives.

The preacher wavered. He was hurting, or at least draining of power. Casey pushed harder, imagining the boost of energy that Sophia had given him in the past. Right now, the placebo was just as powerful. Casey put everything he had in it and shoved hard, and the preacher stumbled backwards.

Suddenly all the wendigos appeared around the preacher, blocking Casey's view of the preacher. Within seconds, Jackson, Crazy Bear, Mingan, and the remaining men and women of the camp turned the tables and together attacked the wendigos. Casey raised his dagger and pierced the blade between the nearest wendigo's shoulder blades, hoping he was hitting its heart.

He didn't know how long it took until all the wendigos were gone. There was no sign of the preacher—he disappeared. Casey was exhausted when he holstered his blade. Mingan's last arrow whizzed past Casey's head, hitting a wendigo as it leaped into the air behind Casey. He would've been dead if it wasn't for Mingan's skill.

"Thanks, man!" Casey said.

"Where's Jade?" Mingan said.

"She rounded up some women and children. I saw her heading to the woods with the elders," Crazy Bear said.

"Where's the preacher? What happened to him? Did you kill him?" Casey asked, looking from Mingan to Crazy Bear, searching their faces for answers.

"He vanished."

"What do you mean *vanished*?"

"He dematerialized like the wendigo," Mingan said.

Together they checked the few wendigo bodies. They were all dead. They had transformed back into naked human bodies that looked emaciated.

"Get some sheets to cover these people!" a man yelled.

"This wasn't us. This was you Casey. Your dagger destroyed the evil and freed the person. I have never seen this before. You, you could have saved Bob," Mitch said, coming out of the common hall.

"But they are all dead," Casey said.

"Yes, but their souls are free. Their spirits will ascend, and they will reside with Great Spirit. The greatest freedom there is," Mingan explained.

A couple of men and women stumbled down the steps of the lodge, obviously injured. The doctor followed behind, cradling his wounded arm. "If we get attacked again by the wendigo and the preacher, we won't survive. We have to leave."

"We need to find where Jade and the others went," Casey told him.

16

JADE: THE SKIN OF THE DARK REALM

Spirit Walker was old, but her movements were fluid, nimble as she weaved in and out of the trees, better than Jade. The group of families moved farther away from the campsite, the woods grew dense, and Jade had to trust the elders knew where they were going. It would be too easy for them to get lost. Jade looked over her shoulder making sure nothing sinister followed.

Spirit Walker glanced at her and smiled. It was like she wasn't even touching the ground. Jade believed magic kept the elders moving in a tireless manner as the families followed Rising Eagle. Jade wondered if they were heading for a particular location.

The occasional glint of jewelry reflected in the moonlight, marked out the location of some people to her, as they slowed down and moved quietly towards a fog that drifted through the trees. Loud rustling came from the treetops. Jade stopped and scanned the canopies for the wendigos that she feared would kill them all, one by one under the cloak of fog. She looked back over her shoulder, unable to see more than a couple of feet behind her. She held her wand and the staff together in her left hand, shining the way for her and Spirit Walker as they moved on.

There had been a moment, back at the campsite, when she thought she felt Kevin's energy. Maybe she should go back. He wouldn't know where she was, wouldn't know about the dangers lurking in the forest. "How many people do you think have turned?" she asked Spirit Walker.

Her breathing labored, Spirit Walker said, "Too many. It's not safe."

Someone screamed on her left. Jade slowed, but Spirit Walker tugged her along.

"This way," an elder yelled from up ahead.

The terrain changed to a deep rise that slowed their pace. Jade's throat burned. Air traveled down her throat like razor blades. A man in his thirties stopped to pick up his child. Jade watched as someone fell not far in front. It was a woman holding the hand of a child. It was Sue and Ruby.

As she paused to help Sue, and Spirit Walker took little Ruby by the hand, a sound like a horn of a ship blasted in the night. It seemed to be everywhere at once, echoing in the trees, tearing through Jade, shocking her to her core, and leaving her quaking in fear. Still, she summoned an encouraging smile for Ruby, who looked much younger than she had a few days ago when they first met.

Jade's arm hurt from the tension of carrying the unwieldy staff. She wanted to rub the raven tattoo on her forearm, it was itchy and uncomfortable, but she dared not let go of Sue. A few men came up on their flank. At first Jade thought they were going to help them move faster through the trees to where Rising Eagle had gone. But they suddenly stopped and dropped to the ground.

Spirit Walker stooped as if to help but straightened quickly and ordered Jade and the others onward. She blocked the sight of the fallen as they hurried by.

Suddenly, a burst of light came from Spirit Walker, and Jade looked back. With her hands stretched out, light traveled around the fallen men, creating a circle, smothering them with light. Jade could smell burning flesh. She turned away from the terrifying scene as the men burned. They had turned to wendigo. They must have eaten the meat the hunters had prepared—it must've been human flesh. Jade tried to remember who she had seen eating meat and vowed she was going to become a vegan again if she made it out alive.

She looked up into the night sky and wondered if God was watching or if Metatron was watching them all on his behalf, and not just Casey. She didn't understand why Metatron connected to Casey only. Her legs were so sore she wanted to stop running. Spirit Walker was pulling them along as they climbed up. "Where are we going?" she asked Spirit Walker.

"To a safe place. A place that is protected by our ancestors," Spirit Walker said through gasps for air. She, too, was tiring. Jade still couldn't believe her stamina.

They stopped at the face of a cliff. "Up there?" Jade said and couldn't imagine Spirit Walker or any of the elders being able to make the climb. But they did, and they moved fast with unusual speed and agility; it was unnerving. They looked like shadows scaling the side of a mountain.

Spirit Walker let go of Ruby's hand. "You now go with the speed of Great Spirit."

Ruby cried. "No, I can't without my daddy! And where's Mitch? I want my daddy!"

Sue pulled her daughter tight. She crouched down and wiped her tears. "Daddy and Bob are with God, and Mitch will find us, honey. Great Turtle's great-granddaughter is here. Trust in her and the elders. Now up you go," Sue said, hoisting the girl up onto the rock. "I'm right behind you."

Other people didn't wait their turn. They pushed ahead and climbed.

"Watch out!" Jade called as a shadow on the face of the cliff tumbled backwards sliding down the cliff face, headed for Sue and Ruby. Ruby jumped off the rock as the man tumbled to his death. His head repeatedly hit the face of the cliff. He was unconscious before his neck broke, landing at Ruby's feet. The girl screamed. Sue picked her up and gave her a leg up back onto the rock for her to scale the cliff face. "Now find the footholds like Mitch taught you. It's okay to be scared, but you've done this a hundred times. This time is no different."

"Try to relax. Connect to the energy of the mountain," Jade said to Ruby. Jade tucked her crystal wand into her back pocket before threading the staff over her back between the arms of her drum bag. She made sure it was secure and wouldn't stick out too far and accidentally push Spirit Walker off the cliff.

Spirit Walker insisted on going last. Jade tried to protest, but the old woman would not change her mind. As quick as she could, Jade climbed up the mountain behind Sue and Ruby. She didn't have the agility of the elders. Tired and out of breath, Jade dragged herself over the top edge of the cliff. Her calf muscles spasmed and her fingers bled.

Jade lay on her stomach and reached over the edge of the cliff down to help Spirit Walker, who refused her help. She actually didn't even look like she needed it. Jade took her wand and held it in front of her so that Spirit Walker could see the next purchase in the rock and hoist herself over the cliff edge.

Jade drew in a deep breath, shocked by the appearance of Spirit Walker's face. She was so young and beautiful, maybe only twenty-five years old. It felt like she had intruded on a secret that was not for her to know. Feeling guilty, Jade put her wand away, but first dared to steal a glance at the other elders, who had waited for everyone to climb the rock face. They all looked as old as they had sitting around the fire earlier in the evening. Ruby helped Spirit Walker up onto her feet, which Jade felt was more for the child than Spirit Walker, but when she looked again, Spirit Walker looked old and frail.

"This way. Rest time is over. We must keep moving," Spirit Walker said, ushering them forward. The others didn't wait to be told twice before they started at a brisk walking pace. Jade waited a little longer for Sue to catch her breath, and it was then that Jade felt the dirt slip from under her feet and heard the pebbles slap against the cliff face on their way down, when Spirit Walker grabbed her arm pulling her away from danger.

Cautiously peering over the edge, she spotted two figures scaling the cliff. They moved with inhuman speed. One creature paused, as if sensing her presence. It tilted its face up towards her and let out a roar.

"Run!" Jade yelled over her shoulder.

A huge moth or butterfly fluttered in her face. Jade slapped it away. Suddenly, Charlie was by her side. Jade could smell her sweet scent that reminded her or magnolias. "Charlie? But how?" Jade said.

But there was no time for her to answer. If Jade could've seen her face, she believed she would have seen a gloating smile.

Spirit Walker stood her ground. "Go," she said to Sue and Ruby. "Charlie, get them out here."

Charlie, quick to act, stretched her arms out and encircled Sue and Ruby, and together they moved as one mass.

"I'm not leaving if you're not," Jade said to Spirit Walker.

"Then you'd better raise your staff," Spirit Walker said.

Jade reached over her shoulder for the staff, ready. Everything seemed to move in slow motion. For a split second, two wendigos stood eight feet tall on the edge of the cliff. Spirit Walker opened her hand and blew as if something lay upon it. Jade hadn't even seen her reach into the pockets of her smock. A snake, with its mouth wide open, darted out of the wendigo's mouth, ready to sink its fangs into Spirit Walker's face.

Struck by the invisible powder, the wendigo staggered back, too far, flailing at the edge, and the snake protruding from the wendigo's mouth was yanked back, missing Spirit Walker as the wendigo fell backwards off the cliff, howling into the night.

The second wendigo let loose the snake-like tongue, and Jade hit it away with the staff, right before the creature leaped high into the air. Jade raised the staff upward to pierce its abdomen; she missed, and gravity brought it down on her. It fell hard, knocking the wind from her.

Pinned down, she gulped for air. Saliva dripped onto her face. Her breath returned with a burst of nausea from the stench of the beast's mouth.

Disgusted, she pushed the creature's head off her and wiggled her way out from under its bulk. Spirit Walker chanted over the creature.

As Jade dusted herself off, a purple trail of energy drifted up and away from the wendigo.

"How did you kill it?"

"My breath is like the dragon. One puff upon the powder of fire will burn like the fires of the demon spirits. Pick up your new friend."

She didn't understand what Spirit Walker meant by her new friend. Jade looked down at the creature and saw a naked, dead man at her feet. Spirit Walker bent down and picked up the staff and handed it to her. "Your new friend."

"What is the powder of fire?" Jade asked, trying to keep up with the old woman.

"We all have our sacred medicine pouches. We do not talk of their contents."

Jade thought about her own medicine pouch, made from the skin of the rattlesnake that had sunk its fangs into her hand when she was only a toddler. Great Turtle had killed and skinned the snake and made her a medicine pouch, adding its first contents—the pieces of the vertebra of the snake. Jade caught herself rubbing her hand at the memory. The verse from her memory stone with the snake popped into her head.

Hisss. Hisss. Hisss. Hunger and pain,
The infernal shall slither,
Into your minds again.
Poisoning your thoughts,
Feeding on your fear,
Luring you into the darkness,
Boiling your blood as he nears.
Hiss. Hiss. Hiss. Hunger and pain,
Feast from the vessel,
Starvation is the game.

Jade looked around at the darkness. "Where has everyone gone?" She kept pace, waiting for an answer, unsure if Spirit Walker had heard her, so she asked again, "Where are all the people?"

Spirit Walker stopped. "Raven Wings?"

"I'm here," Jade said. Something was creeping up her spine. Spirit

Walker could no longer see her. "Spirit Walker!" Jade grabbed her shoulders and Spirit Walker flinched as if touched by something unseen. She couldn't see or hear Jade. Jade was invisible to her.

Spirit Walker started chanting. Jade was frightened. Had something happened to her, or to Spirit Walker? The hair on the back of her neck stood up. The feeling that someone was behind her grew, stronger. Jade turned around with lightning speed, ready with her staff pointed outward—this time she wouldn't miss. "Who's there?"

Spirit Walker stopped chanting; the silence was unnerving. Jade pivoted back around to check on Spirit Walker, who was illuminated with whispers of emerald green smoke that covered her from head to toe. It sparkled with silver light.

Spirit Walker's mouth continued to move, chanting, and praying, but Jade could no longer hear her. Desperately she wanted to draw her crystal wand from her back pocket, to cast light into the darkness, but she dared not lower her staff.

The sliver arrow tip caught the light of the moon. A twig snapped. From her chest starlight glowed, projecting from her, illuminating her being, and joining with the light of her bracelet. Once again, she could hear Spirit Walker's chanting. It was muffled, flat, and dead to her ears. Jades surrounding light grew encompassing the area around her, revealing the shadows amongst the trees. Startled, frightened, and repelled by the emergence of a shadow the shape of a tall man, wearing a hat, standing no more than a few feet from her, Jade stepped backwards.

"I seeeeeee you," he crooned, hissing like a snake. He rushed forward. Jade braced herself for impact when suddenly, she felt a hand on her shoulder from behind, and she knew it was Spirit Walker. Their spiritual bodies united, and together they ran like the wind.

"I have seeeeeeeen you!" the preacher said. His voice was muffled and dead.

Spirit Walker continued chanting as they moved through the woods with phenomenal speed, creating distance between them and the preacher. Once the chilling dark energy seemed far behind, Spirit Walker, and Jade slowed down, the light returned to her chest.

Spirit Walker's glowing green aura folded back into her being and her body solidified. Jade felt and saw the last rays of starlight flow back into her chest, and the brightness of the bracelet dimmed as she felt the weight of her own physical body.

The leaves crunched under her feet while she turned around to check for the preacher.

"What just happened?" Jade asked.

"You stepped over the threshold into the dark realm that is merging with ours. Soon, it will consume our realm," Spirit Walker said.

"How did I step over so easily? I didn't even know it had happened. All I saw was that you couldn't see me. And then I saw him," Jade said.

"The veil is thin, and you are like me, able to step into the different realms. You stepped into the dark realm," Spirit Walker said.

"Why would God create a dark realm?" She had never thought too much about where the realm of lost souls, or another dark realm had come from.

"To keep us safe from those that wish to do us harm— a place where he can banish the evil, but he also promised them a time when they could roam from the dark realm into ours. But it also would be their time of reckoning," Spirit Walker said.

"But, why?" Jade asked.

"Because humans are destroying the earth. You know this, Raven Wings. Many have stopped believing that Great Spirit is in everything. A human removed the physical seal to the dark realms. But our forefathers have spoken of a time that will come for us to return to the place of creation among the seven sisters. Now is that time. Great Spirit has not forsaken us. He means to fool the evil into believing they have won."

Jade knew it was Shaun's father who had removed the seal. "But if you know that, won't the infernals and all the evil entities from all the realms know it too?"

"Let's hope not. And if they do, they'll think they're smarter than Great Spirit." Spirit Walker kept moving, searching for the others.

They came to the clearing, and the moon had travelled through the night sky. It would be morning soon. She couldn't wait for the light of the sun. The pleasure and joy Kevin expressed whenever he bathed in the sun was contagious. He believed he was like a solar battery recharging his internal essences. Jade smiled – she missed him.

Cautiously, they walked through tall grass. A film covered the sky, obscuring the twinkling stars. "What's that?" Jade asked, pointing up.

"It is the skin of the dark realm. In the open, we are vulnerable to all the unseen entities that hover above that fill the air, some good, but mostly evil."

"Where are we headed?"

"See where the sky is blacked out? Where no stars are visible? That is another mountain. There is an entrance to a cave we must pass through," Spirit Walker said.

"Are we headed towards Devils Tower?" Jade asked, thinking it ironic how the place of the portal for an ascension was called Devils Tower.

"It's Bear Lodge. And no, *we* are not."

"Why?" Jade knew sounded like a kid asking a million questions, but she just couldn't help it. She needed to know.

Spirit Walker picked up her pace as they drew closer to the mountain. "Your great-grandmother said you would ask many questions. I cannot tell you more," Spirit Walker said with a slight chuckle.

A wind picked up her hair and ran around her neck. In silence, they continued to rush to the open field. A gust of sour wind blew back her hair. Alarmed, Jade reached into her back pocket for her wand.

"No. Leave it. It will only bring more attention to us."

Jade imagined the white buffalo walking beside her, guarding her from the unseen entities. The wind was chilly, as if it came down from ice peaks. The mountain never seemed to get any closer. Jade stomped her foot down to hear the sound and feel the vibrations. Something stifled the stomping and vibrations. Oh, no, not again. "Spirit Walker?" Jade said.

Jade stopped walking, and snakes slithered over her boots quickly, she batted at the snakes climbing up her legs, but there were to many.

17

CASEY: POISONING YOUR THOUGHTS

In the main community kitchen, Casey turned on the hot water tap, cleaned his blade and tried to catch his breath. He needed time to think, and he prayed Jade, and the others were safe and unharmed. The smell of blood on the knife left a metal taste in his mouth, his stomach turned, and he leaned on the edge of the sink, feeling sick. He was lucky to be alive thanks to the ancient dagger. Saying the banishing prayer as he pierced the knife into any beast's heart would never become like second nature. The thought of killing something made him feel sick. At least now he didn't have to think of the words of the prayer, they just poured out of his mouth. Casey dried his blade on the hand towel slung over the oven door handle and felt all the energy from all that has passed embedded on the cloth. They had good times and prepared many feasts in this kitchen. A lot of wonderful memories were here.

Crazy Bear was in the pantry, filling a hessian bag with canned goods and other packaged food. Casey held open the bag for Crazy Bear. "Do you know where the elders have gone?" Casey asked.

"There is a place, we don't mention to strangers, it's beyond the woods, a safe special place tog to if there's a storm or any other incident that threatens our survival. Before the whiteout we were attacked by a group of men who wanted the women in our community, and that's when the elders told us of this special place. It's where they have gone." Crazy Bear said.

"What's special about the place?" Casey asked looking at Crazy Bears trembling hands.

Crazy Bear shook his trembling hands as if it would stop them from shaking. "This attack has freaked me out. I've never killed anyone before. The place is special because it is concealed. It's in a cave that runs deep, and we are forbidden to pass a certain point, only the elders can go beyond the forbidden point. I'm not even sure if Mingan or Mitch knows what's in the cave. Let's hope Mingan does.

Before all this, Mitch and I trained to rock climb Bear Lodge, it was part of our spiritual development, not just another mountain to conquer, like some rock climbers. I think the elders once through the cave intend to go to Bear Lodge where we can connect to our ancestors and Great Spirit. It is now called Devils Tower, but it was originally called Bear Lodge; from a distance, the rock formation looks like a giant bear had clawed the sides. The bear had been chasing seven girls and the girls prayed to the rock to keep them safe, and the rock rose out of the ground, the bear clawed the sides trying to get to the girls, but the rock went higher towards Great Spirit. If you look up in the winter, you will see the seven girls, which are now called the Pleiades." Crazy Bear kept filling the bag with food.

"What do you mean through to Bear Lodge?" Casey asked leaning against the pantry door frame.

"I think it's a magical doorway, maybe even a portal. Anyway, before all this happened, Mitch and I trained the old and young to scale the cliff, just in case we need to flee the campsite to this secret place. The elders never took part. I worried they would not make it. But Mingan said, 'The elders have strength, an untapped reservoir they will use when needed.' I hope they have left some sign for us to know they have safely reached the first mountain. The second mountain is beyond the open fields, a half day's walk from here; it's going to be tricky in the night. There is a secret entrance which we cannot find unless an elder is with us. Lucky we have Jackson; he is a great tracker, able to find almost anything in the woods, and should be able to track the elders to their special place," Crazy Bear said.

Casey watched Crazy Bear trying to keep his hands from shaking, nervously he fill another sack with food while he talked. "Where do you want me to put these? And if we have to scale up a cliff, how will you be able to carry them with no ropes?" Casey nodded to Mingan as he walked through the kitchen's swinging doors.

"Crazy Bear!" Mingan sounded exasperated.

"I know but—"

What are they talking about?

"You know the rules," Mingan said.

"But—"

"We were told to take nothing when the time came to leave," Mingan said.

"There's a dozen people we are about to lead through the woods; we need to take some food. And you've got your bow and arrows," Crazy Bear pointed out.

"You know it's not the same. We're leaving," Mingan said, looking at Casey's backpack.

"I'm not leaving it," Casey said.

Casey waited for Crazy Bear to relinquish the food he gathered for the journey.

"Maybe they have food where we are going," Casey said.

"You're probably right," Crazy Bear agreed reluctantly.

"Are you always this hungry?" Casey asked.

"Forever. As long as I can remember."

"As long as it isn't a recent thing." Casey waited for Crazy Bear to catch on to what he meant.

"Oh. Shit, no. Definitely not. I'm always hungry," Crazy Bear said.

"I have a friend, Tim. He's always hungry, too. But never seems to gain an ounce of body fat."

As they entered the forest from behind the community hall, away from the lake and the sightings of the preacher, Casey walked behind Jackson, and Emma walked next to him. He could smell her hair every time she passed him by.

"So, what special gift do you have?" he asked Emma.

"None, unless it's how good I can piss off Jackson," Emma said. "I saw what you did, back there with the preacher. Are you some sort of demigod?" Emma said.

Casey tried not to laugh. "No. I'm just like you."

"Obviously you're not," Emma said and walked a little faster, leaving Casey behind.

With the strongest flashlight Jackson was up front, studying the foliage, leading the group, checking the ground tracking the elders. "What's that smell," Jackson said.

Casey could smell something rotten too. He followed Jackson, who sniffed the air and moved in the direction of the scent that grew stronger unit it started to rain.

It had started to rain, making it even harder to see. Casey pulled up the hood of his jacket.

Mingan stopped at a burned-out section of the woods and shone his flashlight around on the ground. "This is fresh. It's still smoking," he said.

Jackson bent down, picked up the dirt, and smelled it. He handed it out to Mingan. "It's still warm."

"Flesh. Human" is all Mingan said.

Casey wondered if Mingan was right, but there was no way he was going to put his hand out, to hold the dirt touch his skin, and instantly feel and see what happened to the people. Most of all, he didn't want to know if it was Jade. The preacher was out there. He could feel it. The force of dark energy the preacher possessed was so powerful.

Mingan looked at Casey. "What do you see with the vision of the night owl? You have a gift; control it and *use it*."

It was as if Mingan knew there was something Casey could do. Emma was impatient; he could feel her frustration. He had to know for himself that it wasn't Jade. *Dammit!* Casey reached down and touched the dirt with the tips of his fingers. Suddenly, in his mind, he saw three men surrounded by light, but their bodies felt like they were on fire from the inside ready to combust, ignited by a light warrior – Spirit Walker. The smell of hair and skin, burning and melting filled Casey's nostrils. He screamed out.

Spirit Walker was the bearer of light that killed the men. Shocked, he forced himself to watch the men perish. A surge of darkness suddenly rose from the men's physical form, the dark energy had possessed, and vanished. Casey experienced the separation of the dark energy and the souls connected to the bodies, and once the dark energy left, the pain stopped, and the souls ascended to a realm beyond his vision.

Casey peeled his hand away from the clump of dirt and studied the night of the forest, then into the light from Mingan's flashlight before he raised his head up to welcome the fresh droplets of rain upon his burning cheeks. "The wendigo had taken over their bodies. They must've eaten human flesh. And Spirit Walker purged the evil wendigo from their bodies and saved their souls," Casey said.

"Spirit Walker did this," Mingan said.

"It's barbaric," the doctor said.

"She only would have done what was necessary to protect the people," Charlie said to the doctor.

"Can you touch anything and know what happened?" Emma asked.

"Not everything. I've tried hard not to see," Casey said.

"So, let's say I had a boyfriend, and I suspected he was cheating on me. Would you be able to touch him and know if he was or wasn't?" Emma asked.

"Emma!" Jackson said frustrated.

"I don't know, I've never tried, and don't think I would want to know," Casey said and walked off. Jackson had gone ahead searching for a sign to confirm what directions the others were heading in.

Jackson looked up at the falling rain. "We have to hurry before the rain's washes away the tracks," Jackson told him.

"But you know where you're going?" Casey said trying to zip up his jacket at the neck.

"Of course, he does!" Charlie said copying Casey and zipping up her windbreaker, as it rained harder.

Jackson looked up from the ground. His hair was soaked. Water dripped off his eyelashes. "I know, but I want to make sure they are on track."

* * *

THE BODY of a young man was at the bottom of the cliff face. *He must have fallen*, Casey thought.

The doctor, cradling his arm, checked the man. "Broken neck. Crazy Bear, grab his feet, and take him over by that tree," the doctor said, watching Crazy Bear.

Casey looked up at the cliff that Jade would've scaled. He could just see the place where it stopped. It was hard to tell through the rain and the darkness of the clouds. "Do we have to go up there?" Casey asked Emma.

"Yep," Emma said.

Casey shone his flashlight around until he saw the doctor and Crazy Bear covering the dead man with branches. Mingan lit a stick of sage from his pocket. It took him several goes to get the lighter working in the rain. He covered the sage stick with his hand and blew on it until it billowed with smoke. Then Mingan waved a trail of smoke over the pile of branches that hid the dead body, to cleanse the body and prepare the soul for departure from this world.

Mingan dropped the sage on top of the leaves and branches and started climbing up the cliff face without bothering to tell Casey how to climb. He grappled for a handhold and wedged his foot into the cracks between the rocks to climb, but then he heard Sophia the first day he tried to levitate. *Push your energy out of the bottom of your feet.*

He shook his head and almost laughed out loud at himself. He had forgotten he could fly. For a few moments, he had forgotten everything he could do. It was all still very new to him. To be sure he was the last, Casey checked behind him; in his peripheral vision, he noticed a figure of a man. Frightened, he spun sidewards shining his flashlight at the figure, afraid it was the preacher. It was the doctor. "What are you waiting for? What's wrong with your arm?" Casey asked.

"I fractured my forearm. Not going to do much climbing with one arm. I just wanted to make sure that everyone reached this point. That you all made it this far at least," the doctor said.

Casey pointed the flashlight down.

"I'll be alright, son. You hurry along. I want to know that you're safe up there with the rest of them." Twigs broke behind the doctor.

"Shh," Casey mouthed. He put his finger up against his lips.

"You go. Whatever it is, I'll deal with it," the doctor said and they both looked back into the gathering fog.

Casey could feel the evil worming into his mind. His body felt heavy. His heart ached with grief and it was hard to breathe. A laughter, filled with madness, echoed through the woods.

"Go, go now," the doctor said.

"Not without you." Casey didn't wait for the doctor to answer. He grabbed his good arm by the elbow tight. "Hold on to me, hold tight."

"What?"

The foliage stirred around them, as Casey propelled himself, and the doctor straight up into the crying sky and landed on top of the slippery cliff; most of the others had already reached the top. The doctor join, the group of from the campsite encouraging them to move away from the edge of the cliff. With his good arm he pushed Brandon and his son Dylan back away from the cliff. There was one more man scaling the rock face. The density of the darkness increased up the side of the cliff.

"Hurry. Move it, Mitch," Mingan yelled down the cliff.

Jackson picked a rock and hurled it over the side, just missing Mitch. Emma followed Jackson's lead and kicked stones over the edge, making it impossible for Mitch to make any progress.

"What the hell! Are you guys insane?" Mingan said to Jackson and Emma.

Mitch called out for them to stop. Casey was sure they had hit Mitch in the head. When the doctor started kicking stones off the edge too, Casey knew something was wrong and started pulling them away from the edge. "Crazy Bear, get them out of here and don't stop. The preacher is here somewhere controlling our minds. Get them all out of here now," Casey said.

Crazy Bear sprang into action and pulled the others away from the edge and away from Casey and Mingan. Mitch continued to climb when a shadow, blacker than the night, hurried up the rock face and covered Mitch's body. It didn't matter how much light Casey or Mingan shone; they weren't able to penetrate the darkness to see Mitch beneath the shadow.

Anger ignited the telekinetic energy that coursed through his veins. Casey pushed out, blasting the shadow off Mitch's back, but Mitch didn't have the strength to hold on to the rock with his fingertips and boot toes as the shadow pulled Mitch off the cliff. With his mind Casey reached out for Mitch and caught him. Mitch dangled in the air like bait.

"What are you doing? Bring him up," Mingan said.

Casey looked at the ground below, imagining what would happen to Mitch's body if he let go. How would the broken body look? Would it be the same as the other man's? Or would it bend differently depending on how many times it hit the rock face on his way down?

"Casey, what are you doing?" Mingan said.

The snakes had slithered into his mind. Casey struggled to bring Mitch up. *Drop him. Drop him. You know you want to. Drop him,* Casey heard in his mind.

They weren't his thoughts, but the desire to drop Mitch was strong. His body shook as he struggled for control. The preacher showed himself at the base of the cliff, clapping his hands.

Suddenly, an alpine white wolf the size of a small horse rushed past Casey and jumped off the cliff, landing on the preacher, severing the connection between the preacher and Casey turned and Mingan was gone. The sudden disconnection caused Casey to rocket Mitch straight up into the air, so high that he lost sight of him. But he heard Mitch screaming as he tumbled back to earth, giving Casey a fix on his location to guide Mitch back to him. He eased Mitch towards the cliff where Mingan had been standing and joined him there.

They looked over the edge, searching for Mingan and the preacher. The wolf battled a giant snake that had wrapped itself around its neck and torso.

"We have to go," Casey said to Mitch.

"We can't leave, that's Mingan. We have to help him."

"I'll take care of this. Go, get as far away from the preacher before he turns you against us," Casey said.

Mitch hesitated for a second, then started running. Casey knew he could blast the snake away from the wolf, but he feared he might hurt Mingan and he wouldn't be able to transform back into his human form.

Casey jumped off the cliff and grabbed the snake with his hands. He needed two hands to wrap around its tail. He wasn't physically strong enough to pull the snake away. Casey pushed out his energy, slamming the wolf and the snake against the cliff. The snake refused to loosen its grip on Mingan.

The preacher watched on as if it was a cockfight. The thick body of the boa constrictor wrapped itself even tighter around the wolf, and Casey heard ribs crack. Somehow, Casey knew the preacher was assessing Casey's powers. It was all a game to the preacher, a test to see what Casey could do. Casey took hold of the snake again and slowly wedged his hand between the smooth belly of the snake and the wolf's coarse gray-white coat. He pried the body of the snake away, freeing Mingan.

Now for the preacher, Casey thought, feeling a lot stronger emotionally than he had a few minutes ago. He drew his dagger, ready for the preacher, but the preacher had gone.

Mingan crouched on one knee, catching his breath.

"You're the wolf, literally. You're not just a spirit wolf, you were *the* wolf. How do you do that?"

"I can explain it no more than you can explain what you do."

He had a point. Casey didn't know how he did things; he just knew he could. "Do you feel human still?" Casey asked.

"My consciousness is there, but I feel the strength of the wolf, the desire to be part of a pack. To protect those around me, for I am their leader. Not like a king, but for love. Power comes from love," Mingan said.

"We must go before the preacher returns. I'm worried he's toying with us," Casey said, reaching out his hand.

"Hell, yeah. I thought you'd never ask," Mingan said, taking Casey's hand, ready to take flight.

Casey didn't look back. He kept an image of Sophia in his mind to block out any intrusion by the preacher, who had become a great, big pain in the ass. The thought of Sophia made him smile. He felt her arms around his waist, just like she had done when he doubled her on the back of the motorcycle back at the estate. He thought about what might have been if she'd lived and quickly stopped because it was becoming cold inside his heart. The preacher was close, testing him again, trying to get control. Casey pushed him out.

"Be careful. The preacher is trying to get into our heads again," Casey said to Mingan as they landed, startling Mitch, who waited in the clearing.

"Is that what's happening?" Mitch said with a sigh of relief. "I thought I was going crazy. While I was running, all I could think about was snakes, snakes crawling in and out of my eye sockets. I'm dead in the image and snakes slither through my ears, out through my eyes, then back in through my mouth," Mitch said.

"I feel him too. Come this way," Mingan said.

It wasn't long before they came upon the others, waiting on the edge of the wide-open grass area.

"We have to cross these fields, and when we do, we will be the eagles' rabbit," Jackson said.

"I think you're right," Mingan agreed.

"Why don't we start a grass fire?" Mitch suggested.

Jackson, who permanently had a trucker's cap glued to his head, pulled it off and scratched his head. "The wind is blowing south. If we start a fire, it will hold back any wendigo headed in our direction, but I don't know about the preacher. Is he even a man?"

Casey had spoken little to Jackson, but it sounded as if Jackson knew what he was talking about.

"I don't really know. If he was, he's not anymore," Mingan said.

"What do you want us to do?" Casey asked.

"Wait here with everyone. I'll tell you when to run," Mitch said.

"I don't think Brendon can keep up," Crazy Bear said.

"Who's Brendon? Are you all right, pal?" Casey asked, following Crazy Bear's gaze. The man, Brendon, doubled over, clutching his stomach.

Brendon spat. He stood tall, wiping his mouth. "I'll be fine. Nothing that a good night's sleep won't cure. That's all."

Casey patted Brendon on the back. "You'll be right." Heat pulsed off Brendon, and Casey wasn't so sure if a good night's sleep was all Brendon needed. "Look after your dad and come tell us if you think he is getting worse," Casey said to the boy standing next to Brendon.

"No need to get the boy all riled up. We'll be fine. Won't we, son?" Brendon asked, putting his arm around his son and pulling him close.

"Ready, everyone?" Jackson said.

"Let's go," Emma said, as if finishing Jackson's sentence.

Hunched, they rushed into the open. As soon as Brendon and his son passed Jackson, Jackson held his hands together and outward and blew down on them. Fire filled the air. Jackson was a human blow torch.

Casey couldn't help watching, frozen to the spot. Jackson was so much more than a tracker. He breathed fire on to the ground like a dragon. The grass exploded into flames, raced out, stretching a mile long. Jackson ran off, creating an arch of fire like a half circle as he headed towards the middle of the field. Casey, feeling the heat of the flames, dashed off and flew over the tips of the blades of grass to catch up with the others. It didn't take him long before he came up behind Brendon and his son. They had stopped. Brendon was down on one knee, exhausted.

"Take my son and get out of here," Brendon said.

"No. I'm not leaving you," Casey said and reluctantly rubbed his hands on the side of his jeans before touching Brendon. Casey pushed back Brendon's personal history as it came flooding into his own body. "Wait up! Crazy Bear," Casey called ahead to the others. "I need some help here."

Brendon was burning up. Casey wrapped Brendon's arm around his shoulders and tried to lift, but he was too slippery. Brendon's skin was peeling. Brendon knew something terribly wrong was happening to him and was concerned only for his son's well-being.

"I'll be right behind you. Take my son," Brendon said.

Casey pulled the crying boy away from his father and lifted him up, shot into the air with such lightning speed that it was impossible for the boy to hold on to his dad. Casey set the boy down as soon as he found the doctor. The boy kicked Casey. Screaming, he started to run back towards his father. Casey followed.

Suddenly, the boy stopped. The grass moved as if a leopard was heading straight for them.

Casey drew his dagger just before he got to the boy. A dark shadow leaped into the air and pounced down on the boy. It was Brendon – the face of a mad man, his transformation into a wendigo had begun. He had started to transform into a mad man, a wendigo. Casey drove the dagger into Brendon's heart.

Brendon's son, swinging punches at Casey screamed like a wild animal. "You killed my dad! You killed him!" the boy shrieked.

Casey pulled him close until he could no longer hurt him or himself. Casey saw Brendon's body transform back into his old form. "Look, your dad is free. He was infected by one of those things."

"You killed him."

Crazy Bear ran with his knees raised high through the tall grass. "Casey!"

"Over here," Casey said.

The boy ran to Crazy Bear. "He killed my dad."

"What happened?" Crazy Bear said to Casey.

"He turned. He was becoming a wendigo. He was going to hurt the boy," Casey said.

"Dylan. I'm so sorry about your dad. You must be brave. We must hurry now. Your dad is on his way to Great Spirit."

"You mean God," Dylan said. He was angry and hurt. "I'm not going anywhere with a murderer!" Dylan spat at Casey.

"We have to go. It's for your own good," Crazy Bear said.

Casey ran towards Dylan. Before the kid could protest, Casey picked him up with his mind and flew him over to Mingan at the far side of the field at the base of the mountain.

The doctor rushed up to Dylan, "what's wrong?"

"He did it. He killed my dad. It all started when he arrived. He is murdering all our people. He's a cannibal eating the children. I saw him. Can't you tell? Can't you see it? He is an evil one. We need to stop him before he kills us all!" Dylan cried.

Mingan put his hand on the boy's shoulder. "Calm down. He's here to help us. If you want to be with your dad and die out there? then go!" Mingan said.

Dylan didn't move. He was too scared and didn't try to do anything else. Crazy Bear caught up with them, huffing and puffing. "Where's the entrance?"

"I'm waiting for the call. I need to listen. Everyone needs to be silent," Mingan said.

Mingan sat on the ground, and everyone circled around him, watching and waiting. The doctor was pacing around behind the circle.

"Can you hear that? It's Rising Eagle, the elder. He is calling out to us. This way," Mingan said, running his hand along the face of the mountain. With the gentlest movement, a boulder slowly rolled away, revealing a hidden opening. They all entered. Mingan and Casey waited until Jackson joined them.

"Can you return the boulder?" Mingan asked.

Casey reached out with his mind and moved the boulder back into place.

Twelve feet in front of him, blocking the depth of the cave, was a vibrant wormhole. "Where are we? Where does that go? I can't leave without finding Jade. I have to find her first. Kevin would never forgive me if something bad was to happen to her," Casey said, looking from person to person as they tried to process the idea of a portal.

"Raven Wings is stronger than you know. She doesn't need your help. She can save herself and us all," Mingan said.

18

JADE: SLITHERING INTO YOUR MIND

S nakes slithered up the leg of Jade's pants, up onto her shirt, quickly she yanked them, but for every snake she removed, another two climbed up and now they were worming up the inside leg of her pants and under her shirt. Jade tore off the drum bag and reached around for the cold and sticky snakes slithering up her back, when one thin snake slithered into her ear. With lightning speed she grabbed its tail before it clung to her inner ear, but she was too slow. She pulled, screamed in pain, collapsing to her knees, still holding onto the tail, trying to pull it free from her ear as snakes covered her head, and the ground opened, dragging her under.

Falling into an abyss of darkness, she wrestled to free herself. She had stretched the snake in her ear to where she expected it to snap in two, when it suddenly let go of her inner ear. She threw it into the darkness and reached for her wand. Instantly, it illuminated. She touched the crystal tip to her chest, and the snakes fell away. She could feel the blood trickling from her ear. Jade placed the tip of the wand on the outside of her ear, and the pain subsided.

Her heart glowed so brightly it blinded her. She called out to God for help, and suddenly, she was back under the starry sky, wrestling the blades of tall grass on the ground. Spirit Walker, by her side, tried to calm her down. The sensation of the snakes had returned, but no longer was she in the abyss. On her back, she focused on the sky above and a snake trailed across her eyes.

"ARHHHHHH!" she screamed into the night. Spirit Walker blew something into her face, choking Jade. It reminded her of her asthma attacks and she gasped for air. She had always feared suffocating. Spirit Walker placed the palm of her old leathery hand onto Jade's head. It was warm and comforting. The sensation of the snakes vanished. But a hideous sight filled her head, and she knew it was the preacher manipulating her thoughts.

What the hell did he have against her? Why was he coming after her? Her airways were clear and so was her mind. It felt like the snakes had been slithering inside her brain. She went to sit up and discovered she was tangled in the blades of grass. None of it had been real. The preacher had poisoned her mind.

Spirit Walker handed Jade a piece of sage. "This will help you, just as Great Spirit helped you when you called out to him. But if you don't believe, it won't work for you. It is all about your belief. Your Faith will protect you," Spirit Walker said.

"I believe." Sophia had given her sage, and so, too, had Chief Thundercloud. She now believed in God so much more than she had when she was a child. The memories of her doubts filled her mind.

"Don't second-guess. You must have faith in yourself, too. Just as Great Spirit, Great Turtle, and I have faith that you can fulfill your destiny," Spirit Walker said.

"He was inside my head. How will I know what is real and what is not real?" Jade asked. Maybe when she had thought she had seen Kevin, it was really the preacher slithering inside her mind.

"We have to keep moving," Spirit Walker said.

Jade looked at the mountain that had seemed so far away. Now it rose up only a few yards ahead of them. It had been like the inside of a nightmare when you walk down a street or up a flight of stairs. They never seem to end. The preacher had been messing with her mind. She had to keep a guard of her thoughts.

"The best thing you can do is call Great Spirit. He will always help you," Spirit Walker said, stopping and looking around at the looming fog. "I hear Rising Eagle calling me. They are safe and we are not far."

Spirit Walker sought direction, looking at the mountain and from left to right. As soon as she had her bearings with certainty, she headed for a single boulder resting against the mountain. Behind the boulder was an entrance. This must be the other entrance that Spirit Walker and Chief Thundercloud had spoken of. The entrance to the cave where she had found Chief Thundercloud.

The size of the cave took her breath away, and she didn't need to draw her wand, for the cave sparkled with light. From the outside, she hadn't noticed a single ray of light. Nothing escaped the cave giving away its location. She was looking into a funneled portal. Spirit Walker moved to the portal's edge.

Jade hesitated. What if she entered and Kevin never found her? She wished so much that he was with her.

"Why you hesitate, Raven Wings? It will take us to the other side of the mountain. To the elders, to the community. They are waiting for us," Spirit Walker said.

"I'm scared my friends won't be able to find me," Jade said.

"It doesn't matter if they find you or not. You will see them after we have ascended," Spirit Walker said.

"But that's weeks away. I need to be with my friends. They're my family. I'm lost without them. We need each other," Jade said, backing away suddenly, afraid of the colorful portal. "This isn't right. I have to go," Jade said, turning to run.

"Stop!" Spirit Walker said.

Jade froze. The tone of Spirit Walker's voice scared her and filled her with uncertainty. The preacher was doing it again. Her faith in Great Spirt returned. Quickly, before she changed her mind, she turned and ran to Spirit Walker, taking her hand and together, they entered the portal.

The energy inside the portal, she imagined was like being in a wormhole. Very different from the portals Kevin created; she didn't feel a fetal embrace. Instead, she felt an overwhelming sense of positivity, and a thought flowered into her mind. The sensation was glorious. Like an awakened dream, it was so clear and real, three dimensional.

It was as if she could reach out and touch herself and Kevin. The clothes were different. Their lives were not the same. They were older, much older. Her spirit connected to the spirit of what she believed to be her future self, and she saw two moons were in the sky, and the sky was washed with pinks and blues. It was sunrise, and they weren't living on earth. No words were spoken, it was like data downloaded from her future self into the now. They had chosen a new place to live out their lives, and when they died, they would be reincarnated in this new world they had chosen to be part of.

The image shrunk and drifted down to her waist. It folded up like a flower and nestled inside her abdomen. Was it a hallucination or a glimpse of a future? She didn't know but welcomed the hope of a bright future, away from the raging dark realm that was smothering the earth. Anything was better than the horrific images the preacher had projected into her mind.

The warmth of Spirit Walker's hand was in hers. "Where are we?" Jade asked.

"We're in the tunnel, traveling to the other side."

"The other side of what? The mountain?"

"Yes."

"But we entered a portal. I don't feel like we are still on earth. I had a bazaar hallucination of my future self, in another world far from here," Jade said.

Spirit Walker smiled and said nothing. Sometimes Jade believed Spirit Walker, like Chief Thundercloud, Great Turtle, and her own mother, knew more than what they ever said. She didn't understand the reasons to conceal information from her.

"One day you will understand," Spirit Walker said.

"Understand what?" Jade asked, still feeling positivity coursing through her body. It was as if she had taken some kind of happy pill; not that she had ever done anything like that before, but she imagined that this was what it would feel like. The energy of the portal changed like a kaleidoscope. "Awesome!"

"One day, you will understand everything. Your thirst for knowledge comes from the awakening of your soul. It is happening to all of you, all the old souls you call friends. We are all spiritual beings, part of a spiritual family. Everyone else still alive on earth will go through their own transformation and will be given the opportunity by Great Spirit to make their own choices. Earth is just the beginning of our soul's journey," Spirit Walker told her.

"So, God is deliberately creating situations for us to transform?"

"Yes, but no. Your soul knows what you need to transform, what will take you to the edge to become who you truly are. That's why I am called the Spirit Walker. I walk amongst the souls."

Jade thought about what she had said. There were too many things to unpack and analyze. Intuitively, she knew she could trust in her soul to guide her through this journey to find the survivors for ascension, if she kept her logical thinking out of it and stayed focused.

They emerged out of the portal and daylight was hidden under dark storm clouds. Jade looked back at the tunnel, wondering how the time had moved forward so quickly. The portal was gone. There was nothing but rocks and dirt. Was there a quickening of time? It was raining and cold. "But I thought we were going to the caves behind the waterfall?"

"Yes, Raven Wings."

They clung to the rock face. Her foot gave way. The dirt had turned to mud as if it had been raining for days. Jade couldn't understand how this was a shortcut. The ledge they were on was at least thirty feet up. She looked down at the plants below. Spirit Walker moved around the bend and part of the ledge had washed away. She turned and looked at Jade. Jade said nothing, passed waiting for her directions. "We will have to jump," Spirit Walker said.

Jade wasn't sure if it was a good idea. She looked down at the ground again. "Let me go first so I can help you across," Jade said.

"Your eyes deceive you, Raven Wings," Spirit Walker said, and jumped. The ground gave way, but she made it across.

That woman never ceased to amaze her. Jade looked at the gap and wiped her hair off her face that was sticking to her cheeks. Her hands were freezing. She blew onto them to keep them warm. Her body shivered involuntarily. How on earth was Spirit Walker able to keep going?

"Hurry, Jade; what are you going to do? Freeze to death?" Spirit Walker shouted over the sound of the rain.

"Aren't you cold?" Jade asked, shaking. Her legs felt like icicles under her cargo pants.

"No, are you?" Spirit Walker said.

Jade couldn't believe she had to ask. It was clear by her teeth chattering and her body shaking.

"What are you going to do?" Spirit Walker said.

Her body was exhausted from the sudden loss of heat. Jade just wanted to lie down somewhere warm and sleep.

"So, you going to lie down and die?" Spirit Walker taunted.

Jade didn't know what the woman expected of her, but she wished she would stop pestering her and just go already. Her wand. Jade reached into her pocket for her wand and held it to her chest, hoping the light would give her warmth. Spirit Walker came close to the edge on the other side. The water cascaded down the face of the mountain like a stream.

"Be careful," Jade shouted.

"Why? What could happen?" Spirit Walker said, edging closer to the fringe of the cliff.

"You know what, you could fall to your death."

"Would I?"

"Please, just move back," Jade said, squatting and hugging her wand.

It happened so fast she didn't have time to draw a breath. The edge gave way under Spirit Walker, and she fell. Jade sprung with instant stamina and dived for Spirit Walker. Jade transformed into a giant Raven and swooped down under Spirit Walker. Jade still felt as if she was Jade, but she also could see through the eyes of the Raven as she flew down to the ground with Spirit Walker on her back.

None of it made sense. As soon as she touched the ground, she turned back into herself. She looked at her arms that had been black wings. "It's impossible," Jade said.

"Nothing is impossible. All that you think you are, you can be," Spirit Walker said.

All things are compressed atoms, which are made of light. Rearrange the atoms and you project different physical forms, because light reflects particular particles. It also reminded her of the second law of thermal dynamics: entropy. "We're in a reverse, living in a state of negentropy," Jade said and looked up to the ledge where they had come from, wondering how they were going to get back up there. Could she transpose into the Raven again and fly back up? She didn't think so. Jade looked up into the rain falling on her face. She felt exasperated with each drop. Spirit Walker watched her intently, as if waiting.

Jade reached out her arms and closed her eyes, feeling her boots on the ground, and imagined connecting with the earth and nature. Thick gray clouds that covered the sky and heavy rain stung like needles. She closed her eyes and imagined she was under a cold shower. She reached out for the tap in her mind and turned the faucet anticlockwise, turning off the spray of water and the sensation of water needling her face stopped. Her face felt a ray of warmth. And in her mind's eye, a rainbow appeared in a blue sky.

Jade heard Spirit Walker gasp, and she opened her eyes. She had forgotten the woman was there and her body jerked to cover her private parts as if she was naked and had just stepped out of a shower. Spirit Walker was looking up into the sky. It was clear and blue. The rain had stopped, and the clouds were gone.

This is the third time that she had changed the weather. Kevin said she shouldn't mess with nature, but Jade didn't want Spirit Walker to be killed by the flu.

"Now you're really getting it," Spirit Walker said, as if she had known Jade could change the weather. "You could have done that while we were up there. Now we will have to climb, unless . . . ?"

"I guess we'll have to walk, because I have no idea how I became the raven, or if it will ever happen again," Jade said, touching her forearm, tracing the image of the raven. "I don't know at all," Jade said.

They walked through the woods to a clearing Jade recognized. It was hard to forget because it harbored slithering snakes at the edge of the water, and they were still there basking in the sun that warmed their reptilian bodies. Jade snapped her fingers in frustration, everything went still. The snakes, the slight movement in the trees, even the water cascading over the waterfall, froze in motion.

The second she felt fear of her own power, the magic disappeared, and the snakes slithered, the water flowed, and the wind touched her face again. "I thought we were going to enter the cave from another way, a secret entrance, but I was wrong. We have to go around the snakes and climb up there. I did it once before with Kevin while searching for my father. The entrance to the cave is up there. Behind the waterfall. Do you think you can make it?" Jade asked, thinking how frail Spirit Walker appeared.

"We are only as old as we feel. I can get up there," Spirit Walker said.

Jade recalled her scaling up the cliff face a few hours ago and believed that Spirt Walker would be able to climb up the rocks.

They tiptoed through the snakes and started their climb. It didn't seem to take as long as it had the first time she had climbed the waterfall, which was only a week ago. She thought about how much had changed in that time. It made her sad, recalling that Sophia was no longer with her.

The energy that she had felt inside the portal, the positivity that had flowed through her veins, was almost gone. The further up they went, the darker the world seemed to be. She looked down at the snakes slithering through the water and on the sandy bank and she thought she saw them rise, forming the shape of a human body. She turned away from the image and screamed.

Spirit Walker was falling. Jade stretched out for her, reaching for Spirit Walker, touching her hair with the tips of her fingers as she fell just out of Jades reach, landing on the rocks and snakes below, her body broken, her legs twisted at odd angles. Jade scrambled down the rocks as fast as she could.

"Spirit Walker!"

Three quarters of the way down, a butterfly fluttered on the edge of the water spray. It was beautiful. Soft purple wings highlighted with black edging. It captured Jade's attention. She reached out a finger towards it and it flew away. She watched it as it went up in the air. Up past where Jade had been standing and from where she believed Spirit Walker had fallen from.

Jade never took her eyes off the fluttering wings. It grew in size as it flew all the way to the very cliff edge they were trying to reach. On the cliff edge, behind the light fall of water, Spirit Walker stood with Charlie.

Jade looked back down, and Spirit Walker's body was not on the rocks at all, it was the preacher standing tall, as the snakes slithering around and inside of him.

"What the hell is it with snakes!" Jade said to herself. "It was you. You're putting those thoughts into my head, making me see horrible things that aren't real." She looked up again, reassuring herself Spirit Walker was safe.

"Go without me," Jade yelled up to Spirit Walker and Charlie. "I know the way."

They didn't hesitate or argue. They stepped back into the sheet of water, disappearing from her sight as fog closed in.

The preacher stretched out his arms. ". . . they shall speak with new tongues; They shall take up serpents; and if they drink any deadly thing, they shall be healed. Come drink from my blood, and you shall walk with me with no judgement forever. For we have inherited the earth," the preacher said.

"You're crazy," Jade said, turning her back on him and starting to climb up along the edge of the waterfall, to the shelf where Spirit Walker and Charlie were last seen. She wished she had her new friend with her, but she had left it up on the ledge when she had turned into a raven.

"You do not turn your back on me," the preacher said.

19

CASEY: BEWARE OF THE WENDIGO

C asey moved forward and entered the tunnel of light, hoping to God it would lead him to Jade. Casey compared the energy in the wormhole to the energy of the portals Kevin created, and there was something very different between the two. This wormhole was more like a train station they had to pass through to get to a pre-established destination, whereas Kevin's portals were a feeling of rebirth, and every single time, it was glorious. This was nothing like Kevin's portals.

He followed up the rear, keeping his eye on Dylan, worried he might try to run back to his father. Casey felt for Dylan, but there was nothing he could do. They were all going through painful losses, and they all just had to get through the next couple of months to be reunited with their loved ones. It still sounded unrealistic. It wasn't long ago, before it the world changed, and they were reading on the internet about communities engaged in mass-suicide to join their loved ones amongst the stars in heaven. But this was different because no one would die. The hand of God would practically reach down and take their body and soul.

Casey hung back and watched the people ahead of him reach a point in the wormhole where they disappeared. Crazy Bear and Emma were directly in front of him, with Dylan between them. Jackson was the first to vanish, then the doctor, the rest of their group with Mingan, and then came their turn. Crazy Bear, Emma, and Dylan paused and waited for him. Casey walked to the other side of Crazy Bear and joined them. "Where do you think they went?" Casey asked.

"I was just about to ask you the same thing," Crazy Bear said.

Suddenly, scaring them all, Jackson's head appeared to hang in the air in front of them, like the cat from *Alice in Wonderland*. "Hurry. We're all waiting for you."

As soon as they stepped through, Casey covered his eyes as night had turned to day with a misty summer rain. He looked down at the forest, then up at the distant rainbow. "Have you spotted the elders? Any sign of Jade?" Casey asked, watching Mingan navigate the narrow ledge of the cliff with a staff in his hand. Casey instantly knew it belonged to Jade. He snatched it out of Mingan's hand.

Jade flashed into his mind, falling. Then, like magic, she glided with wings. "She had dropped her staff and transformed into a bona fide giant raven," Casey said out loud.

"A raven?" Emma said, as if it was no big deal.

Mingan smiled. "I told you she didn't need your help. She can save us all."

"You said that before. How can she save us all?" Casey asked, keeping as close as he could to the edge of the cliff as they made their way further up and around the mountain. There was one tricky part where they had to jump. The rain had washed away part of the ledge.

"This is where it happened," Casey said after he floated across to the other side. "They went down there," Casey said, looking down to ground with the sensation of his feet firmly on the forest floor. Feeling uncomfortable, he shrugged his shoulders and pulled in his head,. The sensation of snakes crawling over him made him dance on the spot, and he nearly slipped off the side of the mountain. If it wasn't for Crazy Bear's restraining arm, he would be dead. Crazy Bear had caught him just before he went over the side. Casey checked his arms and the ground for snakes. He wasn't on the ground; he was still on the edge of the mountain and there were no snakes.

This is what Jade had felt. The preacher had followed her. This meant the preacher wasn't limited by time and space. Casey had left the preacher behind him, and Jade was in front of him. The preacher had more than one way of traveling and could torment him one minute, to disappear and torment Jade the next.

It wasn't long before they rounded a corner and walked up into an open area with boulders that looked like a family of sleeping rock people. The largest rock face was smooth. Casey ran his hand down behind it and felt a crevice they could squeeze between. In a single file behind Jackson, they slipped between the crack into a cave. Ahead of Mingan, the older people and children struggled. Emma encouraged them to keep moving, and Crazy Bear kept watch at the rear, making sure the preacher or a wendigo didn't follow.

"Down this way," Jackson said, standing aside and blocking a side tunnel so everyone could pass him by and enter the cave.

Once Casey was inside the cave, Jackson made his way up to the front of the group, where everyone had switched on their flashlights. He looked down for rats, then up for bats. Kevin and Jade had ventured into these caves only a few days ago, having found a different entrance. Kevin had ended up with mandibles for stitches in his head and back after being attacked by vampire bats. Casey hadn't thought vampire bats were real, but not so long ago he'd thought levitation wasn't real, or even possible. *It just goes to show you anything is possible.*

Crazy Bear wove through the tunnels and Casey kept close behind, wishing he had something to mark the bedrock to find his way out again. He collided with Crazy Bear. "What's up?" Casey said, sensing danger.

"It's Emma," Crazy Bear said, pushing to the front of the group.

Emma had stepped to the side and had slid down the rock wall.

"Emma, what's wrong?" Crazy Bear said.

"Wait up," Casey called up to Jackson.

Emma was on her knees, doubled over, holding her stomach. Casey shone his flashlight on her face. Sweat beaded over her arms and down the side of her face. Her arms were peeling. "Move away," Casey said.

"What is it?" Jackson said from up front. "It's not much further."

Dylan had doubled back and fixed his flashlight on Casey. "It's him. See. He makes people sick."

"Go back, Dylan," Mingan said, making his way through the people.

Emma hid her face from the light. Casey moved his flashlight to the ceiling. Crazy Bear helped her to her feet.

"What happened?" Mingan asked.

Emma moaned.

"It's not far now. Can you walk?" Crazy Bear said, holding her up.

The tunnel opened and different passageways branched off. Jackson ushered everyone to the left. Emma suddenly pulled away from Crazy Bear and bolted down a passageway on the right, heading away from the others. Crazy Bear chased Emma and Casey chased Crazy Bear. The entrance to the passageway stunk of stale urine.

Suddenly, an inhuman screech filled the tunnel, piercing their ears. Pebbles fell from the ceiling, hitting Casey and Crazy Bear on the head. Up ahead, Emma had stopped. She was panting, curled up against the wall, hiding her face from them. Casey shone the light down the passageway and away from her glistening, slimy body. Emma turned back towards them, her teeth and face distorted.

"Move!" Casey yelled at Crazy Bear.

"No!" Crazy Bear said.

Emma growled, her the transformation into a wendigo had begun, she stepped forward and sprinted towards them. At first on two legs, she chased them, then she dropped to her hands and galloped on all fours, picking up speed. Casey started to run, pulling Crazy Bear with him. She slid to a stop. Casey and Crazy Bear looked behind them to see her staring at them before turning and running in the opposite direction down the dark passageway beyond the flashlight beams. Casey imagined her fighting the urge to feed on Crazy Bear's flesh. It wouldn't be long until she gave into those urges and attacked them all. "We have to find her," Casey said.

"No, let's go back. Let her go. She won't hurt us," Crazy Bear said.

"I'm sure Brandon didn't want to hurt his son, but that didn't stop him from attacking," Casey said.

"Let's just go. If she comes back, I'll take care of it," Crazy Bear said.

Casey kept his flashlight on Crazy Bear's face, then lowered it to the ground. Crazy Bear was in love with Emma. How did he not see it before? Casey walked away despite his screaming instincts. If it had been Sophia, he, too, would have let her go.

They doubled back in silence. The stench of urine told him they were heading the right way. Mingan had waited for them at the junction where the main tunnel had opened and led them down the passageway in the opposite direction.

Singing echoed in the passageway. They ducked as the height of the roof reduced. Then the whole tunnel swelled and expanded, opening into a cave furnished with wood, stone, and animal skins. It could've been someone's home. Herb bottles, some full and some half full, sat on a shelf above cooking utensils; two pots, a pan, and a jug hung on nails used for hooks below the shelf. On the ground were transparent water bottles. In the middle was a fire pit with mats surrounding it. The four elders were sitting around the fire on the mats, chanting.

On the other side of the cave, Jade crouched down and gently spoke to Ruby, who was peeking her head into a hole in the wall. The sight of her relaxed the tension he didn't realize he held in his neck.

"It's the fox's den Kevin and I crawled through to find my father," Jade told Ruby.

"Hey," Casey said.

At the sound of his voice, Jade sprang up from her crouched position and turned, slightly losing her balance. Her smile grew as hope turned into recognition. She was pleased to see him.

Sue offered him a drink. "She was worried about you. Afraid we lost you to . . ." Sue glance at Jade.

Jade embraced Casey.

"What is this?" Casey said, taking the bowl from Sue when Jade let him go. He sniffed the contents of the wooden bowl.

"It's a mixture of super leafy greens and essences of cypress, geranium, lime, and ylang. Chief Thundercloud taught me a few potions waiting for Kevin's fever to break. It will help heal your heart before the vision quest," Jade said.

"It's good to see you. What vision quest?" Casey said, feeling connected to Sophia through Jade. Jade felt like home.

"Drink up," Jade said as Mingan whispered in her ear.

Casey sipped the herbs, watching Ruby play in the fox's hole with Dylan, wondering what Mingan had whispered.

Jade sat down on the mat next to Spirit Walker and joined the chanting. It sounded like one continuous note.

Casey sat next to her. "You were a raven! Now I know why you are called Raven Wings."

She didn't answer, but she opened one eye and smiled. She had changed, matured, and looked wiser. It had only been hours since he last saw her. He wondered what had caused such a change. Jade chanted next to him, holding the single note for as long as she could. Then the elders started again. Ommmmm. Jade picked up her drum and a stick of sage that was burning on a rock that surrounded the fire and smudged her drum.

"Just a few days ago Kevin had laid over there on the right, dying. And my dad had laid over there without his soul. Chief Thundercloud helped me to find my dad's soul while he healed Kevin," Jade said, taking out her crystals and cleansing them also with the smoke from the sage. He smiled and thought of Sophia wishing he could've saved her. but could only think about Sophia.

Mingan finished grinding up a new herb mix and made a brew. Everyone stopped chanting and the rest of the group made themselves comfortable against the walls. In the middle with the elders, Mingan passed the brew of herbs to Charlie, on his right. By the time it was passed to him by Jade, Casey expected the bowl to be empty, but there was enough of the mixture, thick with herbs for him.

Mingan must have seen him stall. "It is to simulate your pituitary gland and open your third eye. It's a mixture of purple berries, fish oil, and a few other things."

The brew tasted of sweet, rotten fish. He tried not to gag. Nobody else seemed to have a problem. The elders and Charlie rocked back and forth in time to a silent rhythm.

Spirit Walker got up and rubbed an oil blend over his forehead and the back of his neck. "To open and protect your third eye," she said and moved around the circle.

Jade started tapping lightly at the center of her drum; elders resumed chanting fresh notes, holding each one until they were out of oxygen.

Casey closed his eyes and drifted into the vibrations of the drum and the chanting. Back and forth, his body gently rocked. His legs and groin tingled with energy that wrapped its way up his body like vines from deep within the earth. The tingling energy traveled into his stomach and turned into beautiful fluttering butterflies, escaping up into his throat and fractionating into a kaleidoscope of color behind his eyes, before transcending through and out of his crown.

Gazing into the myriad of colored light, he heard Spirit Walker guiding Jade on her vision quest. Casey felt as though his body was a metronome keeping time. A vision of himself exploded into his mind. With his head bowed, he passed between golden gates behind a man wearing a long white robe and roman sandals. Casey tried to look higher but couldn't move his head to see past the ankles and sandals. He watched the feet from behind and passed through an aisle of people dressed in white gowns and praying as he walked towards sandstone steps. They were outdoors, like in an amphitheater being used as a place of worship, and he had interrupted them. His presence drew murmurs from both sides as he passed.

They went inside and headed for an altar. They went beyond the altar to a side door where Casey followed the ankles down a corridor, where he spied a version of himself sitting at a table in white robes with a golden sash, scribing. Casey was being led up a spiral staircase that went to dizzying heights amongst the constellations.

Suddenly, he was falling back down the staircase. The edges of the stairs cut into his head and bruised his body. He heard screams. Dazed he stood up and went outside. It was a total eclipse of the moon, and the moon was blood red. He was at the base of a stone tower that went up into the heavens, people were falling from windows as the tower burned. He tried to project himself upwards, to catch the helpless people, and to break their fall, but he was powerless and could only witness the destruction of the tower. He had seen an image like this before but couldn't remember where.

It was like a dream movie that started and ended in the blink of an eye, and he traversed from one place to another. He was now standing in an ice castle that was warm and toasty. He touched the ice crystal walls that were shaped like honeycomb. The smell of fresh soap drifted into the room—Sophia!

Casey turned, and in his vision was alone, and suddenly on the deck of a ship in the middle of a hurricane. He lost his balance and slid along the deck. He clutched onto the side rail as the ship rose on the crest of a wave. Another wave and another pounded the deck of the vessel. Casey squinted as the sea water stung his eyes. Men, the ship's crew flashed into existence entering his vision, falling, scurrying to save the doomed ship as a giant wave crashed onto the deck washing the men overboard.

His heart raced. There was nothing he could do. "Why show me these images if there is nothing I can do to help?" he yelled into the storm. The door under the ship's top deck opened and a yellow light illuminated the entrance. Casey hooded his eyes and pulled his jacket tight, pushing against the wind, trying not to slip. He held onto the doorframe as the ship dipped to the starboard side. When he was about to enter the bowels of the ship, the vessel tipped the other way, tossing him down the stairs.

A young man dressed in simple clothes sat calmly and undisturbed by the thrashing waves. He was writing with a feathered pen in a journal. He looked up and dipped his quill. Casey imagined he was recording the ship's journey.

The scene turned into a carouse of images. Century after century went around and around with him at the center, scribing—he was the record-keeper through time. Never did he look the same. Sometimes he was black, sometimes Asian, sometimes white, and sometimes brown, but he was always a man.

Casey reached out to touch the walls of the ship. He was feeling dizzy, and the images vanished. It took him a moment to calm his breathing and collect himself as he stood in a pyramid, touching a wall, tracing with his fingers around etchings. And he knew they were his markings. So many lives he had lived, and in each one he had the dagger by his side. In Egypt, they had given it to him when he was a child, and he had worn it religiously.

Why show him all these past lifetimes? Wouldn't it be better to show his future, so he could take action for the greatest outcome? Or did it mean that he had no future, and he was about to die? Casey struggled to move. To return to his body and end the vision quest.

He felt as though he was still dreaming. Trapped inside the dream. He struggled to imagine the cave and return to his body. Inside his body, in the cave, he felt like he weighed a ton. His legs were riddled with pins and needles, and he carefully stretched them out, trying to make as little noise as possible. The others were in a trance or a meditative state. It would be bad if he startled anyone.

Dylan and Ruby had fallen asleep, along with a few others that weren't on the vision quest. Was this supposed to happen? A shiver raced up his spine. A shadow darkened the passageway from where they had entered. Something was just out of his sight. His heart pounded, concerned the preacher had found them.

Then Emma showed herself. Her clothes were dirty and torn, and her hair had fallen out in clumps, or she had pulled it out. Casey couldn't move his legs. Emma lunged at Rising Eagle's body, who was closest to her. Casey, with his mind, pushed her back, holding her suspended. Mentally, he shoved her, and she fell backwards into the passageway. Nobody stirred. She growled and lunged again. He held her at bay with his mind until he could get to his feet. Once on his feet, he mentally pushed her all the way back down the passageway to the intersection of the main tunnel.

Drawing his dagger, he chased after her. Suddenly, she turned and ran at his dagger. He pierced the double-edged blade deep into her chest. Her yellow eyes locked with his as he recited the prayer, and he watched her eyes turn white as she transformed back into Emma.

"Sorry," he whispered. "Sophia, take Emma's hand and keep her safe."

He crept back down the passageway and into the cave. He found an unused rolled-up mat to cover Emma's body and dragged her remains out of sight, down the dark passageway that stunk of urine.

Back at the cave, he stood in the doorway like a centurion protecting a holy space. Different combinations of colored auras filled the air, swirling around the circle, uniting them on a spiritual journey. Casey rejoined the circle but didn't think he could get back into a meditative state easily.

Carefully he unzipped his backpack and cringed as the zipper teeth opened. Everything sounded super loud. He expected the noise to break the peace, but no one seemed disturbed as he removed his sketchbook from his backpack. Consciously, he drew the circle of elders. It reminded him of the scribes, the record-keepers, in his vision. *I just hoped the pictures would not take on a life of their own like they had done back in London.*

Isabella's notebook—a flash of it sitting at the bottom of his bag abruptly entered his mind that he almost dropped his charcoal. Repeatedly, he blinked away the intrusion and resumed his drawing. Wiping the fragments of charcoal off the page, he surprised himself because he had drawn the cave without a ceiling and replaced it with stars and the constellation of Taurus with the bull and the seven-star cluster. He looked up to the ceiling and there were no stars, only dusty stone.

When Casey turned the page, Spirit Walker spoke, and he drew her face in detail, wishing he had color because shades of blue and green covered her. His ability to see auras was on hyperdrive. Nowadays, he had excellent control over it. He only saw auras when he wanted to see them, and everyone in the circle was a blaze of color. Not just the people sitting around the fire in the inner circle but everyone in the cave.

"My ancestors are from up there," Spirit Walker said, pointing to the ceiling, and as she did, the ceiling opened to a nighttime sky. Everything that she spoke of he could see forming in the stars.

"They are the people of the north, and one day we will all return home. Write the story of the northern star people and our seven sisters," Spirit Walker said, and with her eyes closed, turned her face towards him.

Casey sketched as much as he could. The sky filled with colors and a bright blue star twinkled amid the seven sisters—Pleiades. Casey could easily believe he was looking at a universal rainbow stretching from one side of the cosmos to the other. *This is what a cosmic aurora borealis would look like,* he thought. There must've been something in the potion they had all drunk for his senses to be this heightened. He let the warmth of the images float over him as he placed his pad and charcoal by his side. Jade's drumming and Spirit Walker's voice were in sync.

"The star people, our ancestors, have visited many times since the beginning of the fourth world, to remind us of where we came from and download into our beings new knowledge we are ready to accept. Land has sunk and waters have risen. The buffalo has come and gone. Tropical places have become cold and cold places have come hot. The sky is red with angry spirits," Spirit Walker said.

Spirit Walker floated out of her body and stood before Jade. "Listen to your heart, Raven Wings, and feel the DNA of your ancestors as they speak to you about the coming of the blue star. Then you will know it's time."

Her voice, and the low hum of the drum accompanied by the surge of chanting from the elders, left Casey mesmerized. He didn't even recall when he had joined the chanting that sounded like Tibetan monks on a mountaintop rather than deep inside a cave. As he chanted, his hand quickened and drew all that he saw. An eagle flew around the circle, chasing a rabbit. An armadillo curled itself into a ball as a bear tried to unfold it with its claws. Casey wondered what this all meant. In the middle of the fire, a phoenix rose and burst into sparkles. Casey watched where the embers fell, concerned they would fall upon those who have transcended into the cosmos. Luckily, they fell back into the fire. One landed on his paper and burned a small hole.

Sometimes, he thought Rising Eagle was watching him. He paused with his charcoal, staring into Rising Eagle's face, and saw two sets of eyes. The pair of eyes on Rising Eagle's forehead opened and looked straight at him. Casey pulled back his slouching body and tucked in his chin, shocked. Rising Eagle's whole body bent forward as if he was going to stand, but his physical body remained firmly on the ground as his spirit stood tall.

Spirit Walker's spirit returned to her body after she counseled Jade, rose again, and stood before him. Then Crazy Bear's spirit and Mingan's spirit joined the others before him. Everybody's spirit rose from their body and looked towards him. He felt like a small child, sitting on the floor while surrounded by adults. They parted for him to see.

The drumming grew faster. Jade's arm moved at a great speed that he could hardly even see when she hit the drum. Quickly Casey drew everything he saw. Spirit Walker lifted her arm and waved it across the fire. She pointed to the invisible screen. Stars appeared, and she drew her hand across the sky, joining the stars until a centurion appeared and disappeared. Then an archer wearing a belt with three sparkling diamonds, had two dogs behind him, battling a bull. It was a map of the stars, the three diamonds were Orin's belt. The bull represented Taurus, the archer Sagittarius, and the dogs connected to Sirius, but Casey didn't understand what it all meant.

The universe expanded and contracted like a beating heart. Casey flicked the pages over and frantically drew. Along the edge of each page, he recorded the colors of everything, wishing he had a pack of Derwent colored pencils because he saw multiple colors and multi-dimensions in full technicolor.

20

JADE: VISION QUEST

S oon as Jade and Spirit Walker had emerged from the fox tunnel, she was overjoyed to see the others had already arrived and had started a fire in the center of the cave. She never expected to return to the cave where she had met Chief Thundercloud only a week ago. Rising Eagle had sat in the very spot, along with the other elders. They had prepared for something, and it was as if they had waited for their arrival. There was plenty of room. And when Casey showed up, she relaxed a little.

Once Casey drank the potion Mingan prepared and settled next to her, she had let herself go to the rhythm of the drum. The chanting set the pace until the herbal mix took over, and Jade relaxed from head to toe. She visualized the memory stone with the turtle on it and imagined roots winding down through her body, anchoring her to the center of Mother Earth.

The leathery face of Gray Wolf took shape in her mind. He toked on a pipe, and she followed the trailing smoke up into the expansiveness of the universe that erupted before her, and the weight and movement of her physical body became nonexistent. She was pure energy. A spiritual being in the great cosmos.

In the darkness, a purple flower bloomed, filling up her visual field.

It melted like fresh paint on a canvas, revealing the Milky Way. Millions of stars sparkled like glitter, leading her into the vastness of the universe. Stars twinkled as she traveled through the cosmos. She recognized Sirius, Orion's belt, the Pleiades, over four hundred and forty light years away, and they were going to travel there in the blink of an eye on the day of ascension.

She wondered what was out there for them. What sort of life they could possibly live? She had heard the stories as a child, of the coming of the messiah and peace on earth, along with more traditional beliefs and even some irrational beliefs that we are from the stars and our DNA is part alien. But anything was possible. It was not for her to say what was wrong or right, or what could be. She couldn't imagine life anywhere else but on earth.

Jade pulled her thoughts back from the spiral of random thinking and focused on the vision quest. She had not yet learned the meaning and the memory sealed in the onyx with the maze. She wanted to know why the figure had moved into the maze as if on a journey. Patiently, she waited for a sign, but nothing came. Quietly, she waited for the vision quest to end. She had expected to travel far and wide, finding her last frontier deep within herself, but she felt like she was in limbo, waiting, frustrated. If she could not have a vision, she would let her mind wander.

Kevin. His beautiful soul filled her heart. Rolling green mounds, tall rock mountains, stars that looked like diamonds. Cool, crystal-clear blue water, full moons, and purple fields. Together they walked hand in hand on the water. Her bracelet was gone, but a ring around her wrist where it had been glowed, as if it was still there. It was like she was walking behind herself and Kevin, watching. She wondered if they were in heaven—had they died?

Suddenly, the sense of death washed over her, and she was filled with sadness. There was no image that shouted out a meaning or a metaphor. It was a feeling of knots in her solar plexus. A sense of danger—death. Jade pushed the thought and images away and focused on the situation at hand. They needed guidance on how they were going to defeat the evil entities that were growing in numbers daily. She had noticed Emma wasn't with Jackson. That was not a good sign. No one mentioned her absence, as if they all knew she wasn't coming back.

The hat was the first things she noticed in the darkness. Within her mind, the darkness became absolute. She was being watched. Snakes that hid inside the shadow of the preacher slithered into her mind. Battles between dark entities and the survivors were bloody. The survivors would die. They were no match for the evil coming out of the dark realm that would envelop the earth.

Time was of the essence. How were they going to get to the portals without dying? That was her biggest questions. And what was going to happen to the poor animals and nature? Again, she and Kevin walked in purple fields, when suddenly the image burned, smoldering around the edge until it became a blaze of fire. They burned from the inside out. They were the center of the image, and as they burned, so did the landscape.

It was too much for her to witness. Smothered with depression, she tried to clean her mind like a slate with her sleeve and focused on nothing, but a black onyx popped into her head. She wanted to stop!

Suddenly, she dropped back into her body, aware of her arms and legs. Her head was heavy, and her neck felt as if it could not support its weight. A breeze passed across her face. A push of energy had taken place in the cave. She felt the reverberation of the pulse. Feeling vulnerable, Jade willed her eyes to open as she slowed the beating of the drum, signifying the end of the vision quest for everyone.

Casey was drawing. There was no electromagnetic disturbance. Jade looked at his picture. Dead bodies scattered around the base of a rock mountain. She stared questioningly into his eyes. He closed the sketchbook.

"Show me. Show us all," Jade said, when everyone came out of the meditation.

Casey glanced around, and everyone looked back at him.

Jade expected Spirit Walker or Rising Eagle to say something. Mingan and Crazy Bear also stared at Casey. It was making him uncomfortable.

"You have a message for us?" Rising Eagle said.

Casey shook his head, breaking eye contact, and took out his dagger and held it over the fire, cleansing the blade.

No one spoke. Silence. Waiting. Casey was the only one moving restlessly. She had to save him from the awkward silence. "How did your meditation go?" Jade asked.

"Not so good," Casey said.

"Why's that?" Mingan said.

Charlie made eye contact with her, and it was like she was speaking to her with her mind. "What did you draw?" Charlie asked.

Casey's shoulders relaxed a little, and the redness in his face subsided. Something had happened while they were on a vision quest. He brought out the sketchbook and started at the back, turning the pages until he reached the first drawing he had completed while they were meditating. The images told a story that intrigued the elders. They nodded to each other as if they were in on a secret that she and Casey were not part of. Jade expected them to interpret his images. She noticed he didn't show or mention the last picture, which she had glimpsed as she came out of her shambled vision quest. "What about the last picture?" Jade said.

He shook his head as if saying, "No, you don't want to see that one."

"Show us," Rising Eagle said.

"Hmm . . . ," the elders said one after another and nodding their heads up and down.

"This one is a problem." Rising Eagle tapped on the sketch with bodies scattered around the base of Bear Lodge, wendigos climbing up the side, a dark storm gathering above, with trailing whispers of clouds that looked like dark flying entities. He showed only the elders before returning it to Casey, who quickly stashed it away into his backpack.

"What did you see, Raven Wings?" Mingan said.

Her cheeks burned hot, and she imagined they were as red as Casey's had been. Her vision had been so ambiguous that she didn't know where to start. She told them about the images and feelings she had in sequence.

"There are pathways to two futures, and you, Kevin and your friends are at the center of them both," Spirit Walker said.

Jade didn't know what to say but "Why?"

"It is not for us to know, or we would have had the same vision," Rising Eagle said.

Each one shared their visions. Jade imagined Casey was feeling like she did. The bearer of bad news and clueless as to what was to be done about it. And how was Kevin and the others involved? The further she progressed along this journey, the more confused she became. She wasn't so certain about anything anymore. Her best sense of security was with the belief in entropy and negentropy. That is what she had started with a year ago, the possibility that a shattered bottle, chaos, could be transformed into a mosaic creating order for chaos. She had to hold on to that belief that a cosmic order could still come from the darkness of chaos. But it can't work in reverse. *We must move forward into the future to change the outcome of the past events.* Her head was hurting.

"Listen to your heart. Not your head," Mingan said.

He looked too young to be giving her pearls of wisdom. She felt a little embarrassed at the thought. She was letting his good looks and youthful appearance get in the way. Inside, his spirit was old and wise. She tried to shut off the faucet to the theories in her head and find the rhythm of her heart.

"We need to keep moving. I don't think there is anywhere safe from the preacher and his kind," Jade said.

"We shall eat off the land and fast from meat," Rising Eagle said.

"Who had eaten from the meat of the hunters?" Spirit Walker said.

Three people raised their hands, and Ruby.

"I'm not sure? I ate some meat," Ruby said.

Dylan whispered in her ear.

"No, that's right. I didn't eat any meat," Ruby said.

Her mother tilted her chin upwards. "Are you sure, missy?" Sue asked, sounding afraid for her daughter.

Ruby whispered in her mother's ear.

"Ruby said he is going to kill us like he killed Dylan's daddy if we ate the meat?" Sue said, jerking her head towards Casey.

"Do you have a place for serpents in your belly?" Spirit Walker asked Dylan.

Jade saw Casey clutch his stomach and his face turn into a sour expression, as if lemon was squeezed into his mouth.

Dylan sat back and cried. Sue comforted him the best she could, rubbing his arm and cuddling him to her side.

The elders looked at each other as if telepathically talking. The group grew nervous the longer the question was unanswered.

"I didn't kill his daddy. The spirit of the wendigo did. I killed the wendigo and freed his daddy's soul," Casey said.

"Casey speaks true. And you will have to do it again if anyone else turns," Rising Eagle said, making eye contact with every person in the cave until they all understood.

"We should rest and eat before we begin our journey to Bear Lodge," said Rising Eagle.

* * *

JADE WAITED until she was alone with Casey to ask about Emma. He told her what had happened. "I'm sorry you had to do that. Should we go back to the campsite so Kevin can find us, or should we go with them to Bear Lodge?"

"It's up to you. I'm good either way," Casey said.

"If we go on, we might not see our families again. Kevin is the only way to get back to them," Jade said.

"Until we all ascend. Then it won't matter where you are because we will all be going to the same place," Casey said.

"I don't know which is the right choice. We came here to warn the people and give them the message. We were just messengers, nothing more. It's up to them to get to their ascension point. It's not our responsibility," Jade said.

"What's wrong?" Casey asked her. "You're not telling me every-thing," Casey said.

"My vision and the last picture you drew could be . . . never mind. What does your heart tell you we should do?" said Jade.

"My heart has one goal, and that's getting back with Sophia," Casey said.

Jade wanted to argue with him, but she didn't know what to say because if they all believed in the ascension, then he was right to think it didn't matter if they went with these good folk to Bear Lodge or went back and waited for Kevin; he would achieve his one goal—to be with Sophia again, no matter which choice he made.

"How far is it to Bear Lodge?"

"A month's walk," Mingan said.

"Why don't we drive?" Casey said.

"We believe we should walk. It's all about the journey," Mingan said.

Jade was thinking, believing they should drive, but she was wondering if that was because it suited her needs or theirs. It will take too long if they walk. Jade dusted her cheek with the end of her hair, thinking. Casey waited for her to speak. Mingan turned away and conversed with the elders.

Jade tossed her ponytail behind her head and spoke softly to Casey. "We need to check out Bear Lodge. What if it is a trap?" Jade said.

Casey's eyebrows dipped in the middle. "Why do you think that? Don't you think the elders are in tune enough to know if it is a trap or not?"

"You're drawing. We should scout ahead and check it out. If it's all good, we can then leave to meet Kevin and head back to estate and Stonehenge, once we know they'll be safe and ready for ascension," Jade said.

"We could head back to town and get a couple of motorcycles and be there in a few days. We could be back here in a week. Surely, Kevin would periodically check the campsite until we return," Casey said.

Charlie, Mingan, and Crazy Bear pulled away from a group discussion with the elders. "We will go with you. Jackson will remain here as a tracker," Mingan said to Jade.

"Where's Emma?" Jackson said.

Casey looked awkwardly at Crazy Bear but couldn't make eye contact with Jackson.

"She turned," Casey said, turning away from them.

"What do you mean *she turned*?" Jackson said, pulling at Casey's arm, preventing him from leaving.

"Let him go," Crazy Bear said, stepping into Jackson.

"Get out of my way," Jackson said to Crazy Bear.

Crazy Bear looked down at the ground before connecting with Jackson's eyes. For at least ten seconds, they just stared. "You know how I felt about Emma. I saw her turn. She's gone."

"No. I don't believe you. She was frightened and ran off. You frightened her!" Jackson said, pushing Casey against the wall.

"What are you doing? Stop this, Jackson. He is not your enemy," Rising Eagle said.

Rising Eagle studied Casey's face. The old man nodded with understanding. "Did you free her soul?" Rising Eagle asked.

Casey tilted his head in slight agreement.

"Well then, there's no more to be said. Our beloved sister Emma is waiting for us with Great Spirit. We will see her again at the time of ascension," Rising Eagle said. He looked so old. He didn't look like he was going to make the trip to Bear Lodge.

"I hear the hissing. You must be on your way," Spirit Walker said to Mingan and Jade.

The hissing. She hears the hissing. "Spirit Walker, what do you mean by hissing?" Jade asked.

"These are his days, the days of the devil. Hisss, Hisss, hisss, hunger and pain, the infernals shall slither into your minds again. Poisoning your thoughts, feeding on your fear, luring you into the darkness, boiling your blood as he nears," Spirit Walker said.

"Hisss, hisss, hisss hunger and pain, feast from the vessel—starvation is the game. Great Turtle taught that to me," Jade said, ending the verse.

"As my mother taught me, and her mother taught her. If you hear the hissing, then you are its adversary, as I am. Go, Raven Wings, hurry and return to us with your healing magic," Spirit Walker said.

Mingan picked up his bow and arrows and handed Jade her staff. "I found this and thought you might need it back."

The moment Jade touched the staff, there were a few seconds when they both had their hands holding it, and energy ran through her body. They had energetically locked forces and she couldn't let go of the staff. It had become a conductor. She felt the energy go all the way around her body and into her crystal wand that was in her back pocket. She could feel its tip heating. Charlie opened her hand and small white butterflies flew into the air between them, breaking the connection between her and Mingan, because he let go.

What the hell was that? she thought, shaking her hand. There was only one other person who made her feel like that, and it was Kevin. For a second, she felt like she had just cheated on Kevin. Ashamed, she couldn't look at Casey. She hugged Spirit Walker and headed into the fox's tunnel, throwing her backpack and drum in front of her, along with her staff. She didn't wait for the others to follow.

"Wait up!" Casey yelled into the hole.

"Where's she going?" Casey asked Spirit Walker.

"She knows a shortcut that leads to the upper Catawba Falls," Spirit Walker said.

Jade heard someone enter the tunnel behind her. Unless they called for her to stop, she was going to keep going until she was out and under the waterfall. The bats may have returned and settled in for the day. She'd have to make sure that there were no surprises. It would be extremely unfortunate if one of them got bitten by the vampire bats.

Jade wondered about the creatures that she had seen in the realm of lost souls and wondered if they, too, would be part of the eternal night that was being forged. She didn't like the idea of running into them in this realm. The wendigo and the preacher's kind were enough, not even to mention the shadow man that they had seen at the estate. Oh God, and then there were the giants that looked like a cross between a cyclops with three eyes and an ugly orc, back at the estate. She had forgotten about the giants—shit! She had to get back. Thank goodness they only had the wendigo and the preacher to deal with.

As she wriggled her bag and drum forward, she wondered how Kevin was getting on and if he had found the others at Stonehenge yet. She regretted telling him to go and she would see him again in the stars after the ascension—worst-case scenario. What had she been thinking? She had been hungry for knowledge to learn from Gray Wolf —Mingan—the old ways. But she didn't know Mingan was Gray Wolf then. Mingan's energy had purely taken her, not realizing it drew her to him because he was her teacher.

She felt so stupid and juvenile. Kevin was right; the elders were right. She needed to listen to her heart—and her spirit. Jade wanted to go home, back to the estate, and fight the giants and the shadow men to keep their families safe before the ascension.

She stepped out of the cave and into the waterfall, letting the cold water splash onto her head, soaking her clothes and cleansing her aura.

21

CASEY: THE DEVIL'S COMMUNION

Casey saw the beauty in every living thing as he emerged from the cave and looked down at the water below. Even the snakes that wriggled through the water and bathed on the sand looked magical and glistened in the light. He searched for the sun, wanting to know the time of day. The air was crisp, like a spring morning. He felt so calm and in love with the surrounding beauty. He let himself lift off the ledge where Jade stood looking at the waterfall as he rappelled himself with ease and floated into the air. The higher he went, the more he saw. He held onto the straps of his backpack as he travelled higher and higher at a slow pace to take in the beauty of the trees. Everything looked harmless and glorious. He could hear angels singing.

A twinge in his solar plexus tensed his body, and he stopped in midair, as a sweet scent of jasmine floated through the atmosphere. It would have been divine if it wasn't hiding a rotting smell of dead animals. A pale gray fog hung over part of the forest. It came from the direction of the campsite. Casey followed the stench, but before he went, he heard Jade's voice as if she was far, far away.

"Where are you going now?" she yelled.

"I'll be back," he called down to her. She looked tiny in the distance.

The smell grew potent, and the singing grew stronger as he entered the fog. His mood shifted. It was the same church hymn as the first and the second time he called on the preacher. He tried to catch the words; they were unrecognizable, a different language, like nothing he had ever heard. The rhythm was what he recognized. It was hypnotic—he feared it was the devil's song. A demon-summoning rhythm, which Casey didn't want stuck in his head.

His blood ran cold as he got closer. The fog cleared, and parts of the forest looked dark—burned in the preacher's wake. In between the trees, he glimpsed the choir and their maestro holding up snakes in the air and dancing in ecstasy. The congregation was heading in the same direction as the community and the elders.

Dead trees and plants surrounded their church site. Casey moved a little closer and saw movement in the trees. Wendigos, he imagined, cloaked, perched in the trees like guard dogs. Casey hovered over the trees and looked for a safe place to lower himself to the ground for a closer look. He moved cautiously. Last time, with Jade, they had passed through the fog and into another time in space or the dark realm.

Mingan, Crazy Bear, and Charlie had seen dismembered bodies and the hat on a stick, but he and Jade had seen a mirror of what he was seeing now. The congregation had grown from a dozen or more to twice that. They stood shoulder to shoulder, moving in a hypnotic wave as one, while selected parishioners held snakes and danced and rejoiced. They weren't too far from the cave where the elders were.

What the hell were they doing here? Casey could feel himself getting frustrated. *What the hell*, he thought and walked out of the brush and stood at the back of the congregation. He waited until someone spotted him. It was like a reverse stadium wave as the body of worshipers came to a stop. The snakes dangled at the side of their legs and wrapped themselves around their arms like bracelets. No one spoke. Nervously, he moved, pushing his shoulders back and his chest out. He lifted his head. "You are not safe," Casey said. He watched to see if his words registered, but all he got were blank stares.

"Why do you insist on seducing my congregation, devil?" demanded the preacher.

Casey wanted to know what was going on inside the congregation's heads. The only way he was going to do that was to make skin-to-skin contact or touch something they were holding. Someone's hand or hymn book. Inspecting the books more closely, he noticed they were upside down and the cross behind the preacher was upside down, too. How could they not notice? He had to touch someone, but who? The closest person to him was a middle-aged woman, dressed as if she had rushed straight from work to a service, but her hair was matted and unkempt. Dirty fingernails clutched the hymn book. The books looked worn, tattered embossed covers, spins peeling away as though centuries old. Casey was worried he had gone back in time.

Enough stalling, he thought and grabbed the woman's elbow. Her words sounded English but jumbled, like a record playing backwards. Through the woman's eyes, he saw everything change. Everyone looked clean and there were no snakes. The congregation appeared genuinely loving and holy. At the altar was a man that resembled the image many recognized as Jesus, and behind him, a crucifix. Casey released his hold on the woman, and the world changed back to his reality. He reconnected with the woman and the same images presented themselves to him. Two realities existed. Theirs and his. Which one was real?

While Casey held onto the woman's elbow, she saw from his perspective and reacted to the surrounding horror. "Stay calm," Casey said as he let go of her elbow again. "I'm not the devil." He took hold of her once more. In a gentle voice, Casey leaned into the woman and said, "I mean you no harm, but please tell everyone what you see, so you can be free of this demon that stands before you, claiming to be the Son of God."

"Please let me go," the woman said, trying to free herself from Casey.

"Tell everyone, please," Casey urged, exasperated.

"We are all disheveled," the woman began, her voice trembling, "and the man before us is not our beloved. He is dark. Shadows cover his face and snakes fill his belly. He's wearing a black suit, a white shirt, a black collar, and a black derby hat. A fat pale green snake sleeps upon his shoulders and more gather at his feet. Ghostly dark gray figures stand all around us, feeding on our essence, and the cross, oh—" the woman stopped and covered her mouth.

"What's your name?" Casey asked, as if they were the only two in the woods.

"Sophia," the woman said, smiling.

At the sound of her name, he stepped back away from the woman. It unnerved him. *There are many people in the world called Sophia.* He gathered his emotions and touched her elbow again. "He can't hurt you. Finish telling them what you see."

Reluctantly she placed the old hymnbook to her chest and said, "The cross is upside down, and we are not in a cathedral, we are in the woods—it's damp and surrounded by an infernal fog. It smells of death. Please stop this torture; take away these terrifying images." The woman begged.

"He shows you nothing but lies," the preacher said.

The preacher was enjoying himself. Casey let go of the woman's arm and touched the first person in the next row. "What I show is the truth. What is your name?" Casey asked.

"Sophia," the next woman answered.

Casey pulled his hand away and looked back at the first woman he had touched. He moved to the next row and touched the first person in the row. "What is your name?"

"Sophia," the man said.

"What is your name?" the preacher intoned, raising his hands.

Every woman, man, and child cried out, "Sophia!"

The preacher motioned with his hands for everyone to take their seats upon the fallen tree. Once they had all seated, a woman dressed in a long white gown came forward. She wore a cross upside down and had been carving meat off a blistering human leg on a spit. The preacher nodded, and it was as if everyone, and everything, connected. The snakes moved outward from the preacher's feet and circled the parishioners, heading towards Casey.

"Ignore the voice of the devil. Step forward, those who wish to receive the body and blood of Christ," the preacher said.

The Satanic nun holding the plate of meat stood by the preacher. As each person stepped forward, he performed his twisted idea of the Christian sacrament with the freshly cooked meat. Horrified, Casey backed away, accepting he could not help the people in the clutches of the preacher. For a fleeting moment, he thought he saw the first woman he touched recoil. "Come with me," Casey said.

"It's too late," she whispered, joining the end of the line.

"It's never too late," Casey said.

"This isn't my first communion. Whatever the devil is serving, I have already consumed. I just pray one day I will return to God," the woman said.

Casey touched his dagger. "Come with me and be free."

"I cannot," she said, turning away from him.

"But why?" he said, pulling her aside.

"For he is my husband, and I am his bride."

He couldn't leave without severing the hold that the preacher had over them. He needed help, but what? A chorus of rattlesnakes warned him that if he moved, they would strike. He couldn't help them if he was dead. Casey created a magnetic pulse around his feet, giving him a buffer from the rattlers, and boosted himself up into the air.

"The devil runs! He is no match for your faith," the preacher cried.

Casey looked down at the parishioners lined up for communion. Soon, every one of them would turn into a wendigo. He shook his head and returned to the others.

At the bottom of the waterfall, the others had waited for Casey.

"Where did you go? We've been waiting for ten minutes," Jade said.

Casey couldn't help but notice Charlie's impatient stance. He wondered what they had been talking about. "I saw the preacher. His congregation has multiplied. We have to help them," Casey said.

"You didn't confront him, did you?" Jade said.

He gave her a look that told her he had.

"Why? That's reckless. You're going to get yourself killed," Jade said.

"He's a big boy. I'm sure he can look after himself," Charlie said.

"He can, but that's not the point," Jade said.

Mingan stepped into Casey. "Come with me."

Casey followed.

"Tell me what you saw," Mingan asked.

Casey told him from the beginning: about the trees, the fog, the upside-down cross and the fake figure of Christ, and the communion.

"We can't help them now. It's like the woman said. She has already taken the devil's communion. They will turn," Mingan said.

"Yes. But I can still save their souls and free them from the evil spirit of the wendigo and the preacher," Casey said.

"How many did you say there were?" Mingan said.

"Maybe twenty-six or thirty people. We were supposed to save those people and get them to the point of ascension. Dammit," Casey said, frustrated. "Why don't people listen?"

"They can't hear if the evil spirit is speaking to them," Mingan said.

Crazy Bear had been listening behind Casey. "We can't kill them in cold blood."

"No. We will have to wait until they have taken on the form of the wendigo to kill them and free their souls," Casey said.

"We can't just hang around and wait for them to turn," Charlie said.

"She's right. We have a plan," Jade said and nodded at Crazy Bear.

"We're going to hike to Moto Bikes in town and get some wheels to ride north to the Bear Lodge. We'll have to stay overnight in Nashville and then ride out first light. We might make it to Bear Lodge by nightfall, if we push it. It's an easy twenty-four hours," Crazy Bear said.

Casey stepped back, rubbing his stubbled chin.

"Why don't I head off to Bear Lodge alone?" Casey said.

"Here you go again," Jade said.

"Hear him out," Mingan said.

"If I see trouble, I can come back and tell you faster than all of us riding on motorcycles. But the elders and your community have to get a move on," Casey said.

"Why?" Charlie asked.

"The preacher and his congregation, I think they're heading in the same direction," Casey said.

"What would be at Bear Lodge for them?" Jade said.

"We also known it as Devils Tower, right? There's a lot you don't know," Charlie said.

"I'll go with you," Jade said to Casey.

"I can't carry you all the way. It's too long a distance. I don't even know how long I can stay in the air," Casey said.

"You won't have to carry me. I have wings. I can take on the form of a raven."

"How many times have you transformed into a raven?" Charlie asked with her hand on her hip.

"Once. But I know I can do it again. Give me a few hours. Mingan, you can help me, right?" Jade said.

"I can help you, Raven Wings, but you're not ready for such a big journey. It will take practice, and time; we don't have time on our side," Mingan said.

It started rained again. It poured down soon it would become a flood. Casey was getting fed up with being out in the elements all the time. Everything was constantly changing. Thunder rolled through the clouds and lightning cracked, striking a tree. They scattered in all directions, out of the path of the falling tree. Casey didn't move. He looked up at the tree and it stopped in mid-fall. He eased it down to the ground.

Jade cried up to the sky, "Enough," and the rain stopped in motion. It froze in place, as did the wind, leaves, and the movement of the clouds. A crack of lightning still illuminated across the sky.

Jade avoided eye contact. Casey reached out his hand and touched the water. It hadn't frozen. He parried the rain droplets to the side, and they fell to the ground. Never had he seen Jade do something like this. But how? Jade waved her hand in the air, and the clouds parted.

"Jade?" Casey said.

"Kevin told me not to, until I worked out how, and why, I have this gift to control nature," Jade said. She had her hands on her hips and walked in a circle, as if contemplating her actions. "If I can do it, why not do it?" Jade said.

"It's not for your pleasure," Mingan said.

"So, who's speaking now? Gray Wolf, my teacher, or Mingan?" Jade snapped, rattled.

Strange vibes filled the air. The colors in Jade's aura faded quickly from soft blue greens to orange and red.

"Turn into the raven," Mingan said, challenging her.

Jade closed her eyes and controlled her breathing. Her aura pulsed in and out as she tried to generate the energy to shift into the form of a raven. But she was still angry. A raven flashed into her aura but never materialized. Casey's eyes widened as Mingan's aura became a wolf and Charlie's a giant butterfly and Crazy Bear turned into the biggest grizzly he had ever seen. "Okay, everyone. Stop," Casey said.

Jade struggled. She crossed her arms protectively and looked down at her feet.

"You depleted your energy. You channeled it frivolously to suit your needs. That's not the way," Mingan said. The wolf towered over him.

Casey wished everyone else could see what he could see.

Mingan left Jade to contemplate on his words. "Would you like to know what I see?" Mingan said to Casey.

He had forgotten Mingan saw auras too.

"I see a white owl in your aura, like the bear in Noah's, and the butterfly in Charlie's. It is strong, powerful, and wise, not like Jade's raven. That's weak, unformed, and immature," Mingan said.

Casey hadn't heard Noah referred to by his first name, only his spirit name. The hurt in Jade's eyes was too much for him to look at. Instead, he took her hands in his. He held her pain to let her know she wasn't alone. "I won't be long," Casey said.

"Was that necessary?" Casey said to Mingan.

"Sometimes you need to be ruthless," Mingan said.

Crazy Bear turned his wet hand over, then wiped it on the side of his leg. "The thing you did with the rain was pretty neat," he said to Jade.

"While Casey is away, why don't we track the preacher and his congregation, making sure that they don't go after the elders and the rest of the others?" Charlie suggested.

Mingan stepped back and brought his hands to his mouth as if he breathed into them. "If we track them and they find us, they will kill and eat us."

It was up to Casey. Only he could free the souls. They were wasting time. "I'll be back in less than forty-eight hours. If I'm not, you'll know it's not safe at Bear Lodge," Casey said.

He hugged Jade before accelerating upward into the sky, into the parted clouds that Jade had pushed aside. He knew she didn't do it for herself; she did it for them all.

Once above the clouds, he felt the warmth of the sun. Casey headed in the direction he had once flown in a plane, for a state sports event, in Montana. He wasn't a swimmer or a baller; he had been a high and long jumper. *Ha, ha. Maybe I've been using this powers all along,* he thought as he looked down at the ground and sped up towards the horizon and Devils Tower.

22

JADE: BENT ARROW – SEE NO EVIL

Jade's cheeks warmed as she continued to ignore Mingan. She felt childish but would not give in. Charlie had transformed into a gorgeous huge butterfly. Her wings were shades of violet and yellow. Slowly, she dwindled to a quarter of the size and looked like a giant moth. Mingan had instructed Charlie to go back to the elders to warn them of the preacher and the need to wait a day before heading off. That would keep them out of the preacher's reach by a day.

"What are you doing?" Jade asked.

"Sticking to the original plan. Scouting ahead to Bear Lodge. Casey may need our help. If Casey is right and the preacher is moving west of the river, then we should stay on the other side to pass them by unnoticed," Mingan explained and started walking.

It worried her that Mingan thought Casey was going to need help. He knew something that he wasn't saying. The fog rolled in off the river, hiding what was on the other side. She searched the treetops for the wendigo because she constantly felt like she was being watched. It took all her inner strength not to run, but if she did, she didn't know where she was going. Jade took her wand out of her back pocket and shoved it down the front of her pants so she could feel it against her stomach. Her anxiety grew the further away they got from the elders.

Many times, she turned quickly, thinking she could hear phantom footsteps.

Mingan must have noticed because he stopped and searched the dense woods around them and walked behind her, letting Crazy Bear lead the way. She was glad when they came out onto the road. She walked down the middle because it felt as though they were still being followed. The clouds streamed down from the sky as if raining, but no rain fell. Jade wasn't as tall as Crazy Bear, and she needed to take extra steps to keep the pace. She was sticky and tired.

Two hours of silence seemed like four. Clouds gathered and parted. Jade monitored them. Their behavior was unusual, and she didn't know why. They seemed to cluster. Jade adjusted her drum on her back. The straps were chafing under her arms in the humidity.

They reached the town and were surprised nobody had broken into the motorcycle store. Crazy Bear jimmied the locks and opened the roller door. He saw the concern on her face.

"It's alright. This place belonged to Emma and Jackson's family. They're cool," Crazy Bear said, casting his eyes down.

"I'm sorry about Emma. You'll see her again," Jade said.

"Yeah, I know. There's so many people dead to catch up with once this is all over," Crazy Bear said.

"Finally, Raven Wings," Mingan said.

"Finally, what?" Jade snapped. She knew her voice was too harsh and challenging, but she couldn't help it.

"You rebalanced your energy. When your energy is unbalanced, your arrow is bent. Your aim is the arrow, and your intention is the arrowhead. You must have a straight arrow for it to travel with the intensity you desire. When you do, you become one with the universal energy, and you will reach your target," Mingan said.

She almost asked him how he had come to that conclusion when she remembered he could see and read auras.

"Your heart chakra opened and poured into your aura, balancing the displaced anger," Mingan said.

She felt a little embarrassed.

"There's no hiding around this guy," Crazy Bear said.

"Then why won't you teach me to fly? Spend half an hour with me and we could save hours flying to Devils Tower," Jade said.

Mingan laughed. "You think you can learn how to shift your energy into a bird, then maintain that state for hours on end? Even if you could transform into the raven, your mind will wander, and you will fall out of the sky and break into a million pieces as you hit the ground."

"But I have my wand—I can heal? It's not okay to just dismiss me. I want to try!" Jade said, frustrated.

"Already your energy is out of balance," Mingan said.

"I want to learn," Jade said, and as she did, she felt as though Great Turtle's hand was on her shoulder to steady her. She knew that meant she needed to slow down and breathe.

"If you want to learn, first you must expand your awareness, become conscious of what you are focusing on. Where are you directing your energy? For the last two hours, you focused on the clouds, the possibility of the horror lying in wait in the bushes along the side of the road, and me," Mingan said.

She felt ashamed and awkward that he knew she had been angry at him for not talking during the past two hours. Crazy Bear had stopped actively listening and began sitting on the motorcycles trying to pick the one he wanted to ride out of the showroom.

"Even now you're not focused on what I am saying. Your pride and ego have got the better of you once again. Balance your energy. Expand your awareness. What's in the peripheral field? What is behind you? And what is within you? Then the universe will grant your wish to fly," Mingan said.

She thought of Kevin, and suddenly Mingan's words made sense. It was something Tim had said about Kevin. Kevin's aware that his awareness expands. He knows, most of the time, whose emotions he is feeling, if not his own. Not much takes away his intense focus. She felt the anger towards Mingan shift. Her energy flowed out of her feet and into the ground, balancing her like a tree. She felt strong and flexible.

"Good. Sit with the energy. Maintain that balance," Mingan said, walking towards Crazy Bear.

Jade wandered over to the smaller bikes because she had little experience on motorcycles and had only had a few turns on Casey's back at the estate. She picked a scooter and a protective jacket with zippers on the side for ventilation. She was going to need it. Crazy Bear chose a chopper. He looked like a badass. Mingan picked out a pink open face helmet for her.

She smiled. "No, not quite my style, but thank you."

She knew he was baiting her, trying to force her out of the balanced state she had achieved and maintained for the past fifteen minutes. He put the helmet down and took her hand. Their bracelets pulsed with energy as they touched.

"See what can happen when you align with your higher self and the universe?" Mingan said.

The combined energy of their bracelets joined, creating one large golden bracelet that circled around them. The etchings on their bracelets combined into one continuous Aramaic sentence.

Suddenly, she knew information was downloading into their auras. She felt like she was getting an upgrade that would slowly filter through the layers of her aura and into her chakras. Mingan released her hand, and the combined ring around their wrists faded.

Jade said nothing as she picked a black open-face helmet and a pair of sunglasses and secured her drum on her back. The straps were a little tight, but she was just going to put up with it. She would not leave it, or her memory stones and medicine pouch. Mingan stood next to a small motorcycle that had saddle bags and a windshield. She hadn't noticed the bike before. *It would be a good choice*, she thought. Mingan wasn't getting any protective gear—Jade and Crazy Bear were ready to go. Mingan had merely watched on.

"I'll see you at Bear Lodge," Mingan said.

It took him only a second to transform into a gray-white wolf the size of a pony. He had whispers of purple energy around him, like ghostly vapors, and she wondered how solid he really was. He looked solid, but she imagined he could easily turn into pure spiritual essences in a heartbeat. Mingan left no time for them to protest.

At first, they wondered if they should wait for Charlie to catch up or go on without her. Jade tried to adjust the straps that were digging into the top of her arms. She looked at the bike she thought Mingan had chosen for her and took it instead of the scooter. Crazy Bear helped her take off the drum and tuck it into the saddlebag.

She was a lot more comfortable with the drum in the side saddle bag on the left and the memory stones and medicine pouch on the right. She moved her arms freely, and the windshield would protect her from the bugs splatting on to her face. *Maybe I should've picked a closed-face helmet,* she thought. She bet when they stopped for a rest, Crazy Bear would pick bugs off his face—his bike didn't have a windshield.

They climbed onto the motorcycles and headed down the road. Crazy Bear led the way, dodging rabbits and deer. At first, Jade was nervous and couldn't get comfortable on the bike. But once she leaned to lean her body and the bike into the corners, the ride became smooth as if they were one. It felt like she was flying once she got into the rhythm and enjoyed the curves.

She thought about what Mingan had said and focused on her awareness. As she did, she felt an expansion of her energy. At first, it scared her, and she pulled out by narrowing her focus to what was just ahead. But once she felt safe and let go, she entered the universal energy that was everywhere, and she flowed along like being lifted towards the shore by a gentle current.

THEY GOT a few hours under their belts before the sun settled. Heading into Knoxville, a zebra ran across the road. Crazy Bear pulled on his brakes, just missing the first zebra, followed by two others. It crossed the road in two strides. Crazy Bear's back wheel drifted forward. He was going to slide sideways into the last zebra. Crazy Bear's leg was under the bike as he clipped the back of the zebra's legs. It stumbled and regained its stride. Jade pulled her bike up and veered to the side of the road. Her heart pounded in her chest harder than she had ever hit the drum. She couldn't believe how quickly she had stopped without going over the handlebars or running over Crazy Bear and his bike. She kicked down the side stand and raced over to Crazy Bear.

"Help me get this thing off me," Crazy Bear said.

Jade looked at the bike and wondered how she was going to get the bike up. It was at least a couple of hundred pounds if not more. She could not lift it—she would need leverage.

"What are you doing?" Crazy Bear said.

Jade turned the ignition into the off position, even though the bike had stalled. She pulled down the side stand. Went to the other side of the bike and held the handle and the brake, before crouching down and pushing her back against the gas tank, slowly edging her feet back, lifting the bike off Crazy Bear's leg. She held the bike upright and slowly let it settle onto the side stand.

"Are you alright?" Jade said.

Crazy Bear checked his leg. "Where do you think the zebra came from?" Crazy Bear lifted the leg of his jeans.

Even though his jeans were intact, his leg was grazed and bloody. "That looks painful," she said.

"It is. The rest of me is fine." He locked eyes with her, and a grin grew across his face. "That was pretty awesome. Shit! I'm lucky I didn't go over the top of the handlebars. Things would have gone very wrong, very quickly," Crazy Bear said.

"Did you sense anything beforehand? I reckon you braked a second before the first zebra ran out onto the road," Jade said. She, too, had sensed a need to brake.

"Yeah, I did. I just didn't know why. If I hadn't, I would have hit the first one head-on and the others would've piled up on top. Poor zebra," Crazy Bear said.

"Hold still," Jade said, getting her wand out. The crystal glowed a vibrant emerald over Crazy Bear's leg.

"It feels cool. The burning of the gravel rash has subsided," Crazy Bear said.

Jade left the wand in place over his leg for a little longer, then pulled it away to check the progress of the healing. She took a tissue out of her pocket, wiped the blood off his leg, and revealed a smooth patch of skin where the wound had been.

"You don't think that wand of yours could make the hair on my leg grow back, too?"

"It'll grow back," Jade said, pocketing her wand.

Jade searched the other side of the road for the zebra in case it needed healing. She walked a few yards into the brush but saw no sign of the zebras.

"How's the bike?" Jade asked Crazy Bear as he climbed back on his bike.

"There's no serious damage, just a scratched tail pipe and a bent footrest that I've bent back into place," Crazy Bear said.

He rested his foot on the damaged peg that still looked like it could do with some straightening. Jade put on her helmet, and they traveled a few miles down the road when Crazy Bear pulled into a motel in Knoxville – a Red Roof Inn, down and across the road from the gas station, where they had rooms on the ground floor.

They rode up to the lobby, hoping it would be unlocked and climbed off their bikes. Unclipping her helmet, Jade noticed something just outside her field of vision. She turned around. Off to her left were three monkeys eating strawberries. Hear no evil, see no evil, and speak no evil came to mind. She looked at Crazy Bear, making sure he had them too. "Do you think they're the valet drivers slacking off on the job?" Jade asked, smiling, trying to chase away the fear that was building inside her.

"There has to be a zoo close by. Someone probably let the animals free," Crazy Bear said.

Jade looked around and in-between the trees. "What other animals do you think are out there?" Jade could feel her mind drifting to the possibilities of lions and tigers. Something moved in the bush. Crazy Bear put his finger to his lips and moved towards the sound. She was feeling skittish. She shook her hands by her side, trying to relax the tension building in her upper body, when a meerkat and its friends popped up their heads, giving her a fright.

"You fellows are a long way from home," Crazy Bear said.

"Well, this looks like the place to be. It's all happening around here," Jade said, catching her breath and unclipping the saddlebags.

The motel was unlocked. She shifted the saddlebags over her forearm, wishing she had brought the staff rather than leaving it behind. She tiptoed on the carpet, and knowing it was pointless to be tiptoeing, she continued, thinking she should have left the bags on the bike in case they needed to run for it. Standing just inside the motel lobby, she looked down at the ground and expanded her energy outward, increasing her field of awareness, sensing what else was in the atmosphere.

A slight touch of an unseen presence made the hairs on the back of her neck stand up. She paused, analyzing the energy, friend or foe? She bowed her head down to her chest and asked her heart. She saw a flash of green and thought whether it was friend or foe, it wouldn't harm them right now.

"I'm picking up something in the room, but I think it will be okay for us to stay here," Crazy Bear said, jumping over the reception counter and checking out the keys. "You want your own room?" he asked her.

"I think we should stick together. Why did you jump over? Why not just go around?" Jade said.

Crazy Bear grinned. "I feel energized."

"Why did Mingan go off on his own?" Jade said.

Crazy Bear searched through the room's numbers. "Once he has taken the form of the wolf, he can travel day and night. I'd bet he'll be at Bear Lodge before Casey. He'll probably be there by the time we head off tomorrow at first light," Crazy Bear said. "With or without a balcony?"

"Ground floor. Pick one along the side so we can see our motorcycles out the window," Jade said, adjusting the saddlebags again.

* * *

THE ROOM HAD A SHOWER, two beds, a bedside table with the Bible in the top drawer, a TV, and a desk with a telephone. The bedcovers were orange. Crazy Bear left Jade alone in the room to have the first shower and freshen up. When she had finished and was sitting on the edge of the bed, towel drying her long black hair, Crazy Bear returned with arms full of snack foods. He dropped them onto the other bed and spread them out for her to choose.

"Do you prefer to be called Crazy Bear or Noah?" Jade asked, before tipping the last of a bag of chips into her mouth.

"Being called Noah reminds me of hugs and my family. Especially my brothers. And Emma. But Crazy Bear reminds me of my spiritual strength, the dream lodge where I connect with the cosmos. It reminds me I am part of all life, and the universe loves and supports me in all that I do. So, you can call me either, because they both give me happy thoughts. What about you?"

"My great-grandmother, Great Turtle, was the only one who called me Raven Wings until I came here. Jade is who I have always been. But there have been many faces of Jade. I was an emo for a while—it was a phase but only one Raven Wings. Raven Wings reminds me of a feeling of wonderment, excitement, and connectedness, but I have never known why until the past few weeks. I'm learning to connect to all that I can be. It's hard because I have always come from my head rather than my heart, which is what I need to do to become the Raven. Come from the heart."

"Then I will call you Raven Wings," Crazy Bear said, smiling at her.

The outside lights switched on, and Jade stepped out onto the porch to witness the fleeting beauty of twilight. The monkeys stopped screeching. It all seemed so natural. She couldn't believe in a couple of months, Great Spirit would destroy all things during the cleansing of the earth.

"Hey, Raven Wings, check this out?" Crazy Bear called from inside the room. Jade pushed the door closed behind her. Crazy Bear was standing at a table with a telephone and the welcome booklet containing an array of pamphlets. They were all about what to do during your stay in Knoxville. He held one up: Visit the Knoxville Zoo.

"I told you there had to be a zoo around here," Crazy Bear said.

Jade stared at the picture of the tigers and lions. "I wonder if they let them out, too?" she said, tapping the image of the tiger on the front of the pamphlet.

"Yeah, good point."

"I'm tired. I'm going to get some sleep so we can get an early start," Jade said.

"Yeah, me too," Crazy Bear said, heading for the bathroom.

Jade slipped out of her jeans and shirt and folded them up. Placing them neatly on the chair next to her boots, she dropped onto the bed and listened to the sounds around her, expanding her awareness beyond the running water in the shower and the monkeys outside.

But she quickly decided that sometimes it was probably best not to expand it too far when she felt something chilling just beyond her reach. She didn't want to know what hid in the shadows. It was like her relationship with spiders. As long as she couldn't see them, they were fine to stay where they were.

The rhyme that played itself over and over in her head randomly during the last forty-eight hours intensified, demanding attention. She deconstructed it line by line. It was a warning. Great Turtle knew this day was coming. She knew the darkness was coming.

Hisss. Hisss. Hisss. Hunger and pain,

The infernal shall slither,

Into your minds again.

Poisoning your thoughts,

Feeding on your fear,

Luring you into the darkness,

Boiling your blood as he nears.

Hiss. Hiss. Hiss. Hunger and pain,

Feast from the vessel,

Starvation is the game.

Hissing definitely related to snakes. Hunger and pain could refer to the wendigo. The person possessed by the wendigo was famished. It was the first sign that they had been infected and the fever, boiling your blood. Was that an infernal? The preacher? He commanded the snakes, the hiss, hiss, hissing, and he got into your head, making you see things that were not real—poisoning your thoughts. Jade wondered about the next few lines. She was going to need to use her wand to cast light, but how would that light defeat the preacher? Jade heard the door of the bathroom gently close and heard the rustle of bedsheets as Crazy Bear got into bed.

"Good night, Raven Wings," he whispered in case she was asleep.

"Night, Noah," Jade said, staring up at the dark ceiling.

"What are you thinking about?" Crazy Bear said.

"About the nursery rhyme connected to my memory stone. I'm trying to understand what the line means, 'starvation is the game.' I'm thinking maybe we need to fast, or at least abstain from eating meat so we don't accidentally eat human flesh and turn into a wendigo? Or maybe *the vessel*, being the human, will be starved to death by the wendigo or the infernal?"

"You're thinking with your head. What would have to be taken from you, to starve your heart?" Noah asked.

Jade thought about Kevin and her family. Being starved of love would be crushing.

Jade heard Noah turn over to face her. "I think if I was starved of the light of Great Spirit, my heart would be in darkness and shrivel up and turn to dust.

She heard the voice of Great Turtle telling her she will need to use the light of the wand. All thoughts of sleep vanished as she became all too aware of the darkness.

23

CASEY: READER BEWARE – SECRETS OF THE NOTEBOOK

C asey had never flown more than a couple of hours. It was stinking hot, and he could not stay airborne for much longer. Even though he sorted out how to fire up all his chakra energy centers, and the electromagnetic force allowed him to travel further for longer, it was just too hot. Riding a motorcycle might have been faster after all.

Casey tried to stay above the clouds, which made it difficult to get his bearings but easier to maintain the energy to propel himself forward. He wished he had a compass. Every so often, he would dip below the clouds, searching for towns or familiar landmarks. Some clouds were low and thick, and refused to let him through. He was flying blind until he could penetrate the clouds that seemed to have a different atmosphere. The energy inside the clouds was dark and foreboding. Color seemed to have vanished.

Once beyond the peculiar clouds, he flew low and avoided the scary pockets of turbulence as well, which had totally freaked him out. Sometimes, when he hit a pocket of turbulence, he plummeted, and his stomach dropped. But at this low altitude, it was hard to ignore the ghostly figures haunting the towns. In one town, a woman climbed to the top of a church steeple. Her figure was fragile in the warm breeze, she stood with her hands clasped to her chest, looked up as in silent prayer then toppled over. As she fell, her form weakened, becoming transparent, and before hitting the ground, she disappeared, then reappeared at the top of the steeple again.

Casey needed a safe place to stop and rest that wasn't haunted. It wasn't going to be easy. On his left was a lake, and it tempted him to skim the surface and cool down in the water, but he kept going instead and maintained his altitude. Out of the sun would be good. He came up to Nashville airport, a graveyard for planes. Casey slowed down, not wanting to scare the cooing birds perched on the backs of the planes.

Time had frozen. Nothing moved, no planes taxied on the runway, no luggage handlers packed suitcases into the belly of the jumbos. It was a graveyard. The last time he was at an airport was for the last flight out of the New York airport, bound for Heathrow airport. The airport had been chaotic. He had stood at an enormous window looking over the tarmac, and he watched the reflection of desperate people, without tickets, determined to get out of the New York, harassed, and begged those with tickets offering colossal sums of cash for their seats on the last flights out of the country; soon they'll stop asking, and start taking.

Fear had strangled the airport and anyone in it. He had felt the fear so strong that even now his heart sank with the weight of the memory. He wished he could close his eyes and time would turn back eleven years before the plague.

Casey shot up into the sky, and away from the memories. Nashville was a place he had always wanted to visit. He had wanted to spend his year before college watching and listening to live outdoor music around the world, and Nashville was where he had wanted to start. It was the place to be.

The air whipped past, filtering through his curly head of hair, cooling his scalp as he flew over Nashville. He slowed down and landed at Union Station, platform number eight. As he sat down, he noticed it was like a cool wind tunnel. He welcomed the breeze and leaned back against the brick wall facing the tracks.

His stomach rumbled, and he looked at his backpack beside him.

He was sure he had an orange, but all he could find under the books was an old rocky road protein bar. He opened it and the chocolate had faded to a gray brown as if he had left it out in the sun for too long. It was too old to eat. Sophia had put it in his bag months ago. She had picked it up at a shop while walking through Scotland to the estate in Northmead in England. Her journey hadn't been easy, avoiding the infected, hiking over the Cheviot Hills, through cold dark caves, falling into cold underground water holes, blindly following her instincts with Father McDonald and Joe, until they found the tunnels that ran under Casey's estate.

That was a good day, the day he met Sophia in the flesh and knew for sure she wasn't a ghost or a figment of his imagination. He touched the wrapper and let the weight of the bar sit in his hand. A connection with Sophia, even a flash, would be enough to sustain him.

But nothing came.

He put the protein bar back into his backpack. Casey jolted at the sudden loud sound of a train whistle. He could feel the rumble of the train coming down the track, slowing down as it neared the station. As the train came to a stop, Casey pushed his back into the wall, held his backpack tight, as men and teenagers, not much older than him, dressed in army uniforms, spilled out of the train and onto the platform.

"You got a light, buddy?" a soldier asked Casey as soon as he jumped off the train.

"No. Sorry. Thank you for your service," Casey said.

The young man stood looking at him as if he thought Casey was a little odd. "Where are you off to, boy?" the soldier said, checking out Casey's clothes.

Casey stood up and put his backpack on.

"You're not from around here, are you?" the soldier said.

"No. I'm just looking for something to eat, then I'll be on my way home," Casey said.

The soldier put his cigarette in the corner of his mouth and as he did, another soldier came along and lit it for him.

"Here ya go, buddy," the solider said and took a half-eaten sandwich out of his pocket, and handed it to Casey.

"No. You keep it. My folks are just inside," Casey said.

"Your loss, buddy. My sweetheart made this for me. Fine girl. I'm going to marry her when I come home. Godspeed to you," the young man said, touching his hat and nodding his head.

"And to you," Casey said, watching the young soldier walk down the platform.

Casey relaxed his chest and breathed easy as the soldiers dwindled away, moving to other platforms or simply disappearing into thin air as the train they arrived on left the station. He waited for the discarded papers to settle back on to the tracks before he moved inside to search for a vending machine. Maybe he would get lucky and find something to eat.

Down the track, a light grew brighter, a train speeding into the station. An even brighter light in the cloudy afternoon shone from behind Casey. The two trains were on a collision course. There was nothing Casey could do but jump out of the way, into the station doorway, before they sucked him into the impact zone.

Inside the station, ghostly wounded people lined up against the walls. Other ghostly apparitions rushed to help the survivors of the train crash. Two men covered the deceased with tablecloths. The ghost of a woman cried and cradled the hand of a dying man laid out on the floor. His injuries looked bad—he would not live much longer. Pain and sorrow filled the station. Casey walked outside and took flight, leaving the station with its embedded ghostly memories behind.

The air above the station was thick and turbulent. He bounced around in the air as he flew away to another part of town. He scanned the area, testing the pockets of emotions that were creating the turbulence, and for a moment he wondered if he was alone. A chill went up his spine. He pushed the notion out of his mind and focused on finding something to eat.

The streets were busy with the deceased from all eras. There were no time boundaries. They all blended in this moment and moved as one. Outside of town might be a better choice. Casey headed east and crossed over Cumberland River. He felt peace in the trees as he flew towards another airport before slowing down, thinking he was far enough from the haunted town center. He heard music the closer he got to Gaylord Opryland. Slowly he lowered himself and landed, facing a 'Do Not Enter' sign.

A bus sat empty at the side of the road and cars sat abandoned throughout the large parking lot. He hoped few people had stayed on site at the end to die. He flew over the top of the dome that covered part of the resort and cautiously set down by a green, murky swimming pool. His shirt was sticking to his back from the heat. As he walked by the edge of the water, he let one strap of his backpack slip off his shoulder and he pulled it to one side, allowing the air to circulate over his back.

He ducked under an archway of trees that led into the dome setup as a small town, with arching footbridges over a man-made water way through the center of the town. Casey looked up and scan the huge glass conservatory dome roof, high above that was greater than the size of eight football fields. Casey could feel the sweet dripping down his neck as the heat increased under the dome. The once manicured gardens were now over growing, and the turn of the century buildings along the winding river, were empty of life.

At first, he thought the place was quiet and free of haunting ghosts, until he heard the distant sound of music. He strolled across the footbridge and walked along the sidewalk that overlooked the river while being followed by disembodied footsteps. Quickly Casey turned and caught a flashing image of a woman in an old-fashioned long black dress, flickering in and out of existence.

Despite the heat, he shivered, and tried to ignore her presence. If she kept her distance, he was okay. He hoped she would get bored with him and enter a building or simply vanish. He followed the music and entered the main lobby of the grand motel he was in awe of the sheer size. He trailed his fingers over a beautiful abstract glass sculpture. Dust darkened his fingertips. He wiped them casually on the side of his pants opposite the dagger. Two vending machines stood side by side. One with beverages and the other snacks. The clear glass faces smashed, and only three snacks remained. Two packets of beefy jerky, a lonely bag of potato chips, and a couple of bottles of water.

Casey sat on the stone wall surrounding a stagnant fountain with dying plants, and under a magnificent twinkling chandelier that moved in a gentle phantom breeze. He wished there was air-conditioning. Nothing worked. Someone must have shut down the power long ago. Balconies overlooking the main lobby would have once been filled with people peering down at the impressive lobby. He scanned as much he could while sitting on the edge of the fountain.

Casey sighed and took out his almost empty bottle of water and drank the last few mouthfuls before opening a new bottle he salvaged from the vending machine. The beef jerky was salty and so were the potato chips. This would be as good as any place to stay the night.

He pushed himself off the wall, headed to the reception desk in search of a key, wondering if they would even work. He opened the early check-out box for a used key that might still be programmed; It was his lucky day, there were five keys in the box. Casey took number C2101 and held it in his hand. He felt the emotions of the last person who had held it. A man about thirty-five had returned the key and was sad to leave. He had a good time and had a song in his heart. There should be good energy in that room.

Casey looked around, trying to work out where that room might be. He needed to find it before nightfall, when darkness would prevail. The place was so big he didn't know where to start. He tried to tune into the man who had returned the key and follow his steps in reverse. He had walked down steps instead of taking the elevator to prolong the return of the key. The room couldn't have been to far because he wasn't out of breath. He walked up the stairs to the second floor and searched for room numbers that ended in 01 until he found a door that opened.

Casey looked at his sweaty, dusty face in the concave bathroom shaving mirror and leaned on the ceramic sink, praying for clean water. He turned on the faucet and welcomed the beautiful running water by splashing it over his face. The pipes rattled. He peeled off his shirt and stepped out of his clothes and into a cold shower.

Out on the balcony, he squeezed the water out of his clothes and laid them out to dry in the late afternoon breeze. *They'll be dry in no time*, he thought. With a towel around his waist, he lay down on the bed, resting his hands behind his head, and stared at the ceiling, wondering about all the things that could have been. He scolded himself for the fruitless thoughts and sat up. He had tossed his backpack on top of the table next to the old telephone that connected to reception. Casey got up and took Isabella's notebook out of his bag and sat back on the bed.

Slowly, he turned the stiff pages. The first section was on healing with herbs and potions. The second was about mythical creatures. He quickly passed the image of the sandman, the cause of much of his grief, and stopped before getting to the images of the fallen angels at a subcategory titled Supernatural Creatures. He hadn't noticed the section in the past. The first page was a kind of introduction to the contents. Casey looked back at the other sections, noticing that the first page of each section had an introduction.

He read the Supernatural Creatures' introduction out loud. "Reader, be aware of what you are about to learn, many men have gone mad with the true understanding of the knowledge you are about to receive. It all begins with the Angels, The Jinn, The Watchers—Fallen Angels and The Human Soul—Good and Evil. By now you have learned of the mythical creatures of this world and now you will come to know their fathers, the Fallen Angels. You will come to know of the Jinn, the race before the creation of the humanoids, and last, the most loved and desired by all—the human soul."

Casey held the bottom edge of the page ready to turn it over, but he read through the introduction again, deciding whether or not he wanted to read on. The words, *men have gone mad*, appeared bold and larger than the rest of the text written with a quill. Casey reached out his finger towards the words. He licked his lips, suddenly thirsty. *Stop being a coward. Touch the letters*, he thought. The words captured his mind as he touched the letters. He saw screaming faces, ghostly apparitions, demons and death, lots of death. He quickly pulled his fingers away and shivered as he turned the page to continue reading.

The angels seemed to glow, as if drawn with golden ink. Michael, Gabriel, Uriel, Raphael, Selaphiel, Raguel, and Baracheil, each governing a day of the week and each one a guardian of humanity. They were beautiful to look at, with three sets of golden wings and the light of heaven glistening down upon them.

Casey ran his hand over the images; his head tilted back in ecstasy. The light filled his soul and radiated out through his eyes, hands, every pore of his body. The tendons in his neck strained as he struggled to pull his hand away from the image, and as soon as he did, his head flopped forward, his chest expanding as the light exited.

He panted, as if running a marathon. As he lifted his head up, he pushed his hair back off his face and stood. His legs wobbled, fatigued. He shook his head, trying to release the overload of emotion, light, and energy. He needed to burn off energy. Slowly, he picked up his pants that were on the balcony and dropped his towel as he put on his jeans. Barefoot, he bent his knees, pushed up off the balcony, and flew into the air. At the edge of the ozone, it was peaceful. He closed his eyes and pushed the energy out of every pore. Brighter than the descending sun, he radiated pure energy from the angels over the entire country. Calmer, he watched the golden light falling like raindrops upon the earth. Tiny sparks of light exploded, as if they had collided with something on their way down to the ground. Casey floated down slowly amongst the glittering light and returned to his hotel room to read on.

Must remember not to touch the angels, or next time I'm liable to explode like an atomic bomb.

He approached the notebook. It looked harmless, and he wondered if Isabella knew how much light it contained. Had she ever experienced the purity of the angel's light? He sat on the bed with one leg under him. With great care, he turned the pages over. The first two pages were blank. He turned the pages over to the next spread entitled 'The Fallen Angels.'

The angels seduced humans with their knowledge. The pictures depicted some in flight, performing the sin of intercourse with the females of earth—some human. It made Casey feel sick in the stomach. He turned away from the images and focused on the words. The fallen angels had brought shame upon the heavens and for these deeds, God banished them from returning to the heavens and so to all their offspring. This was the beginning of true evil upon the earth.

Casey turned the page, avoiding making any sound. Drawings of centaurs, the body of a horse with the head and torso of a man. A chimpanzee and the name Lucy scribed in the blue ink of a ballpoint pen under the image. Eagles with the body of a sheep. A goat with the face of a man with horns. A snake slithered around the page with the head of a woman on both ends of the body.

These were the abominations that became mystical creatures through the ages. A horse with wings. It was hard to tell what some creatures were supposed to be. A giant of a man with three eyes ate humans as if they were sheep grazing the fields. Casey turned the page and there was a mix of creatures, and they all had supernatural powers to shape-shift. Could Mingan, Charlie, and Crazy Bear be of these creatures? Was Jade? Dracula was there, an immortal man with the power to shape-shift. A hairy man, hunched over, looked a lot like a werewolf.

Casey turned the pages quicker. Confused to their meaning, were they all the children of the fallen angels? At the top of the book, as if a footnote on the edge of the page, it said, "Evil entities, the emancipation of the human soul."

No way, it couldn't be.

But it was.

It was the wendigo and a mix of other creatures just like it—demon possessions. Evil entities entered the human through the back of the neck, mouth, nose, eyes, or stomach. The script at the bottom of the page said, "And God saw what became of the earth as the children of the watchers populated throughout the earth and destroyed the beauty God had created. The unclean children will become evil spirits chained to the earth." Next to it was a number 5727. Casey wondered if it was a date.

He turned over to the page titled 'The Jinn,' flying gray-black clouds, dark silhouettes, some only whispers of smoke flew in the air, some in the shape of smoky clothed humans and others, hideous, deformed creatures that resembled nothing on earth. Casey had sketched similar images, silhouettes of men, and into these silhouettes poured evil negative energy.

On the next page of Isabella's notebook, people looked up to the skies in wonder as dark ghostly images flew above them dismissive of their presences while other evil, revengeful shadowy human like forms stood beside the passive humans, and whispered evil thoughts into their minds. Casey read the bottom text. "A race before the time of humanoids that were born from the smoke of the flame. Gifted with the emotions to love, they chose to hate. God, after seeing the bad in the Jinn he had created, proceeded against the angels' protests, and created humanoids. Together, the Jinn will live upon earth, but man will be blind to their existence, for if they were to know the evil that walks beside them through all their days, they would go mad. One day, the war to end all things will come, waged by the Jinn, and the Fallen Angels."

Gently, Casey closed the book and went outside onto the balcony that faced the street and searched for the Jinn, the unseen. The turbulence he had felt, the sparks of golden light exploding in the sky, could he have been colliding with the Jinn? He squinted and looked out the side of his eyes to try to glimpse a Jinn. He saw dark clouds in the sky that appeared out of place, nothing more.

You know what? I don't need to know. If God chose for us not to see them, then I don't want to see them. Casey held onto the edge of the balcony. The metal rail was cold to the touch. *What does all this mean? I have supernatural powers. Am I an abomination? Was Sophia?* His head felt dizzy, and his stomach churned. "Oh God, what am I?"

He looked over the edge and down to the asphalt below. Jump. Jump now and end this life. Save God the sorrow. He ignored the strange voice. Why would Metatron protect him? He stared down for a long time. A heaviness weighed on his back. It was like he was giving a child a piggyback. The weight seemed unbearable, increasing by the second, tipping him forward over the rail. His knees buckled. Fear filled his heart. He clenched his teeth, trying to stop himself from tipping all the way over the edge of the balcony. His knuckles were turning white as he held on tight, trying not to fall. He was on his toes, the railing dug into his hips, his body weight bearing down, no longer able to hold on to the rail he teetered over, falling headfirst towards the ground below.

He opened his eyes. The asphalt he expected to feel beneath his body was a bed; the room was golden as the sun shone through the balcony's open doors, where Metatron emitted phosphorus light. Casey sat up. The notebook was at the foot of the bed and the pages turned on their own.

"Read on," Casey heard Metatron's' harmonic voice in his head. "God will bless you in the time of the Great War, when the world will be cleansed, and the earth will be reborn, again."

His heart was racing, he had trouble catching his breath, he believed he was going to die for the third and final time. The illuminous light echoed in Metatron's wake. The air scintillating around the room emerging into the walls and Casey. He took in a deep breath and let it out, grateful to be alive, he turned back to the first of four pages depicting skies overflowing with whispers of gray, ghostly energy, and started reading about the fallen angels.

24

JADE: STRAIGHTENING THE ARROW

J ade slipped her jacket on. It was a misty morning, and she didn't like the idea of riding a motorcycle, she didn't feel aligned with her physical body. She felt she needed to be grounded with the earth. She checked her helmet for spiders and cockroaches. Crazy Bear had dressed earlier and went out for a walk, giving her an hour to dress and practice her drumming. Drumming sometimes helped to balance her energy and focus on her intentions for the day, which were to get to Bear Lodge in one piece, and find Casey.

Jade could hear footsteps outside, heading towards their room. She opened the door for Noah, then went back to packing her drum in the saddlebag, ready to leave. Noah stopped just outside the door and out of sight. Jade froze, waiting, listening. She looked back over her shoulder, energy built up inside her making her hot and extremely uncomfortable with her riding jacket.

"Noah, are you okay?" Jade asked, unzipping her jacket. Puzzled, Jade stuck her head out the door, and turned her head from left to right, but couldn't see beyond the morning fog. She pulled her head back into the room and quietly shut the door.

Ready for an intruder to bust through the doorway, at full force, she adjusted her stance, so she wouldn't fall over. The door burst open, and a tall man, dressed in black wearing a hat, faceless—entered the room and launched himself at her. It was like the darkness of the abyss stared back at her.

Instantly, Jade stepped back and to the side, drawing the man past her using his own momentum to throw him into the glass door of a cabinet. He slammed into the door so hard Jade thought it was going to smash, and he fell to the floor.

Jade could feel fire in her veins as she waited for the faceless intruder to move. She ran for the open door. Concerned she had turned her back on her assailant, she ducked her head in case he struck out at her from behind.

"What the hell are you doing?" Crazy Bear bellowed.

Jade stopped in mid-stride and looked back into the room. Crazy Bear was on the floor, holding his face. His nose was bleeding. Jade watched as he got to his feet. "I thought . . ." Frantically, she looked around the room, searched the bathroom. "I thought you were a creepy faceless shadow man I saw back at the estate. It wasn't you I saw. I saw someone else." Jade's words came slowly as she replayed the scenario in her head.

"Well, it's me, and that hurt! What were you thinking?" Crazy Bear said.

"I'm so sorry," Jade said, trying to move his hands away from his face so she could see the damage.

She winced.

"What?"

"Just hold still," Jade said as she put her hands on either side of his broken nose, ready to put it back in place. "On the count of three. One—"

"Wait. What about your wand?" Crazy Bear said.

Jade dropped her hands down. "Of course."

"What's gotten into you?" Crazy Bear said.

"Sorry, Noah. I don't know what came over me." Her body temperature was declining, and she could feel her perspiration cooling with the help of a slight breeze coming through the opened door. She shivered.

Jade reached into her back pocket and took out the wand. It glowed as she gently touched it against Noah's broken nose, that moved easily into its natural position. Noah yanked himself off the floor and stalked into the bathroom to wash the blood off his face.

She couldn't believe that the faceless shadow man wasn't real. Jade sat on the edge of the bed waiting for Noah, wondering what had happened to her. She avoided the idea jumping up and down in her mind wanting her attention. "I think the preacher has his eye on us," Jade blurted out into the empty room.

"What?" Crazy Bear said, coming out of the bathroom.

"I think the preacher knows where we are, and he pushed those thoughts into my mind. I would have sworn a faceless man wearing a hat had entered the room. Not you. He was taller and slender. You're tall, but not seven feet tall. He had to duck to get into the room. You don't need to lose a few pounds, but you're not that thin, so I don't have any other explanation why I saw what I saw. I'm sorry, Noah."

"We're going to have to guard our thoughts better, and be aware of any changes in our energies."

Jade had been feeling calm and balanced after the meditation with the drum. She couldn't tell when the energy changed. *Hang on, what about when I heard his footsteps?* she thought. That wasn't Crazy Bear, or was it? The sounds could've been an illusion. "I am getting so confused. Let's get out of here. This place is giving me the creeps," Jade said.

They rushed out to their bikes, ignoring the screeching monkeys, frightened by something Jade couldn't see.

* * *

ON THE WET road it was humid inside her jacket, and she wanted to unzip it, but she'd have to wait until their first stop. There was plenty of time along the way to think. They had eight hours of riding ahead of them before dark. Normally she would enjoy the time to mull things over, but now she worried the preacher might enter her mind and encourage her to ride straight off the next cliff.

She imagined Mingan as the wolf, running all night. He would be eight hours ahead of them already. She tried to meld with the bike but was afraid she would lose control and cause an accident. With each mile, it was getting worse. Her anxiety increased. She needed to stop and get off the bike before she fell off.

Dark clouds have been followed them all morning, the road was wet, and Crazy Bear was a half a mile ahead of her, which meant she was going to need to increase her speed, something she didn't feel safe doing on the slippery road. She flashed her lights, hoping he would see her and slow down. The clouds collided; thunder clapped above her so strongly she nearly jumped off her motorcycle in fright. *Enough!*

Jade pulled onto the side of the road and got off, hoping Crazy Bear would eventually notice and come back to look for her. She kept her helmet on and unzipped the jacket. She didn't want to stray too far from the motorcycle, and her belongings in the saddlebags.

Why not move the clouds away and stop the thunder, lightning, and the misty drizzle? Why have this amazing, phenomenal ability if I'm not supposed to not use it? Jade thought and took off her helmet and absently hung it on the handlebar before staring up into the sky. She took off her jacket and laid it on the ground by the motorcycle then while standing she crossed her legs and crouched down to sit on her jacket. Jade closed her eyes and listened to the sounds of life as sheets of light rain began. The wind pushed the drizzle into her face, but not hard enough for it to feel like tiny needles. She focused her awareness beyond her immediate area, stretching out her consciousness, expanding, searching.

She didn't know what she sought when suddenly she was in a forest, running behind a purple trail of energy. It was Mingan in the form of a spirit wolf. He pulled up hard like a horse that had spotted a snake. He slid for a few paces before turning back towards her. At first, Jade didn't think he was aware of her, but the hunched posture of a wolf quickly grew into the tall stature of a man.

Quickly, she pulled back her consciousness and slammed back into her body, hard, so hard it made her cough. *Wow, what the hell was that?* she wondered.

The sound of Crazy Bear's motorcycle was heading in her direction. She raised her arms up and out as if to encompass all her surroundings. She closed her eyes and took in a deep breath, calming her mind and connecting with nature until she felt the warmth of the sun on her face. When she opened her eyes, she could no longer hear Crazy Bear's motorcycle. The clouds were gone, and the humidity too. A cool breeze floated over her, and the sky had a golden glow. Jade let her arms down and breathed in the fresh clean air as if she had been holding her breath for hours. Her stomach rumbled.

When she looked down, she saw Crazy Bear sleeping on the ground next to his bike. Jade walked out onto the road and stamped her foot, testing it was solid. The ground was dry. She stood by her motorcycle and there were no droplets of rain on the light blue tank of the Harley Sportster.

Crazy Bear must've sensed her moving around because he opened his eyes and sat up. "Well, it's about time," he said.

"Thanks for coming back. I just had to get off the motorcycle. It was doing my head in. I couldn't stop thinking about crashing or falling off," she explained.

Crazy Bear crossed his legs. "It's been over an hour. The clouds cleared in a few seconds, but you froze for an hour. I tried to talk to you. I clapped in front of your face. Nothing would make you budge. I went into a meditation, to the dream lodge, to find out what happened to you. I was told to go back and guard you from the darkness."

"Sleeping is not guarding," Jade complained. The self-assurance and balance she had felt unraveled as soon as he mentioned the darkness.

"We have to keep moving. You can turn back. I can go on without you. There's no shame in turning back, Jade. It's important to know your limits."

"I can't turn back. There's never any going back. Otherwise, I would turn everything back ten years, to a time before Shaun's dad stole the emerald tablet and prevented the cleansing of the earth." Jade took her helmet off the handlebars. She left her jacket open and climbed onto her bike.

Crazy Bear followed her lead and readied himself. "The universe loves and supports you, Jade. You just need to let go," Crazy Bear said gently, putting on his helmet.

He pulled out first, and she followed. The road was dry, and quickly she found her connection to the motorcycle and leaned into the corners. "When your energy is unbalanced, your energy is bent," she heard Mingan's words in her head. How had she expanded her consciousness so much that she had spiritually caught up with him in a heartbeat? And he knew she was there watching him before she pulled back, afraid of the consequences of her curiosity.

She was always afraid of the consequences of her actions. Worried that someone else would get hurt or be disappointed. A smile crossed her face, because coming up behind Mingan had felt awesome. She wondered if that was what Casey and Sophia had meant when they said they connected with each other on the astral plane, through meditation, when they had lived on different continents.

What else could she do? Jade imagined her arms were soft, strong, feathered wings gliding on the wind, and she lost all sensation of the throttle in her palm. The motorcycle slowed down. Quickly she stopped imagining the raven wings and focused on the feeling of the rubber and metal of the bike. She fumbled through the gears as she geared down to get control of the bike again and increase the revs. She needed to experiment with the raven, but not while riding a motorcycle across the country.

THE WILDLIFE WAS plentiful the further north they went. Her stomach rumbled. They needed to stop, and what better place than the strawberry fields they were passing?

Crazy Bear made his shirt into a sling to collect the strawberries. "So, you mean to tell me you have done no work to enhance your ability to control the weather," Crazy Bear said, eating the last strawberry he had collected. "Can you gather rain clouds? Make a mini tornado? Or a dry lightning storm?"

"I turned autumn into winter once, and back again. But only once." Jade looked up at the sky, thinking. "And I think once I might've rushed the sun to rise. It sounds silly, I know." She was feeling self-conscious and unworthy.

"Make a tornado," Crazy Bear said.

"No. I can't do that."

"I bet you can."

"I shouldn't mess around with nature."

"Just a small one. Try it?" Crazy Bear encouraged.

Jade crossed her legs, put her hands at shoulder width apart, and closed her eyes. She felt the energy between her hands move, tickling her palms. Expanding her awareness while staying focused, she opened her eyes and watched as the dirt below her hands drew up into a tiny twister; she had never tried this before, and it scared her. She collapsed her hands together, and the dust returned to the ground.

"I didn't mean that small," Crazy Bear said. "What are you afraid of?"

Jade stood up, raised up her arms, and drew the clouds together, pressing them until the center gave way and trailed down to the ground.

"Yes! That's what I'm talking about!"

The power felt good. "It's the power that scares me," she said, raising her voice.

"All the power that ever was or will be, has always been inside you. Use it. Give me lightning," Crazy Bear said.

Jade clapped her hands and green lightning flashed across the clouds, and thunder rumbled.

"Now make it go away," Crazy Bear said.

Jade drew in a deep breath and blew out. The clouds rushed into each other and melted away like candy floss.

Crazy Bear scooped her up off her feet and twirled around. He put her down again and held her face. "Rejoice in the power. Don't fear what Great Spirit has given you."

His joy was infectious. "Okay. Okay. I get it," Jade laughed.

"Don't stop. Hold that feeling. Become the Raven. Now. Do it now!" Crazy Bear let her go, his face split with a wide grin.

It was like someone had flicked a light on inside her. She saw the raven, she felt the wings, the power of their movement pushing the air taking flight. She was one with the raven and one with the sky. Jade as the raven circled up into the sky and flew above the motorcycles and Crazy Bear, who was jumping and clapping with giddy joy. She focused on the energy. She was the spear, the arrowhead, and the bow propelling her into the sky.

It differed from flying with Casey. Her heart pulsed with energy, a connection to all things flowed through her heart. It was beautiful. She thought of Kevin and wished he could have seen the first time that she consciously took flight as the raven. A trail of purple light, like ribbons, seeped from her wings as they disappeared. Her aim was gone, her wings disintegrating into trailing vapors. She had lost her balance and her mojo.

Quickly, the ground rushed up to meet her as she fell out of the sky, no longer the raven. Jade struggled to keep her eyes open in rapid descent. She would crash into the ground and break into a hundred pieces, just like Mingan said, and she felt like a fool plummeting towards the ground.

Jade pushed the foolish thoughts and the disappointing emotions away, expanded her awareness, and calmed herself until once again she felt the wings and power of the raven. She skimmed the ground as she soared back up into the air and flew around for another ten minutes, looking at the world from above. It was beautiful. Dark clouds were gathering up ahead again, and they looked fierce. Foreboding. It was time to get going.

Crazy Bear rushed up to her as she changed into her natural form a few feet from the ground, just as she touched down. He scooped her up and twirled her so much she thought she was going to vomit. They had to steady each other, waiting for the world to stop spinning.

"You did it, Raven Wings! Now you can do it whenever you like. Do you want to fly, or ride the motorcycle?" he asked, looking back at the bikes.

She thought hard about it. Flying in on Mingan sounded like a good idea, but as soon as she had the idea, she felt the power leaving her. The thought, laced with gloating and pride, unbalanced her energy because if she did, she would only be showing off to Mingan, which meant she'd be coming from a place of ego. Her arrow would be bent. Now she understood. "I think I'll ride," she said, smiling at Crazy Bear.

"Well then, we better get a move on, or we will be late for the party. Did you create that storm?" Crazy Bear said, pointing to the north.

"No. You think something is going to happen when we get there, don't you?" Jade said, and the concern in her own voice grounded her instantly.

"Yes. There's a battle ahead, we must fight," Crazy Bear said.

He gave Jade another big hug before mounting his motorcycle.

EXHILARATED with the power within her from becoming the raven, Jade longed for corners to lean hard into. She should've picked a MotoGP motorcycle. Passing through the towns, she looked at everything like a tourist. She wanted to stop and appreciate everything. It was twilight once again, and the stars were coming out. They twinkled so beautifully, it was hard to focus on the road ahead. Without all the city lights, the sky was a glitter of gold. Everything around her seemed glorious as they rode along Yellowstone Highway, and she could see for miles around.

As she rode slowly through Casper, she noticed a stillness. Nothing moved but them. No birds, no clouds, not even a lizard or snake, nothing except the building storm in the distance.

Just like Pavlov's dog, her mouth watered while reading each fast-food restaurant's sign as she passed through the town. *Wood-fire pizza. What I'd do for a pizza!* she thought. Time to top up the gas and find some food for Crazy Bear and herself.

Twilight unfolded its magical light. She had missed out on so much and had closed herself off to the mysterious, precious world most of her short life. It was only eleven thousand five hundred years ago the earth recovered from the last apocalyptic flood that cleansed the planet, why did it have to happen again, no in her lifetime? It was a shame the world was going to be destroyed by the hand of God, just as she was seeing clearly for the first time.

Jade slowed the motorcycle and looked around at the Prairie dogs popping their heads up in the fields. They were so cute; she hoped they would survive, and that Great Spirit wouldn't let them get hurt.

Her awareness had narrowed so much that she didn't notice Crazy Bear slowing down and pulling over at a truck stop. She rode straight past him and had to double back. There were trucks lined up, and she wondered where the people were. She wondered if they died inside the cabins of the trucks, or inside the fast-food joints, or did they just disappeared?

"What's up?" Jade said.

"I've run out of water, and I need gas and food. I'm starving. It's been a long day in the saddle – I need food and sleep. And the beef jerky at the last gas station just made me hungrier and thirstier. I ran out of water a hundred miles back. Let's fuel up and check the place out before it gets too dark. I'll fill up the bikes if you can check Subway for something to eat," Crazy Bear said.

"I'll check Subway, but I don't think we'll find anything in there worth eating," Jade said as she unzipped her jacket.

Someone had pried the door open with a crowbar. Cautiously, Jade slipped through the crack and went inside. The smell hit first, quickly she covered her mouth, it stunk of rotting food, and the place had been tossed. Jade didn't bother searching the rest of the restaurant. Instead, she went into the gas station's main building hoping to find some packaged food.

She rubbed her eyes and waited for them to adjust to the dull light. Jade stepped back outside and grabbed her wand out of the saddlebag and returned to the gas station mart. Jade waited for her wand to illuminate and breakup the darkness so she could see the shelves; some shelves had been overturned. Why people had to trash things she didn't know. Her energy was draining, her body heavy, she just needed sleep. She felt she needed to sleep. In the back was an office and she lay down on the couch. Just a few minutes was all she needed to freshen up a little. The stillness and quiet disturbed her equilibrium, after moving all day, feeling the vibrations of the bike through her whole being for hours on end. Her body started to overheat. She had to get her jacket off.

Suddenly, her senses on high alert she pushed herself up into a sitting position. Her body was heavy, and the preacher stood in the doorway.

"I'm waiting for you," he whispered.

She aimed her wand at him, and he just laughed at her, knocking it out of her hands. He stepped forward, touched her head with his hand, and her eyelids went heavy. She tried to keep them open, but the darkness enveloped her. Still sitting up and awake, she could not move.

She tried to scream. It was useless. Something trapped her in a dark abyss inside herself. She waited, trying to sense movement outside of herself. Willing her body to move, she called out to God to help her, and instantly she was free of the preacher's hold.

She sat up, breathless. In her hand was the memory stone of the man in the maze. It was closer to the center. She didn't know if that was a good thing or a bad thing. She didn't recall taking it out of its box. The power and exhilaration she had felt throughout the day's left her and now she felt totally empty.

Crazy Bear was standing over her as she jolted awake. There was no memory stone in her hand, and she was laying down, quickly she sat up and looked around the office for the preacher. Crazy Bear turned on the lights. She sighed, relieved it was just a dream. She was overtired and her mind was playing tricks.

Crazy Bear had her saddle bags and placed them on the floor next to the couch. He tossed her a Twinkie, a nut bar, and a bag of potato chips. "It's all I could find," he said.

"Thanks, Noah. I'm beat. Wake me when the sun's up," Jade said, resisting the temptation to check her memory stone to see if the man in the maze had moved.

25

CASEY: ST LOUIS: A GOOD PLACE TO DIE

Several times during the night, Casey woke with a racing heart and covered in sweat. He couldn't sleep, but when he did, he dreamed of dying angels, good and bad, the earth trembling, and rivers of lava scorching the earth. The fallen angels had risen. The realm of earth and the realm of darkness had become one. And, as a result, God unleashed his wrath, and there was no going back to what the world had once been. So, Casey gave up trying to sleep, got up out of bed, splashed water over his face, feeling slightly refreshed, he put on his shirt grabbed his things, and jumped off the balcony getting an early start to the day.

He landed in town, and languidly, walked through the center of town, ignoring the ghosts and restless souls that surrounded him. He was emotionally numb. He was in no hurry to get to Bear Lodge. Whatever was going to happen, his presence would not change a thing. Seeing the likeliest fate of the world laid out in his dreams made him wonder, *what was God?*

Casey was becoming resentful. He once heard someone say that they thought the earth was like the mind of God. The idea had filled Casey with wonderment, but not anymore. Humans were only toys of a contemptuous God. Filled with morbid thoughts, Casey got off the road and followed the Cumberland River.

Out of town, away from the concrete jungle, he took flight and continued to follow the river. He set down just out of Lake City where the river ended. Dead fish covered the surface of the lake. His sorrow for the fish was greater than his feelings for the ghosts and souls that wandered aimlessly in the towns. The fish, the trees, the birds, all the animals, and Mother Earth were the true victims—the planet and all its living creatures were going to perish.

He flew over to the Grand River and it was the same—dead fish floated on the surface of the still water. The stench rose to greet him, so he flew a little higher and followed the Tennessee River. A feeling of sorrow that he had never known before weighed him down like oil-soaked wings of a bird. It was as if he carried the pain of every living creature.

Crossing the Ohio River, he passed over the green ponds and cypress trees of Mermet swamp. Beyond the swamp, he saw a campground, and he set down to relieve the pressure on his bladder. He read the sign 'Catch and Release' before wandering over to the trailers, away from the smell of dead fish.

For a moment, he thought there might be another human close by as he looked over the trailers and pop-ups scattered around the campsite. One by one, he checked the trailers for survivors that were too scared to come out. As he passed between two trailers, he walked around a small mound of dried bones and fur that was molding into the land. One looked like a dog.

Before he went inside a trailer, he paused and tried to gauged, by the smell, if people had come to the end of their lives inside the trailer. Those trailers or tents he didn't bother checking.

Towards the back of the park, the furthest away from the lake and closer to the trees, was a trailer with an extensive sunshade he hadn't noticed. Casey had brushed past or checked all the other trailers. He might as well examine that one, too. It was too quiet, as he walked towards the trailer by the trees, he thought that if there were bodies inside, the scent of the forest could mask the stench.

Cautiously, Casey stepped under the sunshade that was like a small outside room, and up the two steps. The trailer squeaked under his weight. So far, so good. The air was fresh. He looked around the clean tiny kitchen and then the made bed at the back. Most of the trailers had spoiled food in the refrigerators and dirty dishes in the sink.

Worried about what he might find, he stood back and opened the refrigerator. A bottle of water and two healthy-looking duck eggs sat on the shelf. *But they're probably bad inside,* he thought. Casey's stomach groaned. Opening the cupboards above the gas cooktop, he found a frying pan. Good start. Then he fired up the cooktop and a blue flame reached up to the base of the pan. Hell, why not? He cracked an egg into a pan, ready for the foul stench that would follow. But it smelled okay. Smiling, he scrambled the egg. His mouth watered as he sat down and ate straight from the pan.

A guitar, propped up against the tiny wall of the shower recess between the kitchen and the bedroom, caught his eye. Scratch marks trailed down the faded bottom half of the guitar body from serious strumming. Casey plucked two strings. He picked it up and turned the knobs, tuning the strings. With his left hand, he formed a cord and plucked at the strings again. The sound was haunting in the emptiness. Casey softly picked the strings, and a tune formed as he recalled an old favorite his mother used to sing. He hadn't held a guitar in his hands for two years.

A flash of a woman playing and strumming the instrument in happier days filled his mind. But his own memories overrode the strangers. He had forgotten how much he had enjoyed making the guitar sing. His mind flashed back to the campfire where Jackson had played. *I could stay here, but I miss the sounds of the living, he thought,* exiting the trailer and taking the guitar with him. He put the strap over his arm and the guitar hung over his backpack with the neck pointing down to the ground.

The sun penetrated his hair, warming his head. It was midmorning and already it was heating. Casey patted down his hair and thought he'd best get a move on, for Jade's sake. She might need his help, and he owed it to Kevin. He never wanted Kevin to feel like he did.

"Get away from there!"

Startled, Casey spun around. The sound of another voice threw him for a loop. He nearly tripped over himself, stepping backwards. It was the boots he noticed first. Red shiny boots that looked out of place with the blue cut denim shorts and a bright orange shirt. She moved out from between the trees, pointing a rifle. She was in her twenties, maybe earlier thirties. Hair looked like she hadn't brushed or cut it for a couple of years, which made his curls look tame. Her dark, shiny skin glowed.

"Put down the gun," Casey said.

"Drop your knife," she said, challenging him.

"I can't do that," Casey said, glancing at its holster.

"Well then, it's a stalemate. Where did you learn to play like that?"

"I taught myself after my dad died. His guitar was all I had left of him. My name's Casey. You live here alone?"

She lifted the gun up a little higher and pulled the bolt back, ready to shoot. "That's my husband's guitar you took it upon yourself to play."

"I'm sorry. I shouldn't have taken it. Look, there's a terrible storm coming. There are other survivors, like you and me, meeting at Bear Lodge. I'm scouting ahead to make sure it's safe. When the others pass through, you should join them," Casey said.

"It ain't called that no more. It's the Devils Tower. You do what you like, but like I told that preacher man, I ain't in need of charity. So put down the guitar and get the fuck out here," she said.

"The preacher? What did he look like?" Casey asked.

She shot at the ground. "I said drop the guitar and get out of here."

The grass moved. Slithering towards him were snakes. Dozens of snakes. Casey pulled the strap over his head and laid the guitar on the grass. The strap turned into a snake. He jumped back a few steps and stared at the guitar, but there were no snakes, and the guitar strap was just a strap. He searched the ground around him and held up his hands. "I will not hurt you. Tell me about the preacher." *The preacher must be close enough to cause a hallucination,* he thought keeping an eye on the ground.

"Like an angel, he came to me in my dreams. Three days ago, he arrived in the flesh with his followers, and he killed anyone who refused to join him. The fish went belly up, and birds died too, they fell straight out of the sky and off their perches. There were twenty-nine people here, and now it's just me. The preacher left me here to wait for you!" she said.

Three days ago, Casey had seen the preacher back at Black Mountains. "He's not an angel, he's a demon. Why did he let you survive? Where did you hide?" Casey asked, stepping forward.

"I didn't hide anywhere. I'm no yellow belly. But I survived because he chose me. He doesn't scare me."

Casey had to ask. "I don't understand. You're not making sense. What did he choose you for?"

"You don't have very good manners. You haven't asked me my name."

He didn't want to ask. "What were you chosen for?"

She fired the rifle again. "Ask me my name!"

"What's your name?" Casey yelled.

The woman smiled. Her teeth were a lovely white, but her smile looked more like a sneer—the cat that had caught the canary.

She pulled back the bolt and cocked the gun again. "Sophia!" She paused and her mouth opened wide, as if ready to laugh. When Casey said nothing and held back his emotions, she dropped her glaring smile and closed her mouth. "Are you sure you want to know what he chose me for?" She paused again, as if dying for Casey to ask again, but Casey kept quiet. He could see his silence agitated her.

"He chose me . . . to kill you!" She was so excited she couldn't contain herself and gave a slight wiggle of enthusiasm. She laughed and laughed. Her laughter turned into an unnatural laughter which wasn't female and wasn't human. She pressed the rifle against her shoulder and fired the gun. In her haste, she missed. She fired again and charged at Casey, screaming.

Casey fled into the air and levitated. Furious, the women raised her gun up into the air. He soared higher, out of range, but he didn't stop until the air thinned, and only then he lowered his altitude and changed his trajectory towards the north. The surge of adrenaline wavered.

Suddenly, he collided into an invisible wall.

Crashing through the treetops, halting his descent, floating in between the canopies, he regained consciousness and tried to get his bearings as he came to a stop. He floated back up into the sky, rubbing his head. He moved as if blind, feeling for the barriers.

The dark storm on the horizon had gathered momentum, and everything in front of him blackened. He backed up as his hands touched an invisible wall. Behind the barrier, the storm churned, like barreling waves continuously breaking at the shoreline, only to get sucked back into the turbulence. He looked from left to right and couldn't see an end to the tumultuous storm. He was going to have to go through it. Slowly, he entered, and the rolling clouds picked him up and flung him violently. He thought he was finally going to die.

He fell hard; the wind knocked from him, landing in what he could only describe as a dead land, all the color of life sucked out of the environment. The bleakness stretched up to an altitude of at least ten thousand feet.

He took flight once again. The borders were rolling, churning clouds that marked the edges of the storm. It was like watching an old black-and-white movie, nothing but shades of black and gray. The forest was still below but looked lifeless.

He needed to get his bearings, find the river. Nervously, he looked up as the dark shadows dropped from the sky above—it reminded him of the Jinn in Isabella's notebook. He flew lower, taking refuge in the canopies. There were no animals that he could see; there was no sound or movement. No wind. He found the river, but it didn't flow. It was still as a piece of glass.

Casey continued to follow the winding river into St. Louis and searched for a way out of the stormy wasteland. Desperately he needed to see the light and color return to the world, it was hard to fly, there was a stronger gravity pull, a dense atmosphere greater than outside of the wasteland. He stopped and looked back and saw black sweeping shadows of men trailing out of the storm clouds above.

Casey sped up and flew even lower, searching for a place in town to hide. They matched his speed.

The highway was a graveyard of motor vehicles, and he ducked and skimmed the colorless vehicles until he accidentally clipped the side of what should've been a yellow school bus, and he tumbled to the ground. He scurried under the bus to hide as six black shadow people landed in pursuit. They were going to trap him. Casey rolled out from under the bus. There was only one way out, and that was to fight.

Casey pushed the cars with all his mental strength and sent them flying into the shadows. They disappeared like clouds of smoke and reformed. *Shit!* They were unfazed by his telekinetic ability. Nothing that he threw at them could hurt them. Casey raised the cars and trucks around him and moved his hands in front of him as if to swipe a huge display screen to the right. Motor vehicles spun around him, getting faster and faster. He expanded the circle to sweep up the shadow men, trapping them inside the vortex of metal. Casey sped up the mass of metal and then flew out of the top of the funnel and didn't look back.

He thought he had evaded the shadow men until a pressure from above suddenly knocked the wind out of him and forced him downward, riding him like a surfboard. He couldn't turn to see his assailant, but his back felt cold and burned like ice. It rode him hard into the ground just outside the city of St Louis—*as good as any place to die,* he thought. His face grazed against the abrasive concrete.

Casey telepathically called out to Sophia and Metatron. No help came. This time, he was on his own. The pressure eased as the beast stepped off his back. Casey lay still on the concrete and played dead. It picked him up by the backpack as if he weighed no more than a few grams. He turned to look up at his attacker. He expected a shadow man, a wendigo or the preacher, at least one of them, if not all of them, combined into some hideous monster from hell. But what he saw was far scarier than anything he could have imagined.

A fallen angel, surrounded in pulsating dark matter. It had sharp teeth and wings of leather. It reeked of death. He wanted to close his eyes, to refuse its presence. But it wanted him to see it. It was a dirty gray with horns on its forehead, naked and muscular with fur or hair covering its genitals. A snake wrapped around its neck, its tail trailing down the angel's shoulder. Its brow was drawn down, its nostrils flared, and Casey could hear the faint sound of a flute that seemed so out of place in the presence of death. The creature's fingernails were long and sharp, and its toe nails were the same. Its ears were pointy, like elves'. It seemed more like a bastard of a fallen angel. But it was strong as a bodybuilder on steroids. Isabella's notebook depicted the pictures of the fallen angels more like humans, but this thing was more like a demon.

Casey reached for his dagger and pulled it from its sheath in one quick motion. He jumped up towards the demon's chest and, with both hands, stuck the dagger deep into its heart. Casey shouted as loud as he could, "Cum postestate omnipotentis, aut spiritum daemonii immundi, et terebrare in te judicia, et non erit ultra ferrum: et hoc non factum est, in nomine spiritus sancti: Amen."

The demon laughed as it plucked the dagger out of its chest and dropped it, then swatted Casey to the ground. Casey rolled like a tumbleweed in the wasteland. The shadow men surrounded him in a blink, surprising him as they raised him up into the air and presented him to the demon for reckoning. From all directions, the dead came like metal to a magnet.

"You are in the realm of darkness. Your toys won't work in here and God cannot hear you. In here, you bow to the fallen, for we are now your God," the beast intoned, twisting his hand as if squashing a plum.

Casey grabbed his chest and doubled in pain. The more the fallen angel squeezed his fist, the more the pain increased. He couldn't breathe through the pain. Casey expelled all the energy he could and blasted the shadow men holding him captive, giving him enough time to retrieve his dagger and flee. He raced over the dead bones scattered across the wasteland, but their spirits walked as the fallen angel laughed, commanding them to rise. "You are mine!" he shouted and turned into the preacher.

"Kill me!" Casey yelled. With lightning speed, Casey flew at the demon, but there was nothing but air.

The fallen angel disguised as the preacher was gone. The dead and the dark, faceless shadow men advanced on him. Casey picked up his dagger and flew straight up. He needed to get out of the dark realm if he was going to kill the fallen angel. It would have to be in his realm, the realm of light and love—God's realm.

Casey held nothing back as he sped up to the barreling clouds. One of two things was going to happen: he was going to break through to the other side, or he was going to snap his neck and die in the dark realm, never to see Sophia again. Casey prayed for the former and closed his eyes as he punched through the dark clouds. He counted each second he was without oxygen. Thirty, thirty-five, fifty, sixty-five. He tried to stay focused as he neared a minute and a half when the sun hit his face as he burst free from the dark realm.

He gasped for air, checking to see if they followed him. If they did, he couldn't see them. But he would not waste any more time. He headed straight for Bear Lodge and won't stop until he finds and kills the preacher. No more Mr. Nice Guy.

His heart stopped racing the further he left the shadow men and the fallen angel behind. He slowed a little, wondering why the fallen angel had let him go. Now, come to think of it, it all seemed too easy. It was as if the fallen angel was toying with him. Guarded, Casey continued flying above the churning dark storm with watching out for the dark shadow men hoping they will emerge or, even better, the fallen angel.

He wondered if the demon that had possessed Sophia had been a fallen angel. How many fallen angels were there? He tried to remember what the book had said. There were twelve commanders and two hundred followers. *What were the shadow men? Demons or something else?*

26

JADE: LOST IN A STREAM OF DARKNESS

In the gas station office, under the window, Jade slept on an old worn couch, with her legs hanging over the side. She woke to the sounds of Crazy Bear rustling, tossing about on the floor in his sleep, as if fending off an unseen attacker. He kicked off the small woven blanket that covered his body. Jade grabbed the tassels of the blanket touching her face and pulled it aside then sliding off the couch to kneel beside Crazy Bear. Gently, she placed her hand on his shoulder, careful not to startle him. "Hey, wake up. It's alright. It's just a dream."

His arm flew up into the air, almost hitting her in the face.

"Crazy Bear, wake up!" Jade yelled and squeezed his shoulders. Suddenly she fell backwards, pushed away by an unseen force. "Noah! Noah, wake up!" Jade turned on the light hoping it would jolt him out of his nightmare. She kneeled back down beside him. "Noah, if you can hear me, call out to Great Spirit for help. It's the only way to free yourself from whatever is haunting your dreams."

The window shook as if someone had thrown a handful of stones against it, as if a major storm cell had released thousands of tiny balls of hail. She peeked through the shades and could see a swarm of beetles flying into the window. Jade picked up the end of the couch and propped it up to cover the window and then quickly turned off the light in case it attracted even more of the strange insects. The beetles rained down on the gas station's roof. The overwhelming sound drowned out Noah's cries and grunts as he continued to fight his invisible assailant.

A pair of noise cancelling headphones right about now would be great, she thought as she pushed her wand against Noah's head. She expected him to come out of the nightmare instantly, but nothing happened. *Shit, what do I do?* Jade reached into her saddlebag for her black-and-yellow snakeskin medicine pouch. She took out her bottle of crystal dust and sprinkled him along the path of his chakras.

Carefully she pulled back Noah's lower lip, even though she was worried he might accidentally bite her, as she placed a few stalks of sage between his teeth and his bottom lip to protect him from spirits entering his body through his mouth. *But what if an evil spirit has already entered his body?* she thought. Jade tried block out the sound of the beetles and started drumming, preparing herself to enter the astral realm to find out what was happening to Crazy Bear.

It was taking her longer than usual to get into the right state. She was unbalanced and blocked. She had to get control and calm down. Breathing in deeply, she slowed her inhalations and channeled her energy into the steady movement of her wrist, and the vibrations of the drum as her brain entered theta. *That's better,* she thought and pushed her foot forward to connect with Noah's body. And with ease, she slid out of her body into the astral realm.

A golden grizzly bear lit up the darkness, it was Noah. Ghostly vapors, maleficent gray entities circled the grizzly, squeezing out its life force, trying to get to Noah. She swung at the swarming entities. More, gray smokey entities came out of the darkness, outnumbering him. Noah, caught in a vortex of evil that grew stronger the more he struggled, was getting tired.

Jade watched and searched her mind for a way to get rid of the evil and free Noah. From her mind, she pushed out at the entities, but still, they didn't budge. They absorbed the energy she had cast out towards them. One stream of darkness loomed out of the gray abyss, circling Noah and headed for her.

The sound of her drum had lost resonances. The energy of her vortex, which allowed her to enter the astral realm, faded and weakened. Her brain shifted from theta back into beta and suddenly she was conscious of the physical sensations of her body. Something crawled up her arm and onto her face. She held the drum tight, bringing herself back into her body smoothly while resisting the urge to fling her arm wildly.

As soon as she was back, Jade sprang to her feet and batted away the beetles. She flicked on the light switch. They had come in under the doors and were dropping from the ceiling. Her drum had fallen on top of Noah's chest. It moved and slid off his stomach as beetles crawled under it, heading for his face. One beetle entered his open mouth. Jade quickly pushed his bulky mass onto his side and fished the beetle out of his mouth.

"Noah! Crazy Bear! Wake up, dammit!"

Under the weight of the beetles, a part of the roof caved in, and they flew into the office. Jade covered Crazy Bears face and head waiting until the assault was over. Light shone between the edges of the couch covering the window casting a shadow over her body. The door bust open, and three men entered the gas station office. Two picked up Noah and the other covered Jade's head. They were both led to an idling pickup trucks. She broke free from the man as he tossed their bike keys to the man in the second pickup truck. The air was foul. She covered her mouth, and her unbraided hair flew out in all directions.

She pivoted around and sprinted back to the office for her drum and bag with her memory stones and medicine pouch. The man sheltering her from the flying beetles helped her to re-enter the building. She was grateful he didn't force her to leave.

The beetles covered the floor and everything on it. They squished and crunched under her shoes as she ran over them to get to her things. Jade pushed the beetles out of the way to find her medicine pouch. The beetles, in protest, pinched her skin with their spiky claws. Once she had her belongings, the man covered her head, keeping her safe with his jacket, and guided her through the invasion and hurried her into the back of the first pickup truck. The sound of the creatures pelting on the roof of the car was worse than any hailstorm, and the beetles grew in numbers turning their attention to the vehicles.

Blindly, they pulled out of the gas station. The wipers smeared dead beetles across the windshield. They had buckled Noah in an upright position. He continued to struggle in the astral realm with the evil entities. His body jerked, and his arm lashed out to the side, hitting her hard in the chest. She heard a rib crack. She couldn't catch her breath. She doubled over, trying to breathe.

Quickly, she reached behind her, with one arm cradling her side, and fished out her wand. She pressed it against her side. The tip glowed. She gulped back air. She screamed out with the acute pain. As her wand repaired the fracture, her breathing became easier. Jade sat back and calmed herself. She looked out the back window of the pick-up's cabin. Jade could barely see the headlights of the second pickup through the swarm of beetles.

"Raven Wings?" the man next to the driver said, looking back at her and meeting her eyes.

"Who are you? How do you know my spirit name?"

He glanced at her wrist, then faced forward. Jade turned her wrist over and covered it with her opposite hand.

The wipers scratched and smeared blood and guts across the windshield as the beetles continued to bombard the windshield, limiting their view of the road.

"Stop this," the man with the braid said.

"I'm not doing anything," Jade said.

"Exactly. You must stop this. Awaken the four winds and disperse the invasion, so we can get you and Crazy Bear safely to Chief Thundercloud," the man said, holding on to the hand restraint above the window. His elbow crashed into the glass as they ran over something big. She just hoped it wasn't an animal. She cringed at the thought.

"Raven Wings!"

"How?" she said, but as the words left her mouth, she knew what she had to do. She didn't need anyone to coach her anymore. All the power that ever was and would be was inside her.

She took out her memory stones and selected the one with the swirls that she had seen dozens of times during the weather report in the old days to indicate *Caution: strong, damaging winds.* Jade closed her eyes and rode the bumps as if she was on a horse and imagined the feeling of the wind running through her hair as they galloped across the fields. The bumpy ride stopped. The crashing sound on the roof stopped and the foul odor that had followed was gone, too. But now she could hear Crazy Bear's moans and tiny cries as he battled the demons in the astral realm.

She tucked her box of memory stones away. "How did you guys know we needed help?" Jade asked.

"Chief Thundercloud saw you and Crazy Mato in the dream lodge."

"What do I call you?" Jade asked.

"Chantan. This is Hotah. Chief Thundercloud is our father," Chantan said.

"What about our bikes? Where are you taking us?" Jade said, sitting forward, watching the squirt of water rise onto the windshield as the driver endeavored to clear the view.

"Your motorcycles are on the pickup behind us. We're taking you back to the Res," said Chantan, looking at her over his shoulder.

She watched him turn and face the front. She could see his hair was black and long. He had a strong face. "What's a Res?"

"Reservation. Where our people are. Crazy Mato needs our help," Chantan said.

"It's Crazy Bear. You are taking him to a medicine man?" Jade asked.

"Mato, same thing. No. He needs a Shaman." He looked back at her. "You're not strong enough—yet."

Jade felt embarrassed and inadequate. She looked at Noah. She had let him down.

They travelled towards the rising sun and left the beetles behind.

Jade slipped in and out of sleep, woken by Noah's screams. They had pulled over and Chantan was pushing something into Noah's mouth. Jade pulled his hand away, stopping Chantan. "What are you doing?" Jade said.

"It will help him till we can get him to the Shaman," Chantan said.

Of course, she knew this. She pulled her hand away and let him replace the sage behind his bottom lip. Crazy Bear settled a little and seemed to slip into a restless sleep without the jerking and screams. His body stunk of perspiration, but Jade dared not open a window.

* * *

THE SOUND of slamming doors woke Jade. She had dozed in and out of sleep for six hours. She glanced at Crazy Bear, but he was gone. Someone opened her door. Mingan offered his hand to help her out of the pickup. Her head felt woozy, and as much as she wanted to refuse his hand, she knew her legs and head were going to betray her. Gingerly, she stepped from the vehicle. Her head was light. Silver light danced in front of her eyes as she looked into Mingan's. Her legs felt heavy. She tilted forward as if she was going to fall.

"Just wait a few seconds," Mingan said.

He would get no argument from her. She closed her eyes and took in a few deep breaths and felt the warmth return to her body. "I'm okay now."

He still held onto her. "We've been waiting for you."

Jade swept her eyes over the area to get her bearings. Scattered across the land were dozens of portable homes on the opposite side of the road, facing the distant hills. It was the early hours of the morning, but there must have been at least a couple of thousand people awake and busy loading trucks. Off to the side of the homes were rows of different food haulers, including refrigerated eighteen-wheelers. Trailer homes were hitched up and ready to move, along with the RVs pulling out and lining up like a convoy.

On the side of the road, where Hotah and Chantan had pulled up, were two huts in the shape of a dome, made of hides. Their motorcycles were on the back of the second pickup. The driver was unloading them. He had even collected the saddlebags and was smacking off the beetles that tumbled into the dirt. He mumbled and winced as he killed them, as if it pained him.

A barefoot man wearing denim jeans tended to a fire. His braid trailed down his shirt and touched the belt threaded through the loops of his jeans. He went inside the dome tent and brought out a dozen large rocks. He put them into the fire.

"He is the fire keeper. It is his responsibility to keep the temperature hot inside the sweat lodge," Mingan said.

Charlie, three other women, and four men stepped out of the closest hut wearing running or sports shorts and tops. Charlie was the youngest. She handed towels out to her elders and then wrapped a towel around her own shoulders. They all looked as though someone had dunked them in a river. They sat silently, spread out on the four logs.

Mingan led her to the hut. "It's our turn. Where are you in your cycle?"

"What? No. I get asthma; I won't be able to breathe in there. And besides, I have to help Crazy Bear," Jade said.

"Soon. But first we must purify you to enter the Shaman lodge. Where are you in your cycle?" Mingan said, kicking off his shoes and removing his jewelry from around his neck before stripping down to his boxers.

Jade, confused, locked with his eyes, trying to understand what he meant by cycle. The first thing that came to mind was the cycle of the caterpillar.

Charlie looked up and took in a deep breath and blew it out. She seemed exhausted. "Aunt Flo . . ."

Jade could feel her cheeks burning. "No. It's not that time of the month."

She quickly gathered her hair and braided it over her shoulder before stripping down to her undergarments. Mingan got on his hands and knees and crawled into the tent. Jade looked at Charlie. Charlie nodded, and Jade followed Mingan. The heat hit her straight away. Chief Thundercloud sat by the fire, chanting with closed eyes. It was just the three of them. The fire keeper brought in the rocks and added them to the pit in the center of the tent. Jade looked up at the roof. It looked like a spider's web. The fire keeper added herbs to the pit. Jade recognized the smell of cedar and lemongrass. Kevin had told her that whenever he could smell lemongrass, he knew his nana was close by, watching over him in spirit.

Jade wondered if she should have brought her drum into the ceremony. Mingan would've told her if she was going to need it. The fire keeper said a prayer as he left, and the flap was closed.

She slowed her breathing and breathed through her nose that she could already feel burning from the heat. It didn't take long before she was perspiring. At first, she wanted to ask questions, but Mingan closed his eyes and Chief Thundercloud had his eyes closed, too. So Jade closed her eyes and cleared her mind. Listening to Chief Thundercloud chanting, she entered a meditative state. She prayed inside her head for Great Spirit to help her connect with Mother Earth and her heritage. To purify her so they may bless her with wisdom from her ancestors to find the power within herself, so she could continue her journey.

They filled her visions with lights and spirals. Flashes of otherworld and lifetimes. See saw into the deeps of the multiverse and all she had ever been. The connectedness that bounded all of humanity to all the worlds that ever were or would be created by Great Spirit flowed within every one of them. Parts of herself stepped forward with projections of the future to come, with fear of failure and doom. All the burdens she carried from life to life, seeking resolution, stepped forward for healing.

When she opened her eyes, it was as if she was seeing everything for the first time. Mingan had already left the tent. She was on her own with Chief Thundercloud. They sat staring at each other, engaged in an in-depth conversation between their spiritual selves. Simultaneously, they smiled and nodded.

Outside, the air was fresh. The others had gone, but Charlie, Mingan and the fire keeper waited for them to crawl out of the lodge.

Charlie gave Chief Thundercloud a towel, then one to Jade before offering water. Out of the second tent, where Crazy Bear was, Chatan exited and greeted his father.

"It's time. The Shaman is ready," he said to his father, Chief Thundercloud.

Jade silently followed Mingan, Charlie, and Chief Thundercloud into the Shaman's hut. A middle-aged man in a ceremonial dress danced around Crazy Bear, and Jade recognized it as the dance of the plains grouse. He was building up the vortex to enter the realm of the lost souls. Chief Thundercloud stretched his hand out and offered her Crazy Bear. She knew what she had to do. He had taught her how to travel to the realm of lost souls to find her father's spirit.

"This time, Raven Wings, I will do the drumming. The Shaman will heal Crazy Bear and hold the doorway open between this realm and the realm of lost souls. Mingan will bring Crazy Bear back, and you must find a way to lure the entities back to the dark realm of lost souls," Chief Thundercloud said, beginning the drumming.

As soon as she entered the trance state, she saw the spiraling energy that led to the realm of lost souls. She had barely made it out alive last time. Mingan, as the spirit wolf, was quick to snatch Crazy Bear from the clutches of the evil entities that had nearly sucked the life force from him. A dim flicker of light remained inside Crazy Bear. Once Gray Wolf and Crazy Bear were gone, the evil turned their attention to her essence.

Jade, the spirit raven, dived into the spiraling vortex, and her spiritual light trailed behind her like the Milky Way. It was too much for evil to ignore. They gave chase and entered the vortex, spiraling down, following her between the realms and into the darkness of the realm of lost souls.

She fell into the sea of tears. Instantly, pain and misery weighed her down. She struggled to break the surface. She reached out her hand, feeling through the dense air, searching for a purchase to haul herself out of the water. There was none. Her face broke through the water and the evil entities snatched her up and dragged her into the air. They had followed her, as planned, but now she had to get free from them or she, too, would end up trapped in the realm of lost souls.

Jade thrust her wand forward, into the center of the dark energy, disintegrating it instantly. Again and again, she thrust her wand into each of the creatures and they, too, disintegrated.

Her light had attacked hundreds of the same entities, when suddenly she heard the preacher's voice echoing across the black ocean, warning her and laughing as if she had fallen into his trap. Jade blasted light from her wand, illuminating the darkness. The vortex was closing. She reached up into the air, touched the tip of the vortex, and let the energy sweep her up. It collapsed into itself as it propelled her back into her own realm and into her body in the tent seated next to Crazy Bear. Mingan was breathing into Crazy Bear's heart charka, returning his spirit to him.

Panting, she watched and waited.

* * *

CHIEF THUNDERCLOUD WATCHED the convoy of trailers, cars, and trucks headed out to Serpent Mound. "You did well, Raven Wings. Now you must hurry to Devils Tower. No longer can we call it Bear Lodge. Now, it belongs to the dark realm where all evil spirits go. The devil is there waiting for you all. Look after each other and I pray I will see you again," Chief Thundercloud said, giving her a hug.

Crazy Bear's dimmed light glowed again after the breakfast they all had. He was shining with a bounce in his step. He once again had a crazy amount of energy. Mingan and Charlie shifted into their sacred spirit animals as Jade and Noah mounted their bikes. Together, they traveled the last few miles to the Devils Tower. Jade prayed that Casey, in his grief, hadn't done something foolish.

27

CASEY: THE DEVILS TOWER

Casey knew he had arrived, but there was no towering rock. The storm concealed everything. The sun, bowing out of the day, cast the world below in a dirty red. He watched as green lightning flared within the barreling dark green-blue storm clouds. Singing floated out of the thick fog that smelled of rot. There was nowhere for him to land, nothing but storm below him. As foolish as it seemed, he flew straight into those clouds with only one thought in mind—kill the preacher.

Casey tilted his body downward and, like an arrow, shot through the veil of fog and into the dense clouds. Blind and out of control, the turbulence turned him over and over. Green lightning struck him in the leg. His whole body went stiff as the current raced through him, searching for the earth. Like an anchor, the lightning traveled through his body until it stuck the ground below, releasing Casey's contracted body. His muscles fatigued; he went limp.

He was still conscious when he tumbled out of the sky into the dark realm that covered the land for as far as he could see. He passed the south side of Bear Lodge named Devils Tower, the first ever national monument. It was at least three football fields wide. He could make out people scaling the hexagonal sedimentary rock face that made up the sides of the tower as he regained control of his body. Wendigo scaled up behind the climbers. Frightened, he gasped as people fell to their deaths and into the clutches of the wendigo below that ravaged their broken bodies.

Casey scoped the dangers as he watched in horror as some climbers tried to hide between narrow cracks in the rock face. Dark masses trailed down from the clouds above the tower and targeted the climbers, knocking them off the face and the top of the mountain of rock.

Determined to save the falling climbers, Casey pushed to accelerate in their direction, but he couldn't move. He was stuck. He looked down. A snake, like a rope, had snuck up and around his waist. A long, thick snake squeezed him around the waist. Casey reached down and grabbed the snake, but the more he struggled, the tighter it held onto his waist.

Holding onto the other end of the snake was the preacher, with his congregation, now in the hundreds, surrounding him. It had multiplied to hundreds. They all tilted their heads up as if watching fireworks on the Fourth of July. Like flying a kite, the preacher tugged on the tail of the snake, lowering Casey to the ground. Every face of the congregation that he looked at was Sophia's. Every man, woman, and child said in unison, "We missed you, Casey."

"Let me go!" Casey said, struggling, propelling his energy away from the ground, stretching the snake like a rubber band until it snapped in two. In the air, Casey regained his balance and headed towards the top of Devils Tower, but the tower of rock disappeared and was replaced with a giant Ferris wheel that reminded him of the Eye of London, and what had happened to Sophia.

Everything around him changed. Confused, he drifted back down to the ground, unsure of what he had taken flight for. He tried to recall what it was he was about to do. He knew it was important. But what?

"Casey!"

He whipped his head around to the sound of Sophia's voice and waited with bated breath. Out of the darkness, Sophia walked towards him. He couldn't believe his eyes as he lowered himself to the ground.

A streetlamp shone overhead. He was standing in the middle of a London street and the camper van was idling behind him.

"Quickly. We have to go," Casey said.

Sophia ran into his arms. He squeezed her tight before rushing her into the waiting camper van.

"Get us out of here," he said to Hugh as he took his seat next to Sophia. He wrapped his arm around her shoulders, pulling her close.

"It's going to be all right," Casey said.

"Yes, yes, it is," Sophia agreed. "Never let me go."

And for the next few weeks, he didn't. They spent every waking moment together. He never saw another living soul at the estate and didn't care. Not once did they have to use their powers. Life was heaven. He wanted to stay like that forever, but each day that passed, he felt like he had forgotten something, and he would spend nights outside, looking up at the stars until Sophia dragged him back inside. She always smiled, but her blue eyes didn't have the same sparkle they once had before . . . before what?

"I can't sleep; my mind is so foggy," Casey said and went to his own room where he sat at his desk and drew a tower of rock, people climbing, and a preacher praying for their journey.

Horror suddenly filled his being and the walls of his fantasy world melted like lava. The floor dropped from below his chair. He was outside under storming clouds. Sophia was gone and death was all around. He couldn't believe the past few weeks that had seemed so real in his mind were only minutes and were the preacher's doing. Fake memories that Casey would've loved to call his own were impregnated in his mind by the preacher, the fallen angel, or whatever damned thing it called itself.

Tears trailed down Casey's face, the hopelessness overwhelming, grief for the loss of a life that never existed, as he tried to cling to the false memories as they faded. Closing his eyes, he regained focus, and when he opened them, the Devils Tower and all its horrors returned in full shades of black and gray. The dark shadows from the sky were probably the Jinn, but he couldn't be sure. Their attentions turned from the climbers to him. Casey had little time to react as they swarmed and entrapped him in the velocity of their spinning wrath. The dark life force trailed up his nose and into his mouth and ears, sucking out all the light and joy inside him.

He could no longer battle; the fight within him was gone. With the last flicker of golden light, he went limp. His head hung heavily as he submitted to the darkness that filled his soul.

Finally, the dark entities let him fall. He was no longer appetizing. As he hit the colorless ground at the preacher's feet, the impact knocked Casey's last breath from his lungs. He lay motionless as the snakes trailed over his body.

"See what you could've had if you'd submitted to me. Now you will be a symbol of the future to those that wish to believe in the foolishness of your God that has abandoned you, as he abandoned us. Where is his hand to catch you? Why has he not reached down and plucked you from my grasp? Where are his heavenly angels? No one comes because they are all afraid of us. Yes, us. I am just the first of the fallen angels to rise and prepare the way for Semjaza, our commander, the head of the watchers. It is only our beloved offspring you have faced," the preacher said.

Casey wanted to struggle, to argue, to speak up, but he had no energy. He had nothing left to give.

"Pick him up. Crucify him for his God to see," the preacher said.

Casey didn't think he deserved a crucifixion, but he welcomed the pain. Two men dragged him over to the west side of the tower. There were no wendigos or climbers on the west side, and there was a calm, gathering of people who seemed to be oblivious to the chaos on the other side. The preacher must have wormed his way into their minds. Casey held his breath anticipating the pain; he screamed as the first nail was hammered into the fleshy lower part of his hand and into the wooden cross, he didn't stop screaming as they hammered in the second nail. He was on the verge of passing out as they finished nailing his feet. They began to raise him up, Casey felt the pull of gravity. The nails tore through his hands, and his body weight pushed into his feet. He looked into the black eyes of the men and women that pushed the wooden cross up.

The pain was excruciating. Casey felt shame, paraded for all to see as the preacher and his followers marched through the campsite of those that had had the dream about the ascension. They bowed down to the preacher as he passed. Those that did not, the wendigo tore apart. Casey kept his eyes open, forcing himself to stay conscious to witness the horrendous crimes the preacher committed against survivors who were ready for ascension.

So many people, so close to returning to heaven, were trapped in the dark realm governed by this maniac that called himself an angel, a god. A flicker of faith was still in Casey's heart for humanity. Casey closed his eyes and searched for the spark he called faith. His throat tightened. He gasped as a snake wrapped itself around his neck.

"Keep your eyes open. I want you to see who God is. If you don't, I will have your eyelids sliced off," the preacher said.

The mention of slicing his eyes off made him think of his dagger. It was still around his waist. He tried to pull his hand away from the wood, but even if he could rip his hand free from the nail, snakes wrapped themselves around his wrists and ankles, binding him to the wooden logs tied together to make a cross. In the dark realm, the dagger wouldn't work.

The earth and the dark realm were one, for as far as Casey could see. The clouds seemed to have moved even further up and out as he looked up. He didn't know if it was a night or day. He blacked out and regained consciousness time and time again.

The congregation below had prepared a feast for the hundreds, if not thousands, of people that had gathered now for the ascension, and had not yet been turned by the preacher's unholy communion. Human flesh sizzled over heated rocks. The flames were gray. Color belonged in the earth's realm. People of all creeds lined up to take the offerings. There was nothing he could do but die. But the preacher would not let him die until he was done with him.

Casey watched the green lightning and wished for it to hit him again. A funnel formed from the clouds above; stretching and reaching down, it twisted its way across the dark land. As it did, the cyclonic clouds moved closer and closer. The space of the darkness was being reduced. Wind penetrated the walls. The cloth flags across the fields danced, and the preacher looked up as hundreds of shadow entities flew to the ends of the dark realm as if holding back the tumultuous rolling walls.

Blood dripped into Casey's eye. He couldn't wipe it away. He blinked rapidly, to wash away the blood, not sure why he was even bleeding. Something was happening. The preacher stopped handing out human flesh as communion and stretched out his arms, as if to push the outer limits of the dark realm back. But it continued to contract inwards, as the twisting tornado moved at a great speed through the dark realm, destroying it. Casey could feel the twister pulling at the cross, pulling at him, trying to lift him up and into its chaos. He was ready to meet his maker. It was finally time to go home to God, his creator.

Released from the preacher's spell, the survivors screamed and ran in all directions. Casey didn't know if they saw the preacher for what he was, or they were fleeing the spiraling tornado heading in their direction. Beyond the tornado, Casey saw the stars twinkle in the night sky. The twister pushed the last fragments of the dark realm towards the west coast, and he could see again the top of Devils Tower. The tornado wasn't part of the dark realm.

Casey imagined bathing in the starlight, allowing it to fill his soul and push out any darkness. He looked down to the east and saw a light illuminating the plains. As the twister swept over him, he could feel the cross shaking, his body being torn from the cross. In unbear-able pain, Casey closed his eyes, waiting for his body to be completely torn from the cross, when suddenly the shaking stopped. He opened his eyes and gazed up through the storm funnel into the eye of the storm. The eye passed and the spinning wall of the twister pulled him free from the cross and flung him into the whirlwind. He expected Metatron to rescue him, as he always did. But as the twister dissolved, he stopped himself from tumbling into a free fall and levitated above the mayhem on the ground.

Hundreds of people had taken to climbing the mountain of rock, but the dark entities returned and attacked. The preacher returned to his natural form as the fallen angel. It stood at least ten feet tall, and its eyes blazing red.

From the illuminated plains beyond fog and the Devils Tower, Jade stood with her wand held high and her hands and aura stretched out, as if commanding a symphony. Out of the brush beside her, a spirit wolf and a huge grizzly bear raced towards the fallen angel and jumped on it from behind. *The cavalry has arrived,* Casey thought.

Jade ran and, picked up by the wind, turned into a huge raven. Casey needed no invitation. Dagger drawn, he dived for the fallen angel, but a wendigo intercepted and snatched him out of the air. Barefoot, Casey rammed the dagger into its heart and recited the prayer before he went for the fallen angel again. He ignored the bolts of pain in his hands and feet as he ran taking flight and joined Mingan and Crazy Bear in their battle against the fallen angel and the Jinn.

Lightning struck Casey, sending him skidding across the ground as soon as he got close. The dark realm was rolling back from the west. In his mind, he heard Sophia's voice, "Save the people." Casey paused in midair, wondering if it was really her or the fallen angel's trickery. The fallen angel took flight. Casey watched it grab and pull climbers of the wall along its way to the top of Devils Tower, dropping them to their deaths.

Casey raced around the face of the tower, catching and setting as many climbers as possible down on the ground. His efforts were almost futile, as he missed dozens. Casey flew to the top, passing a giant spirit bear as it scaled the tower alongside a giant spirit wolf. Mingan and Crazy Bear weren't giving up the chase. Jade's light grew stronger as she rose into the air and headed to the top of the tower to join them. The dark entities protected the fallen angel from Jade's light.

Casey, weak from the loss of blood, gave it all he had and was first to strike out at the fallen angel. The blast pushed the angel off the summit, but it quickly regained its position. Its giant brown leathery wings flapped in the night. The stars twinkled behind it. It was majestic. The sudden blow sent Casey up into the heavens until he couldn't breathe. He blacked out and regained consciousness when the oxygen was rich. But he was used to it now and turned into a dive.

Mingan's and Crazy Bear's spirit animals moved about and flickered in and out of existence, infuriating the fallen angel. It couldn't strike out at them or catch them, so instead it picked up the people who had made it to the summit and threw them off. Casey, with lightning speed, moved around the fallen angel, pushing it into the ground as if he had wielded powerful blow that hurt the fallen angel and threw him off his feet. It flapped its wings, trying to take flight, when suddenly it reached out and, as if Casey wasn't even moving, and grabbed him by the neck.

"You honestly are annoying, but I admire your persistence," the fallen angel said. A dark black mass covered the stars above, casting the summit and everything on it in darkness.

This is it, Casey thought. Mingan and Crazy Bear transformed back into their human forms, and the darkness was in the shape of a giant raven. The wingspan was greater than the fallen angel's. Seconds before it landed, it folded into itself and Jade, with her foot extended and her wand in her hand, touched down on to the summit. *She should have picked up the fallen angel with her talons,* Casey thought.

The fallen angel still had hold of Casey around the throat, and he squeezed. Casey saw more stars than he could count. He watched Jade move behind the fallen angel and Mingan stood in front. They reached their arms out, as if reaching for each other, when lights from their bracelets shone and the lights combined into a ring that wrapped around the fallen angel, placing him in its center. The fallen angel let go of Casey, who raised his dagger up and into its heart.

Casey hit the ground and crawled out of the ring of light that bound the fallen angel. The fallen angel, like a submarine that had penetrated the unknown depths, buckled and compressed into a stone.

The stone fell to the ground, and the dagger dropped beside it. Jade and Mingan let go, and the rings disappeared. Mingan picked up the stone. It was hot, and he dropped it and crushed it underfoot.

Together they killed the wendigo, one by one, and the dark shadows that had trailed down from the clouds disappeared. Casey was sure they would return. The fallen angel had been one of two hundred. The war was not yet over, but for today, they had won the battle.

After Jade used her wand to heal his hands and feet, she and Mingan talked to the survivors until morning, telling them of the future of the darkness that would ravish the earth. Casey listened to the stories while drifting in and out of a light sleep. The sacred site of Bear Lodge had been tainted and they would have to travel to another sacred site that would be a portal to the stars. It didn't take long for the survivors to pack up their tents, RVs, and trailers, ready to begin their new pilgrimage to Serpent Mound, where they hoped to ascend to the heavens, to Great Spirit, the creator of all things, when the portals would be opened on the day of ascension.

"You do not have to stay with us," Mingan said to Jade.

"I know, but first we must make sure the hundreds of survivors make it to Serpent Mound," Jade said, looking at Casey.

Casey looked into Jade's eyes and saw the pain of her decision. He knew what she was going to say before she had even said it. She was going to sacrifice what her heart wanted for the sake of others.

"I have to do this. We are stronger together," she said, looking at Mingan and Crazy Bear. "Kevin will find me. I know he will." She removed Sophia's necklace and put it over Casey's head.

"This belongs to you," Jade said and embraced him.

The end

AUTHOR'S NOTE

Enjoy this book? You can make a big difference.

Reviews are the most powerful tools in my arsenal when it comes to getting attention for my books. Much as I'd like to, I don't have the financial muscle of a New York publisher. I can't take out full-page ads in the newspaper or put posters on the subway. (Not yet, anyway.)

But I do have something much more powerful and effective than that, and it's something that those publishers would kill to get their hands on: a committed and loyal bunch of readers.

Honest reviews of my books help bring them to the attention of other readers.

If you've enjoyed this book I would be very grateful if you could spend just five minutes leaving a review (it can be as short as you like) on your favorite online bookstore, or on Goodreads, which you can access through my website as well as my other books.

https://jmhartwriter.com/buy-now/

Thank you very much.

ABOUT THE AUTHOR

Now semi-retired, JM (Jeanette) moved to a peaceful county town south of Sydney, to focus on her grandchildren and writing.

JM Hart is the author of *The Chronicles of the Supernatural Series*. She makes her online home at http://jmhartwriter.com

You can also connect with Jeanette on social media. Click the links below.

If the mood strikes you, you can send her an email at author@ jmhartwriter.com

OTHER BOOKS BY JM HART
CHRONICLES OF THE SUPERNATURAL

www.ingramcontent.com/pod-product-compliance
Lightning Source LLC
Chambersburg PA
CBHW070111120726
47909CB00002B/562